Praise for *Those Who Return*

'Sensational and deeply addictive,
Those Who Return is a true page-turner'
Karin Slaughter

'A pitch-perfect psychological thriller
of the absolute highest calibre'
Peter Papathanasiou

'Fresh and atmospheric, a mystery as haunting
as its lonesome Great Plains backdrop'
Anna Bailey

'What an extraordinary book . . . both poetic and haunting'
Victoria Selman

'A searing psychological thriller of guilt and redemption'
My Weekly

'Montag's thriller transports you to the vast Great Plains
of Nebraska [where] old secrets spill like vengeful ghosts'
Peterborough Telegraph

'Darkly atmospheric and beautifully written'
Irish Independent

THOSE WHO RETURN

Kassandra Montag is an award-winning poet, novelist, and essayist. Her work has appeared in magazines and anthologies such as *Midwestern Gothic*, *Nebraska Poetry*, *Prairie Schooner*, and *Mystery Weekly Magazine*. Her debut novel, *After the Flood*, has been published in fourteen languages and has been optioned for television. She lives in Omaha, Nebraska with her husband and two sons.

THOSE
WHO
RETURN

KASSANDRA
MONTAG

QUERCUS

First published in Great Britain in 2022 by Quercus
This paperback edition published in 2023 by

QUERCUS

Quercus Editions Ltd
Carmelite House
50 Victoria Embankment
London EC4Y 0DZ

An Hachette UK company

A CIP catalogue record for this book is available
from the British Library

PB ISBN 978 1 52941 683 1
EB ISBN 978 1 52941 684 8

10 9 8 7 6 5 4 3 2 1

Typeset by CC Book Production
Printed and bound in Great Britain by Clays Ltd, Elcograf S.p.A.

MIX
Paper from
responsible sources
FSC® C104740

Papers used by Quercus are from well-managed forests and other responsible sources.

For Rainer and Ansel

'The imagination is continually at work filling up all the fissures through which grace might pass.'

– Simone Weil, *Gravity and Grace*

PROLOGUE

From the highway, it looks like a prehistoric beast settled in a field of grass and fell asleep. Maybe it's the early morning fog that makes Hatchery House appear alive. Or maybe houses are living things – watching you between their walls, holding you as you sleep, feeding you dreams and nightmares alike. It could awaken any minute and come after me.

Last night my partner asked, 'What will you tell our son about your childhood?' I was so unsettled I drove straight through the night to stand with one hand on the rough bark of a cottonwood, peering at where I grew up. The cathedral's spires pierce the sky and its gargoyles taunt the wind.

Three deaths in four days, the newspapers had reported. There was so much else they couldn't say, couldn't know.

I don't want to tell my son about the paintings of monsters that'd stare back at me. About the staff member who'd asked me: 'How would it feel if I cut off all your fingers and toes?' How we all – the students – held our breath at night when we heard a ballad drifting beneath our door, some song about a ghost and a bed full of blood.

Nor do I want to tell him that I still sometimes feel as alone as I did then. As though I'm an island with no shores. I don't want him to know how much I've hidden in order to survive; how much I grew to love it and had to be yanked back to life by almost losing it.

Those stone walls held screams; if I strain, I can still hear them. Inside, it felt crowded, and that restlessness of being trapped follows me. Even now, I can feel the beating hearts of camouflaged animals surrounding me.

Where would Dr Webber begin if she were here? She had known the students' secrets, even the ones they hadn't told her, secrets she gathered while watching them. She'd reminded me of a whopping crane, all tall and lanky, with an abundance of hair the color of ashes and dirt mixed together. A near constant furrow creased the skin between her brows.

During those four days, she'd sometimes go white, and when she was that pale, I'd want to touch her to remind myself she was still with me. Perhaps she'd begin with the May Day festival, the merriment that had turned to menace and then back again. I'd begin with the first murder, which I witnessed from the tall grass.

A figure on horseback chased a boy across the hills. The gap between them shrank and the boy ran harder, his whole body bent forward as if he could lean into some space in the distance and arrive there unscathed.

A thud and the boy toppled across the grass. I threw myself down to hide, hoofbeats rumbling past me so loud I thought my head would split open right there on the ground.

Some of the stars shining above had already died. Still, once it was quiet, their light guided me back home.

CHAPTER 1

Thirty years earlier
May 1, 2007

One hour after the May Day festival began, the wildflowers around the fire pits had all been trampled. I stood apart from the celebration. Though I'd worked as a psychiatrist at Hatchery House for five months now, I still felt like a stranger. Students gathered around the fires, warming their hands as the wood hissed and popped. Some broke away and danced across the prairie, silhouettes under a moon shrouded by smoke. Their voices, drunk with revelry, burned through the night sounds of crickets and owls.

'We're prisoners here,' one said.

'They lock us in!'

'They want to keep us here until we die!'

A frenzy of laughter erupted amid a flurry of elbows and hair as fireworks illuminated Hatchery House and their faces in a flash.

Beyond them, the open plain felt full of eyes; the hair on the back of my neck prickled. A pig roasted over the largest fire, cooking meat mixing with the scent of smashed flowers. The jumping flames made me flinch and the scars on my ankle itch. Someone was going to get hurt.

3

Hatchery House has been called many things over the years, from an asylum to a therapy ranch. The locals in the nearest town called it an orphanage, though funding for those had gone out of fashion decades before. From a bird's-eye view, the two-story Gothic Revival church made the shape of a cross. A hundred years before, it'd been called Our Lady of the Sandhills.

Now it was a nonprofit, renovated and funded by a billionaire, for orphaned or abandoned children with psychiatric disorders. Working with social services, it accepted only the neediest cases, since the House held a mere twenty beds. It was a residential treatment facility that took a holistic approach; school, living quarters, and psychiatric appointments all prepared students to re-enter the world.

It stood in the Sandhills of northern Nebraska, a region so iso-lated you could drive for hundreds of miles and not see another person. The land unfurled into blackness, hills mirroring each other into oblivion. This was an animal kingdom, a space where wild things reigned.

Luis, my favorite patient, stood alone, fashioning a crown from twigs and grasses. He was small for sixteen, with solemn dark eyes and a sensitive face. Often, he could be found making model airplanes in the lounge. The pieces came in boxes labeled with the aggressive names of weapons or warriors – Warhawk, Raptor, Thunderbolt – so unlike the boy who sat quietly assem-bling them.

After tucking a few leaves between woven grass with steady, methodical fingers, Luis set the crown on his head. It transformed him. He looked like a mythic creature banished to a wasteland, who somehow emerges triumphant at the end of a fairy tale.

I smiled at him when he looked my way. Instead of smiling back, he looked at something over my shoulder and his face blanched. I whirled around. A hunched figure hovered on the outskirts of our celebration, standing in the knee-high grass, lurking in the dark.

The witch was in the field again. That's what the students called her: Baba Yaga.

I wasn't sure who'd first told them about the supernatural creature from Eastern European folklore. Baba Yaga was a savage old woman whose personality melded with the wildlife that surrounded her hut in the forest.

Though I hadn't been here long, I'd heard all the rumors. How she haunted the grounds at night, sneaking about. How she threatened to shoot the students when they strayed on to her property. Beyond their stories, I knew little about her. A widow, she lived alone in a cabin a quarter mile east of the House, the only other person living in the area for miles and miles.

On my morning walks, I often saw her out in the hills, once dragging a roadkill deer behind her, presumably for a stew and skinning. But this was the first time I'd seen her so close to the students. She shouldn't be here, stalking them in their rare moment of delight. Like a thief for joy. I moved forward to confront her, to tell her to go home, but someone shoved past in front of me. The wind shifted and smoke blew into my eyes. Stumbling, I rubbed them and blinked, but she was gone.

She couldn't be that fast, old as she was. She looked near seventy and crippled with arthritis.

The face of Owen, one of our oldest students, flared a few yards away. Eighteen, with a shaggy crop of blond hair and startling blue eyes, he often blocked the door during our appointments, clearly enjoying that moment of power.

He first came to us after putting bleach in his baby sister's bottle. A year later, he returned home; eight months after that, they sent him back to us, having spent six months in juvie for assaulting a neighbor girl. Twelve at the time, he'd been with us ever since. Now that he was eighteen, we were getting ready to release him to the world.

Owen looked between the fire and Luis, his eyes making a coil between the two, winding tighter and tighter. The fire pit's iron walls were a foot high and flames leapt several feet above its rim. Don't even think about it, I thought, walking toward him.

A grin spread across Owen's face when he saw me approaching. He charged Luis and hooked his elbow, dragging him toward the fire. Luis's crown fell to the ground.

'It won't hurt. You'll be a phoenix!' Owen cried merrily.

I broke into a run. Luis cried out and twisted, wrenching his arm. Owen pushed him toward the fire pit and Luis stumbled backwards. Owen shoved him again.

I caught Luis by the arm just as his back brushed the flames. Yanking him upright, I ran my hand down his back to make sure it didn't catch fire and breathed a sigh of relief to find it only warm.

Owen laughed and turned away before I grabbed his wrist.

'You're hurting me,' he whined, a gleam in his eyes.

'It's not funny, Owen,' I said.

He ripped free. 'You think you're so good, but really, you're just scared of being bad. We all hate you. You can't do your job—'

A bubble of fury rose in my chest, but I steadied my voice.

'You're done,' I told him. 'Get back to the House. Party's over for you.'

'Oh, wah-wah. This was the best party ever, too!'

'Owen,' I warned.

'We won't get out of here until you've changed us how you want. Well, fuck you.' He swung his arms out wide and turned in a circle. 'Fuck your lessons and pills. I'm rotten all the way through.'

He stepped closer to me, drew his head back and spat in my face. I flinched and froze.

Eyes wide with delight and amazement, he suppressed a laugh. He held his hands up as he spoke: 'I'm going, I'm going!' And before I could say a word, he sprinted toward the House.

Everyone at the festival was too occupied with dancing or eating or scolding each other to notice us. Luis touched my arm gingerly. When I looked at him, he reached up and brushed the saliva from my face with the cuff of his flannel shirt.

Several hours passed and everyone went to bed. Charred bones cooled with the embers, a sacrifice for a good harvest, a request that the summer be what summers should be. Fertile ground for carefree moments.

But I couldn't sleep. I could still feel Owen's spit on my skin. Fires danced when I shut my eyes. I'd report his behavior to the headmistress, but I knew little would be done. Docked points or some other metaphorical wrist-slap.

But beyond all that, Luis brushing my cheekbone burned in my memory. This tenderness needled me more than the rest. I thrashed in bed until I threw the covers off, left the apartment and crept down the open staircase to the lounge. Tucked under a window, an old traveling chest held correspondence from students who'd graduated from Hatchery and begun new lives.

Not all of our former students wrote to us, but many more did than I'd ever expected. Christmas cards held photos: a kiss under mistletoe with a new boyfriend or a snowman built with a daughter. There were engagement, wedding, and baby announcements and newspaper clippings of accomplishments. One letter detailed an artist's first exhibition in a gallery. Another card held a photo of a sold house with a single sentence scrawled on the back: *I never thought I'd have this.*

When I looked through this chest – only in the dark, when everyone else was sleeping – I thought of a game I'd played with my younger brother when he was only a toddler: What do you want to be when you grow up?

'Firefighter!' he'd cry. Or on another day, 'Builder!'

We'd play-act each job until we were spent. Then he'd curl up on the floor with a blankie and stroke his cheek with its tag while I rubbed his back. We both could have become so many things. Back then, the world had felt full of possibility.

Blinking back tears now, I leafed through the chest, ashamed of how proud I was of these former students. I knew their uphill battle; caring for them was the closest I got to loving the child I'd been, who had a childhood not far from many of theirs. I disliked this part of myself – the soft, inner core that was too quick to feel and just as quick to show it, my insides bursting forth without permission. I wanted a letter like this from a student one day. Needed it the way lungs crave air.

A creak came from the stairs and I shut off my flashlight. No one materialized in the dim, blue moonlight. I closed the chest and wrapped a throw around myself. Tiptoeing down the hallway, I stopped in the foyer for an umbrella. A camera perched in the eaves above the front door; I didn't need anyone questioning why I was going outside in the middle of the night. I punched in the security code and slipped around the back of the House.

I laid down in the grass. Chilled fresh air and the night sky would scour my mind clean of those flickering fires. Wild pansy waved beside me in tiny purple shreds, stems bent to the side like broken necks. Sometimes I couldn't stand the safety and comfort of a warm bed.

Grass itched my cheeks as I drifted off. Sometime later hoof-beats startled me awake, thunder striking within my skull. I almost jumped to my feet to avoid being trampled, but the sound disappeared as quickly as it came.

You were dreaming of horses, I told myself. Just dreaming.

CHAPTER 2

May 2, 2007

Leaving the House for my early morning walk, I saw Baba Yaga standing out near the hanging tree.

After hearing the hoofbeats last night I'd only been able to fall into a restless sleep. I kept waking up, thinking of her shape in the darkness while the children, for once, were able to dance and be lighthearted. Rare things for them.

I grew up in a neighborhood where you heard pops at night and could never be sure whether they were gunshots or fireworks. I'd stay awake, listening for the whirr of helicopter wings or blare of police sirens, the sounds both a terror and a comfort because I knew danger was close but someone was attending to it.

So, when she bent down in the tall grass, I started walking toward her. Her figure was small and fuzzy on the horizon, as though the wind had pulled her edges apart. She wore an oversized brown coat and heavy winter boots and carried an ax slung over her shoulder.

Just outside the ghost town of Ennenock, that tree was rumored to be the site of hangings during the Wild West. A single gnarled branch jutted to the side and pointed straight at Hatchery House, a quarter mile north.

A thriving mining town, Ennenock had expected to need a magnificent church, full of gleaming pews and soaring ceilings. Instead, the mine had collapsed, killing half the population. Ennenock never grew; it curled up like a dying dog. Beyond the hanging tree, crumbling, half-rotten buildings trailed along a wide dirt road that had once been the thoroughfare of the bustling town.

Baba Yaga began ambling northeast, toward her cabin. I pivoted my direction and took off running after her.

When I was still a dozen yards from her, she shot a look over her shoulder at me. She stopped then, and turned, stance wide, glaring at me like I'd inconvenienced her. The ax fell from her shoulder and she leaned on it like a cane.

I was panting slightly when I reached her. 'Ms—' I realized I didn't know her real name.

She raised her eyebrows at me, her large nose protruding from folds of skin, her face like a puckered tomato left to dry out in the sun. 'You were going in the right direction originally,' she said.

'Right dir—'

'God sakes, you people. Don't even see what's under your noses!' she barked. She reached toward me as though to grab the collar of my jacket and shake me.

I took a step back, yucca and thistles snaring at my ankles.

'Why are you carrying an ax?' I asked.

'Trees,' she said matter-of-factly. 'Living in this world is like walking a tightrope. Something even slightly off-balance—' She made a cutting gesture with her hand. 'You're gone.'

'You need to leave the students alone,' I said. 'I saw you watching the festival last night. It's inappropriate—'

'I did not watch any festivals last night,' Baba Yaga said. She gritted her teeth and pointed in the direction of the hanging tree. 'You best get over there.'

A vulture circled above. Golden grass swayed around us, making it impossible to see anything on the distant ground.

'I saw you bend down – what did you take?' I knew that she scoured these hills for stray treasures: bits of metal, dead animals, fallen tree limbs, but I didn't want her to take anything after last night.

'Didn't take. Gave.' She spat in her palm and slicked fuzzy white hair back against her scalp. 'A gift.'

'Gift? To whom?'

I had the queasy thought that Ezra had finally been found. Behind cupped palms, students said Baba Yaga had taken the nine-year-old who'd disappeared from Hatchery House two months ago. Little Ezra, gone from the house on the hill. The country sheriff had responded first and then the FBI took over the case. They'd swept through the pastures and talked to people in the closest towns. No one had seen him.

I'd been working at Hatchery House for three months when he vanished in March, and it was so cold then that everyone agreed he couldn't have survived alone in this land without help. There was only miles and miles of grass, nowhere to hide, the nearest town twenty miles east and to the west only birds, prairie dogs, herds of pronghorn, coyotes and the bones of bighorn sheep.

Though the students told tales of a kidnapping, his case file was filled with reports of running away from foster homes, and during his last few months at the House he mentioned plans to run away. He'd even packed a bag but, for a reason no one had understood, had left it at the foot of his bed when he'd run away.

'Ezra?' I asked. 'The boy—'

'Not him.' She chewed what I thought was the inside of her cheek until I smelled tobacco.

'What is it?' I asked.

Impatience tightened her face and she turned and walked away from me. I felt someone watching me, my skin turning to gooseflesh, and I looked over my shoulder. Nothing but the quiet hills and, behind me, Hatchery with its windows smudged into stone walls.

A bell tower, connected to the front of the House on the right side, rose into the mists. The gardener's cottage hunkered a short walk away, beyond a gravel circular drive. It had originally been the parish rectory. On any other day, the stillness could trick me into a sense of peace, but since last night, something sharp had lingered in me, a sensation of having swallowed glass.

Some of the students had been experiencing odd symptoms lately: excessive fatigue, fainting, confusion. I'd double- and triple-checked their medications but couldn't find the culprit. Perhaps one of them had snuck outside last night and passed out in the grass?

Walking toward the hanging tree, I smelled death but told myself it was only a dead animal. Fur dried by the sun; skeleton half exposed by midnight feedings from coyotes. I could hear screeches at night, the quick attacks and even quicker hush between predator and prey. I couldn't get used to how silence made those killings sound so loud and close.

Instinctively I felt my pockets for my phone, but remembered it was back in my room. Even though there was no signal inside the House or out on the grounds, I sometimes carried it with me to check the time.

The scent of decomposition clouded the air and bile built in the back of my throat. The vulture circled above me now, its feathers dark and oily, like something dipped in tar. I swallowed a gag.

He lay face up in the grass, as it splayed around him like rays from the sun; as if he'd been taken up into the sky and dropped back down.

CHAPTER 3

Luis.

I tried to breathe, my mind blank and roaring.

Check for a pulse, I thought, but I stood rooted.

He was pale already, head turned to one side, neck arched. Blood matted his dark hair and stained the grass; a shard of white skull poked through skin. His hands were slightly splayed like claws, fingers rigid. I knew if I touched him, he would be cold. Flies buzzed around his face and one landed on his lip, where a trickle of spit had dried.

It couldn't be. *No, no, no.* He'd already been hurt so much in life; he shouldn't be hurt more. Luis, the quiet boy who never caused any trouble. My eyes burned as wind blew hair across my face and I clawed it back, thick waves knotting in my fingers. I wanted to scream.

A cornhusk doll was nestled in the crook of his arm. It must have been placed there after his death; he wouldn't have fallen with it positioned just so. It was made from the birch bark of a nearby fallen tree and the tall grass that surrounded him.

Baba Yaga had said she left a gift. I looked in the direction she'd gone but she was now a speck in the distance. I needed to get back to the House but I couldn't leave his body unattended. I felt lightheaded and quickly inhaled.

Up north, the old groundskeeper who cared for the House's twenty acres exited his cottage.

'Help!' I cried out. I waved my arms over my head. 'Albert!'

He kept walking toward the House.

I leapt up and down, waving my arms, calling his name. He looked around as though he heard something, shook his head, and continued on. Breakfast would begin soon, all the students and teachers and staff in the dining hall.

Hands clenched at my sides, I dropped to my knees and screamed a high-pitched wail. Albert spun around. I leapt to my feet and waved my arms until he started running toward me.

In his early sixties, he still had the thin, erect body of a much younger man. He kept his white hair slicked back with gentleman's pomade and his checkered shirt buttoned to the top. His carefully maintained appearance made him look like he was trying to ward off the world.

He crossed the paved highway, the only road you could use to reach or leave Hatchery House. I looked from him to Luis's body. What if I were asking the killer to stand next to the body? I wouldn't admit it for some time, but I already suspected – in a subliminal, inarticulate way – that whoever had done this lived in the House. My stomach curdled and I clamped my mouth shut, swallowing acid that rose up my throat. Too late; there weren't any other choices.

I stared at his fists while he ran, as if I could spy guilt or innocence written across the knuckles. Albert had gotten the job because he'd known the headmistress since they were children. I'd heard Hatchery had difficulty keeping employees long-term and I worried this meant warning signs of bad behavior might be overlooked. Albert could be aggressive with the students at times – mostly barking at them to do their chores – but I'd never seen him hurt them. Still, I stiffened as he approached.

When he reached me, I held up my hands to stop him from getting too close to the body. Though I wasn't short, Albert always towered over me.

'Albert, Albert,' I said.

'What?' he asked, his face stern.

'It's Luis . . .' I began to feel like I was unraveling, so I rushed on. 'He's dead. I need you to stand with the body while I get help.'

Albert's face didn't register any change. 'Dead?'

As if I might be playing a trick on him. The students were always pulling small pranks, like breaking into his cottage and rearranging the furniture, or stealing his cowboy hat and tying it around the foyer's taxidermy deer head.

Evidence was decomposing and blowing away in the wind, as seconds ticked loudly in my head. 'Stay here,' I told him.

Confusion spread across his face and then, the first glimmers of fear lit his eyes.

I ran to the House, the image of Luis's face floating up before my vision. I tried to push it back. I needed to first tell Beverly, the headmistress; the students couldn't go outside after breakfast like they usually did.

Inside, down the hall, Beverly argued with Kristin, the eighteen-year-old who always missed curfew. Beverly grabbed her arm when Kristin tried to turn from her, whipping her back around to face her.

'We have rules and those rules will be followed,' Beverly snapped. She wore a faded green cardigan and her long grey hair was pulled into a loose bun at the back of her head. How old was she? Early sixties? I always noticed the veins in her hands when I spoke to her, the way her blood seemed to want to leap from her body.

Kristin rolled her eyes and ripped her arm from Beverly's grasp.

'Don't touch me. That's against the rules.' Kristin spun on her heel and scurried down the hall, sending us a dark look over her shoulder.

'We need to change the security code again,' Beverly said as I approached. 'That girl—'

'I need to tell you something,' I began, smoothing my damp palms down my pant legs.

'I'm telling you, when I was that age—'

'Luis is dead,' I said. I told her about finding his body and how we needed to contact the authorities.

Beverly stared at me, her mouth slightly agape. 'Luis?' she asked, as if she didn't know him.

'Alvarez.'

Her eyes narrowed on me. 'No, he was in bed by curfew.'

I steeled myself against the impatience rising up in me. We didn't have time for denial.

Beverly shook her head, took a step back and pointed in my face. 'No,' she said. 'Not now.'

'Now?' I asked.

But she kept shaking her head.

'How?' she asked.

I shook my head and tried to steer her down the hall. 'The

county sheriff will need to secure the scene until the FBI arrives,' I told her. 'I'll call both.'

The case would be federal – Luis came from Kansas and about half the kids at the House came from outside Nebraska. And they'd all be suspects, particularly the older ones who were on the brink of adulthood.

She whirled around and grabbed my wrists.

'How?!' she asked.

'It . . . it didn't look like an accident,' was all I could manage.

Beverly didn't say another word. I guided her to her office and made her a cup of tea. The teacup and saucer jingled in her shaking hand. I thought she was crying, but when I looked at her face, all I saw was rage.

I called Cedar, an old friend in the FBI who was still stationed back in Omaha, a four-and-a-half-hour drive from Hatchery. I hadn't spoken to him since I'd moved, so when I heard his voice, my chest tightened. He was a junior agent at the bureau, where we worked together for two years. I'd done two fellowships after medical school and residency: one in child psychiatry and the other in forensic psychiatry. At the bureau, I worked as a profiler for violent crimes and a counselor for witnesses and informants in vulnerable situations. Last year, I quit after a swirl of gunfire during a prostitution raid left one of my patients dead. Deborah. The twenty-two-year-old with forehead wrinkles and a laugh like a razor blade.

But before all that, Cedar and I had been childhood neighbors and friends. We both lived at the end of a gravel lane in northeast Omaha, where charming old Victorians gave way to ramshackle cottages and houses with angry dogs behind chain-link fences. He lived with his five brothers and two parents in a large, dilapidated colonial, and I with my might-as-well-be-mute father in a one-and-a-half story stained by my grandmother's cigarette smoke.

'We'll want you in on this,' he was saying. He meant it as a compliment, that he didn't see me as incompetent, even though his actions after the raid had said otherwise. Last we'd spoken, he'd questioned if I were ready for work again and I was surprised he wasn't repeating that same concern now.

I gripped the receiver more tightly and drew dark scribbles in the corner of a notebook. 'I'm working here. Conflict of interest.'

Trouble was, since finding Luis's body, the only thing I'd thought of was catching the killer. I'd be profiling my own patients, like it or not; it was my training. The question was how much I'd betray their confidence. How I'd decide what was relevant to the investigation. They were still under my care, after all. If the students discovered I was using our appointments to inform on them, how could they trust me to keep their secrets? These students deserved to have someone to trust and I'd already signed up to be that person.

'Yeah, but aren't you just on a one-year contract? You could dissolve it,' Cedar said.

'It's not about that,' I snapped.

Two tall windows behind my desk threw light on to my back, lifting the spring chill from my bones. In the summer, I'd crack those windows open and let the scent of milkweed drift across the room, wind ruffling my papers, bringing in a fine layer of dust to coat the bookshelves near the door. There was only a single light fixture in the middle of my office, so the corners always gathered darkness.

Cedar sighed. 'Are you sure you should be practicing . . . working . . . at all?'

I wouldn't dignify this with a response. 'When should we expect someone?'

'Lore, I know I disappeared on you—'

'County sheriff should be here within a half hour to secure the scene,' I interrupted. 'He'll be able to fill whoever is coming in on any details.'

Cedar was quiet a moment. 'An agent should arrive a little after noon. After that disappearance a few months back – that case Burke and Vildera were on? What was his name?'

'Ezra Flores.' In my view, that investigation had been short-lived and sloppy, but when I expressed my concerns, I was told the case wasn't a priority. Ezra's guardian had told the agents he had been planning to run away – he'd talked about it on one of their infrequent phone calls. That, combined with his packed bag, seemed to confirm their assumption. They shoved him on to the missing child list, promised to follow up on new leads, but didn't suspect any foul play so they couldn't stay out in the middle of nowhere forever. While I couldn't disagree that him running away was the likeliest explanation, I still felt uncomfortable when they ended the search.

'Yeah. We'll really need to get ahead of this one before the press starts nosing around. What's the closest town to . . .'

'Augustine,' I said. 'It's on the highway, twenty miles east of the House.'

'Shit.'

'Yeah.'

Augustine had been a factory town, before it closed and the population shrank to three hundred and two people. Soon, it might fade like Ennenock into sepia tones and tumbleweed.

'I know they're helping with your student loans, but I still don't get why you're out there.'

'A repayment plan that helps with half a mil in medical student loans doesn't seem appealing to you?' I asked.

'I'm just trying to understand,' Cedar said.

I made a *hmm* sound and left it alone. Debt felt like being buried alive. Dirt shoveled on top of you, blade by blade until you couldn't breathe. But it wasn't just money that had brought me out into the middle of nowhere. I'd always been the kind of person willing to take the job no one else wanted because I was a scavenger at heart. As any mutt would tell you if it could: a lot of scraps adds up to something.

Besides, after the raid, I took some time off. One morning I'd been carrying laundry upstairs and paused on the top step and found myself wishing I owned a gun, so I could blow my head off. Mild wishfulness, like wanting sugar in your tea. It was the detachment that had scared me more than wanting a bullet in my brain.

I couldn't go back to the bureau. I needed quiet and space. Maybe I wanted to lick my wounds. Or maybe I just wanted to disappear.

Before I moved out here, I stopped by Deborah's grave for the first time. 'I'll do better this time,' was all I could manage, setting a dozen carnations on the headstone.

Ha. She'd be rolling over in her grave now, howling. She was never one for bullshit.

'We're understaffed right now, so if I get assigned, it'll be just me,' Cedar said.

'Sure,' I said. They weren't understaffed; they were trying to use all available manpower to fix the botched raid back in February, and I felt a small pang. Regret was a sneaky bastard, striking unexpectedly, always saying *you're not free yet*.

CHAPTER 4

Crying echoed down the hallway. I poked my head around the door into Helen's classroom, where she was furiously erasing something from the chalkboard between pauses to swipe her cheekbones.

'Hey,' I said softly.

She looked over her shoulder at me, light green eyes shimmering with a layer of tears.

'Do you need to talk?' I asked as I stepped into the classroom.

She shook her head and bit her lip. There was a muscular presence to her, which made sense when I later learned she'd grown up on a farm in South Dakota. Despite this, she was often timid and nervous. When I'd first shaken hands with Helen, her gentle grip had been like a dead bird about to spill from my palm.

'Has this happened to you before?' she asked me. She scrubbed the chalkboard more vigorously. 'Losing a patient?'

I felt the wall go up, high and cold as brick. 'No,' I lied. 'At least, not like this.' A half lie. If people here knew about Deborah, then this wouldn't be my chance to start over.

As the head teacher, Helen taught most of the classes, and social programs sent visiting paras and tutors to help out. There were two classrooms, one for middle school and the other for high school. The setup was not unlike the one-room schoolhouses that had once freckled the prairie landscape, their clapboard walls and bells a statement of civility among the wild.

When Helen stepped back from the chalkboard, I could see the faint remains of a sentence she'd tried to erase: *For I am of the generation of vipers.* It was in the loopy, uncoordinated scrawl of a student not accustomed to writing on a chalkboard. It looked like Kristin's handwriting.

I pointed at it. 'Who wrote that?'

'Who knows – it's another prank. Someone trying to scare the younger students. We don't need this. Now, of all times!'

'Was it there before . . . or after—'

'I just found it this morning, but it could have been from yesterday afternoon.' She wrung her hands. 'God, Lore. Luis was one of the good ones.'

I nodded. I liked some of the students, while others made the clock move slowly during our appointments. I hadn't yet mastered pure objectivity. Not all of the students seemed like precious flowers, tender and fragrant with their innocence and goodness. Some, when I looked in their eyes, seemed callous, and try as I might to reach them, they resisted me.

In residency interviews, when asked why I'd wanted to become a psychiatrist, I gave the standard answers: I want to be able to spend more time with patients; it's the last frontier of medicine; it's more art than science. Nods and smiles had been exchanged.

My answers were almost as bad as the cliché that psychiatrists are trying to solve their own problems. I've got issues like anyone, but I'm not treating myself in appointments any more than a kindergarten teacher is reminding herself of basic arithmetic.

Instead, I could have told them about an afternoon when I was seven and my father sat drinking at the kitchen table. Eyes yellowed with jaundice, his back in an arc of defeat, he appeared ill. I'd thought, if he seems this sick on the outside, what does his brain look like? I imagined it'd be a jumble of wires, some of them shooting sparks, others going cold.

He had stared right through me as I stood, hesitant, in the doorway. 'The trash needs taking out,' he said finally.

I nodded and did the chore. Outside, before I flung it into the bin, I told myself there were other things he wasn't saying. Maybe even *I love you*.

I had been starved for words beyond the TV's drone, which gave me a poor substitute for real communication. Years later, during a psychiatry rotation, when my supervisor told me to *listen for what patients aren't saying*, something clicked. I wanted to be in that familiar space where you try to identify what a person feels or wants beyond what they say.

I didn't know yet that the limits of language can be protective; sometimes you don't want to know what's left unspoken.

Now, Helen began rustling through papers on her desk as if she were searching for something. 'Did you notice anyone on the grounds last night?' I asked.

She shook her head. 'I was up late doing lesson plans and saw Albert poking around. Maybe around twelve? But he always does that.'

After talking to Cedar, I'd met Sheriff Anders by the crime scene, filling him in on the timeline and impending arrival of the FBI investigative unit. A stout, burly man with a mustache, he had unwound yellow tape as he walked backwards through the tall grass. It was this – the border around Luis's body – which made it seem more real and I'd turned back to the House with a tightness in my chest.

The patter of feet above us filled the quiet. When the billionaire had renovated the cathedral, he took down the choir loft and added a second floor, which held students' bedrooms, staff studio apartments, and a study room.

Down here there were the offices, classrooms, kitchen, dining hall and the lounge room that smelled like dirty socks and salted snacks. But this main level kept the vestiges of the church it had been, complete with marble floors, stone pillars, stained-glass windows and the darkened, yellowed stain of years, the kind even paint can't fully cover.

'Look at this,' Helen said, shoving a newspaper clipping into my hands.

May 17, 1997

Today, one asylum shuttered its doors while another asylum celebrated its twentieth anniversary. The anniversary of Hatchery House, located in the Nebraska Sandhills, is shadowed by tales of abuse and overcrowding at the now closed Topeka State Hospital in Kansas.

Reports tell of patients isolated, chained, and confined to their beds for long periods of time. An anonymous source who worked at the hospital claims one patient's skin grew over straps confining them to their bed. For years, TSH has been infamous for forced sterilizations of both habitual criminals and the mentally ill.

Given this history, people are concerned about whether Hatchery

House will also be susceptible to mismanagement and neglect of patients. The founder of HH, Howard Davis, insists this isn't the case.

'Even though inpatient facilities are out of vogue, they continue to be the best line of treatment for recalcitrant patients. Staff – both teachers and doctors – live on site. It's not an institution, it's more like a family.'

Hatchery House is funded by a foundation run by Davis. Before Davis started a billion-dollar energy company, he himself grew up in the cathedral that has now been renovated into HH. Back then, the cathedral operated as a home for unwed mothers as well as an orphanage. Nuns raised Davis in what he claims was a loving home life.

'Not everyone gets parents who care for them. We're here to fill in the gaps,' Mr Davis said.

'I don't—' I started to say as I handed the article back to Helen.

'The abuse and neglect – what if it's happening here? Students are fainting right and left, like they're being poisoned. Yesterday, Carly passed out after lunch in the hallway. And Ezra disappeared. And now Luis has been murdered.' Helen shook the clipping. 'Something is wrong with this place.'

I'd thought the same thing only moments earlier, but now that Helen was saying it, I felt implicit and defensive. I shook my head. 'We don't need to jump to conclusions right now—'

Her nostrils flared and her face hardened. 'Please, don't talk to me like I'm a hysterical patient.'

When shouting erupted from another room, Helen and I froze. It was Beverly's voice, ranting at someone who wasn't responding: *after all I've done, after all I've done.*

*

Leaving the classroom, my spine stiffened involuntarily as I hurried toward Beverly's office. It'd only been two hours since I found Luis's body, but the atmosphere had already become charged. Down the hallway, students' murmurs grew as they crowded around the dining hall door to watch. I waved my hand, gesturing at them to go back and not worry.

I knocked on the open door, but Beverly didn't seem to hear it. She screeched into a telephone receiver and slammed her hand on the desk. 'This place is my life and it's falling apart under me! Everything I've done, I've done for these students and for YOU.'

Howard, I thought. One time I'd overheard her muttering, *Nun in the House of Howard*, her lip curled with disgust. He had a magnetic hold on Beverly somehow; she was a tornado of nerves before, during, and after his visits.

Now, she inhaled sharply and blew the air out in a gust that ruffled the papers on her desk. 'How many years of my life have I given this place? How – how many DECADES? Don't tell me to calm down! I AM CALM.'

I knocked again.

'What?' she roared, whirling around to face me.

'You're scaring the students,' I said. I raised my eyebrows to say, *tone it down*.

Beverly daintily set the receiver on its cradle, took a few steps toward me, and slammed the door in my face. I reared back just before it smashed my nose.

A few students down the hallway giggled. I couldn't just walk away now; I already had trouble establishing authority with them during appointments. Steeling myself, I opened Beverly's door and stepped inside.

My office felt like a dusty, shadowed space, but Beverly's was a miniature chapel. Sunlight burst through the stained-glass window, rendering the room rosy and golden. A short church pew sat in front of her dark, gleaming desk. No cushions or rugs to warm the ascetic space. It even smelled like antiquity from the ever-present scent of wood polish and burning wax.

'You can't—' I started.

Beverly interrupted me. 'So, your colleagues are coming back. Your old job seems to have followed you, as if you missed solving cases.'

It was a weird accusation, but I sidestepped it. 'Actually, my work was in profiling and counseling—'

'I was worried when I hired you that you wouldn't be devoted to our mission,' she said.

When she'd hired me, she seemed to dislike my background in the FBI. 'You won't go looking for problems where there are none, being a kind of busybody, will you?' she had asked. It seemed odd at the time, but her personality had brimmed with a kind of religious fervor, so I thought the intensity was just her disposition.

Now, she pointed at me. 'If I hear one word that you are working the investigation from that side . . . you won't have a job here.'

I had expected Beverly's typical jitters or even a weepy agitation, but this steely anger surprised me. I tilted my head as if to say, *Aren't you overreacting?* but her already upright posture simply hardened with an audible intake of breath. Helen's article and the word *mismanagement* flashed through my mind.

'I know my priorities are to my patients. But I'll comply with the investigation . . .'

She waved a hand. 'Yes, comply, whatever. You know what I mean. This place will already have the media casting us as some backwoods institution; we don't need you informing on us, adding fuel to the fire—'

'Talking to the press is different from talking to the investigators,' I pointed out.

'You need to remember that *was* your job, but now *this* is your job. The students need to trust you to be treated. They need to feel SAFE.'

That word, *safe*, left a vibration in the room, and a vein in Beverly's forehead pulsed along with it. 'Apparently, the press has caught wind of it and is already interrogating the foundation. We were fundraising and Howard said we can't consider expansion now.'

We'd gone through this before when Ezra had disappeared, and I'd overheard Howard asking Beverly: 'How could you let this happen?'

She walked around her desk. 'Last week I had multiple calls from social services in Lincoln, asking when we'd have more beds,' she said. 'They're short of foster parents, so kids are being kept in understaffed hospital wings.'

When I continued to stare at her, my gaze reprimanding, she glared back at me.

'Surely you are also concerned with the perpetrator being caught,' I said carefully. My chest had tightened; I tried to breathe deeper to level myself out.

'Of course!' Beverly spat out, plumping down in her chair. 'But I'm the one who goes through the files of kids who don't get spots here. I'm the one who wonders where they go and what happens.

The system is full of cracks. There isn't enough funding for the treatment these kids need, not enough support structures. You don't know where they end up.'

You'd be surprised, I thought grimly. 'What's the name of that older woman who lives nearby?'

'Oksana Sussel. Why?'

'No reason.'

She seemed annoyed by my caginess, her brow furrowing. 'This place,' she said slowly, 'is important.'

This disregard of Luis made my face hot. The image of his body resurfaced in my mind: dirt under his fingernails, the thinnest sliver of an eyeball under his lashes, a missing button halfway down his flannel shirt. Her threat made me want to reconsider Cedar's plea to join the investigation.

A thunder of footsteps echoed through the House. It was almost time for the assembly.

'I don't think we should make the announcement at an assembly,' I told her. 'There could be an uproar. We may need to sedate—'

'We don't have time for one-on-one appointments,' Beverly said. 'Owen was already asking why Sheriff Anders is hanging about.'

'Owen was bullying Luis at the May Day festival,' I said.

She sent me a sharp look. 'I don't think you fully understand Owen. He cares more about his fellow students than he lets on.'

I'd noticed before Beverly was strangely protective of Owen, always making excuses for him and turning a blind eye to his antagonizing.

'Besides,' she said, giving herself a small shake. 'It isn't anyone from here.' When I looked perplexed, she went on: 'It was a stranger, driving down that highway. Luis was in the wrong place at the wrong time.'

I frowned. It could have been a stranger passing by on that highway, but I'd worked in forensics enough to know it was more likely to be someone familiar with the victim. Several of our students, most notably Owen, already had a history of violence. That was why I'd installed a deadbolt on my apartment door as soon as I moved in.

All of which meant it might – might likely – be someone at the House.

Beverly drummed her fingers on her desk, a twitch above her eye making her look like she was wincing. I'd let Cedar remind her of the statistics. Let him tell her it was more likely the killer walked among us.

CHAPTER 5

Luis would have been surprised by how his death was affecting Hatchery House. I'd written in his files that he had symptoms of schizoid personality disorder – which meant he seemed detached and didn't like interacting with others. But beneath his withdrawn affect and his predilection for being alone, I suspected he secretly desired the affection of his peers.

During our last appointment, shortly after he'd turned sixteen, he'd sat in my office, fidgeting with the cuffs on his flannel shirt, avoiding eye contact and murmuring responses to my questions. Sunlight fell heavy into my office and I almost had to squint to look at him straight.

'I think people like you, Luis,' I'd told him gently.

Luis blinked, his expression unaltered. 'Okay,' he said.

He had been so cold and unmoving, I couldn't tell if what I said had any meaning to him. Yet beneath this chilly exterior, there was a softness, a kindness. His parents had moved from Mexico City to a small Kansas town when he was a toddler, and then before he was twelve, they'd both died of cancer.

In the dining hall now, I stood near the door, back against the wall, where I could watch everyone. Eighteen students sat

34

around small, square tables, where two chairs remained empty. Lanterns hung from exposed beams in the ceiling and cast an orange glow over the students. A tapestry of the Madonna hung between two stained-glass windows, holding a baby that looked like a shrunken old man.

Beverly stood in front of everyone while they warily watched her. 'I'm so sorry to tell you this,' she started. She paused and inhaled, looking down at the floor. Owen elbowed Kristin and rolled his eyes, like it was a big joke. 'Luis Alvarez was found dead this morning near Ennenock.'

There was a sharp intake of breath and stunned silence. Expressions of confusion, shock, fear, and even a distorted fervor broke across their faces. A kind of excitement mixed with terror. No reaction is completely normal, but with these kids, normal reactions were even rarer. In our appointments, I'd watch their mouths when they spoke, and sometimes their hands. So many of the students were already good at practicing personas, but the lips and hands were the first to slip.

Beverly reminded the students that they were safe, meaning to comfort them, but it had the opposite effect. The youngest students began crying first. Carly, the ten-year-old with red hair, began wailing, covering her face with her hands and shrieking into them. Another student knocked his glass from the table and it shattered on the floor. The student next to him began rocking back and forth.

Across the room, Kristin fixed me with a steely glare, seeming indignant more than surprised by the news. Blame, I realized slowly, that was her expression. I felt something harden in me, a worry that she'd lash out in her distress. During most of my interactions with her, she'd bite her nails to the quick while complaining about the food or restrictions at Hatchery. But there were a few times I witnessed her penchant for quick-tempered mania – calling people names in a monologue of grievances before storming away.

Unnerved, I broke our gaze and sat down next to Carly, who sank her face into my shoulder. As her small hand sought mine, I searched each face in the dining hall, looking for remorse or even a gleeful self-satisfaction.

I noticed Dillon, my boyfriend and the only other psychiatrist on staff, was the only person missing from the assembly and it unsettled me. Didn't he know the students would need comfort? He'd been absent a lot lately, nowhere to be found even after I'd checked his office and studio apartment.

A shriek rose above the clamor and a student leapt from the table and hysterically tore at her hair before running out and down the hall. Others stared after her with blank looks of confusion.

'She's guilty!' someone screeched. 'She's done this before!'

I turned. Kristin stumbled as she tried to stand up. She wobbled and leaned against the table.

'She killed a patient before!' She lifted a hand and pointed at me. 'She said it was all her fault!'

I felt pinned by her finger and the stares thrown my way. Carly pulled away from me and a chill rushed in. My thoughts gummed up, but one escaped with clarity: *she couldn't know.*

The cavernous room became a cacophony of whispers. Beverly moved toward Kristin, palms up in a calming gesture, but Kristin stepped backwards. This outburst was different for her – her face wasn't red; it was pale and tired. She looked drugged.

'She told Dillon she killed a patient,' Kristin murmured, the strength going out of her voice. She wavered and then her knees buckled and she fell to the floor.

Beverly dove toward her and caught her head before it struck the floor. I hurried forward to help, but when Beverly waved me away, I halted in a partial crouch and stood back up. Carly, still seated at the table, now with her knees curled up to her chin, lifted her tear-streaked face to me. 'Did you hurt somebody?'

I ignored her question. 'Everything is going to be okay,' I assured her.

All eyes locked me in place. Kristin lay unnaturally on the floor, arms windmilled, legs splayed.

'I think it'd be best if you left,' Beverly told me when I tried to approach again. She whisked a lock of grey hair from her eyes and glared at me. I nodded and took a step back. They thought I could do that to Luis. It seemed so absurd, I wanted to laugh, but there was a tightness in my chest and a hot flush on my cheeks.

After leaving the dining hall, I walked down the long hall and tried to tell myself the accusation didn't matter; it would all pass. I'd blamed myself for Deborah's death before but hearing those words from someone else's mouth brought thrashing denial to the surface. Exposure made the accusation feel true.

At Hatchery, I'd told only Dillon about Deborah. I poked my head into his office and pushed back a rising agitation when I found it empty. He could be trusted; he wouldn't have shared my secret with a patient.

Despite this insistence, my pulse hammered too quickly; my

breath had gone shallow. It was overreaction, plain and simple. Sometimes, my body seemed to have a mind of its own, at odds with what I wanted and actually thought.

I burst into the foyer, heading for the outside door, when I saw someone out of the corner of my eye. Dillon stood near the door that led into the bell tower, fiddling with the handle, as though trying to get it open. Only Beverly had the key and the door was always kept locked. She had told me the stairs leading up the bell tower had never been renovated with the rest of the House and were dangerous.

'What're you doing?' I asked sharply.

His cheeks bloomed scarlet. 'What?' he asked, one hand still on the handle.

'With the door,' I said.

Dillon jerked his hand away and stuffed it in his pocket. 'Making sure it's locked. Feel nervous with what happened.'

He looked so bewildered and sheepish, I almost didn't confront him. 'Did . . . did you tell Kristin about Deborah?' I asked.

His face had that stock-stillness of making silent calculations. Then he reached for me. 'Hon—'

I knocked his hand away. 'What I tell you in private isn't meant to be shared with anyone, let alone your patients.'

'Whoa, slow down,' he said, hands out in front of him. 'I never told her anything. Maybe she overheard us? The acoustics in this place aren't the best for secrets.'

I frowned. 'She would have had to stand just outside the door.'

'Which is possible when you all live in the same building,' Dillon said. He was gentle when he said this, and it reminded me of how I hadn't liked him at first. I'd dismissed him, thinking him an all-American golden boy, like a bouquet of baby's breath.

He still looked like the athlete he'd been all through high school and college, when he ran cross-country and played lacrosse. He radiated an ease that made me feel off-balance before I got accustomed to it.

His family was from Connecticut and medicine was the family business. For him it was never a question of what he'd do, but what branch of medicine he'd specialize in. When I thought of his family, whom I'd never met, I imagined a 1950s magazine photo of a mom holding a casserole.

But eventually, his charm had won me over as he'd taught me how Hatchery worked, how life here could be at odds with my training. Psychiatrists are taught not to get personally involved with patients, yet here I was, eating in the dining hall with students, hearing them down the hall as they gossiped before bed. The boundaries would be more permeable, he'd told me. He'd arrived at the House two years before I did and had more experience with the unconventional setup.

We'd begun dating shortly after that. Being in a confined, lonely space brought us closer together, but a new relationship was also a faster way to put my old life behind me.

I'd been surprised by how quickly we fell into a rhythm. He'd bring me coffee in bed, teasing me about my messed hair, which sprang around my face in a mane when I didn't have it tied back. He'd kiss my fingertips before moving closer, rub my feet when they ached, cook when I needed to write patient notes. When I had a bad day, he'd tell me not to doubt myself so much, and I felt his confidence rubbing off on me, bolstering me. He began to feel like a prescription for recovering from everything that had gone wrong the previous year.

I stared now at the wreath of thistles on the bell tower door, trying to decide how much to say. 'They looked at me like I did it, Dillon. I can't establish trust with them if—'

'Everyone's scared,' he said firmly, taking my hand. 'Sometimes you come at me with guns blazing.'

I had an urge to pull my hand back, but remorse stopped me. He was right and I'd already decided that this relationship wouldn't be like my old ones – I'd be more trusting, not so quick to assume betrayal and sabotage everything. This time, it would be different.

I squeezed my eyes shut. 'I'm sorry,' I said. 'For accusing you—'

He shook his head. 'Don't worry about it. How are you holding up?'

I brushed past this question. 'Who told you about . . .' I couldn't say *Luis*. The morning had to be almost over; Cedar would be arriving soon.

'I was in my office this morning and Helen stopped by to tell me. I think you were on the phone with Cedar. I'd . . . I'd just gotten news of a grant I applied for.'

'I didn't even know you were working on a grant,' I said. 'Did you get it?'

Dillon suppressed a smile, the corners of his mouth twitching. 'Yeah.'

I pulled him into a hug and whispered congratulations in his ear. He squeezed me tighter, burying his face in my neck, and then he released me. His eyes were so bright, they almost glistened.

'What's the grant for?' I asked. It felt so good to talk – and think – about something other than Luis's death. A brief reprieve. Ever since dawn, I felt like it'd swallowed me up.

'I started it before you came here – I've been working on it for years, actually. It's for research on the relationship between anxiety and memory in a pre-adolescent and adolescent patient population. Specifically, how loss of memory plays a role in alleviating anxiety symptoms.'

I frowned slightly. 'As in, memory loss as a treatment for anxiety?'

'Well, research into the defensive biological mechanisms already built into memory loss. If we can better understand its role, we can adapt treatment to make use of it.' His eyes took on a distant, overcast look. 'I became obsessed with this place when I first heard about it. Couldn't wait to work here – the possibilities for research. So many controlled variables that you can't get elsewhere. And now look what's happening. It's enough to break your heart.'

I fingered the collar of his Oxford, tugged him closer to me and sank my head against his shoulder. I was attracted to him even now, despite the circumstances. But maybe the tragedy heightened it rather than diluted it, attraction sometimes being the means to escape the present. Lifting my head, I gazed at him. He had the tawny eyes of a cat, and a lock of hair fell over his forehead. I brushed it back for him, lingering over the soft skin at his temple.

'Take a breath,' he said. 'You're tense.' He rubbed the muscles between my neck and shoulders, then thumbed my chin up and

41

kissed me. Relaxing, I let my weight rest against his, inhaling his scent.

Cold air shot through the foyer. I turned to see Cedar holding the door open.

'Hey,' he said ruefully. 'Good to see everyone's in mourning.'

CHAPTER 6

Cedar looked better than the last time I'd seen him, a rosy flush brightening his brown skin with a healthy glow. But he still had the same wide shoulders and the open, earnest face of a much younger person, reminding me of how his mother would call him 'apple cheeks' with an affectionate chuckle.

The air in the foyer shifted, taking on a pre-storm stillness. I couldn't read Cedar's face; his expression held both contrition and a kind of wonder. I restrained from two opposite urges – to back away or to embrace him – and stood my ground.

'Hey, Lore,' he said softly, not bothering to acknowledge Dillon.

Cedar leaned forward to give me a hug, and after hesitating, I bent toward him and patted his back clumsily, as if he were my frail grandmother with dementia. His familiar scent clouded my mind for a moment, and I remembered how his fingertips had been calloused in high school from playing guitar; his touch had left invisible etchings on my body.

I shook loose from this and introduced him to Dillon. Cedar asked if I could give him a tour outside before he interviewed Beverly, and I agreed. His shoes clacked in staccato notes on the marble floors until we exited the House.

'I wanted to talk to you first since you found the body,' Cedar said. He nudged my arm with the back of his hand. 'Good to see you again.'

I nodded and kept a brisk pace. If he were just an ex, we could play at being buddies. Exes were forgettable, but Cedar was not. Our romance over the years, on and off, was as the Milky Way is to the rest of space. Miniscule, almost meaningless. But those years of friendship, of shared experiences and trust, of millions of words flung between us creating an imperceptible web, that was more than a single galaxy.

Pointing up at the eaves, I said, 'Camera was installed after Ezra went missing. Howard told Beverly we needed increased security. It records for twenty-four hours and then tapes over the previous day. Beverly stopped it this morning.'

Cedar's sedan was parked in the circular drive, behind an FBI crime scene van. Two techs crouched in the distance, one holding a giant camera and the other opening a large black bag. Bluestem grass and milkweed quavered in the wind and the high noonday sun bleached the landscape.

'Did you already . . . examine the body?' I asked.

He nodded. 'It's getting sent back to Omaha with a rush on the autopsy. I spoke briefly with Sheriff Anders when our men took over the scene and he gave me Luis's file.' He gestured to the front door. 'Does it have a security system?'

'Unlocked during the day, but after curfew it locks both from the inside and outside. At night, you can only exit or enter the House by entering a four-digit code. Only the staff knows it. But students sometimes watch us and figure out the code and we have to change it. When Ezra ran away . . . we weren't sure how long he'd known the code.'

'Who counts as staff?' Cedar asked.

'Beverly, Helen, Dillon, Albert and I. Albert lives in the cottage –' I turned and pointed at it, 'and the rest of us have apartments upstairs, next to the students' bedrooms. Albert is technically a maintenance man, but he also surveys the place like a security guard and keeps the students in line. There's a housekeeper and a cook who live in Augustine and commute in. They aren't given the code and don't really spend a lot of time with the students.'

Cedar scribbled down notes as I rattled off their names. 'And Beverly runs the whole place?'

I nodded. 'She also keeps her nursing license up to date, so she can administer chemical restraints if need be.'

'Physical restraints are used here?'

'There's a locked cabinet of wrist and ankle belts, mitts and vests—'

'By vest, you mean straitjacket?'

'Basically, yeah. We'd only use them in extreme cases.'

Cedar pointed at the windows. 'Can someone get in or out through those?'

'They can only be opened four inches. A security device was installed years ago, so the kids can't sneak out after curfew. And none have been broken.'

'So, he must've gone out through the front door,' Cedar murmured, more to himself than to me. 'Anyone else live around here?'

I pointed to Baba Yaga's cabin and told him about her strange behavior during the May Day festival yesterday. Telling him her real name was Oksana Sussel, I also explained why the students had given her her nickname. Sage-colored grass undulated over the sandy knolls and I tasted grit in my mouth as wind whipped topsoil into the air. 'What's the May Day festival?' Cedar asked.

'Irish nuns used to work here back when it was an orphanage and home for mothers. Guess they always celebrated that Gaelic festival – Bentane? Beltane? It's a pagan spring celebration. You know – dancing around the Maypole with ribbons, garlands of leaves and flowers, a big feast. Bonfires were lit to protect crops and cattle, keep the witches at bay. Howard likes that we continue the tradition. The fire pits on the other side of the House have been there over a century, and we roast a hog and light fireworks and the students stay out late and eat treats and act like goons.'

'Walk me through the rest of last night.'

I told him how I'd showered to get the smoke off me, then gone to Dillon's apartment to sleep.

Cedar stopped walking, a slightly stunned expression on his face, and he looked at me inquisitively. I stared back, refusing to answer a question he wouldn't ask. He registered this and sighed.

'So, you'll be each other's alibi?' he asked, pencil poised above his notebook.

Shit. I'd been so distracted by him, I'd forgotten to consider what I was willing to tell and what was pertinent to the investigation. I rubbed my hands on my sweater sleeves until the clamminess loosened. Back when I was a kid, I'd sometimes sleep outside because I felt trapped indoors. Occasionally, after we became friends, I'd stop at Cedar's house and rap on his window, asking him to come out. But more often, I'd lie down alone in the field between our houses. He'd find me in the morning, grass etched into the side of my face, dew damp on my clothes.

I couldn't bear the look of concern on his face, the worried questions: *you're still doing that?* Cedar had always had a tendency to view me as a bit ... broken, and it made me feel like pushing him away. Besides, Dillon wasn't involved in the murder, so it didn't matter if I gave him an alibi.

'Yeah,' I said and then walked him through finding Luis's body, including my odd interaction with Baba Yaga.

'So, she was with the body before you? Technically, she found it,' Cedar said.

We now stood in the quarter-mile stretch of sand dunes between Hatchery and Baba Yaga's cabin. Two coyotes trotted toward her barn, where a steep Dutch roof jutted beyond walls covered in chipping blue paint. The llamas began screeching first, high-pitched and piercing. Then the horses joined in, shrieking as they skittered in place, hoofbeats thunderous against their stalls.

We both glanced in that direction as Cedar ran a hand over his head. He seemed distracted and I guessed that something other than the investigation was keying him up.

'When was the last time you had a hallucination?' he asked.

I glared at him. 'I've told you before, they're really not a big deal.'

I'd had my first hallucination at age six, though I didn't know what it was at the time. I was with my little brother in my mother's house and I thought the hallucination was telling me what to do.

'You've seen a doctor since they started up again?' he asked.

'Of course.'

I hadn't. But my lie seemed to give Cedar a new determination. 'Will you go with me to interview Oksana?' he asked.

I tossed him a look of annoyance.

'Just hear me out,' Cedar said, palms up. 'Given how the last investigation went out here, what do you think are the chances this will go cold too?'

I didn't say anything.

Cedar continued. 'I need insight into these people and this place. It could make or break a case like this. Who are Luis's parents?'

'You know they're dead,' I said irritably. Sheriff Anders had given him Luis's file and I was certain he'd briefed Cedar on the basics in it.

'Right, so the parents won't be calling Mitchell three times a day to see if he's done enough. How long before Mitchell calls me back to focus on something higher profile, like the next raid? An agent's not going to stay on the field out here forever. You know the slow timeline of these things. We have to speed it up.'

Mitchell was Cedar's boss at the bureau. 'I can't view my patients as suspects and still treat them,' I said.

Cedar reached out as though he were going to touch my shoulder but dropped his hand. 'Just this one interview then. I need a second pair of eyes.'

I crossed my arms. He thought my curiosity would overtake me once I got started, but he was wrong; I'd stay loyal to my patients.

'I can't,' I said.

'Our last three solves together were because of your insights, because of your work with assets.'

'That's an exaggeration,' I said, though I did feel a tiny swell of pride.

Cedar stopped pacing. There was something he wasn't telling me. A new wrinkle creased his forehead and his eyes glowed like coals beneath heavy eyebrows.

'Sheriff Anders found something else,' I guessed. 'During the preliminary examination.' I was crossing a line, but my curiosity was indeed getting the better of me.

He stepped away from me; chewing the inside of his lip, he said, 'Lacerations on his back. Some old, some newer.'

'Newer? As in, since he's lived here?'

'That's what we're thinking. Made by something thin and hard, like a whip.'

No, that couldn't be. Someone here at Hatchery couldn't have abused him right under my nose. 'Maybe . . . maybe someone from his past? Has come here to visit and . . .'

Pity crossed Cedar's face. 'And no one saw this mystery person? I know you don't want it to be someone here, but the scars are over a long period of time – from the distant to the near past.'

I shook my head. 'How did he—' I began.

'Blunt force trauma to the head. We already found the rock dropped just a few yards from the body.' Cedar kicked a clump of dirt and it split open, powder-fine and pale. 'Something feels off. This feels larger, like there's something important we're already missing.'

'You need a partner on this,' I said.

'Mitchell might send me one later.' Cedar rubbed the back of his neck. Under his gaze, my skin felt like a dimmer bulb being twisted into full brightness. 'How long are you going to hide out here, Lore?' he asked.

'Did Mitchell assign you this case or did you ask for it?' I asked.

'I asked for it.'

'Why?'

I was scared he'd make a joke, something lame about wanting a good steak in the heartland. Instead, he tilted his head and asked, 'What do you think?'

Before I could respond, a gunshot went off and Cedar and I flinched. Baba Yaga stood in the open field between her cabin and the barn, shotgun at her shoulder, bloodstained apron around her waist, grey hair waving in the wind.

The coyotes ran from the barn, their bodies grey streaks across the golden grass. She followed them with the shotgun's barrel and fired again. One lurched and fell. The other disappeared over the hills.

CHAPTER 7

By mid-afternoon, I'd returned to my office while Cedar went to interview Beverly and I was now eavesdropping on students in the hallway.

'Owen said he saw her drifting down the staircase last night. Pale white with blood stained all the way down her nightgown.'

'I heard she goes to each room and knocks softly on the doors, looking for her baby.'

'Carly said she heard her humming a lullaby in the study room.'

Helen's soft voice interrupted and said something about seeing things that weren't there. Footsteps receded into silence. For months, students had been talking about this bereft mother they called the White Woman who haunted the halls, but their voices carried a greater trepidation today. I suspected there would be nightmares tonight, shrieks in the dark and wet beds by morning.

Sometimes, during a bad storm, collective anxiety would surge and terrified voices would wake me. And once, Dillon told me a story of a manic student who'd jumped straight through his second-story window, and when found bleeding in the grass, asked politely for a lullaby. Night bore the day's understory, the floor we walked on but rarely observed.

Though the students called Hatchery a prison, many also seemed attached and reluctant to leave. They talked big about wanting to live on the streets alone, but I suspected their real desire was to feel they could survive anywhere. Or maybe it was that they knew too much about where the funds came from. Their beds and meals and classes and appointments all paid for by those tax-paying middle-class families they hated, the ones they disdained for their garages and yearly vacations. As though it were alright to be cared for by your family but not anyone else, certainly not a stranger who wrote checks to the government.

'You identify with them too much,' Dillon had said many times.

I'd been annoyed by how right he could be. 'They don't want to be tossed aside,' I said.

'They don't want help?' he'd asked.

'A gift feels different from a birthright,' I'd told him.

Cedar acted like I was working here to voluntarily punish myself, so maybe he thought it was a prison too. But this rankled me less than his concern about my hallucinations. Of course, he was curious now that I wasn't filling his voicemail with reports of them. And all that time I'd wondered why for the first time in our almost three decades of friendship he wasn't calling me back.

Back in medical school, I'd seen a psychiatrist, expecting a diagnosis of schizophrenia. Instead, he told me I had PTSD and the hallucinations were traumatic interruptions to the present, a way the past reinserted itself.

'They can be exacerbated by stress or the perception of a threat,' he'd explained. 'But they can also worsen when you have moments of extreme cognitive dissonance. Some hallucinations are caused by sensory deprivation, but yours involve a kind of emotional deprivation. When you try to negate a reality you don't want to accept, you can actually intensify its presence in your life. For instance, if you ignore negative emotions or negative past experiences, you're not integrating them into your life. They find another outlet.'

He'd suggested exposure therapy, which would involve me spending time around fire, and I refused.

'Nothing will make me do that,' I'd insisted. The psychiatrist had warned me that if the hallucinations worsened, I could veer off into psychosis. I had the same fears my patients had: that I could lose everything, that something in me would spiral, dragging my better self along with it. This low-grade worry permeated any moment when I wasn't distracted or working and I wished there was more space, more forgiveness, for these fractures. An acceptance that being human sometimes meant you'd splinter before being put back together again.

I slid my box of dictation tapes into its hiding place under the desk and glanced at the clock again. Albert was never late for his appointments and I hadn't seen him since this morning. Since I was the only psychiatrist for two hundred miles, my job duties included seeing staff, if they needed treatment or therapy. Unless they preferred telehealth, Dillon and I were their only options.

I glanced out the window to look for him but found only the unending prairie. The hills undulated one after another, waves of grass so indistinct they looked like a mirage if the light fell just so. Like being out at sea with the sky pressing down, existence could warp around you.

Hallucinations used to be called a wandering mind, but it was more my fears that returned again and again, like rubbing the same spot on a teddy bear until the plush stuffing comes out. The world became a funhouse mirror, giving off a reflection of myself that didn't mimic my body. Because I only hallucinated myself and she was always dead.

My last one had been five months ago, right after moving into Hatchery, while I was unpacking my apartment. The floor dropped out from under her and she floated before me, suspended up high, where sung hymns once collected among the rafters, before silence snuffed them out. As though the cathedral wanted to insert its memory into me – an aggressive, domineering chant of *this is how I once was*. I stayed in bed the rest of that day.

I went outside to look for Albert. To the south, techs milled around the crime scene, dwarfed by the gnarled branches of the hanging tree. A group of students stood together between the garden and picnic table, where the grass was worn down to dirt patches. Owen stood on the picnic table, entertaining the small crowd.

Albert crouched several feet away, a clump of pulled thistles in one hand and an expression of distaste tightening his face. Beneath Owen's swagger, his practiced casual attitude, there was always a pressure in him that he liked to release on other people. I walked closer to the table.

Owen let his eyelids droop as though he were sleepy, imitating the often sedate expression Luis would wear. 'Oh, I don't have places to go home to,' Owen said in a mock Hispanic accent, turning his head side to side sheepishly, the way Luis would whenever he was forced to speak to someone directly.

No, he will not be your target today, I thought. I stepped forward but Albert cut in front of me. He bulldozed toward Owen, grabbed him by the front of his shirt and tossed him to the ground.

'Little shit! Think you can make fun of him now that he's gone?!' Albert roared, standing above Owen.

'I'd make fun of him when he was here, too,' Owen said flatly.

Albert's face darkened. He balled his fists and pulled back his foot as though to kick.

'Albert, please!' I said, stepping between them. 'What the hell? What are you doing?'

Albert glared at me and pointed at Owen. 'No one has stopped to teach him a lesson.'

I shook my head. 'We'll discuss this later. Go to my office. Go!' I pointed at the House.

He looked at Owen with such contempt, I thought I'd have to pry him away. But then he straightened, threw his shoulders back and muttered, 'This whole fucking world,' before walking away.

Once Albert was out of earshot, I told Owen to get up.

'I'm hurt,' Owen whined. He clutched his hand to his chest. 'I want to press charges.'

I inhaled sharply and told the rest of the students, 'Get inside in the next five minutes or you'll all be docked twenty points.'

The teenagers scattered. Owen just lay in the grass, gazing at me, the frown on his face softening into a grin.

A vision of Luis sprawled against the grass flashed before me.

Pale, all his blood pooled on his backside against the warm earth, as if heat were drawn to heat.

He deserved better. Luis would never send a letter to be tucked in that chest; his death was the worst kind of theft. This case couldn't go cold. Cedar was right: I did know this place and these people. I knew how investigations worked and knew good leads from bad ones. And if I owed Luis a debt, now was the time to pay it.

Deborah's grave wasn't the only one I'd visited before coming out to this land of erosion; I'd also stopped by my brother's. I'd placed daffodils on his tiny headstone and couldn't bring myself to say a word.

When he was three, he'd been terrified by monsters in the closet and he'd shake so bad, his teeth would rattle. One night, I told him that he needed to scare them away himself, so he opened the door and shouted into the shadows, 'Monsters, get out of here!'

I'd trembled with silent laughter at the sight of his saggy diaper butt and small frame dwarfed by the closet darkness. But years later, it was the image that heartened me when I'd lost my nerve. Turns out, good memories don't just keep people alive; they keep the good parts of you alive. They can urge you to approach your own closet full of monsters as you battle your doubts.

I knew I needed to work the investigation from inside Hatchery with a quiet certainty that felt like still water in my bones. I'd just have to find a way to play two roles at once: psychiatrist and informant. Counseling FBI informants had taught me about working both sides, so I could pull it off, right?

Owen stood up and brushed off his pants. Small cuts on his palms left smears of blood, like a bird's faint tracks in snow.

'What's that from?' I asked. I didn't believe he got them when Albert tossed him to the ground.

Owen thrust his hands in his pockets and shrugged. 'Mysteries abound,' he said and sauntered off.

CHAPTER 8

Back in my office, I sat in a plaid armchair opposite Albert, who dwarfed an antique wingback.

'What's gotten into you?' I asked him. Beneath my irritation at his outburst, a small part of me was pleased Owen had been humiliated in front of his admiring crowd.

'Little shit up to his usual,' Albert said mildly.

When I'd first come to Hatchery, I'd found Xeroxed copies of a drawing of Albert sodomizing a goat tacked up in hallways. Owen's docked points from that simply meant he had to clean the kitchen or do laundry. Unlike most of our students, Owen's parents were both alive and stable, with a house in a good school district and volunteer activities on weekends. *Born bad* was the phrase no one wanted to use, as if rot had darkened his veins at conception.

'Do you often struggle with anger?' I asked Albert.

'Do you often miss the point? That shit killed Luis. Or that old bag out east.' Albert jerked his head in the direction of Baba Yaga's cabin. Then, his eyes narrowed on me as if to say, *or you*.

I fumbled with my pen and set it down on top of my notebook. 'Why her?' I asked.

Albert fidgeted with the hem of his flannel shirt, rubbing his thumb over the edge again and again. 'I heard a horse last night.'

I sat up straighter, remembering the hoofbeats I'd heard outside, startling me awake after I'd fallen asleep.

'Yeah,' Albert said. 'Hoofbeats and a horse whinnying. I was out west, around the Indian tree, doing my rounds. When I heard it, I started walking toward the sounds, up near the bell tower. It was almost a full moon, but cloud cover made it too dark to see anything. By the time I rounded the front of the House, it was quiet again. But that old bag is the only one with horses for a twenty-mile radius.'

'Could it have been something else? Pronghorn?' I asked.

He scowled at me like I was an idiot. 'Pronghorn don't walk like horses. Just because they have hooves, don't mean it sounds the same.'

'What time was this?'

He squinted, as if trying to remember. 'I got back to my house around 12:40, so I reckon it was 12:30.'

I let out the breath I'd been holding. The hoofbeats had been real. I'd slipped outside around 12:15, and if I'd been more observant, or not so quick to doze off, perhaps I could have seen something.

'Did you see anything else?' I asked, hoping he hadn't seen me.

'No,' he said, but something in his eyes said otherwise.

My cheeks burned; I pulled my cardigan more tightly across my chest. 'You'll need to tell Cedar— Agent Knox about the horse.' When I held his gaze, he swore under his breath. 'I know how these things go. He's going to treat me like a suspect. He'll think I killed that boy.'

'Don't jump to conclusions; this is all just protocol. You can't impede an investigation, Albert,' I said.

The way he hoarded this detail made me think of Beverly's nervousness about the investigation. They had grown up together out west, in a small town close to the Wyoming border. I'd even heard rumors he'd dated her sister back in high school and had defended Beverly when she was bullied by a classmate. She'd given him a job when he got back from Vietnam and since then, he'd become a cross between a loyal servant and curmudgeonly brother to her.

He kept to himself and worked when he didn't need to, picking up sticks in fields that people only walked through, trimming bushes that weren't near the House. I could relate to those constant, small tasks, which quieted inner voices one needed to silence.

'Are you going to tell Agent Knox I attacked that shit?' Albert asked.

'Owen?' I asked. Due to everything Owen had done to others, him being flung from the picnic table hardly seemed worth reporting. 'Do you want me to?'

Albert didn't respond to this, which was fine by me because I wanted to hear more about his other suspect.

'I hear Beverly and Howard have been trying to buy Baba Yaga's land for years now. For the expansion,' I said.

'What of it?'

'You think it's upsetting Baba Yaga?'

'No telling what upsets people.'

I treated him for depression related to chronic pain from an inflamed spine, but clearly this appointment was for something else. I closed my notebook and leaned forward. 'We haven't talked about Luis. Were you two close?'

Albert bristled. 'He was one of the better ones. Did a good job weeding. Very exact. Always pulled the whole taproot up. Not like the others, just plucking leaves.'

'Beverly thinks it's a stranger,' I said. 'Not someone who knew him around here.'

Albert started chuckling, his bushy eyebrows low over his eyes, no mirth in the sound of his laugh. He'd never speak out against Beverly, not in her presence and not when she was absent. Wouldn't outwardly disagree with a word she said.

'You're not asking the right questions.' He scowled at the tissue box on the coffee table between us.

'How so?'

'Asking what I was doing, where I was at. What I saw. What did *you* see?'

His gaze held suspicion, unadorned and sharp, heavy as an object he placed on my lap. So, he had seen me outside last night. My spine stiffened and I raised my chin.

Kristin's accusation at the assembly flashed through my mind. How each person's face had tightened on me in a cold grip. Looking back at Albert, I realized Beverly had told him to keep this appointment to spy on me. I shuddered as if hit by a northern wind.

'Let's return to your new dose of Paxil. Was it 40 mg?' I asked, paging through my notes.

'That's not why I kept my appointment today,' Albert said. 'I want to tell you about something that happened years ago.'

No, you don't, I thought. You want to bait me. Outside, clouds drifted across the sun and the room gathered darkness.

Albert started speaking with the rhythm of recitation. 'Thirty-seven years ago, I almost killed someone. Not by accident, but because I wanted to. When I got back from Vietnam, my wife left me and took our daughter. I was drinking a lot and I was driving home from the bar drunk, and this guy . . .' He lifted his hand and gestured to an invisible someone. 'Just stepped out on the road. I saw him and for a split second, my foot stayed on the gas.'

His jaw worked hard and the sound of his teeth grinding filled the room. 'I slammed on the brakes at the last minute and the man dove out of the way. Rolled over the hood of another car, got banged up, I think. I don't know, I didn't stick around.' Albert ran a hand over his face and glared at me like I'd forced him to confess. 'Was so drunk, took me a few minutes to even realize what I'd done.'

I inhaled slowly. 'Why . . . why are you telling me this now?'

'On my mind,' Albert said, too quickly. 'With what's happened here.'

'When you say "wanted to", you mean . . .'

'Killing someone,' Albert said.

'Is that still how you feel?' I asked.

He shook his head involuntarily and leaned back in his chair, as though repulsed. Then, like an actor remembering his lines, he sat up straighter and said, 'Sometimes.'

The confession was too sudden and forthcoming, too labored and false. If my instincts were right, Beverly had asked him to confess to a violent impulse. So she could test me, watch what I'd do with it. Carry it straight to Cedar or keep it locked in my confidentiality code. I felt I was on a high wire and needed to step very carefully.

'I know what you're doing,' I said softly. 'Does it bother you that Beverly is using you like this?'

Albert's nostrils flared and he gripped the armrests, his knuckles whitening. 'Beverly's always been good to me. You can't even understand what those days were like. I killed more people than I know and was left in a daze. Every day since has been penance and nothin' will be enough.'

'Then maybe we should talk about your time in the war,' I said.

'You wanna talk about the jungle and the bodies? All the heat and ammunition? It was all I could smell – sweat and steel. We thought if we survived, we'd leave 'Nam and go home.

'But some places, you never leave. It infects your life – part of you stays there, locked up. After that night, I kept dreaming of his body on the pavement, as if I'd hit him after all. I couldn't sort out what I had and hadn't done anymore.'

'You're more than what happened in the war, Albert.'

'I'm not asking for your positivity bullshit. I'm not talking about myself. I'm saying the war was bigger than me, and when you hold something bigger than yourself, it finds a way out of you. I'll tell you something else, doc.' He leaned forward, elbows at his knees, hands clasped together in front of him. His hazel eyes bore into me. 'If you wanted to kill somebody, out here would be a pretty good place to do it.'

'What does that mean?'

'It means the killer wanted to be found. There's no easier place to hide a body but in these hills.'

'So, it was a display?' I asked. The doll nestled in the crook of Luis's arm had given it the quality of a tableau, a sense of intention.

'Or laziness. Lotta people lazy.' Albert leaned back and broke the string of energy between us. 'But I don't think that's it. It takes a real amount of anger to leave him facing the sky that way.'

Soon after Albert left my office, a high-pitched scream echoed down the hallway, startling me. Hurrying toward it, I found students crowded in the kitchen around the open door leading down into the cellar. Smashed fruit smeared the stone floor beside an overturned copper bowl, leaving an aroma of sweet-sticky pulp. Several students shrieked in response to the screams from the darkness below.

'Move aside,' I said, sidling past students toward the stairs.

'She said she was going down for jam,' a student told me. 'Kristin finished the last jar up here.'

'Who?' I asked.

'Carly.'

I hoped it was nothing more than a shadow that had startled her. Carly was scared of everything, so anything could set her off. She was so terrified of going outside that she sometimes wore paper bags over her head. Safe bags, she called them, so the world couldn't get to her.

I ducked my head to avoid hitting it on the short doorframe and descended. The musty air tasted like a wet blanket pressed over my mouth. A single lightbulb hung from the ceiling, sending long shadows behind barrels and crates filled with root vegetables. Glass jars of preserves glinted from the wood shelves lining the stone walls.

Carly was facing the far wall, where the light dimmed to dusk.

She had stopped screaming but was shaking, the sharp intake of her breath audible above my soft footsteps. Her body blocked whatever she was staring at on the wall.

Each footstep kicked up swirls of dust, and I coughed. A large spider skittered across a barrel and disappeared inside. A putrid odor filled my nostrils; I resisted gagging.

'Carly,' I murmured. 'I'm right behind you. It's okay.'

I reached out and touched her arm and she trembled against my hand, her whole body vibrating like a harpsichord that'd been plucked. She gripped a single tomato so tightly that its juice dripped to the dirt floor in soft plops. I took another step forward and peered around her.

My arms went loose and gummy. There was a hook in the stone wall once used for line-drying herbs. Now, a small wood cross with a crucified rat dangled from its hook. Its arms splayed, feet nailed together, head dropping over its chest. The rat's sharp yellow teeth had been pulled from its mouth and stuck into its own head. A kind of crown. And under the crucifix, a single word was written in white chalk: *atone*.

CHAPTER 9

I handed Cedar a list.

'What's this?' he asked. We walked down the hallway and paused in the foyer.

'Students with antisocial tendencies.' Owen's name was at the top. Cedar stared at the paper until he must have memorized the names.

'You think it's connected to Luis?' I asked.

Cedar shrugged, seeming reluctant to speculate aloud. 'It's possible. Though it could just be an attention-getting strategy from someone who knows something.'

After the rat had been bagged as evidence and the students calmed down, I told Cedar that I'd changed my mind and wanted to help with the investigation. He'd said that was great news, but his voice hadn't conveyed enthusiasm. Instead, he had traced an eyebrow with an index finger, a gesture he'd made since childhood whenever he felt conflicted.

But his hesitation didn't dissuade me. I was too busy hoping that my earlier confrontation with Baba Yaga wouldn't come up and embarrass me. Early interviews could be crucial. As trepidation tugged at me, I reminded myself that I didn't need to prove myself to Cedar.

66

We both looked out the window next to the front door. If I squinted, I could see the police tape flickering around the crime scene.

'The rat – what's with the religious symbology?' he asked.

'A student could be taunting Beverly. She's the only one here who's really religious. It's how the students mock her.'

'In my interview with Beverly she seemed purposefully unclear with her answers. Either that or she's too scared to think straight,' Cedar said. 'Tomorrow I'll interview Albert and Helen. What're your thoughts on her?'

I shrugged and stuffed my hands in my pockets. 'She's known as a good teacher; Beverly always says one of the best Hatchery has had. She's a bit mousy but really nice, Midwestern-style. Seems meek sometimes, scared of her own shadow.'

'Hello, Agent Knox, hello, Dr Webber.'

I looked over my shoulder. Helen stepped past us and opened the front door, giving us a shy wave before she ducked behind it. She was a picture of spring, with a flowing chartreuse blouse and her blond hair in a braid over her shoulder.

'Shit,' I muttered. 'Can't say a damn thing around here.'

'You didn't say anything too mean. Slightly condescending, though.'

I glared at Cedar and he chuckled.

'Let's get going before anyone else sees us talking,' I said.

We stepped outside and headed toward Baba Yaga's cabin. The bell tower loomed above and threw its shadow long and dark across the grass.

'I like the new boyfriend,' Cedar said.

'No, you don't,' I said.

'I don't?'

'You never like my boyfriends.'

'Hmm. True. So, I'm guessing my crew will have to stay in that shit motel on Eighth Street?' Cedar asked.

'That's the only one,' I said.

'Do they call it Eighth Street because there are only eight streets?'

'Now you're just being rude,' I said, but he did get a smile out of me. A familiar warmth spread from my chest to my limbs. It almost felt like we were children again, watching the cars that drove by his bedroom window, giggling over whatever absurdities we'd invented for the people inside. *Her new fiancé bores her, so she still talks to her houseplants. He once got so drunk he fell down an escalator and still made it to the top.*

'Learn anything helpful during Albert's appointment?' Cedar asked, elbowing me lightly in the ribs.

Wariness descended on me. I thought of all the informants I'd counseled at the bureau. Keeping a foot in two worlds was harder than I'd given them credit for. Homicidal ideation wasn't a crime, but if I did tell Cedar, he'd still question Albert about it. Beverly would tell me to pack my bags and I'd be out, not just of a job, but of the investigation. Besides, I believed it was all an act to manipulate me. I could tell Cedar later, if it seemed pertinent to the case.

'Not really,' I said, before remembering the other thing Albert had told me. 'Albert said he heard a horse last night.'

Cedar pulled out his notebook and wrote something down. 'I'll make sure to ask him about that during our interview.'

'Fair warning – he can clam up,' I said. 'He's already convinced you'll treat him like a suspect.'

'He *is* a suspect.'

'You might want to tread carefully. Some people out here . . . take a while to thaw,' I said.

'We did find hoof prints near the body, but it was impossible to date them. Dust keeps blowing around. We thought it looked like the blunt force trauma came from above.' Cedar squinted into the distance. 'That fits if someone was on a horse when he was attacked. According to Sheriff Anders, Oksana's horses are the only ones for miles. She'll probably say someone stole them.'

Old woman, living alone. If she did it and it went to court, her lawyer would plea insanity. Insanity defenses were tough to pull off, but juries already thought everyone out here was crazy.

'She found the body. And I think she left the doll,' I said.

Cedar nodded. 'Innocent bystanders don't normally leave objects. At least not at active crime scenes.'

As we got closer to Baba Yaga's property, we ducked between her barbed wire fence, one wire left sagging by a leaning wood post. A crow perched on a tree nearby; its head rotated to watch us.

We walked past a half-acre vegetable garden. The rows had been recently hoed, the soil dark hued with loam and peat. A feral cat twitched its tail between the wheels of a wheelbarrow.

'Do the students go to Ennenock sometimes?' Cedar asked.

I nodded. 'They slip away, go down there and destroy things. Throw rocks through windows, break old glass bottles. They're not supposed to, but they do. Owen likes to find birds' nests tucked in the eaves and toss eggs into the air and watch them split on the ground.'

'Geez,' Cedar muttered. 'I figured. The techs reported that there are footprints everywhere but it's hard to get a good sample. The ones that aren't blown apart by the wind are trampled by some animal. We think the crime started someplace other than the – what do you call it?'

'The hanging tree?'

'Yeah, and that Luis tried to run for his life. Initial body examination showed strangulation marks on his neck.'

'So, someone tried to strangle him, and he escaped and fled?'

'It's a working theory. We're searching Ennenock for the original crime scene but it's hard to find signs of a struggle when that's this whole fucking place.'

True, I thought. Wind whittled these hills, and eroded soil bleached in the sun like bones.

'The only family I could reach was an uncle in Dallas. Didn't know Luis well. Said family was nice, but religious in an extreme way. Made him uncomfortable a few times but wouldn't say why. "Don't speak ill of the dead" was all he'd say. Kept confirming his brother was a good dad to Luis.'

'Luis had been really close to his dad. He wouldn't open up about a lot, but he did say that.'

'Lore!' Cedar cried out, catching my arm and yanking me hard against him.

'What?!' I clutched the collar of his jacket to keep from falling.

Cedar pointed at the ground, where I'd almost taken my next step. A rusty animal trap lay open, its iron teeth partially covered by grass.

I cursed and released my grip on Cedar. 'Thanks,' I muttered.

'She probably has more. Watch your step,' Cedar said.

Baba Yaga's cabin was made of rugged tree trunks and a tar

shingle roof. Smoke snaked above the stone chimney, hardly visible against the ivory sky.

Beyond the barn, a rusted metal windmill creaked. As a child, I'd visited an uncle's farm on slaughtering day. This place reminded me of that. That solid, unsparing hostility you found in a bull's eyes before you butchered it.

Once we were on the porch, we could hear heavy footsteps from within the cabin. A scrape and rustling, as if things were being moved aside. When Cedar reached forward to knock on the door, it swung open and a rifle's barrel nearly poked me in the chest.

I yelped and jumped backwards, and Cedar scrambled off the porch, tripping and sprawling across a patch of dirt. I stood frozen with my palms up. Baba Yaga didn't lower the gun. She wore a faded blue dress, black boots and a white apron with bloodstains that cradled her round belly.

Behind me, I heard Cedar yank his revolver from its holster.

'Ma'am, I'm with the FBI—' Cedar started.

'I know who you are.' Her voice was a wire brush on a potato. 'I'm not going without a fight.'

'You're not under arrest,' I said.

'Whaddaya mean?' Baba Yaga's eyes flitted between Cedar and me. She seemed unconcerned that Cedar was pointing a gun at her.

'I'm just here to ask a few questions,' Cedar said, a quaver in his voice. He didn't scare easy; this had to be the first time he'd pulled his gun since the botched raid.

'I don't have answers,' barked Baba Yaga.

'Ma'am, if you don't let us have a word today, I'll just have to come back. You're a prime witness in a murder investigation,' Cedar said. I heard his footstep behind me.

'You're not here to arrest me?' she asked.

'No, ma'am,' Cedar said.

Her eyes narrowed to slits. 'Didn't witness nothin.' He was already dead.'

'I believe you, but we still have some questions,' Cedar said.

Baba Yaga looked between us one last time and then sighed and lowered the gun and opened the door wider. She propped the rifle against a corner. It was old, with a heavy wood stock and long barrel, the kind I'd seen pictures of in history books.

She caught my gaze and nodded. 'Husband's father used that when he went to fight in the South. Don't make guns like that no more.'

The cabin smelled of blood, smoke, and lilacs. Glass jars of lilac sprigs sat on an entryway table, making the cabin feel cozy despite the austerity. Baba Yaga waddled toward the kitchen sink and gestured to a headless chicken floating in hot water. 'You interrupted me. Now the skin will tear when I pluck the feathers.'

'I'm sorry, ma'am. We didn't have access to a phone num—' Cedar said.

'That's cuz I didn't give it to you,' she said.

Undeterred, Cedar introduced us, and Baba Yaga barked at us to sit down, gesturing to a wood table. The front door opened into a living room that held only a rocking chair with a quilt thrown over its back. A hallway led to the back of the cabin, where I assumed there was a bedroom and bathroom. My eyes adjusted to the dim light, which came from a small window over the kitchen sink and the fireplace.

The flickering fire made my hands go clammy; I wanted to leave. *The fire is in the fireplace*, I reminded myself. I started to sweat but managed to beat back a rising nausea.

'Did my trap almost get you?' She seemed aware of my discomfort, her face shining with mirthful hostility.

I raised my chin. 'Almost.'

Her lips peeled in a smile to reveal yellow teeth. 'Those damn c'yotes.'

Cedar cleared his throat. 'Beverly Testa told me you've visited Hatchery House more often recently. Requesting to speak with her about Howard wanting your land—'

'Only a few times. She's the one who comes here constantly. Wants a chat. Lonely.' Baba Yaga shook her head. 'That woman's made fear a twin sister. And the kids there don't know how well they got it.'

Did she really think this or was she lying? I'd seen Baba Yaga on the grounds more often in the last few weeks, red-faced as she squabbled with Albert while he trimmed bushes or glaring steely-eyed at the students as she marched down the House's steps.

'Ms Sussel, can you tell us where you were last night?' Cedar asked.

'Here.'

'Can anyone confirm that?'

'No.'

Cedar rubbed his forehead with his palm. 'What time did you go to bed last night?'

'I don't go to bed. What's it those kids call me?' She looked at me.

When I said *Baba Yaga*, she grinned, clearly pleased by this name. 'I have insomnia,' she announced. 'I wander at night. I tried those drugs to make me sleep a while back. They made me drowsy the next day, so I stopped.'

'Then did you see or hear anything unusual?' Cedar asked.

'One of my horses, Adrik, was stolen. I left a bag of seeds out by the garden and didn't want critters getting into it. So, I go outside and hear the horses whinnying. It's pitch-black and I can't see nothing, but I hear the barn door creak. So I grab my gun and flashlight, but he's already taking off by the time I get back outside. See this damn leg . . . had polio, slows me down when the weather's changing.' She jabbed her right leg aggressively.

'Were you able to get a look at who stole the horse?' Cedar asked.

'It was him.'

'Him?'

'That boy. The one who got killed by the hanging tree.'

CHAPTER 10

The fire's crackle filled the room.

'Luis? Luis Alvarez stole your horse last night?' I asked.

'Only had my light on him for a few seconds before he was outta sight, but yah. So when I saw him lying there the next morning, I thought he'd been thrown.' She frowned and chewed the inside of her mouth for a second before continuing. 'Seemed like a good rider, but I guess anyone can be thrown.'

Luis's grandfather had a ranch in Mexico. We'd never talked about it, but maybe he had spent time with horses when he was younger, before moving to the States.

Cedar fumbled in his pocket for his notebook. 'What time did he steal the horse?'

'How would I know?' Baba Yaga asked.

A grandfather clock stood against the wall near the fireplace, but none of its hands moved. Baba Yaga caught us looking at it. 'I have a working clock,' she snapped. 'But when you're my age, you realize time doesn't matter so much.'

'Can you take a guess?' Cedar asked.

Baba Yaga burrowed down in her chair, tucking her chin into her neck like a toad waiting for flies. Finally, she raised her chin. 'Between 12 and 12:30.'

75

'Did you hear anything else last night?'

She gave me a long, measured look, and I felt a hot flush. Like Albert, had she seen me outside? But she turned back to Cedar and shook her head no.

'And what happened this morning?' Cedar prompted.

'Not much you need to know about,' Baba Yaga muttered. She pulled at a loose thread on her apron and pushed her cloud of white hair back. I winced when she placed her hand back on the table. Beneath the knobby knuckles and thin skin, crippling inflammation knotted her fingers into crooked angles. Only degenerative arthritis could twist a hand into a claw like that; it was one of the worst cases I'd seen. Since she lived way out here, I doubted she was getting the pain management she needed, and I admired her refusal to let it slow her down.

'Woke around four to find Adrik pawing the grass outside the barn, wanting his breakfast. I figured the boy must not have taken him too far since he found his way back. So, I fed the horses and llamas and put Adrik back in his stable. Then I went walking out west. Saw vultures circling. Was hoping it was a roadkill deer I could haul back to my place. Sometimes they get hit on that highway and wander into the grass to die. Meat stays good at least a few hours unless critters get into it.'

Cedar checked his notes. 'Dr Webber here says you had an ax with you. Why?'

Baba Yaga glared at me. 'Hatchet,' she corrected him. 'Fallen birch out there. Wanted the firewood. It's not my property, but no one's using it.'

'What happened when you found the body?'

'He lay there.'

I swallowed a laugh and a choking sound escaped me. Her matter-of-fact manner combined with the stench of the dead chicken made it all feel absurd and surreal. I pulled my body into compliance, straightening my face into a sedate expression, and apologized.

Cedar shot me a look before returning his attention to Baba Yaga. 'Did you leave anything with the body?'

Baba Yaga stiffened. She pulled her hands from the table and crossed her arms.

'What of it?' she asked.

Cedar didn't ask her again; he simply kept his dark eyes on her. His face was so neutral and passive, it felt like he'd erased himself until he became a shell, a receptacle for other people's stories. You could deposit a piece of information in him and get no reaction. He'd gotten better at this since the last time I'd seen him.

Baba Yaga held his eyes defiantly. 'His was a bad death, not his own. Not his time. Bad omen that he died on May Day. Won't have a good harvest now, only storms.' She shook her head violently, the skin under her jaw swaying. 'The doll is for his spirit. So it isn't vengeful for his bad death.'

Baba Yaga let her eyes wander the cabin, bored with us and our questions. Cedar raised his eyebrows at me as if to say, *Can you believe this shit?* The doll had been made from the same birch as the fallen tree and I imagined her standing beside Luis's body and fashioning it. I couldn't tell if she believed her own hocus-pocus or was performing her role as the prairie witch. I couldn't tell if it made a convenient story to hide other, darker motives.

Baba Yaga placed both hands on the table and hauled herself upright. 'Be off with you. Chicken is almost sour.'

'Ms Sussel, I have a few more ques—' Cedar began.

Baba Yaga waved her hand in wide swipes like she was erasing us. 'We're done.' She shuffled toward the sink.

Cedar gave me a meaningful look. We needed more. More context, more information; even just her perspective could provide a clue to chase down.

'I'm going to have a quick look around your barn, if that's alright,' Cedar said to Baba Yaga's back.

'Llamas will spit on you,' she muttered.

I grabbed Cedar's arm when we reached the door and leaned close. 'I'll get more out of her. Just wait for me outside once you're done,' I whispered in his ear. Interrogating witnesses had always been my favorite part of the job.

Appreciation flickered in his eyes. 'Don't think I should leave you . . .' The sound of sloshing water filled the cabin as Baba Yaga lifted the chicken from the sink.

'Don't worry,' I whispered. 'We'll enjoy a few martinis and girl talk.'

He smiled and squeezed my hand before stepping outside. Baba Yaga had hung the chicken upside down above the sink by slinging its tied legs over a hook in the ceiling. She stood before it, ripping feathers out with fast, practiced pinches.

'People keep stealing my horses, I'll have to set traps for them as well as the coyotes,' she said.

'I don't think traps discriminate,' I said.

She gave me a look that said, *Who the hell invited you to this conversation?*

Family photos covered one wall from floor to ceiling near the fireplace. Apart from these, a single photo hung in the kitchen.

In it, Baba Yaga was young, with smooth, tan skin and dark hair. She wore a mid-century nurse's uniform, a starched white dress with a crisp white cap.

'Thought I told you to leave?'

'You were a nurse?' I asked, sidling closer to the photo.

Her mouth flattened in a tight irritated line, but she seemed unable to hold her words in. 'Stationed outside Saigon in 1959. Only twenty-one years old at the time. Terribly hard work, but I enjoyed it.'

'I work in medicine, too,' I said.

Her expression didn't lose its bitter shape. 'S'pose they have woman doctors now, too.'

'Do you like living close to Hatchery House?' I asked.

Baba Yaga yanked the chicken from the hook and flopped it on the counter with a thud. The bloody feathers in the bucket gave off a metallic odor. The gooseflesh was yellowed, and the talons were so large against its shrunken body, it looked reptilian.

'Would be better if they left me alone. Yadda ya. Yadda ya. Always talking.' She bobbed her head with this imitation and a sneer twisted her lips. 'That headmistress and her henchman. Should watch those kids closer, if you ask me. They don't know those children from their own asses.'

I suppressed another laugh, but a smile still escaped. 'How long have you lived here?' I asked.

'Born in that room back there.' Baba Yaga jerked her head down the hall as she gutted the chicken. 'Father's father got the ranch back when land was a quarter or so. My father found Mother's picture in a newspaper and she took a boat over from St Petersburg. Three children died in the womb, and then me. So,

79

I got the land when they passed on. Husband and I raised cattle on it for years until he died. Kids all grown . . .' She wiped sweat from her brow. 'Living their own lives. None of them interested in ranching, so I farm it out.'

'Have you ever thought of moving? After living here so long—'

The sound of blade on bone filled the cabin as Baba Yaga started hacking the chicken. 'You don't know what it is to have roots, do you? I'm part of this land; it's part of me. Why would I want to leave? You need someone, or something, to belong to. Otherwise you're—' Baba Yaga waved her hand around in a circle.

Untethered, I thought.

'Just yourself,' she said, the shadow of a Slavic accent sharpening her consonants.

For how much Baba Yaga insisted she wanted to be left alone, she talked like someone who craved company. I inched closer to the photos near the fireplace, my curiosity so intent I could almost ignore the heat. In one, Baba Yaga held a baby, and three school-aged children clustered around her. Her face was blank; her eyes sightless. Her sallow skin and dark eyes reminded me of the painting of Christ that hung in Beverly's office. The look of someone not fully in this world.

In the photo just below it, she sat on the floor, holding a baby to her breast and laughing, her head tilted back, pale neck catching the sunlight. Her eyelids were half closed. My hair prickled in its roots. I'd had patients who looked like this – gleeful, insane, seductive. It wasn't a look of disconnection or being off-kilter, it was one of the expressions of psychosis.

'Get back from that!' Baba Yaga barked.

I stumbled and tripped on a rug. 'I'm sorry—'

'Think you can snoop around here because some kid got killed? Get outta here.' Advancing toward me, she waved her knife.

I was desperate not to lose the little ground I'd gained. 'I – I have years I don't really remember, too,' I said, guessing that her life had ellipses as well. 'I know how it feels to need a life – not just that you want to remember, but that you can bear remembering.'

She halted and her face softened as her eyes shifted to the photo. Her expression became animal and wary, a wolf when offered food on a doorstep. As she looked at her past self, she grew smaller before me, shrinking down from the legend of Baba Yaga to the person Oksana.

'I'm sorry to intrude,' I said.

Two competing visions of her fought for attention. In one, she wanted to catch a thief, and rode her horse into the night until she knocked him out. In the other, she wandered the hills as the students said, but looked at Hatchery, hazy in the moonlight, and wished them well as they lay in their beds.

'He'd been here before,' she said when I reached the door. 'Him or someone else. Few days before, I saw footprints around the stables. Don't know if that helps you.'

'It does. Thank you,' I said.

To my surprise, she opened the door for me. 'Don't get many visitors other than that Beverly,' she said, perhaps by way of apology.

'Does it get lonely?' I asked.

'I didn't use that word,' she snapped.

Out on the porch, the crisp air was a relief from the stuffiness of the cabin. A hawk sailed across the sky, arcing in a wide loop back toward a smattering of cottonwoods to the east.

'I know what kind of doctor you are,' she said quietly, her coarse voice barely above a rasp. 'Good they have that kind of doctoring now.'

Oksana said this with such surprising tenderness and something akin to affection that I turned to respond, but she slammed the door in my face.

CHAPTER 11

On the way back to Hatchery, I told Cedar what I'd learned from Oksana.

'You did good,' he said, not quite meeting my eye.

We paused in the circular drive. White thistles swayed in the wind, reminding me of the dry tufts of white hair around Oksana's face. Cedar's eyes were so often filled with merriment that they almost glittered, but now they were shadowed. The warm sheen of late light made him look vulnerable.

'Get a drink with me in Augustine? Been a long day,' he said.

Part of me wanted to; but I also needed to protect myself, so I didn't end up in the same spot as before. Besides, I needed to check on the students and spend the evening with Dillon.

'I should—' I started.

'All I want right now is a few minutes sitting across a table from you,' Cedar said.

I blinked. This was new; the old Cedar didn't tell me what he wanted. Something had changed during those months we hadn't spoken.

'Okay,' I said. Out of the corner of my eye, framed by a thin window, I saw a figure in the House, watching me. But when I looked again, no one was there.

'What is it?' Cedar asked.

'Keep getting the feeling someone's watching me.'

The smells of stale coffee and artificial citrus hit me as I climbed into Cedar's car. A few grocery bags filled the backseat. I smiled; Cedar was the only agent I knew who stopped at local stores to stock up on real food while he was traveling on a case. Most filled their cars with gas station fare or empty McDonald's bags and their luggage with heartburn medication. Even as a child, Cedar had been mindful of what he ate, teaching himself to cook as soon as he moved out of his parents' house.

As I snapped my buckle, a pressure built in my head and I heard a faint ringing. Heat pressed against my skin. Oh shit, I thought.

Opening up to Oksana had knocked my defenses loose. Now my phantom was gathering steam, insisting on being let out. I stared out the window, motion sickness catching me in its sway, even though Cedar hadn't started driving yet. I tried to beat back the rising terror but sweat still gathered at my hairline. She was coming.

Whenever this happened, my whole body clenched, as if I could will her away. Even if I squeezed my eyes shut, I could feel her near me, daring me to look at her. Irrationally, I worried she would reach out and touch me with ice-cold, faintly blue palms.

Cedar was saying something, but his voice was far away and faint. He was circling the drive now, about to turn on to the gravel access road, when the old well came into view.

It'd been dry for decades. It was a circular stone well with cracked mortar. A hollow feeling opened in my chest and there she was. Perched on the rim of the well, blackened with burns up one side of her body, clean and clear on the other. Patches of red, raw skin puckered around charcoal flesh. A hazy, thick film covered one eyeball and that eye fixed on me.

'Lore? Lore? Shit, Lore.' Again, Cedar's voice, distant and clouded. He stopped the car and grabbed my shoulders; he turned me to face him. 'Lore, look at me, now.'

His face seemed far away too, but it was still a comfort. The rough seat fabric had imprinted on my palms and I loosened my grip. The world was clearing again. Soon, a lark's trill was the only sound above rustling grass.

I leaned my head against the seat and closed my eyes.

'Did you lie to me?' Cedar asked.

I lifted my head. 'I don't get them as often—'

He swore and hit the steering wheel with his palm. 'Your psychiatrist said if they worsened, you could have trouble telling if they're real.'

'He wasn't able to spell out what constitutes "worsened", so there's no reason to panic.' I breathed into my joints and shook my hands loose.

'Does Dillon know? Someone here should know,' Cedar said.

'We're not yet to the part of our relationship where we share our visions of dead things,' I said.

'This isn't a joke, Lore.'

Other people couldn't stop the hallucinations, so what was the point in telling them? Everyone lives with things: with obsessions, tragedies, disruptive thoughts. I wanted to believe everything could be treated for all people, but knew there were limits, or at least, limits for me. I knew from my work that sometimes patients got worse before they got better. Like risking inflammation to cut out an infection. I couldn't gamble with a nervous breakdown, not now, after I'd come so far. So I told myself to always move forward, keep my eyes trained ahead.

Cedar launched into a speech on how he was having doubts about me being so involved with the case. While I wasn't listening, I squinted at the well. Most wells in this region had pinewood walls, crumbling inward from rot and the weight of gravity. But another well, on a homestead four miles west, looked identical to this one. I'd visited it one cold winter day when I'd gone driving to find a distraction.

'You said you think the crime started elsewhere?' I asked.

'Yeah.'

I told him about the homestead. 'It's abandoned and isolated. Perfect place for a crime. You said you haven't found anything at Ennenock, yet.'

Cedar frowned. 'But why would his body end up close to Ennenock? Four miles from the House is a distance to travel, even on horseback.'

'Would only take a half hour or so, a lot less at a gallop.'

'I just want a fucking drink,' Cedar said.

'You disappeared on me. If we do this at all, we'll do it on my terms,' I told him.

I'd been holding that card for a while, but my satisfaction dried up when I saw the pained look on Cedar's face.

'I made a mistake – I was thinking it could be like old times. Working together. I wasn't taking your needs into account.'

'You don't know my needs,' I said. 'We'll get a drink after. Here, let me drive. Country roads are tough to navigate.'

I got out of the car. Cedar exited the car and put his hands on the roof.

'When I said I was interested in your insights, I didn't mean I wanted you to take over the case,' Cedar said.

We switched places and I pulled the car on to the highway.

Soon we were crossing the river, tires rattling on the open-grate steel bridge. The water seethed below us and gnawed at the bank. We were both quiet. Once Cedar spoke, his voice had gone pensive.

'Luis . . .' Cedar said. 'His body looked the same way Warren's had in my nightmares.'

'You never told me you dreamed he'd died,' I said quietly.

Warren was Cedar's older brother, the brightest in the family, with a full ride to college. The summer before his freshman year, he and a cousin had been playing ball in a neighborhood park when several men attacked them. The cousin had run, thinking Warren was behind him, but Warren had been hit overhead with a bat and had collapsed in a coma on the damp grass.

When he woke from his coma, Warren had the cognitive abilities of a four-year-old. Today, he lived in his mother's house, the one he was meant to leave twenty-five years ago. That summer – Cedar was eleven and I was ten – other hate crimes had struck our neighborhood and Warren's attack was added to the unsolved list.

That night, I had sat up straight in my bed, moonlight coming through the parted curtains, the stale smell of unwashed dishes wafting upstairs. Cedar's mother's wails had vibrated in the night sky, held aloft like a constellation.

I'd lost my own brother four years before and Cedar knew this because it'd been in the papers. I kept a certain aloofness between us, my way of assuring him I wouldn't make him suffer that generous sympathy people pour on you when your sides are splitting open. I'd just be in the same space as him, another breathing thing, something warm and rooted as a houseplant.

He began to seek me out, inviting me to play in his driveway. In the evenings, he'd knock on my window and we'd slip outside and sit on the grassy slope between our houses. From it, we could see an overpass littered with graffiti and neighbors' backyards, filled with broken grills and children's lost shoes. When nights were warm, we'd sleep next to each other, waking wet with dew, squinting from the sun in our eyes.

One night, I'd woken to see him watching me, eyes full of tears, face so tense, I knew he had been holding in a scream. I pulled him into my chest and held him as he wept. I felt his sadness like a great pressure in my chest, as if my rib cage had shrunk and now my heart couldn't beat properly. The city lights always dimmed the stars. Sirens and the screech of tires crowded us. I wished I could hold him somewhere else, somewhere darker and quieter, where the stars could be seen.

We turned on to the homestead's long gravel drive, overgrown and knotted by buffalo tracks, bumping and jolting until we stopped abruptly before a one-and-a-half-story clapboard house. Further back, a barn had partially collapsed, its roof caved in the middle. A bucket with a rope lay on its side near the circular stone well, as if someone had recently dropped it.

The house itself felt familiar, not from when I'd last been here, but in my deeper past, reminding me of my mother's house that sat outside of a small town in northern Nebraska. My parents had divorced the year after my brother was born, when I was four, and we would stay with my mother over Christmas and during the summer. The rest of the year, we'd live with my father in the same neighborhood as Cedar's family.

'I'm trying to say,' Cedar said, 'it's not just my abysmal clearance rate and how Mitchell is always going on about desk duty if I don't turn it around. This case also reminds me—'

'I'm not going to mess it up,' I promised him.

'That wasn't what I meant—'

I leaned toward him and pressed a finger to his lips and pointed. Beyond a broken window, a figure moved in the house.

CHAPTER 12

The figure disappeared from view.

'My God, Lore,' Cedar whispered. 'You were right. This could be the crime scene. That could be the killer.'

I felt a thrum of triumph until Cedar pulled his cell from his pocket, saw the 'no service' signal and cursed. He picked up his radio.

'Agent Knox here. Need to relay a message to Sheriff Anders—'

A crow cawed and alighted from a fence post into the reddening sky.

'Thanks. We'll be standing watch.' Cedar set the radio down.

'They already know we're here; what if they make a run for it?' I asked. 'We should go in now.'

'Sheriff Anders will get here in twenty minutes or so.'

'It'll be almost dark then. Dusk shifts to pitch-black fast out here.'

Cedar's face remained placid.

'You've never been out here when it's dark,' I said. 'You'll never find someone with just a flashlight or your headlights.'

'We don't know—' Cedar started.

I wasn't going to lose this person, so I slipped out of the car.

Cedar followed and unholstered his revolver. He popped the trunk and pulled out two flashlights.

'You will stay behind me,' he said. His normally melodious voice had turned brittle and clipped.

I held up my hands to say, *fine*.

The front door was off its hinges, propped against the house, and the stench of feces, rotting food, and ash hit us as we crossed the threshold. A fireplace smoldered with embers, leaving the room dim with smoke. Cracks ran in deep fissures up the walls; piles of trash littered the floor.

In the corner of the room, a glass jar lay on its side, quivering from movement within. I knelt in front of it. Instead of a lid, a rag with tiny holes had been fastened over the jar's opening with a rubber band. Smudges of leftover peach preserve stuck to the glass and thousands of ants scuttled inside.

I stood and stepped back. Someone was trapping insects. A scuffling sounded from behind the wall.

Cedar and I exchanged glances. We crept toward an open archway separating the living room from the rest of the house.

There was the sound of teeth grinding together. Then, a clatter like a dropped dish. Sunlight glinted off Cedar's gun as he raised it before crossing into the next room. A snarl sent a tremor up my spine. I thought of fur and glowing eyes in the night.

Cedar leapt backwards. He stared at whatever crouched behind the wall; his expression a mixture of astonishment and revulsion.

From where I stood, I could only see a window with no glass behind a kitchen counter. Wind burst through this split seam and whirled dust around our feet. Lowering his gun to the ground,

Cedar held out his other hand as though to calm a wild animal or a violent person.

'Easy,' he said softly.

Someone had drawn a monster with a stout body and short horns on the opposite wall in soot. A rancid, acidic smell came from the kitchen, where a rusted handsaw was stuck midway through a table, a small pile of wood dust beneath it.

Grinding teeth again, then a growl. Cedar wouldn't look at me and I couldn't read his face anymore, so I stepped forward.

A small boy squatted on the counter next to a farmhouse sink, shoving a fistful of ants into his mouth.

My hand flew up to cover my mouth. Lightheaded, I reached out to touch the wall. The boy glared at us before scooping the rest of the ground-up ants from his tin bowl, all those mandibles and exoskeletons mashed in a jumble of tiny legs. He swallowed them, smacked his lips, and set the bowl down carefully at the edge of the sink.

Ezra.

I couldn't believe he was alive. Underneath the shock, relief swelled in me. His file said he was nine years old, but he looked much smaller than that. He had thick black hair, tanned reddish skin and gaunt cheekbones that turned his eyes luminous. Defiance in the set of his chin and certainty in the tense muscles of his face gave him an older, aggressive appearance.

But then the relief passed when I thought of how a kid at dusk should be reading a bedtime story in pajamas, snug under artificial light, or playing ball with friends, evading his mother's call to come home. Heat filled me to the brim.

'What the hell . . .' Cedar whispered as he holstered his gun.

'The runaway,' I said softly, keeping my eyes on Ezra. I worried he'd leap from the counter and dart away as soon as I released my gaze from him.

Cedar looked back at Ezra, astounded. 'He – he's . . . alive?'

Ezra picked at something beneath his fingernails and licked his fingertips as his eyes darted between Cedar and me.

'We should get him to the nearest hospital. Renbolt is two hours north.' When I took a step gingerly toward Ezra, he bared his teeth.

'It's okay,' I murmured. 'It's going to be okay.'

Ezra backed further against the windowsill, knobby knees up to his chin, feet gripping the counter's edge. Sweat plastered hair to his forehead; dirt coated even his long eyelashes. He smelled rank and I tried not to grimace as I stepped closer.

'I'm just going to help you down. You're going to be safe.' I reached out to touch his arm. He snatched my hand, yanked it toward him, and buried his teeth in my wrist. His teeth struck bone and I screamed.

I wrenched my arm back, stumbled, and fell. Blood trickled into my elbow crease. Cedar lurched forward to grab him, but Ezra slipped through the open window. There was a tumble on the ground and then the soft footsteps of bare feet running on grass.

Cedar squeezed through the window; I scrambled to my feet and ran out the door. Ezra was already over a knoll and ascending the next. Cedar and I sprinted after him. The distance between us widened and I pumped my legs harder, muscles burning. Dust clouded my vision and my eyes watered.

Half a mile on, the gap between us shortened. I could barely see him in the fading light and fixed my sight on his black crop of hair, swishing with each step, the lone dark spot in the expanse of golden grass. Grass whipped against our legs and I panted for breath.

When Ezra was close, I reached for him. My fingers grazed his arm and I stumbled. Cursing, I charged forward, caught his arm, and we toppled to the ground.

Ezra wrestled to get free and I grappled for a hold of him. We rolled and turned over and over. His hands were out like claws; he swiped at my face.

Cedar lifted Ezra from me and pushed his chest against the grass. With one hand, he held Ezra down, and with the other, he pulled out handcuffs.

'Don't,' I said. My breath clogged in my throat.

'Lore, we need to restrain him. It's for his own good, too.'

'As long as we carry him,' I said. I pointed to the soles of Ezra's feet. Small cuts oozed blood; a burr's thorns bit into his big toe. Beneath the dirt, veins and bones bulged in a way I'd never seen in a child's feet.

Cedar blinked down at them and then said, 'Of course.'

Ezra didn't fight once the cuffs were on him. At first, he made a strange hissing sound, a weak, wordless threat, but then he went silent and limp, as though playing dead.

Sheriff Anders had arrived once we got back to the homestead. Loading Ezra into his car took some time because his fighting spirit had returned. He bared his teeth and writhed free of our grip, collapsing to the ground. When we finally got him restrained in the back, he sat in a crouch, as if hoping to spring through another window.

While Sheriff Anders drove Ezra to the hospital, Cedar and I stayed behind to check out the property. My bite wound throbbed when I touched it, but it no longer bled. Cedar applied antibacterial gel to my arm and bandaged it with supplies from the first aid kit in his car.

'Strong canines,' Cedar said.

'I'll let you approach him first next time,' I said.

'We're lucky for your long legs or we might not have caught him,' Cedar said.

'Glad they came in handy,' I muttered.

'I didn't know you still ran. Your high school self would be impressed.'

I knew he wanted me to chuckle; I knew he needed a moment of lightness, but I didn't have it in me. Mirth disappeared from Cedar's face as he gazed at the well. 'I'm going to start out here and then canvas the inside,' he said.

I nodded. 'I'll meet you in there.'

Twilight erased the horizon as grass and sky blended together. Inside the house, a photo of a corpse – a man in Victorian clothing – decorated the mantel. In front of the fireplace, a stockpot full of water steamed.

Ezra had boiled the ants before grinding them in his bowl. Smart kid.

I climbed the stairs. Covered in a fine layer of dust and soot, the walls felt soft beneath my fingertips. Old wood groaned under my feet, the scent of vinegar and grit reminding me of a barn.

The upstairs was a single room with a gabled ceiling. In the middle of it, a small bed stopped me in my tracks. Threadbare blankets on the floor. An old sweatshirt rolled into a pillow. Urine stains. Small lines carved into the wood close to the pillow, as though he were counting days or trying an image to comfort himself.

My throat threatened to close up; the sense of ruin here felt familiar. Ezra camped out in a room where he felt safe, high up, as though in a tree.

I started to look away and then I saw something. Kneeling, I fished a crumpled, sepia-toned photo from the dirty bedding.

Twin girls in Victorian dresses stared back at me. One of their faces had been scratched but I could still see they were identical. I thought of the dead man's photo down on the mantel and wondered if these had been his daughters. But then I noticed what the girls were standing in front of: the bell tower of Hatchery House, when it was an orphanage. I tucked it in my pocket.

A small door separated this room from the unfinished attic space. I knelt in front of it, pushed it open, and peered inside.

Two large snow owls watched me. My heartbeat staccatoed against my chest and I gripped the door tighter.

Twilight burst through the partially caved-in roof and illuminated their bodies. If they opened their wingspans, they would be five feet wide, taller than the boy they slept next to at night. Their eyes glowed yellow in the gathering darkness and they were perfectly still except when they blinked. Talons protruded beneath their alabaster feathers.

Cedar's footsteps filled the silence and his flashlight beam swept across the gables. I stood up and blood rushed to my head.

'The kitchen pantry's full of empty jars of homemade fruit

preserves and pickled vegetables. I think hunters might've used this as a camp-out a few years back, because I found empty cans of expired beans and soup in the cellar. Kid must have raided that stuff before moving on to insects,' Cedar said.

'Water?' I asked.

'Used that bucket to haul some up from the well. Actually looked fairly clear.' He kneaded his forehead.

'Owls are nesting in that attic.'

'This is messed up—' Cedar said. His face was too compassionate and it was irritating me.

'I think they kept him company,' I said. My voice sounded high and cheery to my own ears. I struggled against a rising pressure in my chest. I wouldn't have lasted as long as Ezra had. I, too, had once scavenged for food, slept without a bed, and submitted to the weather's whims, but only for a few days.

'I don't know why, but this reminds me a bit of your mom's old house,' Cedar said.

'That's a bit hyperbolic,' I said quickly.

'Lore . . .' Cedar reached out to touch my arm.

'Oh, I'm fine,' I said and threw a fake smile his way.

Space between us widened and I was somewhere else. Frozen ground beneath my feet. A locked door. I'd split my knuckles against it, pounding. My little brother, Carson, was inside.

No, we weren't going there. This wasn't about that. Cedar might see straight through me, but I wasn't going to indulge his sympathy. My eyes burned as I turned from him and looked out the single window between the eaves. I could already smell the coming darkness, the night animals that would emerge, their bodies warm and feral, leaving only faint tracks on these hills.

CHAPTER 13

'Tomorrow morning meet at the diner in Augustine?' Cedar asked me after he pulled up to Hatchery. Full darkness had fallen and pressed around us. 'Say nine-thirty?'

'Yeah. Bring the case file and we can review it together,' I said.

'Hey,' he said as I started to get out. 'I'm glad you were there today.'

This dispelled some of the heaviness in me and I smiled. 'I told you that you needed me.'

He grinned. 'Get out before I start driving.'

I entered the security code and headed straight for my office. I left the hall lights off, so I didn't disturb anyone. At night, the House felt haunted by its days as a cathedral. I could almost smell incense and see flickers of votive candles against the walls. Heavy drapes over my window caught the wind and swished against the floor like a priest's robes. I thought I heard scuffling footsteps outside my office door, but when I looked up, I didn't see anyone.

When Ezra had disappeared, Dillon made a copy of his file for me. I opened it on my desk now. *Ezra lived with his grandmother for most of his life other than a few brief stints in foster homes. Grandmother suspected of verbal abuse. Mother only sporadically involved in son's life, often homeless, and addicted to opioids. Currently living in homeless shelter. Father unknown. Ezra ran away from grandmother's house soon after his ninth birthday and when found, he had selective mutism.*

The notes went on to describe his living conditions while he was a runaway, for a period of two months last summer. After stealing a small camping tent from a neighbor's garage, he'd built a camp in the woods near the Missouri River. I could picture him inside it, huddled in a pile of blankets, the sound of water rushing past. Many kids threatened to run away, but Ezra actually planned it and did it – he packed food, water, and warm clothing in bags later found at his encampment.

Investigators pieced together his routine from items at his campsite and Ezra's reluctant nods during questioning. At night, he'd sneak to the nearby neighborhood, digging in the trash like a raccoon. He found empty milk jugs in recycling bins and used outdoor faucets to fill them with water. He took packages off porches and repurposed their contents: a scarf tied between two trees for a small hammock, a briefcase as a pantry for scavenged food.

After he was found, he wouldn't speak at all. A few months later, he'd utter monosyllabic words in brief phrases, though only if he was with someone he knew. In groups or with authority figures, he wouldn't speak at all. He liked to draw and occasionally could be compelled to write a few words. Mutism was often caused by social phobia, but in Ezra's case I wondered if it wasn't also an exercise of power, of refusing to engage in a world that didn't seem to deserve it. So little was under his control, but his speech – or lack of it – was.

Police interviews with his grandmother revealed Ezra's

motivation to run away. Her house was dirtier than his camp and she flung curses at him with an expectation of gratitude. *Can you believe this sonofabitch, just like his good-for-nothin' father, can't be trusted for a minute, after all I'd done for him*, she'd told the police. *Just go and keep the little rat.* What she, and no one else, could reveal, was the source of his determination to live.

The police report mentioned finding insect traps made from empty food containers and an old Folgers tin can near the ashes of a fire, presumably used as a pot for boiling the insects before grinding them up. When they asked Ezra what made him think of this, he'd smiled and written two letters: TV. His grandmother confirmed he loved those survival shows where people filtered water through their socks and used their sunglasses to start a fire.

Not long after, his grandmother had died, and his legal guardian became a great-aunt who lived in Sioux Falls. In her late sixties, with mobility issues, she'd decided Ezra would be better off at Hatchery House than living with her.

The grandfather clock in the foyer chimed and I dropped my pencil. A shadow slipped beyond my doorframe. I squinted at it and decided to ignore it. Night always spun my imagination into high gear.

Back in December, when I'd first started work at Hatchery, I had met Ezra outside by the river, where we were both taking refuge from other people. He sat at the edge of the cliff bank, legs dangling over the side. I started to ask him to scoot back, but he held his finger to his lips, shushing me before pointing to the frozen river below.

I had leaned forward but could see only fog. A bellow ripped through the icy air and a crash vibrated up the cliff walls. My hair prickled as the fog thinned and two buffalo emerged. One grazed on a small island in the middle of the river, pausing only to bellow at the other, whose hooves slipped on the ice as it tried to reach the grassy island.

The ice split in a thunderous crack. Water whooshed around the buffalo and swallowed its hind legs and rump, leaving it to claw the ice around the island, flailing and finding nothing to catch. I knew how that felt, had felt it so acutely, my own hands grew cold and I stuffed them in my pockets. When I looked at the boy and he looked back at me, I saw that he knew too. How it felt to be hungry when someone else was fed. To flail in humiliation.

Finally, the buffalo pulled itself up on a bank opposite the island. When it emerged from the icy water, its whole body steamed, as if covered in fog once again. I shuddered. Bodies steam when they go through fire, too, a vaporous shadow you never fully shake.

Later I'd discovered that there was a wildlife refuge twenty miles northwest of Hatchery and the buffalo were sometimes allowed to graze down by the river during drought years. That night, I'd dreamed Ezra and the buffalo stood face to face and the buffalo did not crush him with its hooves. The dream revealed my admiration of him, maybe even my acknowledgment that on some level he intimidated me. Later, I saw that it even held some envy of his gumption, his willingness to leave the place other people put you in.

My door creaked and I jolted. The sound of breathing echoed down the corridor; footsteps pattered on the marble. I knocked the file to the ground as I stood up and called out, 'Hello?'

Silence, then a tapping. I heard the front door open and stepped out of my office in time to see a figure disappear into the night.

I dashed into the foyer, punched in the code, and yanked the door open. Black surged before me, the person nowhere in sight. Breathing heavily, I reminded myself not to overreact. Beverly had already changed the security code, so it was likely Albert, checking on the House before turning in for the night. He often did that. This was normal.

Despite this, a tiny hard curl of foreboding unfurled in me as I walked back to my office. Flipping off my light, I felt like a deer in the rifle's target and couldn't stop myself from pulling back the drapes for one last look.

At first, it was too dark to see anything. But as my eyes adjusted, a shape began to form faintly, a hazy figure against a sea of darker shadows. The person stood in the tall grass staring back at me.

CHAPTER 14

May 3, 2007

I awoke from a restless sleep in my apartment, still trying to convince myself that Albert had only been roaming the field last night. But I couldn't shake the feeling that if he'd been keeping watch, it'd been on me.

Distracted and dazed, I kept dropping things as I got dressed. I couldn't tell Cedar about being stalked because he'd get concerned and pull me from the case. I considered telling Dillon, but brushed it aside. He was busy, preoccupied with his own coping during this tragedy, and besides, we were still getting used to each other. I didn't need to burden him with this. I had moods when I wanted to be alone; he had moods when he was snappish. He was working on something big he didn't want me to know about yet and he had a tendency to slam his laptop shut when I entered the room at the wrong time. If I didn't respect his privacy, he'd go tense and side-eye me with a warning look.

Dillon was my fresh start and I wasn't going to squander it or scare him away with undue neediness. However, I was curious about where Ezra would be transferred, and since Dillon was his physician, I assumed he'd been updated.

On the way to Dillon's office, I passed Carly in the hallway. She smiled maniacally; lips spread to show almost all her teeth. 'I've gone into the tower, but my mouth is sewn shut,' she said. She tapped her lips with her finger and sauntered past me.

I stepped into Dillon's office and asked him if Carly was doing okay.

'She's adjusting to a new med regimen,' he muttered, shuffling papers on his desk. There was a charged feeling in the air and Dillon seemed tightly wound.

'You had a busy night last night,' he said, not meeting my eyes.

There was something odd about his tone and I didn't respond to this quip. I'd sent him a quick email last night, filling him in on what had happened and explaining I wouldn't stop by like I normally did since I was working late. I wondered briefly if it had been him, checking on me in my office, but brushed it aside. He wouldn't creep outside my window like that.

'How's your old friend?' he asked.

I drew out the word 'good' in a way that I hoped would jar him into the present, but he didn't look up. What always surprised me was how even though Dillon and I had training in communication, we still got caught in patterns, still couldn't escape the hold of our own conflicts. Naming things could help, but sometimes words felt powerless, an endless stream passing us by as we were caught in the grips of something greater than language.

'You just seemed to disappear for a long time yesterday,' he said.

I frowned. This was curious, coming from him, because there were often long stretches of time when I couldn't find him anywhere. Before I could respond, he asked, 'Could you take Kristin on? My patient load is still impossible. And I think she'd be more comfortable with you.'

'I've already taken a lot of your patients; at this rate, you'll only have Carly soon,' I said in a teasing tone, hoping to lighten the mood.

Dillon's face darkened and he straightened up to his full height. 'Now, of all times, you're going to whine about your workload?'

Shocked, I shut my mouth before I could tell him to go fuck himself. I inhaled deeply and told him it was a joke; that I'd take Kristin on if it'd help him. I was so off-balance, I almost forgot why I'd come here in the first place.

'Is Ezra still at the hospital?' I asked.

'He's here.' Dark circles under Dillon's eyes gave him a hunted appearance.

'Here? Why?'

'The doctors evaluated him for dehydration, injuries, malnutrition and psychotic symptoms. Other than the selective mutism, he's surprisingly healthy.'

'We aren't transferring him elsewhere?'

Dillon sighed. 'This is his current home. The closest inpatient facility has no beds open, and we need to establish continuity of care. Students respond best to routine and familiarity. Also, his guardian insisted he be kept here. She doesn't want more paperwork.'

He sounded like Beverly. She'd sent out an email this morning asking all staff to *help life return to normal as much as possible.*

'He ran away. Aren't we worried that – it could be related—' I said.

Dillon finally looked up at me. 'He ran away months before Luis's murder.'

I wanted to believe this, but something was bothering me. 'He left his packed bag by his bed. Why would he do that?'

Dillon shrugged. 'He was probably nervous while trying to sneak out and forgot it.'

A protective instinct in me began to expand, a frisson of energy. 'Can I see his medical report?'

'Why?'

'Did he . . .' I couldn't say *have scars on his back*. 'Did he have any signs of abuse?'

'I thought he was living out there alone.'

'I meant older signs of physical trauma – from back when he was living here, before he ran away. Cedar is considering Luis's killer could be someone inside the House.'

'Does Agent Knox have reason to believe it's someone inside?' Dillon's tone sharpened with defensiveness.

I feigned ignorance and shrugged. That moment with Ezra on the cliff lingered in me and brushed up against this new vigilance. I wanted to be the one to treat him; the one to make sure he was okay. 'Could I take on Ezra instead of Kristin?' I asked.

Dillon tilted his head. 'Don't trust me with him?' He clearly wanted it to be a joke, but it came out accusatory and I didn't want to admit to either of us that this could be true.

'I just . . . it'd be a good challenge for me. I haven't worked with mutism before.'

I could tell Dillon didn't buy it, but I wouldn't back down. His fists rested on the desk as he leaned against it. 'Are you sure you're not more interested in investigating than being a doctor?'

'Part of treating a patient is assessing their safety,' I shot back.

He grabbed Kristin's file and tossed it toward me. 'Take both of them. That'll lighten my load.'

I caught the file and felt a second of detachment, looking at that man in a crisp Oxford shirt, a single hair never out of place, and wondered who he really was.

Dillon cursed and rubbed his forehead. 'Look, I'm sorry. Just struggling here. We're all under a lot of stress.'

I nodded, but uneasiness still rested like a cold hand on my back. Stress was a catchphrase for a lot of negative emotions. Negative emotions, I told my patients, could be messages. They could reveal what was there all along.

I found Helen in the lounge, behind the transept, where the high altar and choir had once been. She wore a slightly translucent yellow blouse that quivered from her shoulders, like a leaf that trembles under gravity as it falls.

'Helen, can we talk?' I asked.

She kept sifting through old photographs, as though she hadn't heard me. Something about the way she held her head down, blond hair shrouding her face, made me suspect she was stone-walling me. I knocked on a pillar, the raps echoing around us.

'Oh, hello,' she said softly.

'I wanted to apologize for yesterday,' I said.

'Yesterday?' Helen asked.

'I thought – perhaps you'd overheard – when I was talking to Cedar . . .'

'Oh.' Helen shook her head. 'Don't worry. We're all out of sorts and prone to being a bit more harsh with each other.' Before I could respond, she went on: 'Your boyfriend and old friend sure don't get along.'

'What?' I asked.

'They had a fight in the dining hall yesterday. Well, argument. Dillon didn't want to be interviewed and insisted he didn't know anything. Cedar kept pushing. They didn't tell you about it?'

This unsettled me and I wondered if it were the reason Dillon had been testy with me, when normally he was so easygoing and supportive. Cedar could get assertive; it was part of why he was so good at his job – he knew how to press past someone's defenses. But Dillon probably smelled it from a mile away and took it as an affront.

'There's a lot going on,' I told her, hoping this minimization would comfort her. 'I should get back to my office.'

Helen held up the photos in her hand as if I hadn't spoken. 'Beverly asked me to go through these and get rid of the most disturbing ones. They're photos from the asylum days.'

She laid them out on the coffee table, and I knelt in front of them. There was a man in a restraint chair, drawings in excrement next to a bed with straps, a hand reaching out between window bars, and a baby in an iron cage. The last was a photo of a woman in a bathtub, water up to her neck, a vacant expression on her face. Hydrotherapy, I thought; the water had been icy-cold, and she froze half out of her mind.

'But Hatchery had only been a mother's home and an orphanage,' I said.

'Before that, it was an asylum for a short time. Makes me wonder what the future will say about us?' She looked at me expectantly.

'Do we offer any treatments quite this bad?' I asked. I was sensitive about the comparison, but didn't want to show it.

Instead of answering, she asked, 'Do you think some of them liked it?'

'Liked what?'

'Breaking people.'

I was taken aback. 'We're not saints, but we're not devils, either. These treatments were of their time. Most did the best they could.'

'One bad apple,' she murmured. She carried an odd stillness, her face clouded and eyes blank, as though transfixed.

This made me feel defensive. 'Besides, we get consent for most treatments, now.'

She seemed humored by this, giving me a lopsided smile as she refocused, her tone turning harsher and more confident, asking, 'What does consent mean to an addled brain?'

Before I could respond, she spoke quietly. 'When the people of Ennenock built this church, they never could have foreseen what'd happen. That mine explosion was like Sodom and Gomorrah. Now it's a city of ghosts, holding so many souls.'

It felt manipulative, the way she kept shifting the conversation with her steady, sedate voice. I followed her gaze to the wall, where carved wooden angels with hostile faces hung between the stained-glass stations of the cross. 'They look like birds of prey,' I said.

She nodded solemnly. 'In the Bible, angels weren't cherubs.'

CHAPTER 15

When I asked Cedar for the file, he hesitated. I sat opposite him in Huck's Diner, in a cheap vinyl booth, where white fuzzy stuffing burst from splits in the seat. Stray cats loitered between rusty trucks in the parking lot and a layer of grime on the wide windows turned the sunlight grey-hued.

'You wanted me in on this,' I said. 'I'm the one who found Ezra.'

'I have to do things by the book here. The bureau is already under too much scrutiny, ever since the raid—'

'So, we both have reasons to keep this quiet,' I said. Scanning the diner, I told him about Beverly threatening to fire me.

He chewed the inside of his lip. 'Why'd she assume you'd work on the case as an informant?'

'She's paranoid about staff leaving after they've been hired – a lot of people won't stay out here. With new hires, she's scared they aren't dedicated to the job and becomes a bit controlling. That's what Dillon says, at least.'

'She seems pretty obsessed with keeping the case quiet too.'

'For years she's been trying to expand Hatchery, but bad media coverage from Ezra's disappearance led to social services in the state withdrawing support for expansion plans. Howard and

Beverly are trying to gain it back. Operation Public Relations,'
I said.

Our waitress, a stout woman with fire-engine-red hair, took
our orders. Toast for Cedar and a steaming pile of eggs, sausage
and hash browns for me.

'You know, if things hit rock bottom, you could always stay
with me.'

'Yes, I'd love to lose my job and couch-surf at your place,
thanks.'

'I actually meant that I could rent a different place. Something
you like, somewhere quiet.' Cedar rushed on. 'And Mitchell would
take you back if you need another job.'

'I'm not setting foot in that station again,' I said.

He sighed and pushed the file toward me; I skimmed it quickly.

Cedar twisted his coffee mug in a nervous gesture. 'The agents
searched that homestead months ago, right after he'd gone
missing. How'd they not find him?'

'Kids like Ezra – they know how not to be found. Ezra has run
away and hid before. Maybe over time he let his guard down and
that's how we found him.'

'But how did *he* find the homestead? And why run away in the
opposite direction of the road? I'd think he'd head for Augustine,
hitch a ride somewhere else.'

I ran a finger over my bandaged wrist; pressed my lips together.
'The first time he ran away, it was toward nature, away from civ-
ilization. So, he's repeating that behavior. But I worry . . . could
Ezra running away be related to Luis's murder? Because he saw
or heard something?'

'I suppose . . .' Cedar frowned. 'But we don't have evidence linking them, so we shouldn't jump to conclusions. Have you started a profile on the perp yet?'

'Barely,' I said, gulping down coffee. Somehow, even the coffee smelled like oil and fat in this joint. 'Any evidence on the body besides the doll Oksana left?'

'Not really. Some blue fibers we're getting processed.'

'Autopsy?'

'I'll get preliminary results tomorrow.'

'I forgot something when I gave you the tour,' I said. 'There's technically more than one exit – but no one uses it that I'm aware of. There's an extra door in the foyer that leads into the bell tower. Beverly always keeps it locked – apparently, the bell tower was never renovated; it's dangerous – and only she has the key. But, if you get into the bell tower from the foyer, you can get outside because there's a small yellow door at the base leading outdoors.'

'Same key for both doors and only Beverly has it?' Cedar asked.

'That's what I've heard. I'll try to double-check in a way that isn't obtrusive.' I thought of what Albert had said about leaving Luis to face the sky. 'If the killer felt guilty, leaving Luis's body the way they did is not typical. Normally there is some movement of the body or covering. But strangulation suggests intimacy; blunt force trauma does not. The different modes of attack and position of the body contradict each other.'

I shuffled through the file and pulled out large photos of Luis's body. A close-up of his hand with bruised knuckles and cracked fingernails. A bright red scratch on the side of his neck, like someone had gone after his face and missed. Defensive bruises on his forearms from blocking blows. 'Does anyone at HH have wounds on their hands?'

'No, but they could have been wearing gloves.'

'Which would make it premeditated. Though it'd be hard to scratch someone with gloves on.'

Cedar nodded. 'It wasn't cold that night. Low 60s?'

Dishes clattered on the counter and our waitress set plates in front of us. A portrait of Jesse James hung above us, slightly crooked. Next to it, there was a black and white photograph of a Native American burial, with a body up in a tree and the sky a swirl of chiaroscuro.

'What can you tell me about Luis?' Cedar asked. 'Anyone upset with him?'

'I doubt it. He . . . seemed scared to exist. Didn't say or do a lot, much less enough to upset someone.'

'Yeah, but with some people, it doesn't take much. Take Owen. Give him one weird look and he'd start beating a person.'

'Maybe the profile should start there.'

Cedar brushed toast crumbs from the side of his mouth. 'Where?'

'Narcissistic injury. Extreme reaction to a minor episode.'

'So, who at Hatchery displays high levels of narcissism?'

He probably expected me to list several patients, but I thought of Dillon first. During arguments, I'd glimpsed a frailty that transformed him into a snarling version of himself, a mirror reflection gone rogue. Often it appeared when something challenged his accomplishments. On better days, he joked that he was married to his career, that he'd been groomed for it since he was a child, and that's why he took it so seriously. Devotion to a job could be healthy, I told myself. Besides, we all had our shadow sides.

This was magnification; I focused on his less desirable attributes because he'd upset me this morning.

'I don't want to give names until I've thought about it,' I said. I forked sausage into my hash browns and changed the subject. 'So, you think Luis was targeted? That if anyone else had stolen Oksana's horse that night and ridden away, they wouldn't be dead?'

'Both my theories so far posit it's a victim-specific crime. And right now, I'm assuming whoever cut up his back is the one who killed him. Which narrows it to someone who has been around him for months; not someone outside Hatchery. My bigger question is whether it was spontaneous or planned. If it were a hate crime, it was planned—'

'But since Luis stole the horse, not the killer, it seems spontaneous.'

'Right. So, the other theory is Luis stole the horse intending to meet someone somewhere.' Cedar pointed to the photos of Luis's defensive wounds. 'He and another student meet but get into a fight. It escalates.'

'It could've been someone other than a student,' I said, thinking of Albert's face when he threw Owen to the ground.

'Lore, if you overidentify with your patients, you won't be able to give an unbiased evaluation.'

'Got any other nuggets of brilliance for me? For the record, the media is always linking mental health with violence, but the mentally ill are more often victims than perpetrators. If they hurt anyone, it's most likely to be themselves.'

Cedar sighed and fell silent. He'd always done that: brushing past what I said, half listening and then ending a conversation with silence. What was worse was when he pretended to listen, nodded attentively, and then proceeded as if I'd never spoken at all.

'So, who'd Luis spend time with?' he asked.

I gave him a flat, annoyed look and drummed my fingers on the table. Luis would often sit by himself at the picnic table outside and stare at the horizon like an old man waiting for his last day. If other students approached him, he'd stand up and walk away. 'He seemed fond of Carly,' I told Cedar. 'But they didn't spend a lot of time together. Once when she was crying, he went and stood next to her. Didn't comfort her or anything. But he also didn't leave the room, which was a big deal for him.'

'I've watched the footage from the camera,' Cedar said, keeping his voice down even though the diner was empty except for the waitress and cook.

My spine stiffened and my toes curled inside my boots. I'd been so preoccupied with Ezra, I had forgotten about my nighttime excursion.

'So, Luis leaves Hatchery at about 11:45. About fifteen minutes later, Kristin and Owen leave. Then – and this is the weird part—'

I'd gone unnaturally still, my eyes smarting from not blinking enough. Cedar pulled a grainy photo from the back of the file and slid it toward me. Timestamped at 12:17 p.m., it depicted someone exiting Hatchery and holding an umbrella as if to shield their face from the camera. Cedar pointed to the photo. 'It drizzled a little that evening, but not enough to need an umbrella. This is our guy.'

'Cedar—' I started.

'Then, no more comings and goings until 1:30, when Kristin

and Owen go back inside. When I interviewed Owen and Kristin earlier this morning, they refused to say what they'd been doing. The person with the umbrella returns around two a.m. Based on the preliminary examination of the body, we're guessing time of death was between midnight and two a.m. Do you think Owen and Kristin were going to meet up with Luis?'

I shook my head. 'I doubt it. They weren't exactly friends. Owen just tormented Luis and Luis avoided him.'

'Which leaves mystery person.' Cedar pointed to the umbrella photo.

My temples throbbed; I had to tell him. He was going to be pissed that I'd lied, and now I was pissed with myself too. We were finally just starting to get close to our old rhythm.

When we worked at the FBI, we had slowly rekindled a newer, more mature version of the relationship we'd had in high school. We'd broken up to go to separate colleges, but came back together tentatively, reacquainting ourselves with the same, yet changed people we'd loved before.

I'd never really reached out to him when I needed him; even when we were kids, he usually sought me out. But after the raid, I called and called, and he wouldn't pick up. Our ritual was to meet at a local bar every Tuesday, and after the raid, I showed up, trying to squash hope in my chest even as I held it there, balancing on a barstool like some wrecked vessel drifting to sea. I felt even more pathetic when he never came; my need laid bare, mocking me.

When we were kids, he knew I slept outside because I had flashbacks to that night in the house with my brother. I'd sweat through my sheets and have to get beyond four walls. He knew all about it.

The best part of my relationship with Cedar had been him knowing what things meant. Now, him knowing what things meant was the worst part. We were too close and too distant at the same time, a foot-wide rupture in the ground with a mile-deep chasm between us.

'If we find this person,' Cedar started, 'we find—'

'It was me.'

Cedar's coffee mug halted inches from his mouth. 'You?'

I brushed someone else's crumbs from our table, not able to look at him.

'You . . .' Cedar set his coffee mug down with a thud. 'You were Dillon's alibi. You could be a witness. This—'

'I didn't witness anything. I heard hoofbeats, which I thought were a dream. But you already got that from Albert.'

'I trusted you, Lore. We can't work together if you're keeping things from me. Even when we were kids, you'd do this – hide things, tweak what happened if you didn't want to be exposed.' He waited for me to defend myself, but I didn't.

'You should have told me earlier.' He pointed in my face and I winced. 'Are you hiding anything else?'

I thought of Albert's homicidal ideation and gritted my teeth. Cedar only gave second chances, and for me, this was that. But I wouldn't be played by Beverly, pushed out of the case or out of my job.

'No,' I said.

Cedar ran his hand over his face and leaned back, surveying me. 'I can't believe this. Dillon has no alibi now.'

'It's not Dillon.'

'That's not the point. Why didn't you tell me?'

'So you can pity me and ignore me like before?'

'That was a hard time for both of us, Lore.'

'I've never disappeared on you.'

'You've disappeared on me in other ways,' Cedar said.

I tilted my head in bewilderment. I assumed he liked that I disappeared when I was troubled; that way, he didn't have to deal with whatever was bothering me.

When the waitress walked past a rubber fish mounted on the wall, it began singing and swimming, its fin flapping aimlessly in the air.

'Shut it!' the waitress shouted, slapping it until it stopped.

When the diner grew quiet again, I caught Cedar's irritation softening, an expression of warring disappointment and relief. I realized my betrayal confirmed who I was to him, still the tormented girl across the street. My lie was easier to accept because it wasn't a surprise. It placed him as the stable one in our relationship, the one who didn't go fleeing terror to gaze at the night sky. And this was exactly why it had been so hard for me to confess; I didn't want to admit to being her anymore.

Maybe the past that bound us also kept us apart: he was a mirror to me – showing me my younger self, making me feel I couldn't grow beyond her. We both wanted to escape being the person the other one had loved. We hadn't learned the art of growing together.

With a smirk, he said, 'Never would have guessed we'd dine together at such a fine establishment.'

Under the sarcasm there was something glowing and sincere; a feeling passed between us like gratitude. I wondered if he wanted this to be our second chance, but before I could share this yearning, I snuffed it out. He looked out at Augustine. 'Funny place out here. People kept staring at us when we checked into the motel.'

'You're a stranger. We aren't used to seeing new people around here, makes people suspicious. They stared at me when I first came, too.'

'We?' Cedar asked playfully. 'Identifying with the locals already?'

I laughed, a pleasant, loose feeling reaching my fingertips. No one else could flip my mood like him. Being with Cedar could feel like being submerged in warm water until my whole body was drowsy with comfort. I wanted to tell him I'd missed him, but I bit my tongue. Can't lose what you don't have.

CHAPTER 16

Ezra perched on the edge of the wingback chair, his feet touching the floor. He seemed to hum with energy; a restrained, bottled pressure. Students didn't normally have his kind of control, this feral self-possession of a large cat stalking prey.

I folded myself into the opposite chair, tucking my feet under my hip to show him he could relax and get comfortable in my office. He stared at my bandaged wrist and then looked up at me unapologetically, his gaze level as a razor blade.

We'd already been staring at each other in silence for over ten minutes and I needed to help him speak, even to utter a random word, just to break the wall of reticence for future visits.

'Look,' I said, leaning forward. 'I know you don't want to be here. But this is a safe space. You're not going to be punished – yelled at, called names – for anything you say or do. I know you're scared right now, but when you ran away from your grandmother, you were brave enough to try something new. I need you to be brave again.'

He looked past me and around my office, his eye flickering back to me as he gripped the armrests, his nails now neatly trimmed back from the claws they'd been yesterday. I thought of him perched on the kitchen counter, smashed ants in his palm, dirty feet on the sink.

'Did you run away from Hatchery because someone hurt you?' I asked.

Ezra's brow furrowed in confusion.

'The police said that's why you ran away from your grandmother,' I explained. 'Did someone here hurt you?'

He shook his head. His hospital file hadn't reported any significant scars or recent wounds, which had eased my worries some.

'Did you run away because you don't like this place?'

He shrugged, glanced at the clock, then out the window, like a prisoner waiting for time to pass. I guessed this wasn't the worst place he'd lived. In his file, I read an incident reported by a visiting neighbor. One day, his grandmother spilled water on the stairs and when Ezra warned her about it, she ignored him as though he hadn't spoken. But once she slipped and fell, she blamed Ezra, screaming at him that he'd distracted her and made her slip.

Projecting blame was a hallmark of verbal abuse and it didn't surprise me that Ezra fixated on withdrawing his words as a way to cope. Words violate, even the best ones; they burrow into you and make a home without your conscious consent. I needed not just to help him feel safe or understood, but to remind him that he had more power than he felt.

'You ran away because you like being outside and on your own, right?' I asked.

He seemed to consider this, and nodded, but after this answer, I felt him withdraw further into himself. I mimicked his unnatural stillness and asked more questions, all of which went unanswered and unacknowledged. He wouldn't move an inch, sitting frozen and defiant, eyes fixed out the window.

I pulled the photo of the twins out of my pocket. He lurched forward and tried to snatch it from me, but I yanked it back.

'I know this is yours; I just want to ask some questions before I give it back,' I said. 'Did you find this in the house you were living in?'

He hesitated, then nodded.

'Why were you sleeping with it?'

He began disappearing on me again. I wanted to reach out and pull him into this conversation with both hands. I shoved the photo closer to him. 'Why do you like this photo?'

When he looked at me, I saw a flash of desperate longing before he carefully concealed it with studied indifference. He pointed at the girls' locked hands.

'You like that they had each other?' I asked.

He shifted his weight and his toes moved in slow circles on the floor. His anxiety felt like an extra person in the room; exhibiting itself in these small, controlled gestures. I was so distracted by his discomfort that I didn't press him as hard as I should have.

'Let's go outside,' I said, standing up.

Clearly surprised, he leapt to his feet and watched me cautiously, as if I were playing a trick on him. All the other students were in class with Helen and the grounds were empty. The morning fog hadn't lifted yet; it obscured almost everything except the Indian tree a quarter mile west. Legend said that the Ponca tribe had used it as a trail marker, pointing toward the Niobrara River with its trunk, which bent toward the ground before rising up in the shape of a serpent before it strikes.

Ezra plucked a dandelion, and instead of blowing its seeds into the world, he bit its head off and ate it. As his cheeks bulged with those wispy seeds, I realized the tension in him earlier hadn't just been fear; it'd been anger. His grandmother had deposited hers in his small chest like an unwelcome package, waiting to detonate or be defused.

'You're more angry than other people realize, aren't you?' I asked him. 'Because life is unfair.'

When he looked at me, I saw a defensive caution on his face, as if he too worried about all that was within him. Before we knew it, we'd passed the circular drive and stood among the blossoming milkweed that stretched west toward the fire pits. Hundreds of monarchs perched on pale pink flowers, the honey smell of nectar filling the air as orange wings trembled all around us. Ezra stood perfectly still, his hands at his sides, his head tilted like an antenna picking up some sound I couldn't hear. His scowl was gone, replaced by a peaceful expression, a looseness in his stance. With all these butterflies between us, he could relax.

The sky filled with flurry. Another swarm of monarchs flew over the hills, shrinking and swelling like a lung before descending to the field. It made me think of Luis and the Day of the Dead, a Mexican holiday that celebrated monarchs as the souls of ancestors returning to the earth.

The flight was contagious; it made me feel free. Ezra must have felt it too, because he beheld it with joyful, rapt attention. A single monarch landed on his cheek and when his eyes met mine, they were buoyant. I smiled at him and delight hummed in my bones.

But then I felt a resistance to all this beauty, a warning that it wasn't mine to enjoy or that it couldn't last. Suddenly, the monarchs thrashed into the air, wings violent in their ascent until the fog swallowed them. Plodding footsteps tore through the milkweed, as a figure emerged through the mist with a strange, unsteady gait and a burlap sack on their head.

I moved in front of Ezra to protect him. The person whimpered and stumbled but didn't throw out their hands for balance, and then I saw why – they were wrapped in a barbed wire straitjacket.

CHAPTER 17

Blond hair was visible beneath the sack and the person's fingernails were painted hot pink. *Kristin.* I rushed forward to help her, my heart in my throat, fingers trembling. I tore off the burlap sack and plucked a sock out of her mouth and she leaned into me, sobbing.

The barbs punctured my skin and I steeled myself against the pain as I smoothed her damp hair back. I scanned the open field, Hatchery's windows, and each curve of the horizon. It felt like we were in a fishbowl, a tableau of suffering for whoever did this to watch and relish. I wanted to find them and push their eyes back into their head.

The wire ripped my palms as I unwound it, as gently as I could. Kristin flailed and jerked, her body shuddering against me.

'Stop moving,' I told her, more harshly than I'd intended. 'It's going to hurt more unless you're still. Calm down.'

It wasn't actually a straitjacket, though it looked that way when she stumbled toward us, arms folded across her chest with the wire holding them there. Ezra watched us wrestle her out of it from a safe distance, his neutral expression unwavering. He could run and run, I thought, but not get far enough from where he started.

'That little son of a bitch, I'll get him back this time,' Kristin kept muttering, half to herself, half a promise to the whole world, it seemed. I assumed she meant Owen but wasn't going to question her with metal thorns in my hands.

When I freed her, I walked her to Beverly's office to report the incident, taking Ezra with us. Blood on my palms had half dried and gone sticky. I thought of how Luis's blood had congealed in his hair, how the rat's had dripped from its skull where its teeth had been stuck in. The iron smell seemed to mock our fragility, seemed to ask, *Why are you not made of metal?*

I dropped Ezra off in Helen's classroom, where he glowered in the corner as if furious with me for abandoning him. An on-call internist from Augustine examined Kristin before Sheriff Anders and Beverly questioned her about the incident. I reported everything to Cedar, promising to relay any significant developments, and then the internist sterilized and bandaged my hands. Thankfully, the cuts weren't deep, but pain still radiated up my arm when I gripped something too tightly.

Returning to my office, I glanced at the milkweed field, all those seed pods that split open in the fall, white fluff bursting forth. The image shifted: soft seeds gone hard, as if the milkweed had harvested baby teeth, somehow, and offered them to the wind, only to drop them on infertile ground.

'Stop,' I said aloud, wrestling my mind back to reality. I noticed my body; how stiff my shoulders were. I live so deep in my mind that sometimes I forget I actually exist in space. Some thoughts have a hunger for rot; I have to pull their hooks out and reorient myself to my surroundings.

An hour later, Kristin stood in the doorway, arms crossed and pinpricked with dried blood. Her eyes were bloodshot from crying and her voice was hoarse. 'What the hell? I'm supposed to be with Dillon.'

'Dr Edwards,' I corrected her. I sat in the armchair. 'He asked me to take you on.'

'That's bullshit,' Kristin said. 'First, I almost die, and now I have to see you?'

I wasn't sure which she thought was worse.

Kristin had just turned eighteen and was preparing to leave Hatchery and move back to Lincoln with her father. For the first time in a decade, he had a stable job and home, so she would live with him and work part-time at a local car wash. Part of our sessions were intended to prepare her for the transition home, along with treating her for acute anxiety and managing panic attacks, but today's appointment would be damage control.

She threw herself into the chair opposite me and launched into a litany of her past abuses and crimes. I'd read it all in her file already and wondered if she thought they'd shock me into handing her back over to Dillon. At age six, she'd been taken to the hospital for a drug overdose from cocaine that'd been left on the coffee table in her parents' house. Her father had been in prison from when she was seven to thirteen years old. At fifteen, she was arrested for shoplifting and discovered to be in possession of drugs. By seventeen, she'd attempted suicide twice.

'So, I'm sure you can imagine,' she said, 'how thrilled I am to head home early. Old Bev called dear old Dad to tell him what happened, and he's picking me up in two days. I was supposed to have a month left, but now that's all ruined because someone else was an asshole.'

'Are you sure you wouldn't be safer and happier at home?' I asked.

A hard glint came into Kristin's eyes. 'I already told you, Owen did it, and I can deal with him and his temper tantrums.'

'Let's . . . let's walk through what happened.'

Kristin gnawed on her thumbnail before she spoke, and when she did, it had a monotone, flat cadence. 'I was in Albert's shed looking for tools to work on the garden. I heard footsteps behind me. I thought it might be Albert – he's yelled at me for being in his shed before. But before I could turn around, someone threw a burlap sack over my head. I tried to scream and they shoved a sock in my mouth and held my wrists down. Their grip was so tight.' Kristin paused and shuddered. 'I . . . went into shock or something and I just . . . went limp. They folded my arms in front of me and turned me round and round and the barbed wire pressed into my skin. And then . . . they must have left the shed. I stood there a while and then stumbled out.'

My first thought was why she hadn't fought more, and I scolded myself for this. Since Luis's death, everyone was more scared than they wanted to admit. And sometimes, submission felt like it could save your life.

'I'm sorry someone did that to you,' I said honestly.

Kristin glared at me. 'You don't believe me either, do you?'

I raised my eyebrows inquisitively.

'Old Bev thinks I'm just trying to get attention. She always says I bring things on myself. I thought if I moved, the person would get upset. That's what happens, you know? If people don't get what they want from you, they get really mad.'

'It sounds like you've been in that situation before. Where someone else takes control.' I paused. 'Why do you say it was Owen?'

'None of your business.' Her knee jiggled and she stuffed a piece of gum into her mouth. I waited and watched her. She yanked at the collar of her shirt and shoved her hair back, and then pulled it forward again. Her knee became a jackhammer.

'Fine,' she muttered. 'I'm seeing someone. Someone older.' That hard glint returned, a smile playing on her lips and not reaching her eyes. Her index finger stroked her collarbone.

'Older? In Augustine?' I frowned and made a note in my notebook. Hatchery had a bus and occasionally Beverly planned excursions to Augustine, to shop in the grocery store or go to the lone steakhouse, just to remind students of life outside. But I couldn't imagine how a few afternoons there could give Kristin enough time to develop a relationship with someone. Other than escaping to Ennenock occasionally, students stayed at Hatchery.

Kristin's eyes darted left and she paused. 'Uh, yeah. Duh.'

'And Owen found out?'

She nodded. 'We're supposed to have an open relationship, but he got mad. Says this is a different kind of cheating. You know Owen can't let something pass without revenge.'

'Are you going to press charges?' I asked.

'For what? Being bullied? Being turned into a fence like I'm a fucking cow pasture? Where are you from?'

Beverly would report the incident to Hatchery's board and they'd decide what action to take against Owen. Throwing a student out of Hatchery was rare because, to a degree, bad behavior was expected. But I suspected Owen's time here was dwindling with each prank.

'Did Owen crucify that rat?' I asked, before I could stop myself. I shouldn't talk about a patient with another patient.

Kristin burst out laughing, covering her mouth with her hand, squinting her eyes shut. Her whole body shook. 'My God. Prolly.'

'Probably? He didn't tell you?' Kristin's jerky movements and sudden glee reminded me of Deborah and the way she'd bob her head as she spoke.

'He doesn't tell me everything. That's what it means to have an open relationship.' She raised her eyebrows at me as if to suggest that someone as old and dour as myself couldn't understand such dynamics. Her expression turned serious. 'He didn't kill Luis, if that's what you're thinking. He's not, like, evil.'

'No,' I said softly. 'I didn't think that.' The way she swung from world-weary to naïve and back again reminded me of myself at that age. I was about to ask about her handwriting on the chalkboard in Helen's classroom when she sat up straight.

'Or maybe it was Albert. Dude has real anger problems. He screamed at me last week about stealing tools out of his shed. And I'm, like, what gives, man? They're school property; I can use them.' She shrugged, as if growing disinterested in her attacker, and then she grinned wickedly. 'I think he's mad all the time because he's jealous of Old Bev's affair with the rich man.'

My pen stilled over my notebook after having written *double-check Zoloft dosage*. Don't take the bait, I told myself, but the question was already on my tongue, irresistible. 'Beverly is having an affair with Howard?'

Kristin rolled her eyes. 'Has been, for, like, a century. They're so . . . old.'

I laced my fingers together and studied Kristin. She smacked her gum and rolled a strand of hair through her fingers.

'Owen will be pissed with me for telling you, but whatevs. I'm so tired of how controlling he can be.'

It probably wasn't true. Howard and Beverly had been close for years, and twisting their intimacy into an affair sounded like the kind of rumor students would tell. 'I'm surprised Owen could keep a secret like that,' I said.

'Right? I mean, we all know loyalty isn't exactly his beat.' A beam of sunlight fell through the window and illuminated Kristin's face. 'Old Bev and the rich man are weird. Maybe, like, they did it. To Luis.'

My pulse quickened, but I kept my tone neutral when I spoke. 'Why would they do that?'

'Dunno. Maybe Luis was going to tell the world about this place.'

'What about it?'

Kristin smiled dreamily, her eyes becoming half-moons. 'How they lock us in and then drug us to make us forget.'

CHAPTER 18

'Something's not right,' I told Cedar over the phone. Back at his hotel in Augustine, he was meeting with the tech team before they returned to Omaha. 'I don't think Kristin's attack was just the usual bullying that goes on here.'

The theatrical barbed wire straitjacket suited Owen's style, and it was believable that he would lash out at Kristin in revenge over a romantic quarrel. But it also felt too neat, too easily explained. Maybe I was just paranoid from being stalked last night, but I'd felt another presence breaking up the migration around us, someone watching as I'd tried to free Kristin. I'd witnessed so many of Owen's pranks, but my instincts told me this wasn't that. Or if it were Owen, it was a harbinger of something more, a sign of him escalating.

'Yeah, I know,' Cedar was saying. 'But we can't begin to shut this place down and get the kids out until we have something substantial I can take to Mitchell. I have something to show you, so let's meet in Ennenock this afternoon. It'll be more private than the diner.'

After hanging up, I kneaded the back of my neck, trying to dismiss Kristin's insinuations about the affair and mistreatment at Hatchery, but I couldn't shake their subterranean pull. I remembered the morning I'd found Luis's body; how Helen had said something was wrong with this place. I hadn't wanted to believe her.

The rumor explained some things – blackmailing Beverly with her secret affair might have earned Owen his special treatment. People could go to great lengths to protect themselves.

Chemical fumes wafted from Beverly's office and I gagged when I stepped inside. She bent over a painting on her desk and dabbed varnish on it.

I discovered, to my dismay, that I was now uneasy being in a room alone with her. Often, Beverly controlled conversations, modulating her voice like the orators who filled the church pews of her youth, manipulating people with monologues and appeals for goodness. Goodness always being equated with what she wanted them to do. Before, I hadn't cared too much, content to wait out her pushiness and get on with my work. Now, I needed some answers.

'What're you doing?' I asked her.

She bolted upright; her shoulders hunched up to her ears. 'Oh, you,' she said. 'Someone thought it would be funny to vandalize a painting in the study room.'

The painting was titled *The Chimera* and featured a three-headed beast with a lion's head and front paws, a goat's head and body, and a snake for a tail. The horned goat looked like an evil spirit that had latched on top of the lion, deforming it as each head twisted in opposite directions. Someone had slashed the lion's neck, as if to behead it.

'James Sevelt, a former student, painted it. Wasn't our finest student, but he was a fine artist. He had delusional psychosis; said he had different people living inside him.' Standing erect, her skin mottled from her exertion, Beverly eyed me.

'Where is he now?' I asked.

'Dead,' she said flatly. 'Suicide in prison.' She leaned over and picked up a half-hidden newspaper from her desk and shoved it toward me.

Feral child found outside Hatchery House, read the main page headline. I could feel her pressuring me for a reaction, so I simply dropped the newspaper back on the desk and said, 'Feral is more of a folkloric designation.'

'Regardless, it makes us sound like we let the children run wild,' she said.

'Beverly, someone's been stalking me at night.'

'What does that have to do with me? Maybe you shouldn't be up and about at night.' She fixed me with a steely look.

I didn't want us to talk about my being outside the night of Luis's murder, so I asked about the bell tower key and if there were copies of it.

'It's never left my ring. No duplicates, only the original. It's not a key you can copy in a machine – it's one of those old iron keys with real teeth. Why?'

'No reason.'

'The FBI don't seem to know what they're doing. Did you know that Agent Knox? He's so fixated on Hatchery, when he needs to be looking into Oksana or drifters or something. But no, he uses up valuable time on a fool's errand.'

'I'm not sure a seventy-year-old widow will be part of the criminal profile,' I said.

'Not even when she killed her own child?' Tension dropped from Beverly's face when she saw it on mine, but remorse quickly replaced it. She made a spastic, fluttering gesture with her hands and flung the varnish cloth on to the painting.

'I didn't mean . . . she intended what happened,' she said. 'There was a lot of gossip around it. Only . . . she went through a spell. Years and years ago. I just want Agent Knox to be looking in the right places.'

A storm of irritation rattled me. She wanted me to be her errand boy, pivoting the investigation in a new direction. And she was willing to use a terrible tale to do it.

'Speaking of rumors,' I said. 'There's one floating around that you're having an affair with Howard.'

Beverly went still and balled her fists. 'Salacious rumors like that will ruin Howard's reputation. And my own,' she said to the painting, her voice as raw as wind-burned cheeks. 'He grew up here, you know, when this was a convent. His mother was . . . what did they call them? A fallen woman. This place saved his life, that's why he reopened it. And now they're slandering him after all he's done. After all I've done.'

She kept mentioning herself as an afterthought. Unable to be angry for her own sake, she had to shroud it in holy anger for someone else. I saw her as a young woman when Hatchery first opened, standing in front of its tall doors as it towered over her. Pet projects have a way of growing, of taking up so much space in your life, you can't see past them.

Her job was the loneliest and most demanding of any of ours, and I wondered if she'd stayed all these years because the children's bad fortunes had drawn her with their whiffs of purpose.

I knew sacrifice for others could provide distraction from your own troubles, but it also built a crawl space where resentment could grow.

'You and Howard have been close for years,' I said.

Beverly snorted. 'I just run this place for him.' Her bitterness was palpable, a fine layer of vinegar coating food already gone to rot.

Tiptoeing around her hadn't worked; I needed to be more direct to get somewhere. Trying to conceal my apprehension, I inhaled and lifted my chin.

'I think you've been so lenient with Owen, despite all his bullying, because he's kept that secret for you. Until now,' I said. 'You've protected each other.'

Beverly shoved the painting from her desk, fingers covering her face as it clattered across the stone floor. Her loose-fitting blouse trembled around her elbows. Dropping her hands and gazing at the painting, she murmured, 'Look, how you've distracted me.'

Then she leaned forward, palms clasped as though in prayer, her blue eyes bright as cornflowers. Behind her, a Gothic portrait of Christ hung on one wall, the crown of thorns so snug, blood trailed along his temples and cheeks. His eyes were so deep-set and shadowed, they became two black holes in his face.

'You want to know about Howard and me?' she asked. She launched into how when she'd first come to Hatchery, she'd seen him standing in front of the cathedral, backlit from the sun, looking like a man cut from marble. His bluster hadn't intimidated her; his grand statements of the nuns who'd saved his life when he'd grown up there had only won him her respect.

And then they'd stayed in the gardener's shed during renovations, the long days blending together. Once, when she'd gotten off the phone with a social agency, she had hung her head and kneaded her temples, unaware of him until she felt his hands on her shoulders as he asked, 'When have you ever rested?'

She ended here and fixed me with a triumphant stare. In someone else's mouth, this would have sounded like a candid story, but Beverly fashioned vulnerability as a weapon, forced intimacy like a wedge between us.

I scrambled to make sense of what this meant. What was apparent was that beyond the affair and whatever it meant to her, Howard had won her loyalty through his recognition of her piety and devotion, cleaving his ambition to hers. She must have felt seen. Howard, Hatchery, who she wanted to be, all became wrapped up together.

About a month ago, when I'd complained to Dillon about how uptight Beverly could be, he told me she'd originally wanted to be a nun and Hatchery had become not only a job, but a kind of calling.

'Her mom left the family when she was young to sing vaudeville. She raised her sister and she's made comments about how they were one step from the poorhouse. Her words, not mine,' Dillon had said. 'I think Beverly's always wanted some kind of stability. Following rules – or holy commandments, as she sees them – offers some security. A sense of certainty.'

I thought now of how the shame of breaking the very thing that made you safe would be engulfing. As a secret, it was compartmentalized, kept separate from her.

'Soon as we pay off your loans, I know you'll be gone,' Beverly said. 'I can't get people to stay and really care about these kids. After you left the assembly yesterday, I told the students to ignore Kristin's accusation against you. That it wasn't true. I think we can all agree we have things in the past we don't want dallied about.'

I felt shoved into a corner. 'A patient of mine died in an FBI operation. That's all,' I said firmly, but my hands had gone clammy. A voice in me said: *that is not all.*

CHAPTER 19

February 2006

The first time I met Deborah, she had sat slumped forward in her chair, blond hair shrouding her face, snapping at an agent that she had a headache and wanted to be left alone. Sleep-deprived from nightmares, she always had purple shadows under her eyes.

When I came in, she glared at me and sneered, 'Is talkin' to you supposed to help?'

I shrugged and sat across from her. 'What do you think will help?'

'Going back in time; getting a new life. Short of that—' She made a gesture with her fingers opening up from a fist, as if to say, *poof, nothing*.

But she wasn't as recalcitrant as she wanted to appear. I could tell as soon as I was in the room with her that she was one of those people who are dying to open up, who don't even really need encouragement to speak. Some people like to talk, as if all the words are built up in them and need to get out somehow.

But she didn't want to talk about her room in the old farmhouse off the interstate, or the johns, or the pimps, or even the other girls. She mostly wanted to talk about her life before she started working, as she called it.

'My mother named me Deborah because she's in the Bible. The only judge who's a woman in the whole thing,' she told me.

'Was your mother religious?' I asked.

Deborah shrugged. 'Isn't everyone's mom religious somehow? They all act like they got answers.'

On the streets she was called Ruby. 'I had thought you'd be a redhead,' I'd told her after we'd been working together a few weeks. 'Aren't the names normally . . . fairly literal?'

Deborah threw back her head and laughed. 'They called me Ruby because Lamberg gave me this ass-ugly red ring, and lied to me, said it was a ruby. So, it was a joke with the girls. I'd hold it out and tell them to look at my ruby and they'd laugh their asses off. Him being so stupid to think we'd fall for that shit. Yes, Daddy, I'd love a diamond next.'

'So, your name was about him?'

'Aren't they always?' she had said, the smile faltering on her face, a faraway look glazing her eyes.

For months, the FBI had gotten leads on girls working along I-80. An agent had approached Deborah outside a gas station and gotten an inkling she wanted a way out, so he asked her if she'd come in for questioning. After insisting he buy her a pack of cigarettes, she surprised everyone by saying yes. We picked her up from that same gas station several times a week, trying to learn whatever we could, build up a report. She only stayed at the office for a few hours each time, so her absence wouldn't be suspicious.

Deborah wanted out and was willing to talk if Victim Services would set her up with a new life. I was brought in to treat her for PTSD and facilitate her work as an informant. A few months into our treatment, the FBI needed Deborah's help for the sting operation they'd planned on the prostitution ring's hideout. The leader of the prostitution ring, Lamberg, transported drugs along I-80, and the agency had been trying to catch him for years.

The bureau needed Deborah to bring in an agent, disguised as a john, to start the raid. She didn't want to do it. She was skittish, insisting there was a mole. She thought it was a police officer, not someone in the bureau. Soon, Mitchell pressured me to convince her to help with the raid.

I was hesitant. It wasn't my job and I couldn't in good conscience guarantee her safety. But other girls were kept in that farmhouse, and drugs piled up in small towns along the interstate. We were doing good work in shutting it down.

'I'll be right there, in the operations room, watching you on camera. We'll get you out if it starts to go south. The agent will be in there to protect you and the other girls; that's why we want him in before it starts,' I said.

That was a lie. We actually wanted him on the inside in case Lamberg tried to make a run.

'Normally, we just do it in the car,' Deborah said. 'Only take johns back to the house if they want drugs with the trick.'

'That'll be the agent's story,' I assured her.

Normally I wasn't allowed in the operations room; I'd have to ask for higher security clearance. But I knew Mitchell would get it for me if it meant Deborah complying. The more I assured Deborah, the more she relaxed. It would help her heal, I told her. She would remember it the rest of her life. It would empower her. It'd help with moving on.

That part wasn't a lie. I'd watched victims come to life when they'd reversed the power dynamic and locked abusers behind bars. Deborah finally agreed.

Before the raid, she talked about her mother a lot. Her mother had disappeared on her when she was ten, but before that, they'd had a strong relationship.

'My mom always wanted me to have a magical life. A strong life. I've never been as strong as she wanted me to be. Always disappointed her.'

'That might not be true, Deborah,' I said. 'Maybe that's just how you see it because she's gone. Sometimes when something negative happens – like your mother disappearing – we see everything around that person or event as negative too. We blame ourselves for a reality we don't want to accept.'

In our previous appointment, I'd asked her if she owned anything that represented the life she wanted after the raid. So today, Deborah brought a snow globe and set it on the table in front of me. Her favorite toy as a child.

'I like this snow globe because it's a little world that isn't even real. When they get on top of me, I just shut my eyes and I'm inside the snow globe, and that's the real world, beautiful snow and no cold,' she said.

The fluorescent lights made her skin sallow. She looked older than twenty-two. Tracing her finger along the curve of the snow globe's glass, her mouth twitched into a faint smile. She pushed it across the table to me. I had thought she wanted me to keep it safe for her, but then she said, 'In case I don't come back.'

'You're coming back,' I snapped.

Another twitch of a smile. 'So you'll remember me.' She shook the snow globe, sending the snow spiraling. 'What I want for my life after the raid . . . is to break this. To not really need it. To be so strong, I don't need to be in an imaginary glass globe.'

I didn't have the heart to tell her she may never get to a point in her life where she didn't want an escape. I wanted her to hope for something impossible, to let the hope feed her and drive her. It'd get her further than reality ever would.

The raid took place on a bitterly cold day in February. The gang's headquarters was an old farmhouse tucked a mile back from the interstate, where Deborah lived with four other girls and a few pimps. Based on her intel, we knew it was an evening Lamberg would be at the house, discussing accounts with a few of his men.

The house squatted on a crooked foundation, a boarded-up window on one side like a shut eye. Private and serene, it was in a clearing surrounded by cottonwoods.

Back at the bureau, I sat in an operations room with two other agents, three monitors in front of us displaying the undercover's camera, Deborah's camera, and a camera on an agent outside the house. My office chair creaked as I shifted my weight. The stale air pressed around me and I tried not to think of what could go wrong: Lamberg's head jerking up, as if he could smell the agents a quarter mile away, pimps pulling bombs or large firearms we knew nothing about, outside bolts on the back door trapping Deborah inside.

It started just as we'd planned: Deborah brought an undercover agent in as a john. A guard outside the house frisked them. I kept seeing flashes of Deborah's face when the undercover agent turned toward her. Her blue eyes looked strangely bright in the dim light. All the windows were covered with heavy curtains, and artificial light stained every surface. Even as I watched her, knowing it was her last time there, I wanted to snatch her out of that house. It couldn't be over quickly enough.

Old beer bottles and empty fast-food bags littered the house. I could almost smell it all: the rancid odors of old food, the musty scent of upholstery that hadn't been cleaned in years. Or ever. Bright, cheap clothing scattered across the floor. A tattered floral couch loitered in front of a coffee table littered with drug paraphernalia. Deborah's room held only a bed and bookcase with two busted-out shelves. Clothing was stuffed in the shelving that remained. A paisley rug covered the dirty, tattered carpet, giving the room an almost homey appearance. The window in her room had bars over it on the inside.

The undercover agent spoke into his headpiece, telling us that the pimps and Lamberg were in his office near the front of the house, adjacent to Deborah's room. Our men were parked half a mile away, behind an outcropping of cottonwoods. Several agents would burst through the front door while others would cover his office window in case he tried to slip out. The undercover agent would block him as he tried to exit the office, while the rest of the agents would arrest the pimps. Deborah had already told us where hidden firearms were located around the house, or at least the ones she knew about.

Nausea clamped my stomach in a vice and I clutched the edge of the table as I watched the monitor. She and the undercover agent had ten minutes to move quietly through the house; to collect the eight guns from under couches and inside cabinets, and hoard them in her room. I watched as they found the first, metal glinting in the dim light. Suddenly, both Deborah and the under-cover agent jolted, as if shocked by a sudden sound or movement.

We asked what had happened. Just a telephone ring, the undercover agent reported, pocketing the revolver he'd found. Uneasiness spread among us in the operations room, tangible as an unwanted hand on your back, pushing you where you didn't want to go. Our lead agent told them to continue on. Bile built at the back of my throat. I wanted to speak to Deborah myself, privately, but she had no microphone.

Two words echoed over and over in my mind: *get out, get out, get out*.

The agents outside had just begun to creep toward the house, expanding in a circle around it. Gunfire erupted. Deborah was facing the undercover agent when the first shots rang out, so I saw her expression. The look on her face – wide-eyed terror – was quickly replaced by a sort of glossy acceptance, and that replaced by an animal instinct for survival. It was in that moment that I realized just how much I'd lied to her. How she must have suspected this was how it would go, played it over in her mind, imagining herself hiding amid gunfire.

The rat-a-tat of gunfire made a storm around them. The under-cover agent scrambled to get her out the front door. She was a few steps ahead of him. He tried to cover her as they dashed toward the front. A bullet caught Deborah.

Her shoulder jerked and she spun in a half circle. Toppling furniture could be heard in the pauses between gunshots. Then her camera faced the ceiling. The undercover agent lurched to the side and fell. His camera pointed toward Deborah's chin, neck and upper chest. No wound was visible, no blood ran in a rivulet along her collarbone. Only stillness amid babel and tumult, more jarring than seeing her face or where she'd been shot. Her skin, smooth and pure against the mangy, stained carpet.

Four agents had been wounded on the field before they pulled back. Lamberg disappeared into the night, despite the choppers overhead. Cedar let me see photos of the crime scene later, one of the agents dead next to Deborah, knees tucked almost to his chin with a bullet burrowed in a kidney.

Of all the places to die, that shithouse had to be one of the worst.

We couldn't trace the phone call to Lamberg in his office, but we did find the guard's cell on his dead body and were able to extract a text from Lamberg: *Raid, 2 minutes.* The text had come in thirty seconds after the phone call, and the gunfire started almost exactly two minutes after the text had been received.

The local police had helped with the raid and were investigated first. But I couldn't shake the suspicion that a rat was among our own ranks, that I'd passed him or her in the hallway as I walked to my desk. That paranoia grew until I even flinched at the ring of a cash register in the grocery store.

I never went back to the bureau after that. Lots of people on the job have stories like that. They process it and move on. But my mind caught on it like a woodpecker hammering the same spot in a tree.

She knew the risks, Cedar told me later. Had she? The line between knowing and not knowing is not always clear.

That night, Cedar had been in the field. Blood from a wounded agent was still on his uniform when he burst into my office. I remember the outline of his familiar shape in the doorway, but not much else.

He'd said I was almost comatose, slumped in the corner. I'd been holding the snow globe upside down, so all the snow drifted back up into the sky.

CHAPTER 20

When I left Beverly's office, I needed to get some fresh air. I could no longer see people straight with the swarm of distrust that hovered around each of us. A thought snagged me like a handshake that wouldn't let go: whoever killed Luis had also toasted to a good summer at the festival, had rejoiced as dusk deepened around us.

Outside, I skirted around the bell tower toward the small yellow door in the back. Checking to make sure it was locked, I jiggled the handle and threw my weight against it, but it didn't budge. Pear-colored grass met an almost white sky; above me, a gargoyle poised open-mouthed, waiting for rain to end the drought. Several yards away, Dillon crossed the gravel drive, head down as he studied a piece of paper in his hand, a boyish expression of concentration etched on his face.

I stayed tucked behind the corner of the bell tower and realized how little I knew him beyond the walls of Hatchery. Only once we'd gone to a dive bar in Augustine, where he'd relished the homespun virtues and good-natured charm he saw around us.

'No competition between people here,' he'd said, and I thought he was wrong. He admired the patrons for a smallness he shrank them down to, a quaintness of his imagination more than their lives. But I could relate to the root of this impulse: how he needed a place where he could break away from his veneer of competence, how their apathy toward him could feel better than approval.

Now, Dillon stopped in front of the stone well where I'd seen my dead self. Cursing aloud, he tossed his head back, face to the sky. Then he crumpled the paper in one fist and threw it inside the well.

After Dillon returned to Hatchery, I peered inside the well. Darkness hunkered below with the smell of roadkill – a smashed thing with insects in its eyes.

It was probably just a rejection from a different grant proposal, but I didn't step away from the well. I could ask him about the paper, but I realized with a sinking sensation that ever since our quarrel in his office, I wasn't sure he'd tell me the truth. Suspicion and curiosity held me in their grip even as I resisted it. I thought of the initial disquiet I'd felt around him when we first met, and how later, after we began dating, he could be evasive by brushing me off when I asked a question. Other times he was so charming, so articulate and easy to connect with, that it felt practiced to perfection. An act.

Everyone had secrets and I wanted to know who I was tethering my future to. I grabbed a flashlight out of Albert's shed and returned. Years ago, Albert had partially filled the well with dirt, leaving the bottom about seven feet below ground. The well's wood cap now leaned against the stones. Small animals could get trapped inside when the cap blocked the opening, and I imagined a possum hunting in that dark hole, its rat tail trailing the dirt floor.

Stop imagining things, I told myself.

Hatchery's windows were cracked open and students' voices drifted toward me, softened and disembodied. Everyone was eating lunch in the dining hall; they'd be finished within a half hour. Rocks scratched my palms as I crawled on to the rim. I found a foothold on a jutting rock and lowered myself into the well. Something small and warm brushed against my shoulder, and featherless wings fluttered against my ear.

Squeals erupted around me and wings beat against my legs and shoulders. My fingers slipped from the rocks, the ground came up, and my boots hit the dirt. Bats shot up and all I could see was the circle of their ferocity in the sky.

Their high-pitched calls faded as I struggled to my feet. Gravity felt heavier at the bottom and the air was muggy. It smelled like mud during a rainstorm, despite the bone-dry stone walls around me.

Panting, I picked up the dropped flashlight. The beam illuminated a mouse scurrying between two stones, a mass of cobwebs, an old book, a cow skull, a high-heeled shoe, and at the edge, a crumpled piece of paper. I crouched down and grabbed it, avoiding a centipede scuttling past.

Cold sweat had already dried on my back and my temples wouldn't stop throbbing. A foul odor began to permeate the well, growing so noxious I covered my nose with my arm.

The note was short. *I told you I want more money. This is your last chance. Melissa.*

Behind me, a long, low-pitched growl filled the well. I whirled around but saw nothing. Something scraped above. Light dimmed as someone pushed the cap across the well's rim.

'No! Stop!' I called out. 'I'm down here!'

I waved my arms, but the circle of sky shrank to a crescent moon and then to a new moon. Darkness dropped around me and I screamed out again, my voice echoing. A snarl joined the echo.

An animal. My stomach went hard, my chest tightened, and I turned in a slow circle. My flashlight's beam caught the pink tongue first. Then, bared teeth and claws, long and distinct as a child's fingers.

The badger backed into its burrow, dirt caked on its eyelashes, a thick white stripe down the middle of its face. It growled again, a low warning that sent panic to my fingertips.

No. Get out, get out.

I grabbed a jagged stone above my head. The badger shot out of its hole toward me. I lifted myself up, my feet jostling and slipping against stones. Mortar crumbled and a rock fell from the wall. Claws scratched rocks; breath fumed against my ankle.

I found footing and launched myself up. I pushed with one hand against the wood cap, but my other hand was slipping from the rock. Each muscle burned and my hand started to spasm.

Skidding through time, I saw the red forked lightning of my brother's eyes when the window wouldn't budge, felt the heat of a house on fire.

A claw caught my boot and I almost careened backwards. Grabbing a different rock with both hands, I rammed my back against the wood cap. It lifted and jostled to the side. I caught the edge, pushed it off, scrambled over the rim, and toppled out of the well.

It'd be a half hour before my nerves stopped twitching and I could fully exhale. Blinking up at the bright sky, I touched the note in my pocket.

CHAPTER 21

'*Psychiatry Today* wants an article on agency and patient consent, but I'm already swamped with research and the new grant. More publications could put Hatchery on the map,' Dillon was saying.

And establish your name, I thought.

We were in my apartment, in the kitchenette tucked under steep stairs that led up to a bedroom loft wedged between two eaves. We often ate with the students in the dining hall but on Thursdays we kept a running lunch date so we could catch up privately. I cooked, hoping to manufacture a serene domestic backdrop before I dropped the bomb. I'd already showered, but the well's stench clung in my nostrils. An ache had settled in my gut, along with my reluctance to bring up the note.

In those lighter, brighter, early days together, I'd had sleepless nights, going over patient notes until dawn, and he often stayed up with me, making coffee, filling in gaps in patient histories. Sometimes just looking across the room at me with quiet wonder. I'd felt so supported and wanted to continue that way, buoying each other on a rushing river that didn't end.

'Mmm. You smell good.' Dillon wrapped his arms around my waist and buried his face in my neck. I tensed.

'Did you just flinch?' he asked, pulling back.

'No.' Burnt garlic released a bitter odor. Turning from him, I smacked my head on the stair's underside. Cursing and rubbing my forehead, I told him about finding the note at the bottom of the well.

'You crawled down into a well to retrieve a note I threw away? What the fuck, Lore?'

'I know it seems odd, I just—'

'Is this what you meant when you said you sometimes do strange things?'

I crossed my arms and set my jaw.

'Lore, it's just an old patient. A raving old patient.'

'You've never told me about her.'

Dillon stepped back and ran a hand through his hair. 'And you've told me about every difficult patient you've ever had? She's been threatening me for years; I just ignore it.'

We'd all had those appointments, the one that turned rancid as sour milk. Voices going hard, faces tightening in hostility. Afterwards, there'd be threatening emails waiting for me. Or patients with a history of violence sometimes stood between me and the door, blocking the only exit, making me feel as powerless as they did before relinquishing their stance.

A bird flew into the window; the thud on the glass made me jump. It rolled in the air and flapped its wings before tumbling to the ground. Dead birds littered the perimeter of Hatchery.

'But why does it say *more* money? You gave her money?' I asked.

'Melissa was psychotic. She got a reimbursement payment after insurance filed a claim and thought the money came from me. She's been hounding me on and off ever since.'

This summoned a story he'd told me about an ex-girlfriend, the love of his life, who'd dumped him during medical school because they never spent time together. *She was always hounding me. She couldn't understand how much I was willing to sacrifice for this work.* His voice had been wistful more than angry, and I guessed his single-minded nature only grew from this loss, his life whittled to a narrow shape.

'If this patient was from so long ago, how'd she know where to send the note?'

'I'm on Hatchery's website.'

'Have you reported her?'

'To who? She's annoying, not a criminal. You're treating *me* like a criminal. Luis's case has you paranoid. Stop catastrophizing.'

Shifting blame, making me feel like something was wrong with me. Calling each other out on cognitive biases had been our inside joke, but now it felt cutting. I hugged my arms more tightly over my chest while Dillon paced the living room and avoided eye contact, lifting his knuckles to his chin and unconsciously brushing his jawline.

Even today, he looked like he belonged on a college brochure. I remembered my initial impression of him; the thought that we'd been born on different planets and had only by chance arrived at the same place. Once, Dillon made a passing comment that some families bought extra houses with their disposable income, but his liked to travel. I'd stared at him, bewildered and slack-jawed. It'd seemed insulting, and then almost charming, like a preteen who still believed in Santa Claus.

'Are you just with me because you're lonely here?' I asked.

His face took on a *stop it with the insecure bullshit* look. 'You've been emotionally holding me at arm's length and then you hunt down a private note of mine and ambush me with it.' He held out his hand, palm up. 'The note. Give it to me.' The command in his voice made me stiffen.

'I left it down there,' I lied. 'I had trouble getting out and was distracted.'

He looked at me like I was insane, so I told him about the cap and the badger.

'You think someone trapped you down in a well with a badger?' Dillon started to laugh and I wanted to join in, to double over at the absurdity, but the wooden spoon was still shaking in my hand.

I hoped we were home free, on the brink of resolving this, but when he straightened, he shot me another sharp look.

'You'll have to be careful of countertransference with Ezra.'

'Why?'

'Before he ran away, he'd always sneak around Hatchery when he was supposed to be in class or bed. Apparently, he searched Helen's desk once and ransacked Albert's storage shed. Beverly used to say: "Kid doesn't talk much because he knows too much." You overidentify with the patients; that's why you're all strung out now. It leads to bad decisions.'

Cedar had also accused me of over-identification, so it stung even more. 'Yeah, I probably do. I suppose their lives are a bit alien to you.'

'Oh, God, this again. Why do I always have to apologize for where I come from?' His nostrils flared.

'You don't,' I said. 'But it is your responsibility to realize not everyone comes from the same place.'

'Yeah? Feeling permanently guilty also seems to be part of the responsibility. Not everyone has your savior complex, Lore.'

'I guess altruism is a construct of vanity, too?'

'It is if you're using it to fill your emptiness.'

'Fuck you.' I pointed the wooden spoon at him. 'Just keep labeling everyone until you can flatten them enough to walk over them. Pinning antonyms on people's motives doesn't make you insightful; it makes you a bully.'

'You display such restraint and maturity.'

I had to put the brakes on this before it spun out of control. Turning back to the hot plates, I flung diced chicken and vegetables into the skillet and watched them sizzle. The burnt garlic made my stomach turn over. Dillon walked over to the window and opened it. A wave of irritation passed over me.

'We need to be an example, Lore. Half of homicides go unsolved. Everyone here will have to find a way to return to normal even if we don't get closure. The students will keep acting out until they feel a sense of security again.'

'It will be solved. Cedar does his job better than anyone I know,' I said, looking over my shoulder at Dillon.

This unabashed belief in someone else, uttered like a threat, seemed to flip a switch in Dillon and his jaw tightened. 'That smells like shit,' he said, nodding at the hot plates.

My body went rigid and I grabbed the skillet handle. The skillet sailed between us and crashed against the door, food splattering across the entryway floor. The metal clattered, wobbling until it stilled, upside down.

As Dillon looked at our meal on the floor, something shifted in him; a stillness came over him that I couldn't interpret. 'You're not better than me because you've suffered more,' he said.

I had a sense of being lowered, slowly, deep into the ground.

'I don't feel like life is one big competition just because of where I'm from, because you feel that way too,' Dillon said. 'It was difficult to live with parents who were always on the verge of being disappointed with me. I get to have that, Lore. I get to have my experiences and the emotions that come with them. You don't get to discount that.'

These words were true, but something else twisted remained in the air between us. Dillon took a step toward me. I pressed myself further back, against the hot plates, warmth radiating against my spine. I wanted him to leave.

'I'm sorry,' I said, blinking hard against his presence. 'You're right. I've been jealous of your childhood.'

'Honey.' He squeezed my arm in a comforting gesture, but his grip felt like a vice. 'I want to be able to trust you. Promise me you won't sneak around anymore.'

It didn't sound like a request; it sounded like a warning. 'I promise,' I said.

CHAPTER 22

Yellow tape twitched around the hanging tree. The crumbling ghost town lay a quarter mile south of Hatchery, and Cedar was waiting in the saloon. I kept looking over my shoulder, but I was the lone moving figure on the horizon, as if I traversed the moon's surface.

Osage orange once separated the town from the graveyard, but since the mine's collapse, this barrier between the living and the dead had grown wild, as thorny branches reached around headstones in an embrace. I'd read that it'd taken weeks to remove all the bodies from the rubble and toxic fumes, most half rotted by the time they were buried.

Some towns were built with an air of insecurity; Ennenock was one of those towns. The extra-wide Main Street and the shiplap false fronts shouted overcompensation as I passed the sheriff's office, hotel, town hall, and general store. Wagon wheels leaned against a broken fence, a rusted automobile squatted among tumbleweed, and wind hissed between buildings under an unending sky. It felt like a cemetery, all the empty buildings holding vestiges of lost life: half-empty dressers, a camisole left behind on a bed, wedding china brought over on the Oregon

Trail and abandoned by descendants who'd moved on, searching for better fortunes.

The Watering Hole stood at the end of the dirt thoroughfare and inside, Cedar leaned against the bar, one elbow propped up on it. Just as he had at our Tuesday night bar.

'You look like a regular cowboy,' I said.

He tipped an invisible hat at me and said, 'Hey, good-looking.'

A mirror spanned the wall behind the bar, somehow still intact after all these years. Shattered remains of bottles littered the shelves along the mirror, caught light and sparkled. Cedar followed my gaze and nodded at them. 'They made things different back then.'

Amused, I said, 'That's what your mom would say. You're becoming your mom.'

He grinned and shrugged. 'Worse people to be.' There was a smudge of dirt on his jaw; I wanted to brush it away for him, but I didn't feel steady yet.

Part of the ceiling had collapsed and scattered plaster across the wood floor, which also held an inch of dust, cigarette butts, a partially decayed sparrow and a few broken chairs. Water dripped from somewhere within the walls.

'I interviewed Dillon this morning,' Cedar said, wiping sweat from his brow. 'Then I canvased these old buildings again and found footprints in the bank, around the old vault. It's locked with a combination code, so I'm going to have to get someone down here.'

'You think it's the original crime scene?' I'd passed the vault before – it was one of those giant Wild West safes you could walk straight into, but it'd always been locked so I'd never seen inside.

'I'm hoping it has something that'll help. They rushed Luis's autopsy and finished late last night. I just got the results.' He slid the coroner's report toward me. 'Time of death is officially one a.m.'

I scanned the report and found a longer list of drugs in his system than I was expecting.

'And we have another method of attack,' Cedar said.

'Wait – in addition to strangulation and blunt force trauma?'

'Preliminary toxicology report indicates he had three drugs in his system. Coroner said two of those drugs are strong sedatives, but the lab doesn't have an in-depth analysis yet. Will take three weeks. He wouldn't be prescribed two separate sedatives, would he?'

'No,' I said. 'And he wasn't prescribed any sedatives. I had him only on a low dose of Prozac for depression.'

'Who all has access to medications?'

'Dillon, Beverly and I have keys to medical cabinets in our offices. Dillon and I have these security keys that can't be tampered with or copied, and Beverly has master keys to everything.'

Cedar watched me closely with that infuriating look of concern on his face.

'What?' I took a step back from him and crossed my arms. My eyes darted around the saloon.

'Dillon was evasive during our interview. About how he spends his time and where. He does group therapy a few times a week, but otherwise only sees three patients a day—'

'He has a major research project. He got a grant,' I said quickly. But a sinking knowledge pulled at me: he claimed to do research in his office, but I rarely saw him in there.

'I know it's hard to accept people we're close to could have a darker side,' Cedar said gently.

I swallowed my irritation and said in an even voice, 'Don't accuse me of delusional attachment. Let's review what we do have. The May Day festival ended around eleven. Everyone went inside to bed. Luis left Hatchery and stole Oksana's horse around twelve. He rides somewhere – either of his own volition or because he was forced. Someone sedates him with two drugs and tries to strangle him in an unknown location. He breaks free and makes a run for it. The perp grabs Oksana's horse and runs him down and hits him over the head with a rock, killing him. Luis dies around one.'

Cedar leaned back against the bar, knuckling his eyes. Despite the dim light, clouded with suspended dust, I caught the muscle twitching in his throat. I knew he was thinking of his brother again.

'I'm sorry, Cedar—' I reached out and gave his hand a squeeze.

He shook his head. 'Don't apologize. You were one of the only people really there for me during all that. You knew – you knew how to just be there.'

Wind hissed through a busted window. Along the wall opposite the bar, a staircase led up to a landing that spanned half the saloon, behind which I suspected were tiny rooms with tiny beds. The landing's railing was busted in places, but it still looked like a fence. My hair prickled; I could feel someone up there.

A hole yawned in the middle of the staircase, as if someone had fallen through. My hands had gone nervy, a tingle in my fingertips, and I quickly rubbed my palms together to loosen them.

'No one has real alibis for the middle of the night,' I said. 'But only a small group of people were outside of Hatchery at the time of Luis's death: me, Albert, Kristin, Owen and Oksana.'

'And Ezra.'

'He was four miles away.'

'Just trying to keep track of everybody. How is Ezra doing?' Cedar asked.

'Hasn't uttered a word,' I said. 'I can't get it out of my head that he saw something and ran away because he was scared.'

'When I spoke to her, Beverly insisted he didn't want to be moved from Hatchery. Wouldn't he want to leave if he saw something? Or be acting out more if he was scared?' Cedar asked.

'People don't all act out in the same way. This place is familiar to him, so maybe he wants to stay here rather than go to whatever unknown place they'd send him. Or maybe he repressed whatever he witnessed while living at that homestead. Or maybe his baseline is scared, so we aren't seeing new symptoms,' I said.

Tumbleweed rolled into a corner. I told Cedar about the rumor of Oksana's child, Beverly's affair that Owen kept secret, and the note Dillon claimed was from his patient.

'Beverly sharing that rumor about Oksana feels like distraction more than something real.'

I nodded. 'Beverly's wound tight, acting like Hatchery is threatened. Keeps lashing out. Maybe Luis didn't report the whippings because the person he'd report to is the one who did it.'

'And she has the key to the bell tower, so she could have gotten out of the house without being spotted on the security camera. She claims she can't ride a horse, which could be a lie, or maybe she's hiding who can,' Cedar said. 'You think she's protecting Owen?'

'Or Albert,' I said.

'Oksana's lived there since Hatchery started. She's not attached to the place, but knows it. We need to get her talking.'

Oksana's cabin was almost as rough-hewn as that homestead where Ezra had been living. He might feel more relaxed there, and I'd wanted to spend more time with him, particularly outside of the House.

'I could take Ezra and go talk to her,' I said.

'Why?'

'If Ezra saw something and he reacts to her in some way, it could tell us something. Or, if he's comfortable being somewhere different from Hatchery, maybe he'll open up some. Get him in a new environment.'

After considering this, Cedar nodded. He squinted at the empty whiskey bottles and shards of glass on the shelves along the mirror. 'Can Dillon ride a horse?'

'His family did the whole equestrian thing – dressage, I think.'

'That different from ranching?'

'Haha,' I mock-laughed, which got a smile from him.

'Can you go through his office? See if you find anything strange?'

I inhaled and stiffened. He wasn't suggesting anything I wasn't already considering, but I still felt reluctant. Dillon was right about my emotional absence and how I pushed him away. So much for not repeating previous patterns.

'I know you're on as an informant, and investigating is asking you to step over a line—'

'It's not that,' I said. 'With Dillon – our relationship – it's already tense with all that's happened; I can't afford to jeopardize things.' I paused before throwing the dart. 'I don't want to bail the minute things get tough.'

Cedar reared back like he'd been slapped, even though I hadn't even been thinking of us. 'Lore—'

A footstep sounded on the landing above us and we startled and looked up. Still only broken railing and a spider web.

'Are you sure no one followed you?' I asked.

'From that shit motel?'

A click. Someone's handheld Kodak camera pointed down at us. The camera withdrew and running footsteps pounded on the landing.

Cedar's eyes caught mine in disbelief and I tore away, running for the stairs.

'Don't!' Cedar called after me. 'That floor isn't going to hold.'

Climbing the stairs, I leapt over the split wood in the middle. Once I reached the landing, the floor groaned under me, straining with near collapse. In the corner, an open door swung in the wind and an outdoor staircase twisted below it. Private entrance for the patrons back in the day. Still, I checked each room for the photographer and halted in the doorway of the last.

Above a thin wrought-iron bed, photographs were taped on the walls. Each one was a portrait of a sleeping student in their bed, and someone had shoved black thumbtacks into the photograph where their closed eyes had been. A year-old *Augustine's Archives* lay neatly folded on the stained mattress.

'Well, if you're going to die, did you at least catch the person?' Cedar asked, coming up behind me.

'They escaped,' I said.

Cedar stopped short when he saw the photos. 'Shit,' he said.

'Owen has a Kodak camera like that,' I said.

'So, this tableau is his.'

'I assume so.'

The headline on the year-old newspaper read: *Augustine Citizens Request Hatchery House Closure*. The article went on to detail how the town council had been petitioning for Hatchery to close or move for years, due to safety concerns.

'Those students cannot control themselves. One vandalized my yard on one of their field trips through town,' said Mirna Clark.

'I didn't know there was so much animosity between Augustine and Hatchery,' I told Cedar as he read over my shoulder. 'What if we're wrong about the crime being victim-specific? What about mental health stigma as a motive?'

Cedar considered this. 'A hate crime.'

'Kind of. Maybe even specific to Hatchery, not necessarily to Luis.'

'But what about the scars on his back? You think the abuser and killer could be two different people?'

Floorboards moaned as I shifted my weight, and Cedar took me by the elbow and steered me back toward the stairs. A board creaked and another cracked, wood grain snapping as we hurried down.

'Never thought I'd be the victim of paparazzi in a ghost town,' Cedar said once we reached the bottom.

I grinned, but it was frozen, lodged in a tense, flat line. I was concerned about the photo making its way to Beverly, but more troubled about who had taken it.

'Hey,' Cedar said, rubbing my neck where I always had strained muscles.

'Someone might be following me. I mean, more than just today,' I told him.

'You mean yesterday when you felt someone watching you?'

'Not just that.' Biting my lip, I told him about being stalked last night and how someone had pushed the cap over the well when I'd retrieved Dillon's note. When I described what the note said, Cedar started shaking his head in disbelief.

'I don't want to assume malevolent intent – maybe the person didn't know I was down there—' I said.

Cedar tossed his hands out wide. 'Because that's not coincidental at all. Someone just happened to replace the cap during the few minutes you were down there. All of this is likely the same person, targeting you.'

'That's a pretty big assumption.'

'Lore.' Cedar's eyebrows pinched together. 'What is it you call this?'

'Minimizing.'

'Yeah. Stop it. I'm worried about you.'

CHAPTER 23

'Dillon's notes indicate that stressful events can destabilize your mood. Have you struggled with that since Luis's death?' I asked.

Helen pursed her lips and nodded. 'I'm . . . I'm thinking of suicide again. I haven't hurt myself – not like before; it's just the thoughts . . .'

Dillon had transferred Helen to me months ago, after she'd asked him out during an appointment. She'd been diagnosed with bipolar disorder during her early twenties, while working on her teaching degree. Dillon prescribed an odd medication, one more commonly used as an antipsychotic or mood stabilizer. Her file detailed highs of maxing out credit cards and staying up all night talking on the phone, to lows accompanied by suicidal ideation and self-harm. But she'd been stable for the last year and even now she looked well – her eyes were bright, her affect calm but animated as she folded her hands in her lap. She was curvy, with a wide, almost blank face, and an abundance of pale hair; she carried a certain warmth you sometimes saw in Dutch baroque paintings, when peasant women stood pouring milk from pitchers.

She'd never struck me as bipolar, but perhaps that was only

because her medication was working. Now in her early thirties, her file described a happy childhood on a wheat farm in South Dakota with three older brothers. I'd called her mother to get a collateral report, but she'd been evasive, only citing insomnia as a symptom in line with a diagnosis. Then again, bipolar doesn't always emerge in adolescence.

'It's normal for those thoughts to resurface at times like this,' I told her.

'I don't imagine you've ever struggled with these thoughts,' Helen said.

I ignored this. 'How often do they occur?'

Helen squeezed her hands together. 'Once a day?'

'I see you're on a high dose of Risperidone, which is an unconventional choice for bipolar disorder. Maybe something else would work better, particularly with the lows you're experiencing?'

'I've tried everything else, and it's the only thing that helps.' Helen studied my reaction and then rushed on, 'Honestly, I'll feel better once the killer is caught. I think . . .'

She complained about the stresses of the investigation, but I could tell something else was actually bothering her. Maybe it was how jittery she was becoming, how flashes of unruly emotion could be seen in her eyes before she quickly replaced them with something more acceptable: worry, anxiety, sadness. That wingback chair could be a stage; this room could be a theatre.

'Sometimes I just feel everyone else is out there living life and I'm just . . . in this facade.' When I didn't respond immediately, Helen tried to laugh at herself and shook her head. 'Since Luis's death . . . it reminds me not everyone gets it all. The works. Great job, house, family. I see all these happy people and I think: I'll never have that. Luis didn't get all that either. Was never given the chance. We have to say goodbye to the people we thought we could be.'

I could relate – discontent made your heart pulse with hunger for the things you didn't have. But the past could also skew your perception of the present, squeezing it into a thin, unyielding passage. I wanted to help her uncoil a bit.

'Maybe we can start with focusing on what's in your control – your future choices, rather than the investigation. You could have some of those things.' I smiled gently. 'Some fears are just failures of the imagination.'

'I thought they were prophecies.'

Something shifted – the air sharpened and wariness crossed Helen's face. I wanted to steer our session back to positive change, so I asked her if she liked working at Hatchery.

'Beverly always tells me you're the best teacher they've ever had,' I told her.

Helen looked to the side, blond hair catching the light and shining golden. 'The work we're doing here . . . it doesn't really happen anywhere else. These kids get chances they'd never have otherwise, and I get to be part of that.'

She wrung her hands and gave a soft laugh. 'I never even told Dillon this. Dillon.' She rolled her eyes like he was an inside joke between us. I caught a whiff of jealousy; it was the first real emotion in the room, tangible as another figure pulsing blood and radiating warmth.

'This is not all I want. I've been reading these self-help books about how I'm a bigger and better person and I can reach for higher goals. I want to move somewhere completely different – Chicago or San Francisco or L.A. It might be easier to join the CIA in a big city – I've always thought I'd make an amazing spy. I figure I could head up a team somewhere, then move on to something else.'

I assumed I'd misheard. 'Spy?'

'I took a Russian class in college and had a knack for it. I could even stop a war. Those Russians.' She chuckled as though they were an unmanageable terrier.

I tried not to look shocked and dismayed. She'd never displayed grandiose delusions before, but they were possible with a bipolar diagnosis if one was in a manic state. Maybe her medication wasn't working as well as she thought.

'My finances have been affected by my highs but I'm saving up my money.' Helen paused with a small smile. 'I have a plan.' She gestured toward the window. Kristin stood up from the garden and brushed dirt from her pants. For the past few weeks, she and Owen had been tending seedlings in their own small plot, and it'd been jarring to see how gentle Owen could be with something so fragile. Catching our stare, Kristin glared at us.

'That girl,' Helen murmured in a way that reminded me of Beverly when she'd caught Kristin blowing off curfew. 'She's always following Dillon around. His little shadow.'

An uncomfortable weight settled on my shoulders. When Helen looked back at me, something mischievous played in her eyes, a suggestion that there was something untoward between Dillon and Kristin.

I frowned. 'I don't think—'

'Sometimes, when I look at these students, I wonder: where will they end up? What lives will they lead?' Helen asked.

I thought of that trunk of letters and clippings, the evidence that some of them would be okay, and how much I leaned on it during bad days.

'We do so much,' Helen said softly. 'But we can't do everything.'

Earlier today, I'd peeked inside Helen's classroom to check on Ezra. There had been a pressure in the air, a tightness on the students' faces. Helen had been slumped in her chair, her head tilted to the side in defeat, as she traced the tip of a pencil across her throat from ear to ear. She surveyed the students beneath half-closed eyelids, with an expression either of disdain or fatigue. The students were difficult to control; perhaps there'd just been an outburst. We were all worn out.

Students were rattled, claiming the White Woman had haunted the halls and hummed her ballad last night. In the dining hall, Owen stood on a table, arms spread wide, head back as he belted the final verse: 'He asked is Lady Margaret in her room, or is she out in the hall, but Lady Margaret lay in a cold black coffin, with her face turned to the wall.'

'I heard that her baby suffocated in the wardrobe in the study room,' a student said.

Normally, Ezra gulped his food down, but now he would only dip his spoon in his soup and swirl the vegetables around.

'Hey, someday you're going to look back on all this and be amazed at how far you've come, okay? I promise,' I told him.

He looked at me skeptically. In between appointments that day, he'd sat on my office floor, reading books and coloring. His favorite book was *Madeline*. He liked how she wasn't afraid of the tiger.

I'd point to objects and name things and he'd watch me,

seeming mildly amused at this waste of time. He knew words; what he didn't have was the desire to speak. But he loved listening to me read aloud, nodding and smiling up at me as I flipped pages. Language seemed to affect him like music, the cadence of certain phrases making him tilt his head with delight.

It was better than the blank stare and blinking he'd given me earlier, an absolute refusal to connect. But I was growing concerned about how attached we were becoming so quickly, the boundary between doctor and patient blurring.

Chairs scraped the wood floors as they were pushed into tables, cutlery jangled on plates, footsteps became a small stampede as the students dropped their plates off at the kitchen window. Ezra dropped his spoon on the floor, and when he reached down to grab it, he touched my ankle. A jolt shot through my body and I jerked my foot back. My wool trousers had ridden up above my boot, showing a sliver of skin.

'Don't,' I said sharply.

Curiosity glittered in his eyes.

'It's nothing,' I answered.

He stayed crouched, half under the table, and peered up at me with patience. I knew he wanted to connect, that it might open him up, but I couldn't cross that barrier. Patient boundaries existed for a reason – the longing to be known created a shadowland that distorted expectations. Loneliness bought me clear vision. Better to cut out the impulse and fling it into the wind.

Besides, it wasn't a story for a child. My mother's house wasn't a house for children.

It was a ramshackle two-story with a chimney protruding from the steeply pitched roof. A gravel road stretched west toward town, five miles away. To the east, a thousand-acre farm churned under a wide sky, cycling each Christmas and summer between death and rebirth, like an optical toy you spin between your fingers, two images blurring together.

Inside, it was sparsely furnished, with a rocking chair and stained yellow couch in front of the fireplace. A few paintings of cowboys hung on the walls. My mother had enjoyed arts and crafts before the drugs snared her and these relics from her former life could be found through the house: blue-jean woven rugs, needlepoint pillows, knitted doilies, and crocheted afghans.

My brother and I never liked being there because we were guests in her home and my mother was no hostess. She'd disappear for days at a time, telling us to fend for ourselves, find food in the cupboards. When she was home, she'd sit in the rocker, the television erupting with fake laughs in alarming regularity.

She hadn't paid the electric bill, so three days before the night of the fire, the power went out. The furnace sputtered toward cold; my brother and I huddled under a mass of blankets on the couch, able to see our breath before our faces on the second day she hadn't come home.

We were lucky to be on city water despite being out of town, so the taps still worked. But the dark and the cold got to us, making us feeble and tired, playing with our minds as we clung to each other.

CHAPTER 24

'Watch out for coyote traps,' I warned Ezra as I searched the grass for those metal teeth. I'd expected him to be excited to go to Oksana's, but he kept glaring at me as we walked.

He was sore with me because after dinner, I wouldn't give him the claw I'd found in my mouth. It had been hidden in a spoonful of soup and once it lodged in my throat, I'd hacked it into my palm. Glancing around the room, I waited to see a student burst out laughing but no one was looking my way and hiding a giggle behind a palm. Still, someone, somewhere, was taunting me. I should have been more scared, but I must have spat my fear out along with the claw, leaving me to chew my own teeth with a brewing indignation.

Too short for a badger. Perhaps a coyote or possum. I'd dropped it in my water glass, let it settle on the bottom, and took a sip.

Now, carrying crayons and the twin photo in his pocket, Ezra followed me like a shadow, keeping slightly behind me, mimicking my movements and refusing to meet my eyes with a pointed chill. A carrion hawk perched on the dead coyote Oksana had shot, and pecked its eyeball until it loosened from the socket. After eating the eyeball, it stuck its beak back inside the socket to lick it clean.

Up ahead, Oksana dragged what looked like a human body behind her, dropping the legs once she reached the edge of her garden. A large cross had been erected there and it tilted to the west, as if trying to follow the sun's descent.

Wary, I paused, uncertain if I wanted to go through with this, but the claw pushed me forward. When we got closer, I saw the body was only a scarecrow and felt silly for assuming the worst, for seeing things that weren't there.

'Thought you'd welcome some company – you said you don't get many visitors,' I called out.

'Didn't mean I need them.' Oksana stared at Ezra and he scowled back at her. 'He's that boy. The one who ran away. I heard about him being found on the morning news.'

Ezra squirmed under the attention, which was so typical for him, I was almost disappointed. He was the same curious, unruly, apathetic, vulnerable boy I was growing too fond of, with no telling overreaction in sight.

'You left the carcass out,' I said, nodding at the dead coyote.

The look on her face asked, *Were you born yesterday?* 'Want me to set it up at my table and pour it a cup of tea?' she asked. 'He scares the others off. That's why you just have to kill one. Coyote's not good meat anyway.' She pointed to the scarecrow in the grass. 'You hold its arms and I'll tie it.'

Dust flew into my eyes as I held up the scarecrow against the cross. Grit coated my tongue and I spit it out. 'Is it always so dusty in the spring?' I asked Oksana as she roped its limbs snug against the wood.

'No, that's the drought. This year's nearly as bad as the Dust Bowl years. Parents barely survived on potatoes and dry beans.

Need to do a controlled burn or there'll be wildfires come summer.'

'Controlled burning?'

'Set the grass on fire.' She slashed her hand through the air and made a whooshing sound. 'Indians would call it the red buffalo. If lightning didn't start one in so many years, they would.'

'Wa . . . why?' I asked. The hills around us were a tinderbox.

'Keeps prairie healthy.' She ticked reasons off. 'Removes old plants, pollinates seeds, manages invasive species, fertilizes soil. But most of all – when grass is too dry . . .' She opened her fingers like an explosion going off. 'Wildfires are stronger and more prevalent. So, you light the fire, you control the fire.'

Dizziness gripped the back of my skull. 'How do you do a controlled burning?'

'Firebreaks and wind. You let the wind push it toward a firebreak – ploughed dirt or a river or canyon – so it will stop. Direction of the wind needs to be steady. Or, you light the fire at a firebreak and burn it against ground winds. It will burn a bit but get driven back to where it started. Won't get out of control. And you do it when it's not too hot and not too dry.'

Evidently bored with us, Ezra pulled a stalk of rhubarb from the ground and started munching on it. 'See that fine red color?' she asked him. 'Spilled blood gave it roots, so you know what the earth asks of you. Walk lightly where others have fallen. That's what my mother would say back when the world was better.' She scowled at us like we had spoiled it.

The hung scarecrow's head flopped forward and Oksana jerked her thumb at her cabin. 'Have water boiling.'

*

She didn't invite us, but we followed her anyway and I detected a hint of pleasure on her face when we stepped inside.

Today the cabin smelled like sweet, decaying fruit. A large stockpot steamed on the stove and Oksana rushed past us toward it, commanding us to sit. Ezra's eyes darted around the cabin while I pulled paper out of my satchel for him. Dried rosemary and lavender hung from an exposed beam in the ceiling, tied together in bunches with twine. Glass jars full of crushed herbs lined the open shelves of her kitchen.

Oksana knifed chopped ginger into the pot. Ezra raised his eyebrows at me and then tilted his head toward the stove.

'We're curious what you're making,' I said.

'Medicine. Elderberry syrup,' Oksana muttered, stirring furiously. She scooped up dried berries and dropped them in the pot. 'Send it to my grandchildren.'

This was the opening and I almost let it pass by, eager not to incite her, wanting to win her approval more than I cared to admit. But I shored myself up and nudged a toe into the roiling surf. 'How many children do you have?'

Stained red from the berries, fingers crooked in their joints, Oksana's hands looked raw and injured. She wiped them on her apron before turning to me. 'So, where'd you hear the gossip?'

'I don't mean—' I stood up, hands out in front of me in a gesture of submission.

'You're not good at this.' She crossed her arms and looked at the photographs by the fireplace. 'I wonder if even you could have helped me then?' She looked back at me like she pitied me, chin lifted in defiance, eyes burning, body tense as coiled rope. 'My body made her and then my brain betrayed me.'

'Postpartum psychosis,' I said, fighting to keep sympathy out of my voice. Ezra hunched over his drawing and pushed down so hard, he broke a crayon.

Oksana poured honey into the stockpot. 'They didn't have those names back then. As if when your body makes someone, you can take care of them. It's two different things.'

I apologized, but she waved away my words. 'This is what you came for. You'll keep buzzing around me until you pierce your way through. Fine. My youngest was born six years after my last son. My husband was always out on the ranch while I tended house. I felt strange with her pregnancy – fuzzy, confused. After she was born, I was in such a thick fog. Couldn't see what was right in front of me. Got the shocks.' She pointed to her wrists, where restraints would have been placed during electroshock therapy. 'Helped after a while, but I started it too late. By the time I came out of it, Sophia . . . was already different. My husband said I didn't tend her. Didn't feed her, didn't touch her. I don't remember any of it. Other people tell me who I am, what I did.'

Oksana paused and rubbed her palm over her face. 'So, she was different from my sons. Doctor said it was from neglect and her brain went bad. I saved men with limbs blown off but couldn't take care of my own child.' She shook her head sharply, jaw set tight. Eyes brittle and hard as glass, staring beyond me, into another time and place. 'But I still tried to give her a good life. She lives now in one of those assisted homes and the other kids look in on her. I had a few other bouts like that later over the years. Pump was primed, as they say. So now you can tell your detective friend I didn't kill my child and I didn't kill that boy.'

'I never thought you killed either of them,' I said, meaning it.

She appraised me and a flicker of fondness crossed her face before she hardened again.

'You remind me of myself. Stupid.' She shook her head. 'Naïve.'

I wanted to claim I wasn't naïve, but she would've called me on my bullshit. She told me about her other children – how her oldest had earned a doctorate in microbiology and her second and third born had beautiful children and thriving careers in business.

While she talked, I could see the other parts of their lives, the sides children learn to hide from their parents when they age. How they all carried the disappointments of her life in their bodies, how when they cried, they said to themselves, astonished: *I am restless, I cannot feel good an entire single day*, how they longed for little else other than relief from fatigue, how they grasped the edges of their dreams when wakefulness pulled at them, how their work couldn't save them and they knew this and denied it on moonless nights while their children slept, how they longed for disaster as much as they feared it, longed for a problem so big it could eclipse the smaller ones that threatened to swallow them up. These were the burdens of their resilience.

An ant ran across the table and Ezra smashed it with his thumb and licked it clean. Oksana brandished the wood spoon in Ezra's direction. 'You're better than a cat.'

He tried to flatten his smile, but I could tell he was proud. He'd drawn a picture of the twins, their hair curled about their ears, four perfectly round blue eyes. I thought of my hallucinations, that eerie doubling and the way she often felt more real than my own body. When Oksana had talked about the controlled burning, I could feel her pressing close, wanting to appear.

Oksana set tea on the table in front of us in fragile porcelain cups. Scrubbed free of the berry juices, her hands looked more delicate now with their deep lines and knobby knuckles, their light touch after working decades, as if the nerves themselves had learned grace. I saw both toughness and tenderness in her skin's map of gestures – the forking of hay, tending of plants, fixing of fences – a quiet acceptance of what we cannot change.

It made me think of Beverly and her bitterness, how she could unexpectedly lash out. I hesitated, not wanting to gossip, but wanting to understand. 'What do you know about Howard and Beverly?'

Oksana gave me a sharp look. 'He became a widower about a year ago. Beverly changed after that. She came by more often, like for a visit, 'cept she'd collapse crying in my rocker. Talked in circles. She'd repeat something a lot: *it can't have been for nothing, it can't have been for nothing.*'

I frowned. 'What was she talking about?'

Oksana pointed in my face. 'This isn't for spreading around. She thought the affair wasn't an affair. More like a pre-marriage. She told me he'd promised that after his wife died, he'd marry her.' She shrugged. 'Then he didn't.'

'Why not?'

She shook her head. 'I didn't pry. This tale is old as time. It soured her a bit. On him, on Hatchery. She clings to the House but also squeezes it pretty tight.'

I didn't like the reference or the visual it gave me. Hatchery was the one thing Beverly shared with Howard and I didn't want to think about the students getting caught in the crosshairs of all this.

Outside, the barn door slammed shut in the wind. Gazing at

the barn, I asked Oksana, 'When this was a ranch, did you use whips to herd cattle?'

'Rarely. But we did occasionally have a stubborn bull.'

Those marks on Luis's back – Cedar had said they looked like they'd been made with a whip. 'Do you have any of the old whips in the barn?'

'Little bastard stole the last one,' Oksana muttered.

'Luis?' I asked.

'No, that tow-headed big one. That one that causes trouble.'

Owen.

CHAPTER 25

Back at Hatchery, Helen told me she'd seen him walking toward Ennenock, so I waited until Ezra was settled in bed and then set off under an orange evening sky and darkening violet clouds. Soon, the landscape would become a silhouette, blackening as light faded over the horizon. An owl swooped low, casting a shadow over me, before disappearing over the hills.

Voices came from the abandoned sheriff's office. A metal trough rusted out front, dusk lengthening a wagon wheel's shadow across the wood plank porch.

One of the voices belonged to Dillon, but the other was so soft, a kind of murmur, that I couldn't place it. Nothing like Owen's. I crossed the dirt road and walked closer.

After our fight over lunch I'd avoided Dillon, which hadn't been difficult since I'd been so busy. On some level, I suspected we were going to break up, that there was no going back to before, but I kept this packaged and tucked at the edge of my mind. I couldn't be winded with that failure right now.

At the end of the porch, I recognized the other voice: Kristin. I froze, hand up on one of the porch's pillars. A spider scurried over my hand; I shook it off. Hesitating, I told myself to walk away. What you don't know can't hurt you.

But Helen's comment about Kristin being Dillon's shadow pulled me forward and I slipped my boots off so I could move silently across the porch toward the window. It was shattered, the glass blown away over the years, leaving a soft layer of dust to cushion my footfall.

'I don't want to go home. Will you even miss me?' Kristin asked. 'I gave you that photo and you're not even acting grateful.'

I leaned toward the windowsill, steadying myself with a hand on the wall, and almost bumped a wind chime made of flattened spoons. Kristin moved toward Dillon, but he backed away, holding his hand out between them. His expression in the dim light looked irritated and almost regretful.

'I didn't ask for that,' he said.

'No, but you were curious,' she said. She flicked a photo in front of his face and turned in a half circle, facing the window I peered through. I ducked behind the wall. Across the drive, a branch quivered from a bird taking flight. I focused on it to slow my breathing.

'Kristin, this has to stop,' Dillon said. 'No more meeting in private—'

'My leaving early will affect your research.'

'It's more important that you're safe.'

'I AM SAFE. Why are you pretending you don't care about me?' It was that familiar whine Kristin used in my office, tilting her head and hugging her shoulders close to make herself look smaller. 'Are you worried about me telling? I only made a scene that once in the assembly. And I didn't really believe she killed a patient; I just wanted to humiliate her. I hate her.'

Dust in the air became thick and caught in my throat. He *had* told her about Deborah and the raid, and he'd stood next to the bell tower door, lying to me while I simpered like a weak idiot.

'I should never have told you about that. I'd hoped it'd help illustrate what we'd talked about, how—'

Something far off in the distance wailed, a high, agonized shriek, and I jolted, hitting the wind chime with my shoulder. A jangle of erratic notes rang out and I stumbled off the porch.

'What's that?' Dillon asked.

'Stop pushing me away,' Kristin snapped.

I struggled with my boots, my hands now gummy and joint-less. Running down the dirt road, the grass and my breath both rasping, I fought back a memory of Dillon and me in his apartment, his hand on my waist, pulling me closer to him.

With Kristin, had he really . . .

The screech startled me again, bringing me to my senses. Red foxes screamed in the night, I reminded myself. Things can sound worse than they are – calm down. I pinched the bridge of my nose and squeezed my eyes shut.

Dillon and I had keys to each other's offices – we often borrowed books or medications – so I reached into my pocket and fingered my ring of keys until I landed on his. I would go through his office and look for signs of something amiss in notes, voice-mail, a left-behind token of affection.

I nearly collided with Helen at the bottom of Hatchery's front steps.

'Lore, you okay?' Helen asked, her brow furrowed. I must have looked frenzied to her: hair askew, so wide-eyed I looked half insane.

'Me? Great – great – great, thanks,' I said, tripping over the first step and catching myself on the porch.

Once inside Dillon's office, I whirled in a circle, taking the whole room in. Kristin seemed like the type who would write effusive love notes, scribbled with hearts and words like *forever*. So I shuffled papers on his desk, opened all his drawers, checked under the two armchairs, and felt under his desk. Standing on the coffee table, I ran my hands along the tops of the bookcases. I moved the rug under his desk chair and felt for loose floorboards.

Orange- and clove-scented aftershave lingered in the room. As I searched, a thought circled my brain: you couldn't be with someone who would do something like this. No, not him. You couldn't . . .

Children's voices came from another room. Hatchery's front door slammed shut with a thud and footsteps sounded in the hallway. I watched the glass-knob door handle, heart in my throat, but it did not turn.

Leaning back on my heels, I rubbed my forehead. Kristin had mentioned an older man in our appointment and Helen had made that comment, with a glint in her eyes, one corner of her mouth lifted like it was a joke. If I'd overlooked this, I'd overlooked other things.

History of Asylums, near the top of the bookcase, was thumbed forward. I opened it. The pages had been cut in the middle of the book, forming a small box which held a stack of notes and a gold key. I twisted the key so it spun. It was the old-fashioned kind with brass teeth sticking out of a cylindrical rod, the kind Beverly had described when I'd asked her about the bell tower key.

I clenched my jaw, nerves raw, the metal smooth between my fingers. I imagined a hideout above my head, a pink bed tucked around a bend in the stairs, a room for captive lovers, stone walls thick enough to soundproof swoons.

But the notes suggested something else. Two were written on index cards in tight handwriting.

Hi Dr Edwards, I sent you the signed forms last week. Did you get them? I know in my heart Carly's mama in heaven will want her to be part of something special like this. When does the money come in? Thanks, Melissa.

Hi Dr Edwards, Carly called me today and said she was fainting in class. Are you sure this medicine is what she needs? I know we agreed to two hundred a month but I'm not feeling so good about this anymore. I think I'm going to need more money. Melissa.

Under these two notes was correspondence from Kristin's father and Luis's advocate, a woman who'd written tersely: *Luis Alvarez isn't really a great candidate for the treatment, but I signed the forms anyway, assuming you know what you're doing. Thought you should know my professional opinion.*

Students' footsteps echoed overhead as they readied for bed, and laughter strained against the walls. The room dimmed as clouds passed over the sun. I stuffed the letters back into the book and tucked it on the shelf. Someone knocked on Dillon's office door and I froze. My heartbeat skipped like a rock on water as I tucked myself behind the bookcase. 'What do you need, Carly?' Dillon asked just outside the door.

'Feeling tired again. Dizzy.'

'I told you it'd take a while to feel normal. Your body's

acclimating. Let's get you a snack before bed, raise that blood sugar.'

Their footsteps receded. When it was silent, I opened the door just a crack and peered out, gripping the bell tower key so tight, it bit into my palm.

CHAPTER 26

The air in the bell tower tasted like damp earth and was so silent, even the stones seemed to wait for sound. A stone spiral staircase twisted upwards in front of me. To the left, the yellow door that led outside moaned against the wind.

Dillon could have snuck outside the night of Luis's murder and evaded the camera over the front door. I wouldn't, not yet, let myself connect this observation with the next possibility: that he'd ridden the horse, held the rock, and bashed in Luis's skull.

After unlocking the bell tower door, I'd returned the key to Dillon's book, so he wouldn't suspect anything, and grabbed a flashlight from my office. I needed to hurry before anyone noticed I was missing.

The flashlight's beam brushed over deep fissures as I climbed the steps. They were smooth from decades of footfall and there was a crisp edge to the night air. The pungent smell of rodent nests grew stronger and the walls felt like they leaned inward against me, threatening to suffocate me, the darkness heavy against my back. Halfway up the bell tower, I stopped on a landing with a small door. Carly's doll lay in a corner with a long crack running from its forehead to tiny chin and a black hole where its second glass eye should have been.

Something creaked above me, and I froze. Tiny footsteps, the scamper of small claws on stone. Swallowing, I reached for the glass doorknob.

The room was tiny and almost bare. At the back of the room, two file cabinets stood against the wall. A small table with two chairs held candles and dried pools of wax. I could see Dillon sitting at it, facing a student who fidgeted, sensing violation on some level just below awareness. Research. He had always talked about this rare patient population and its controlled environment.

I had to take a minute to gather myself and breathe past the anger.

Matches lay next to the candles, but I didn't light them as I walked past the table, toward the file cabinet. My hand shook on the metal handle before I could pull it open. I wouldn't find just surveys; Dillon could have conducted those in his office. A room like this was a place for a different kind of research. I yanked open the first drawer.

Week 2 of Treatment
Patient 2A: Kristin Wilson
Patient responding well to medication. Complaints of mania have subsided. Side effect of memory loss is minimal.

Week 1 of Treatment
Patient 3B: Luis Alvarez
Patient is not responsive to questionnaire. Began at half dose this morning.

Week 4 of Treatment
Patient 1: Carly Howard
Patient fainted in cafeteria today. Also falls asleep in class. Sedation is impairing daily functions though it continues to be successful in treatment of PTSD as panic attacks and social anxiety have lessened.

At the back of the cabinet, there was a file labeled: *Questionnaire and Medication Description.*

What is something you remember from one year ago? Do you feel tired or energetic during your day? Do you have trouble controlling your impulses? What situations trigger panic attacks? How has your sleep changed since starting the medication? Have you thought of hurting yourself or someone else?

My palms dampened the paper with sweat and phrases jumped out at me, jumbled and out of order.

Minzepam . . . off-label . . . longer acting Benzodiazepine . . . hypnotic sedative . . . binding with neurotransmitter gamma-aminobutyric acid . . . possible side effects . . . memory loss . . . inconsistent dosing . . . aggressive behaviors may present in some patients . . .

Bile built in the back of my throat. I reached out and placed my palm against the damp stone wall, rough as an old tombstone and smelling of moss.

They drug us to make us forget, Kristin had said with a slight smile, her eyes half-moons.

A drug trial. The students were too young to give legal consent.

That's what those handwritten notes were about – Dillon securing permission from their guardians, avoiding an electronic trail. Perhaps he was paying all of them, or only the ones who needed incentive. Melissa, Carly's guardian, must not have been willing to keep it confidential once Carly suffered side effects, and that's when she began writing for more money.

This was one of the sedatives found in Luis's toxicology report. Sedatives suppressed the nervous system and could damage neurological development in young patients. This drug had tunneled through Luis's veins, slowed his blood and breath, made it harder for him to flee his attacker.

I couldn't believe I'd dated – almost fallen for – someone who had done this. I remembered the early days – Dillon and I laughing at breakfast over how neither of us could poach eggs, the yolk always running into the white before it set. At his ridiculous shoes, too expensive and stylish with their pointed toes and Italian leather. Of how his aftershave smelled like clove and oranges, bright and exotic amid all this dust and half-dead grass, like we could be fruit, ripening, growing heavy on the same branch.

My fantasy that this relationship would be different, would usher me into a different kind of life, hadn't just been folly; it'd been blinding. Shame clotted in me, sticky as mold in my marrow.

Something clanged below me and I jumped. A heavy door shut with a thud. Tiny, high-pitched noises from within the walls filled the room as I crept toward the landing and looked around the doorframe. The steps spiraled down into darkness and footsteps sounded on them.

Freezing in the doorway, I clicked off my flashlight and dashed up to the belfry. Four arches opened to the night sky, wind whipping through them, hissing and sending dust swirling about my feet. A giant bell hung in the middle, its rim four feet above a wooden platform with missing planks.

Below, the door to the small room opened and footsteps echoed upwards. Cursing myself for replacing the key in the book, I pressed my lips together so I wouldn't make a sound. I tucked myself into a corner between two arches and tried to slow my breathing.

Hurt and embarrassment lay beneath the outrage and fear, common and mundane as a bruise with a dull edge and tender throb. It dazed me that I'd missed so much right under my nose.

The footsteps grew louder. 'Lore,' Dillon called. 'I know you're up here.'

He came into view slowly; when he emerged into the moonlight, his face was so symmetrical and placid, it didn't look fully lived in. He'd look handsome even when dead. He didn't immediately see me in the corner, and I felt like I was back at Carson's funeral: pressed up against a wall, shoved past insignificance, straight into invisibility.

That was fine for me, but not for these students dozing beneath my feet. Luis had climbed those stairs up to that small room, sat at that table by candlelight, trusted the man in front of him.

I imagined Dillon slipping through the yellow door while I had lain in the grass, only yards away, drifting to sleep. I needed to erase that image.

I stepped out of the shadows and he startled.

'Just tell me,' I said. 'Did you kill Luis?'

CHAPTER 27

Carson had been cremated after the fire, so I didn't understand why there was a casket at the funeral. This wastefulness felt mildly insulting, a kind of statement: his body would be here if it hadn't been ruined.

My aunt, who performed umbrage frequently, had a tower of hair and a wart on her cheek and spoke in the booming tones of a sports announcer.

I was standing against a wall, half tucked behind a heavy curtain as people surveyed the tragedy with tones of practiced, empty sympathy.

'He was the sweetest boy. Someone should have been taking care of him,' she told everyone who sidled past her.

My head rang as though a door had been shut on it. *Lorelei should have been taking care of him.* Surely that's what she meant. Erasing myself, I slid further behind the curtain.

I had never stopped to consider she'd meant my mother, who'd of course been the parent in charge that night. No one in the family had ever counted on my mother for anything, so she wasn't really part of the equation when accounting for responsibilities.

But beyond that, it was easier to blame myself than my mother.

She was my origin and wellspring; if she were kept sacred and separate, maybe I could inherit some good spark from her. Believing in her had meant believing in my future.

Now, as then, I couldn't stop shaking. Couldn't escape the falling sensation that I'd failed to protect Luis too. Hoofbeats sounded in my head, getting louder and louder.

'Did . . . did Luis threaten to tell someone about the drug trial?' I asked.

Dillon jerked his head back and threw out his arms. 'God, Lore. Are you accusing me of murder?'

'I just need you to answer,' I said.

I was more scared than I could feel, my mind filled with questions my body didn't want me to ask. My body yelled for me to run, but my mind said, *I can make sense of this. It isn't how it looks.*

When I was at Oksana's, my eyes had tricked me and told me a scarecrow was a dead body. That's all this was: misinterpretation. I couldn't have been trained to read people only to misread the one person I was close to here.

'You're losing your mind. I didn't kill Luis,' Dillon said. His face creased in disgust. 'God, how could you even think that?'

'I don't know what to think.' I hated how my voice sounded small and beseeching.

'Well, I didn't do it.'

It was what I wanted to hear and I took it with both hands. An exhale shuddered through me. I knew this habit of denying the guilt of someone close to me had its claws in me and wouldn't release. But still, I believed him and wondered if I'd regret it.

*

The belfry grew wavy around me, undulating and blue as an ocean, and I had to place my hand on the wall to recover. A crow perched on an archway ledge, its beak piercing the night when it dove back into the air. I knuckled my eyes, energy and clarity slowly returning.

'I asked you to stop nosing around,' Dillon said.

That buzzed under my skin. 'How'd you know where I was?'

'Kristin saw you in Ennenock and I figured you'd assume the worst and search my office. The book with the key was pushed all the way back.'

'I know you conned the guardians to get consent, but I wonder: why seduce Kristin too?' I asked. 'Isn't using her in one way enough for you?'

Annoyance crossed over his face and a muscle twitched in his jaw. 'I didn't seduce her. And I didn't peg you as someone jealous of teenagers.'

I took a step toward him. 'So you start testing drugs on her, she starts spending time with you up in the bell tower. Romantic. You do realize that in addition to medical fraud, you could be tried for statutory—'

'She's eighteen.'

I stared at him, aghast. 'My God. Is that what you tell yourself?'

'Fuck you. Nothing happened. She came at me—'

'How frightening that must have been for you. So defenseless.'

Clouds passed over the moon and the belfry grew so dark, I couldn't see Dillon. I listened to his breath and felt my pulse hammering away on the inside of my wrist. I could hear movement, his soft footfall, but couldn't see where he was going.

'Whatever you think is going on, isn't,' he said. 'She follows me around. I can't exactly get away from her here, can I?'

'That's a weak defense.' I spoke to the darkness, and when the wind blew my hair into a frenzy, I flinched. I didn't think he would hurt me, but the sweat on my temples said otherwise.

The moonlight grew brighter. Dillon sat in an archway, air and a fifty-foot drop at his back. I thought of what a slight shove would do to him and my whole body jolted with the terror of it.

'Was it how much she adores and respects you?' I asked. 'You couldn't back away from that.'

'Yeah, I would like some respect instead of the constant competitiveness from you.'

'I'm reporting all of this.'

Dillon leapt to his feet and barreled toward me. I backed up against the wall; he stopped inches from my chest, his breath hot in my face. He slammed his palm on the stones and cursed, wincing and shaking his hand out.

'I told you. We spent too much time together—' He stopped abruptly, face tightening, not able to say *during the drug trial*. He shook his head and continued on, 'She wanted to confide in me about everything and we crossed a line without me even realizing it. It's difficult, seeing a patient outside of appointments; I didn't know how to maintain distance. She has a crush. There's more transference than there should be, that's all. I swear to you, nothing happened.'

His chin jutted out as his flinty gaze held my eyes. If he'd been all apologetic and defeated, I'd have known he was lying. But this – this evasive non-apology – was trademark Dillon and it told me he was telling the truth. Besides, I'd heard the story before of a man keeping a girl encouraged enough to do their bidding.

'You let her flirt with you and daydream about a future with you. You wanted to appease her, so she would stay compliant in the trial,' I said.

'I never touched her,' Dillon said. 'I kept her at arm's length.'

'And within arm's reach.'

'After Luis's death, I stopped the trial, okay? Carly and Kristin are coming off the sedative.' Dillon kneaded his palm and glanced down at me, a lock of hair falling into his face.

'How'd you get the key?' I asked. 'Beverly said there's only one and she has it.'

'I'm not telling you where I got it.'

Beverly wouldn't have given it to him. She'd never approve of a risky drug trial, not when she was trying to protect Hatchery's reputation and plan for expansion.

'How'd you get Kristin, Luis and Carly to keep this quiet?'

Dillon paced in front of me. 'I told the students I'd pay them once the trial is done, okay?'

A reward for their silence. I remembered Carly outside of Dillon's office, saying, *I've gone into the tower, but my mouth is sewn shut.*

'Both physicians and patients are often paid in clinical trials; it isn't illegal,' Dillon said.

'It's not done under the table like this, Dillon; you know that. You're experimenting on children.'

'I wanted to bring you in on this, but I knew you'd be this way.'

'Glad you knew I wouldn't recruit underage patients who don't even need sedatives and pay guardians for consent and silence.

You were drugging students and when side effects were clearly affecting them, you didn't stop. Why would you do this? Luis never needed a sedative.'

Then I remembered his grant for research into memory loss as a treatment for anxiety. He was doing it secretly because Beverly wouldn't give him permission, but it wasn't even about the drug trial. Drug trials don't need controlled variables, but a case study does.

'You're not doing it in spite of side effects, you're doing it because of them. You were using the sedative to observe how their memory loss affected anxiety levels.'

Dillon flushed. 'You of all people are obsessed with practicality. Why waste this opportunity? You should understand. Besides, any of these students could quit at any time. Once the trial is successful, then Hatchery's involvement can go public—'

'Beverly won't want that.'

'She will if Hatchery can be positioned as a leading research facility. This drug – and my case study – is going to help people.'

The full moon cast a faint glow on the stones and its reflection bent on the brass curve of the bell. Dillon began walking toward the stairs and waved for me to follow. 'Let's go have a drink and calm down.'

He still thought he was in control, that he could just talk his way out of this. I stood rooted in place. Once, he'd told me how when he was a teenager, he got a bad cut on his arm. He took his mother's needle and thread and stitched it himself, eager to show his father when he got home. It had been a challenge, he'd said, and he wanted to see if he could get away with it.

'I know,' I said and he stopped. 'I know why you did this. For you, the moment doesn't matter; it's what you have to show after the moment has passed. The reaction from people who are watching. The object you got out of time spent. The proof. The proof you set on someone's desk and can point to, and say, right there, this is why I matter. But no one is watching.'

I lifted my hand to the open archway and night sky beyond. There was a steady thrum around us, tiny movements and beating hearts of animals we couldn't see, the bats above, the rodents in the walls, the owls that flew silent amid stars. 'There is no audience. No one is judging if you matter or not.'

Dillon shook his head. 'You've never lived a moment of your life like no one's watching. You even watch yourself.'

The hairs on the back of my neck lifted. He couldn't know about my hallucinations.

'Yeah, I know how you are,' Dillon said, stepping toward me. 'The way you monitor each action, measure it against how good or bad it makes you.' Dillon held out each hand, palms up, moving them up and down in an invisible scale. 'You spend so much energy trying to discern where you're at. Whether or not you can allow yourself to feel good after you've done something. It's why you've never been able to move on after something doesn't go well—'

'Doesn't go well? Deborah DIED. Died. Why the fuck doesn't that have any magnitude for you?'

'Maybe you should ask why you have to make her death all about you.'

'Because I take responsibility—' I said, jabbing my chest with my finger.

'You are obsessed—'

'I'm turning you in.'

Our eyes locked. We stood a few feet apart, the giant bell gleaming beside us, our reflections tiny and distorted on its surface. The belfry felt like it was vibrating, but it was my nerves that were jangling.

He shook his head, a chuckle escaping from his pursed lips. 'No, you won't.' He walked in a slow semi-circle around me and I turned, not taking my eyes off him, the bell behind me, the open archway behind Dillon.

The night pressed against me. I clenched my hands into fists and released them, urging my blood away from the pounding in my head.

'Yes—' I began.

Dillon rammed into me, driving me against the bell. My heel caught the edge of the platform and I fell back as he pinned me against the cold metal. It tilted with my weight and in a breathless second, I waited for it to ring. It didn't. There was only the thud of my bones against brass as I tried to squirm out of his vice-like grip on my arm.

He pulled something from his pocket and shoved it in my face. A photo of Cedar and me talking in the old saloon, a file on the bar between us, twitched in his hand.

'Kristin knew I was curious if you were helping with the case and snapped this. It will prove to Beverly you're informing on Hatchery to the FBI. Treating patients as suspects; that's a pretty big conflict of interest. You'll be let go.' Releasing me, Dillon leaned back. Blood flooded down my arm and my fingers tingled. 'Reporting the drug trial won't accomplish anything because I've already pulled our participants from the study. And you need this job. We both know you can't go back to the FBI, and Hatchery is paying your student loans. You have what, half a million? So you'll need to decide if you want to go down for nothing.'

I slid off the bell and almost fell, but Dillon caught me by the arm and lifted me up. Our faces were inches apart and I saw myself in his pupil, tiny and caught like an insect in a black trap. Then he blinked and I disappeared.

CHAPTER 28

Dillon escorted me down the steps and locked the door behind us.

'Those notes you found are already destroyed,' he told me. 'The files up in that room will be shredded before the sun rises. And my contract with the pharmaceutical company doesn't prove any misconduct. Beverly will be upset Hatchery was involved but . . .' Dillon shrugged at this.

He had the presence of mind to be self-protective and I could barely find my feet. He left me standing in the foyer, shell-shocked and unsteady. Only one place to go now.

As I drove to Cedar's hotel, I half hoped a deer would leap in front of the car and force me to swerve into a ditch. I wanted to hurl through darkness like a torpedo, to have a second of exist-ence so extreme it would wipe everything else out.

Once, as a child, I'd stepped on a log in the forest that shat-tered under my foot. Thousands of ants crawled among the ruins, wood reduced to the texture of sawdust, and I'd been astonished something could look strong, yet be so hollow. That was my rela-tionship with Dillon. Or maybe, that was me.

I would report the drug trial to Beverly; the only question

was when and how. The students weren't in danger from it now and I didn't want to get fired before the investigation was over. I could report his bribery to the medical licensing board, but I had no proof.

Fleeing to your friend, my father would say derisively if he saw me now. He hated neediness. I could still see his face – deprived, resigned – before I shut the door on Christmas morning and disappeared down the icy street.

The cultural expectation of happiness, glitter and gold during the holiday season made me feel like someone was drawing blood from my veins. My father and I would eat canned soup, only slightly warmed on the stovetop because he was always impatient. He'd toss me a few gifts meant for a younger child – a broken Hot Wheels car, a doll with matted hair – and we'd go our separate ways. He'd go to the local bar and I'd go to Cedar's house, where I could hear laughter and songs all the way from the sidewalk in front of their house.

His siblings were always piled on the couch, squabbling over cookies and treats, their mother swatting their hands away. The whole house filled to the brim with aunts, uncles, cousins, and people who had somehow been adopted into the family over the years. Nat King Cole sang bright melodies and lights glowed on the tree, the whole beaming room impossibly picturesque, a fable I had wanted to believe in.

Cedar's mother always had a small wrapped gift for me. Nothing extravagant, but still something I needed: a sweater or pair of boots.

One time, I had to hide in the bathroom while they opened gifts, stuffing a towel in my mouth to cover the sobs, splashing my face with cold water to reduce the redness. The warmth in that house could be too much if you weren't used to it.

But that house was the reason I made it. Cedar's mother tended to me when she was already heavy with her own burdens and children. When I made it into medical school, she had been the first person I told and the only person who'd ever cried out of happiness for something good I got. She knew chaos and chaos knew her, and I watched her wrestle it, watched how when her children gathered around the fire, it bowed to her, if only for a moment.

My headlights came upon feet and I slammed on the brakes. Someone stood in the middle of the road, her back to the car. The figure held something, cradled it as though it were a baby, and kept her head down to watch it; a pieta on a country highway in the dark.

She slowly began to turn toward the car and my own face stared back at me. A sulfurous odor wafted from her burnt hair as her dead milky eye fixed on me. She didn't hold a baby. She held a funeral pyre of thorns with the crucified rat on top.

I bit my lip so hard, I tasted blood. There'd been no pressure or heat to announce her coming, no faint ringing in my ears this time. She, or I, was changing. She lifted a lighted match to the thorns and the wind fanned them to flames, the rat blackening as smoke billowed around her face.

The hallucination had left me more desperate and intent on hiding it by the time I knocked on Cedar's hotel room door. When he opened it, my body betrayed me, leaning toward him, my face tightening with emotion, a quick hitch in my breath of relief.

'Hey, hey,' he said softly, taking me by the hand and ushering me inside. His T-shirt had shrunk in the wash and strained across his chest, making him look unfamiliar. 'Are you okay? What happened?'

'Nothing,' I said reflexively, standing in the middle of the room and looking around like a lost child.

It was so clean and organized, I almost laughed. He had files stacked neatly on a cheap desk, next to a photo of Warren, and the lone chair in the room held a box labeled *confidential*. On top of the dresser, he'd arranged apples, bananas and protein bars.

'You're shaking,' he said.

I was shaking? 'Oh, I'm fine,' I said, in what I hoped was a reassuring voice. 'I have info.' I touched my forehead with my fingertips and found my skin cold and clammy.

'Sit down,' Cedar said, gesturing to the bed. 'What happened?'

'I – I need a minute,' I said, still rubbing my forehead. My concentration was shattered; I couldn't string sentences together and explain the last few hours. I could tell he was curious, but he knew not to press me into talking too soon.

I was like Ezra, rabid with silence, listening to my life tick away in my ears with each heartbeat. Loneliness closed me in more than that bell tower ever could.

Sitting next to me, Cedar tucked a stray hair behind my ear. 'Tiny army general.' It had been his nickname for me, borne from my habit of surveying the neighborhood from my father's front porch with the seriousness of battlefield planning.

I shook my head. 'Not so fierce anymore.'

'You weren't always so fierce then.'

'Oh. Thanks.'

'I mean . . . it wasn't all fierceness. You were vigilant. Because you were scared, a lot of the time.'

I didn't like that he knew this, so I laid down and turned away from him. On his nightstand, there was a copy of *Black Elk Speaks*.

'Biographies are the epitome of dad books,' I said, wanting to tease him toward lighter topics.

He resisted my pull. 'Maybe I'll be a father someday.'

'Don't look at me.'

'But I like looking at you.'

Grinning, I rolled over to face him and traced his hairline. 'Give me a line,' I said. He often memorized favorite lines, something I envied with my faulty memory and lack of discipline when reading.

'"I knew that the real was yonder and that the darkened dream of it was here,"' he recited. His eyes, intense under his long dark lashes, wouldn't leave mine. My hip joints had gone loose and a warm ache pulsed in my stomach.

'We can't go back to how we were,' I warned him.

How we were. Fifteen the first time, and I'd felt like a hot pearl had been dropped in my stomach where it just glowed and glowed. No kissing or nakedness, just touching in the dark, so it would be easier to pretend afterwards that nothing had happened. We knew that our friendship mattered more than some pleasure. For years, until the raid, we returned to each other over and over, our hunger an insistent hum, a chorus to our lives.

He lay down next to me. 'Let me help you feel better,' he said.

'Penance?' I asked, a small smile escaping.

'You can call it whatever you want.'

I rolled closer to him and when he tucked me against his body,

I missed how he used to smell like clove cigarettes and pepper-mint gum.

Our clothes rustled and the warmth of his breath was against my ear, heavy and quick. His fingers traced my spine, stopping at my waist and pressing me against him. Smelling faintly of salt, his skin still made me think of the sea, of worn driftwood that had lost its bark.

'I should have been there for you,' he said. 'I know that's—'

I kissed him so he'd shut up. Soon, I felt tremors down in my marrow. My body began to ring like a bell, and I thought of the bell that wouldn't ring in the tower, of the night sky that stood alert.

That first time in January, Cedar and I had driven out to the country property where I took care of horses. My part-time job in high school had been mucking out stables and riding horses out on the green when they needed exercise.

We'd carried sleeping bags and a small tent up into the hay loft of an old barn, where we looked down on a small field circled by pines. We built our own world in the tent and stayed warm under the pile of blankets. Joined, we were the green seedling that uproots itself when stretching for sunlight.

When we woke that next morning, there was snow all around us. Thick and heavy, it transformed everything. So white it was blinding, so pure I imagined we'd been reborn into a snow globe and would never have to leave.

CHAPTER 29

May 4, 2007

We talked until the early morning hours.

'You know when I told you I dreamed Warren had died? That wasn't exactly right. Well, I dreamed he died and now encourages me – the way he would when I was a kid, playing catch or whatever. The part of him that is gone – his intellect, his enthusiasm – I dream of that still being here, can hear his old voice cheering me on, telling me to keep going. As though you could halve a person and keep the best parts of them.'

He told me how his mother had changed after that, getting touchy and discouraging when he or his siblings talked about their dreams. 'She was scared to put her hope in us after the attack, scared to imagine a bright future and scared for us to bother trying. But that's what Warren had always stood for,' Cedar said.

There was something expectant in his face, perhaps for an intimacy I didn't know I had to give anymore.

'He would be proud of you,' I told him. I placed my palms on his cheeks and kissed him, pushing against a luminous sensation in my chest, stuffing it back down.

'We should discuss the case,' he said, and I nodded. His hotel room had become a shelter to me and I was ready.

He told me there was a second raid on Lamberg tomorrow and the FBI was sending someone to open the safe in the bank. When I told him about Dillon's drug trial in the bell tower, Cedar paced the room for almost an hour as I sat on the edge of the bed, staring at the carpet. He swore when I admitted that I didn't have evidence of the bribery and I cursed myself for not stealing the book full of letters.

'Medical research always has casualties,' I said softly.

'What?'

'That's what Dillon said once, under his breath, when he didn't think I was listening. I had no idea what he was talking about at the time.'

An uneasy silence settled between us, interrupted only by the irregular whoosh of a car passing outside.

'I can subpoena the pharmaceutical company for records and get statements from the students' guardians, but that'll take time we don't have. They'll stall; it'll be a mountain of paperwork. Besides, establishing that he ran a drug trial without Beverly's permission doesn't prove that he committed a murder. It's circumstantial at best.' Cedar stopped in front of the window; headlights flared on his face before trailing the wall and vanishing.

'You're sounding certain it was him.' I saw it in my patients all the time – assumptions leading to unsound conclusions. There was such a need to understand what happened that it often led to a false understanding. We had to be wary of that.

'Lore, everything adds up. You're in denial. He has motive and method – he got outside through the bell tower door and that's why we don't have him on camera.'

'Don't treat me like some battered woman, defending her man,' I said.

'Don't act like one.' When he saw my face harden, he quickly said, 'I'm worried about you.'

'Stop saying that. I don't give two shits about your worry. You can't just throw that out there so I'll do what you want. You don't listen.'

'Yeah, I know, sorry. But he's the one who's been stalking you.'

I considered this and shook my head. 'I'm not sure . . .'

'What about Kristin wrapped in barbed wire? He has a motive for that, too. Maybe he wanted to shut her up.'

'I want to shut you up so I can think.'

Cedar swore and returned to pacing. The killer had lured Luis away in the dark, on horseback, to somewhere private. Was the other sedative meant to make the kill easier or more merciful? The attack was intimate, then a frenzied burst of fury. His body left out in the open, where it would be quickly found, uncovered. Lazy, Albert had said, or angry.

It felt, somehow, like the killer's heart was in it and Dillon didn't really have a lot of heart to spare.

Or maybe, something else. I was thinking of revenge and guilt, of vendettas and atonement. How each were a kind of fever, stoked by suffering; how they could rage unabated for years.

'He might be our top suspect, but he doesn't fit the profile,' I said.

'Profiles can be a guide, but they're rarely the full picture,' Cedar said.

'I think this person relates to the students, is reacting to them in some way. If Luis's death was simply to silence him, it would have been done differently.'

I told Cedar about Owen stealing the whip from Oksana's barn. Cedar had learned Owen could ride horses because he had spent time at a therapy ranch in Wyoming after he got out of juvie the second time.

'So Owen has been bullying Luis, even whipping him, and eventually kills him. But what was going on between them?' I asked. 'Why would Luis let him get away with it?'

The bed creaked as Cedar sat down and shook his head. 'I don't know but I don't think the drug trial is unrelated. You think Ezra saw Dillon taking students up to the bell tower and it spooked him?'

'It's possible, but then wouldn't he act skittish around Dillon now?'

'He's still not talking?'

'No.'

Ezra's face flitted before me, the defiant way he raised his chin and narrowed his eyes. His intent gaze on paper, hand in a fist around the crayon as he drew.

I thought of how he liked to draw pictures under my desk while I worked on patient notes. He was expressive and responsive in the twitch of his jaw, the arch of his eyebrows, the careful gestures of his hands. I was convinced he did want to communicate – but not until he felt secure. His guardian could insist Hatchery was safe for him, but children didn't stay silent for no reason.

Cedar's mother had opened her life to me and that had opened me up. Maybe I needed to do the same for Ezra.

*

Ezra and I weeded the vegetable garden outside Hatchery as dawn broke the sky into a brilliant orange. When I'd left Cedar's hotel room early in the morning, he was getting dressed, intent on spending the day searching the bell tower and interrogating Dillon until he had something substantial.

'We need enough to bring him into custody,' Cedar had said.

Now, a pile of dandelions built up between Ezra and me as I struggled with my confession. It wasn't that I hadn't spoken of the fire in years; it was that I hadn't spoken of it ever.

Ezra worked with absorbed intensity, brow furrowed, hands pawing at the dirt around a weed to better pull it up by the root. When he noticed me watching, he swiped dirt on his cheeks and giggled, and I couldn't help smiling in return.

We dropped the weeds in a rusted bucket at the edge of the garden and I gave him the tin of coffee grounds to sprinkle around the seedlings. I crouched in front of the potato row and patted the dirt back into a trough. Ezra stared at my scars when my pant legs hitched up to my ankles again.

I sat down near him and resisted the urge to pluck the new sprouts. Instead, I asked him, 'What are you scared of?'

His gaze was steady, with no movement or answer in those brown eyes. He was waiting for me.

Nausea bloomed in my chest as I rolled up the hem of my pant leg, the reddened, rippled scars extending down my shin to my foot.

Do it for Luis, something in me insisted. Speak.

'I'm scared of fire,' I said. I left out certain details, so as not to scare him. My story could be paired down to a dark fairy tale:

213

my brother and I were in an oven with a locked door and no one was coming to shut it off.

I'd leave out how wood smoke smelled like fate. How you kill the witch, even when the witch is you.

CHAPTER 30

December 1976

Carson. He had been born in the winter and he looked it, all pale and bright with translucent skin and grey eyes. Like a silver bucket left outside, waiting to be filled with snow.

We'd been staying at my mother's house for Christmas. I was on break from school, halfway through the first grade. Carson would turn four in a month. He normally spent his days at a neighbor's house and couldn't wait to be in classes like I was.

My mother didn't come home from the bar the day after Christmas. Early morning light bled through the paisley curtains and Carson and I ate cereal in silence at the kitchen table. We knew what it meant, but I was intent that it wouldn't ruin our day.

We played puzzles on the hearth; the bricks cold beneath our fingers as we fitted pieces together. Then I read Carson the one book I'd brought, no other books in the house, only a pile of year-old newspapers to fuel the fire. After this, we started to grow bored. We suited up in our coats and tried to play outside, but the wind blew bitterly from the north. It whipped our skin raw and stole our breath. We came back inside after only twenty

215

minutes. Later, I discovered that it had been record low temperatures that December.

Our mother's house smelled like cigarettes and canned food and cheap beer. There was an old bottle of perfume on my mother's dresser and I sprayed it around the house, hoping it'd improve the stench. Instead, we sat in a terrarium of decaying flowers, Carson gagging on the fumes as I waved the noxious odors away.

By the evening of that first day, my mother hadn't come home; Carson and I were sitting on the ratty couch together when the lights went out. It wasn't pitch-black yet, so I could see Carson's face, the round vulnerability in it.

We flipped all the light switches. I unplugged appliances and plugged them back in. I didn't know yet about paying bills to electric companies, so we thought that maybe something had broken. An hour later, we'd checked every outlet and switch in the house, and it was still dark. I pulled a chair up to the fridge and grabbed the flashlight.

We slept together in the same bed that night, and when we woke, I smelled urine and shuddered away from the wet sheets. Carson had stopped wearing nighttime underwear six months earlier and this was his first accident.

But when I pulled the covers back and stood up, I realized it had been me.

I scrubbed my clothes and bedding in the bathtub as sunlight stretched across the walls. The house chilled until it felt like we were standing inside a refrigerator. When finished, I rummaged through our suitcases for extra clothes and we put on every item we'd brought.

That's when I learned that after being cold for a long time, everything starts to taste like metal. Your tongue goes thick and stiff in your mouth. The nerves in your hands clamp shut; your skull starts to feel hollow. Your body closes off from the world and your mind runs slow.

Carson sat on the couch with me, wanting to cheer me up. He blew his breath out and it clouded before his face. Making ghosts, he called it, but I wouldn't play along. Night would fall soon, and the house was getting colder.

I wanted to walk to town, but it was too far. Five miles. Even if the weather had been warm, it'd be tough for Carson to make it and I wasn't going to leave him.

It's up to you to figure this out, I told myself.

And that's when she appeared for the first time.

Light brown hair, curly and tangled. Too thin for her age, with pants a bit too short. She had a face like a deer's, narrow and watchful, nose slightly too large.

She knelt in front of the fireplace, stacking wood inside. Her full lips pursed thoughtfully, and her movements were graceful. She pulled a match from a small box, the kind you once got for free at restaurants. Once the fire was lit, she held her hands before it as though warming them.

'Carson,' I whispered.

'What?' he said, indignant that I hadn't joined him in making ghosts.

'Do you see her?'

'Who?' he asked, looking around the room.

She was a vision, I thought. I'd heard of visions. The neighbor who watched Carson read us stories from the Bible about people seeing things. *Divine presence*, was what she called them. If you were holy, you could see things.

When I turned back to the fireplace, she was gone. But she'd told me what I could do to help us. A kind of salvation.

I'd watched my mother make fires many times before. You put the tinder and kindling on the grate, then stacked the wood around it, so the smoke heats and dries the wood. I gave Carson a stack of newspapers to wad up in balls for tinder. He liked having a job to do and sat on the blue-jean rug cross-legged, brow furrowed with intent, his little palms sooty with newsprint ink.

Logs lay stacked against the side of the house and I carried a few inside. I went back outside to gather sticks for kindling. Stars glittered overhead, hard knots in the sky, making the cold somehow colder, illuminating the ground in brittle light.

Inside, I pulled every blanket from our mother's bed and our own and piled them on the couch. I made the fire, adding kindling when the wood smoked instead of burned. I stoked it with the iron rod and flames jumped.

Finally, warmth radiated around the fireplace. We pushed the couch closer to the hearth, I tucked Carson against my chest, and we huddled under the blankets.

Light from the fire flickered over the surfaces of our mother's house. It no longer looked grey and dirty and worn. Carson looked up at me and grinned; I dipped my face to kiss the top of his head. My last thought before I drifted to sleep was how peaceful it was, like a night before Christmas.

My own coughing woke me. The fireplace was dark, filled only with ashes. But flames roared outside it, climbed up the rocking chair, and crawled across the carpet. Black smoke billowed on the ceiling. It was as though the fire had simply stepped outside of the fireplace and into the living room.

I shook Carson awake and we leapt over the back of the couch. His hands trembled as he clutched at me. We stood inside a fever, flames writhing like limbs in pain, heat so strong, we could barely keep our eyes open.

The fire blocked the front door, so we ran to the dining room window. I pulled a kitchen chair against the wall and pulled the window crank, but it wouldn't budge, the window stubborn and stuck in the cold. I heaved all my weight against the crank. The window split open and cold air flooded the room. I wound the crank again and again until the window yawned wide enough for us to fit through.

The fire inched closer to us. Once I got the screen out, we could jump. I shoved Carson into the corner and away from the fire. Returning to the chair, I sweltered in a daze as flames climbed up the chair's legs and licked my left foot.

The screen was frozen in place. In a wild lurch of desperation, I threw my shoulder against it and the screen burst out and took me with it. Falling through the window, I toppled on to the frozen ground below.

Steam rose from my burns. Standing up, I screamed at Carson through the open window, urging him to get on the chair and jump through. I'd catch him, I told him. Don't be scared.

But Carson didn't appear in the window. I called for him, pleading with him. When I got no response, I ran around the house toward the door and yanked at the handle, but it wouldn't budge. I twisted and jerked the door handle again and again until it grew warm against my palm from the fire on the other side.

I stepped back and stared at it. I'd locked it on my way back inside the house when I came out for the wood.

I pummeled the door and screamed Carson's name. The flames had begun to roar, and I couldn't hear anything else. I collapsed to the frost-covered grass. Cold burned my skin as black smoke filled the sky.

My mother had been at a friend's house, sheltering from the cold in a drugged stupor. When she came out of it and discovered what had happened, she disappeared again. A few years later, my father told me she'd been found dead of a drug overdose in Texas. It was easier to blame myself than her.

Smoke had alerted the nearest town's fire department and they'd found me half-conscious on the ground. They told me Carson had passed out from smoke and hadn't felt any pain. But I couldn't get it out of my head – him trapped in that burning house. I'd made the fire; I'd locked the door.

CHAPTER 31

After finding Ezra in the homestead house, I'd thought of Carson even though they looked nothing like each other. Ezra was dark and wild, with thick hair like a buffalo hide. But they did share that wary expression, a determination not to be disappointed by someone else.

Now, Ezra leaned forward and placed his hand over my scars. I winced. Taking my hand, he hauled me up and tugged me away from Hatchery.

I resisted being pulled like a prize heifer and asked him if he'd seen anything frightening around here. But he ignored me as he led me west toward the Indian tree, which he began to climb. Once he settled on a thick limb about ten feet up, he looked down at me expectantly.

He wanted to show me something.

I clambered up the tree after him, much less gracefully. A herd of pronghorn grazed around the deserted buildings of Ennenock, the hills beyond a deep violet under an ivory sky. When the sun burned all the blue away, it felt more ominous than darkness, that cream-grey soft as the plumage of a just hatched bird.

When I opened my mouth to badger him again, he placed a finger against his lips. 'Shush,' he said.

I blinked. It was the closest thing to a word that he'd spoken. He turned and pointed to the old bridge over the Niobrara, which had been steady back in the day but was now dilapidated and too fragile to hold a car.

The river cut a deep, wide ravine through limestone rock and had been named *water spread-out horizontal* by Sioux tribes. Beverly once told me settlers used to ford the river when they ventured west, but so many of them had drowned in crossings that Ennenock had elected to build a bridge rather than dig a new cemetery. The students claimed the wind stirred their watery graves, sending their whispers up from the depths, in search of loved ones. Now, droughts left the river slower and shallower than before, sometimes safe enough for students to swim.

I tried to bite back my impatience with Ezra. I didn't have time for a tour of things I already knew.

'Do you want to go swimming this summer?' I asked.

He frowned and made a sound with his tongue against the roof of his mouth: *clip clop clip*. The canter of a hooved animal.

I glanced at the herd of pronghorn and thought of Albert saying they didn't sound like horses. They were too light on their feet, as though their bones were hollow.

Ezra shook his head and held up one finger. My chest grew tight.

'One horse?' I asked.

He nodded, clearly pleased I'd understood him. But for me, everything slowed and narrowed. My world became Ezra's ear and shoulder, the sky beyond him, the jagged bark biting into my palms.

I pointed to the bridge, rickety and narrow, but strong enough to hold a horse if the rider were careful. 'Did someone take you on horseback across that bridge?'

A nod.

'Did they take you to the abandoned homestead?'

He shook his head.

'Where—'

He moved his hands in an undulating gesture, like waves of grass.

'A person left you in the prairie after crossing the bridge.'

He nodded and pointed to my ankle.

'And that's your scary thing.'

Thoughts skipped like rocks across a shallow riverbed, jolting me. He never ran away. It didn't begin with Luis; it began with Ezra. Someone here at Hatchery didn't think it was a miracle he was alive; someone thought it was a mistake.

'Ezra, do you know who it was?'

He looked past me, toward the hills. I should have seen this. Should have somehow pieced it together.

'Please, this is important. Who—'

He closed his eyes and breathed heavily as though he were snoring.

'You were sleeping? Then how did you know someone took you over the bridge on horseback?'

He lifted his head, cupped his hand to his ear, keeping his eyes closed.

'You woke up and listened but pretended to be asleep? So,

the person already had the horse; you didn't go with them to get it?'

Ezra nodded.

'Did the person . . .' I felt sheepish, but placed my hands around my neck in a choking gesture.

He furrowed his brow, shook his head and pointed to the grass.

'They just took you off the horse and set you down?'

He made the *clip clop clip* sound with his tongue again.

And then they rode away.

I asked him more questions: about the person's clothes, the sound of their voice, the smell of their breath, but he tucked himself away, the filament between us broken. The air became charged, as though a storm had rolled our way. The branch I sat on quavered. Ezra gripped the bark like he could claw it away from the trunk and his hair trembled, his gaze fixed on the space over my shoulder. I turned.

The herd of pronghorn stampeded toward us, leaping more than running, carrying the musk of their sleek, tawny bodies, black horns flashing in the blinding sunlight. The ground shook; our tree shuddered.

They felt like a warning, dropping thunder in our bones. The grass below dry as a corpse's hair, the invisible stars overhead eyeing us like indifferent gods. And we, stuck between, rattling in the limbs of a deformed tree.

When it was silent and still again, I had only one thought: get him away from here.

CHAPTER 32

I considered telling Beverly so she could help me get Ezra somewhere safe, but abandoned this idea. Everything had toppled when the mole called Lamberg right before the raid, our men in the field betrayed by one of our own. The fewer people who knew, the better. After searching for Cedar and not finding him, I tried calling, but it went straight to voicemail.

My mouth is sewn shut, Carly had said. I was beginning to know what that felt like as I dialed Karen Iden, Ezra's guardian, and told her who I was.

'They track you with these things. So they can hunt us down, keep us in the scope,' she said, unhappy about me calling her cell phone.

'Uh-huh,' I said. I needed to convince her Ezra had to leave Hatchery, without revealing too much about the investigation. 'So, I guess you've heard about the case we have here at Hatchery?'

'Sure. Nasty business.' Beyond her, I could hear voices and artificial dings, like a cash register.

'Well, things are getting more . . . chaotic . . . and we're asking some of the guardians to watch students for a few days to give them some space from Hatchery and all the commotion. To give students a break, that is. Until things settle down.'

Another ding and then the sound of hands slapping a table.

'How 'bout next week? I'll come by for a visit.'

'No, Ms Iden—'

'Mrs!' she barked.

'It actually needs to be sooner. And not just a visit, but for Ezra to return home with you for a while.' I took a deep breath. 'I'd like you to come pick him up tonight.'

'I'm playing bingo right now.'

I gritted my teeth and ran my hand over my face. 'Mrs Iden, you are Ezra's legal guardian and Hatchery is not currently equipped to care for him during this stage of the investigation. We need you to watch him for a few days until things stabilize.'

'Well, I've got to go get my leg,' Mrs Iden said.

'Excuse me?'

'My pros-thee-sis,' she enunciated. 'Lost my leg several years back in a car accident. Partly why I couldn't be caring for a young'un. Also never like them. There's that too. My neighbor Ralph has it, fixing it up. Some metal piece was squeaking, giving me a headache. And I can't drive in the dark. And it's a four-hour drive. So I wouldn't be able to leave until morning.'

'That's fine,' I said. 'We look forward to seeing you in the morning.'

After I hung up the receiver, I kneaded my temples. It was fine. One more night. He could stay with me. Anyone could get in or out of the students' bedrooms, but my apartment's door had a lock and deadbolt. Albert had a camp bed in his shed I could set up in my living room; we could pack a small bag with Ezra's favorite things.

Waves of fear radiated from Ezra's small frame.

'Don't worry. You can stay in my apartment tonight. Like a slumber party.' I frowned, uncertain if that would make him more nervous.

Instead, he gave me a reproachful look that said, *don't even pretend this is a fun game*. I couldn't tell if he understood the impact of what he'd told me, if he'd been aware all this time of lurking danger. I got the impression he knew something was off, but in a childlike way had made an excuse for it.

After we stuffed a backpack with his things, we stepped outside, where a bird with a beak like a long, curved blade lifted its head above the tall grass. A student danced across the circular drive, wearing a white summer dress, red hair flying underneath a paper sack. Since Luis's death, Carly had worn that mask almost constantly when outside to ward off panic attacks.

Pirouetting and spinning, she flung out her hands and threw her head back, gaiety so great, it somehow felt melancholic. The display you make to hide misfortune. She leapt, her head blocking the sun, splintering its rays around her before she touched the ground again. On any other day, it would be a resplendent morning.

She stopped and tipped the paper bag off her face. Red lines marred her cheeks and forehead and lips.

'I'm dizzy,' she said, red even on her teeth.

Blood pulsed in my ears and my throat constricted as I rushed toward her. 'Carly, are you okay?'

'I cut some of my hair, too.'

I reached out and touched her cheek, paint smearing on my fingers. 'Why did you do this? Go wash it off.'

'It's my death face.'

'What are you talking about?'

'Owen found her.'

'Found who?'

A whip cracked and someone screamed.

In front of Albert's cottage, Owen wielded a whip, bringing it back behind his head for another strike as Albert cowered in front of him. Owen swung it, but Albert charged forward, caught Owen's arm and swung him in a semi-circle, flinging him to the ground.

I dashed toward them. Owen scrambled to his feet and whipped Albert's legs, knocking him down before Owen leapt on him and pummeled his face.

'Owen!' I called out. 'Owen, stop!'

The blows of Owen's fists rang out on the silent grounds. I stumbled, caught myself, and dove forward, prying Owen from Albert with such force that we both careened backwards and fell in a tangle of limbs.

Owen scrambled away from me and back on to his feet. Gasping, I stood. Blood trickled from Albert's chin and dropped on his undershirt.

'That son of a bitch killed her!' Owen charged me and we toppled back into the grass. 'He killed her!' he screamed in my face.

I wrestled him off me, shoving my knees against his chest. Owen rolled off me and collapsed, staring into the bright sky before lifting himself up to look at me. A chill spread up my spine.

'What happened, Owen?' I asked quietly.

He picked a piece of grass off his pants, brushed dirt away. 'Found her body in Ennenock. In the safe of that old bank. Like she was a fucking deposit.' Owen paused and glared at

Albert. 'He always looked at her funny. Like she was a slut or something.'

'Who?'

Owen spat in the grass and rubbed his face. 'Kristin,' he said flatly. 'I found Kristin's body in Ennenock.'

CHAPTER 33

Two hours later, sounds of hysteria burst from the dining hall, where Beverly held another assembly. While Luis's death had caught them off guard and they responded with denial and confusion, Kristin's death appeared to sink in immediately and threaten them. Primed for loss, they no longer found it unbelievable.

Though the students had reacted to Kristin's death, I couldn't. Numb and dazed, I leaned against the doorframe of my office while Cedar stood in the hallway, telling me about how he and Sheriff Anders were moving into Hatchery, setting up makeshift sleeping quarters in the lounge, so they could patrol overnight. Antlers flung sharp shadows against the wall and the putrid smell of stilled blood hovered above us.

'I was too late,' Cedar said. 'Maybe if we'd gotten into the safe sooner, I don't know, this wouldn't have happened. Might've scared the killer into thinking we were on to them.'

I wanted to reach out and squeeze his arm, or say something comforting, but someone could walk past at any minute. There was also a new distance between us. It felt familiar; we'd been here before, disoriented and aloof.

I'd already told Cedar about Ezra's kidnapping and he had

taken the revelation wordlessly, hands limp at his sides. I knew he felt the investigation was slipping through his fingers. He had already secured the crime scene and questioned Owen, who would soon be coming my way for a psychotherapy session.

'I hope you can get something more out of him,' Cedar said.

'I'll try,' I said, but I wasn't feeling optimistic. I couldn't stop replaying things Kristin had told me, normally in the dining hall when her defenses were down.

Once, she told me about buying corn with her mother at a farmer's market. Afterwards, they sat in the driveway and talked while they husked it, her mother telling her about traveling the world as a military brat, relocating from Italy to Japan to Saudi Arabia. It had been one of the few times her mother had told her much about her life, recounting the twisting cobblestone roads along canals or the dust storms whipping through the desert.

The husks fell at their feet, corn kernels gleaming in the sun. Kristin had gestured with her hands as though she held corn, in awe that it had been grown in the ground, telling me about how it tasted after they grilled it. I understood what she meant. I grew up on canned food like Kristin, that mushed plastic taste in your mouth, as if you didn't need teeth to eat it. I, too, could always remember the instances of my childhood when I got real food, the sliced lemons, the blanched tomatoes, flavors like a handshake welcoming you into a new life. Maybe that's what the garden with Owen meant to her. A new life.

'We found strangulation marks on her neck, just like Luis, except with her, we're guessing that's what killed her. No other signs of bodily trauma. The murder seems to have taken place in the safe, where she was left. Also, we think . . .' Cedar started and shook his head. 'Based on the preliminary examination, we think the killer held her after she died.'

I waited to have a reaction to this, but nothing surged past the detachment.

'There were these impressions on the dirt around and under her body, but no signs of sexual assault,' he said. 'We think it's an imprint of someone lying next to her. What do you make of that?'

I shrugged. 'They feel close to her. Or want to feel close to her.'

'That doesn't give me a lot to go on.'

Rubbing my forehead, I tried not to picture her now. If her wrists had bruises or her fingernails were cracked. If like Deborah, her hair were a blond swirl like a comet's tail across the floor. Deborah's manicured hand had unfurled beside her face. She always had the most beautiful nails, in shades of fuchsia and scarlet, and I never understood when she'd find the time to paint them. Mine were always bare, often with blood crusted near the cuticle from a torn hangnail.

But that was Deborah. She was more a part of this world than me. She always seemed to find time to do small things, reminding herself of her body, of being in a certain time and place, all those small acts of decoration a kind of celebration. Instead, I barreled through time, trying to mark my existence with accomplishments, while feeling more and more ephemeral.

'There were a few strange things we found in the safe,' Cedar continued. 'Up on the shelves, where bankers used to keep the cash, there were these drawings.' He pulled up photos on his phone. Pen and ink drawings of twin monsters with spikes coming out of their heads like halos. Another of a little boy with his chest opened up and a smaller version of himself inside. Cedar kept scrolling until I grabbed his wrist, pausing on a charcoal sketch of the same chimera painting I'd seen in Beverly's office.

'The boy who did these had been a patient here,' I said. 'Years ago. He's dead now.'

'That's not all.' Cedar showed me a photo of grass dolls, same as the one Oksana had left next to Luis's body, though these were dirtier and more tattered, the grass coming loose where it had been tied down. 'Why are Oksana's dolls, once again, next to a victim's body?'

I shook my head. 'Maybe someone else made them. Besides, she already told us she left that one doll with Luis's body. So why wouldn't she have told us about these?'

'She admitted it once we'd already caught her – you saw her out near Luis's body.'

There was some barrier in me; I couldn't consider Oksana had hurt anyone. When she had said I reminded her of herself, I'd believed her and felt it was true; that had created some bond between us even though we were still nearly strangers. 'Did Kristin have scars on her back?' I asked.

'No. And I questioned Owen about the whip. He claims he had stolen it from Oksana's barn when he tried to scare some of the younger kids with it about a year back. Then he got tired of it and left it on the grounds. Then today he found the whip while rummaging in Albert's shed, looking for evidence after finding Kristin's body. Claims Albert has had it all this time. For whatever reason, this made him certain Albert had killed Kristin, and he pulled Albert from his house and started beating him with it. That's about all I got out of him.'

Wind shuddered around Hatchery, scouring the stones, and the hallway dimmed as clouds swelled. The patterns of the damask wallpaper seemed to move, twitching between lanterns.

'A series of thunderstorms are forecast for the region, so I need to get back to the crime scene quick. A forensic team should be here within the hour. Better not get heavy rain tonight and lose evidence. Keep an eye on everyone for me?'

I nodded. Ezra's guardian was still picking him up tomorrow morning and though Cedar didn't want people leaving, he didn't argue with this. Right now, Ezra sat in my office coloring.

'With Ezra, I knew something was off, but I didn't trust my instincts. I should have realized—' I began.

'You're getting him out now,' Cedar said.

Under this consoling phrase, I caught a whiff of his disappointment, a sense that he felt I'd failed him. Normally, this would make defensiveness surge through me, but I was feeling unmoored, indifferent to myself. Instead, I looked at his face, that beloved face, and tried to memorize it.

CHAPTER 34

Owen bit his nails to the quick as sobs and footsteps reverberated through the House. I didn't want to look at him, so I studied the photograph behind him of a skeletal tree in a winter prairie. From a bird's-eye view, the tree would look like a single dark blot, faintly feathered as it expanded outwards, like a wound on a pale chest. Unbeknownst to Owen, I'd tucked Ezra in my small coat closet with a flashlight and pile of coloring books.

'Crazy bitch had to go and get killed,' Owen continued. He'd been going on and on about how stupid she was. That she made bad decisions and brought things on herself.

'It's her fault?' I asked, not bothering to look at him, still staring at the painting.

Owen shrugged, yanking his hand from his mouth. 'She was going to tell about this place. Said she had a secret about how they were mistreating us. She shoulda been more scared.'

Dillon's drug trial. *Shoulda been more scared.* This made me pause. I'd never thought of Kristin as brave, but maybe she was.

'Did she tell you what she knew?' I asked.

'No. Something to do with our medications.'

Escalation. Ezra's kidnapping and Luis's murder had been two months apart. Now, Luis and Kristin's bodies had been found only two days apart. It was common enough, moving from manslaughter to murder, crimes growing closer together in time. Success breeds success.

Owen hadn't stopped talking. Now he was fingering possible suspects.

'Maybe it was Beverly. She couldn't stand to lose this place. Has nothing else to live for. Gave her whole life to this hellhole.'

'If you think that, why did you attack Albert?' I asked.

I wasn't going to do this right; I'd already accepted that. This appointment should be bereavement counseling, but I wasn't in the mood to comfort him. I couldn't care about protocol or checklists or questions; we were running out of time.

You should be concerned for Owen, something in me said. I stared at him blankly, unmoved. I kept trying to remind myself he was a person, but Luis and Kristin were surfacing in my mind and they felt more real and alive to me. I could feel the beat of their hearts, while Owen seemed made of some manufactured material, some plastic contraption that didn't work quite right.

'Because Beverly wouldn't do it. I mean, she'd ask Albert to. He does all the dirty work.' Even now, Owen smirked, and I wished I could slap his face until his mouth flattened.

'How did you find her?' I asked, hoping this would deflate him.

Owen lifted his chin and anger flashed in his eyes. 'She told me she was meeting someone in Ennenock and then we could work on our garden. So, I waited.' Owen gritted his teeth. He didn't like admitting he was willing to wait for anyone. 'When she didn't come by, I decided to walk to Ennenock. Thought I'd wander around, see who she was meeting—'

'Did you see anyone? Did she tell you who she was meeting?' I asked.

He glared at me. 'No,' he said. 'I walked down Main Street and noticed the door to the bank's safe was open—' His head jerked down on an audible swallow. It took him another minute before he could lift it back up. 'She was lying on her back, arms folded over her chest, like she was a mummy. She had red marks—' Owen choked up, making a gurgling sound with his tongue. He gestured to his neck. 'Fingernail impressions and scratches on her skin. Bruises the size of someone's thumbs.'

I pushed the tissue box closer to him. Fury tightened his face and he knocked it off the table. I felt tired. So very tired.

'You know that crucified rat? I did that.' He crossed his arms over his chest and leaned back.

'Why did you do that?' I asked. I'd been curious before, but now I felt hollow and indifferent, a heaviness settling over my bones.

'Kristin told me she liked Doc Douche. He spent so much extra time with her; made her believe he liked her too.'

My stomach clenched at this and it felt good to be able to react to something.

Owen shook his head. 'All you people who run this place think you're so holy. You're no different than we are. Beverly has her religion, and you and Douche Central think you're helping us. Ms Lewis thinks she's teaching us things we can use – like we're all going to sail out of here and become fucking mathematicians, joining those Ivy schools with kids who were raised on horseback lessons and Mandarin Chinese. You're not *better* than we are. But you run around like fucking martyrs. So, I don't know, I crucified a rat. *That's* what I think of your holiness.'

I stayed quiet, not liking how his defiance made me fonder of him. I had resented some people who'd tried to help me too: school nurses who asked too many questions, the occasional social worker's practiced kindness. They were good people, doing good things, but they also reminded me that I'd been born into a life other people pitied. So, at times, I gave them a dollop of bitterness in snide remarks or cold shoulders.

'Are you going to report Dr Edwards?' I asked.

Owen shrugged. 'Maybe. I don't know. Haven't decided.' He jiggled his knee and ran his hands over his pant legs. 'She also knew you're helping with the investigation.'

'She knew a lot.'

'Yeah, I'll give you a goody you can take back to that black cop. I saw Luis whipping himself in Albert's shed.'

I tried to conceal my shock, but some leaked through and Owen grinned. This sent a dull ache to my chest – for Luis, but also from the realization of how much Cedar and I had assumed, how much we got wrong. I'd never stopped to consider Luis had done it to himself because I wanted to believe he'd been doing okay – maybe not great, but not suffering that much. If he was suffering that much, then I wasn't doing my job.

'Yeah, in April or whatever, before he died,' Owen said. 'What's it called Beverly goes on about every spring?'

'Lent.'

'Yeah. I asked him what the fuck he was doing and he wouldn't answer until I threatened to punch him. Said his father and grandfather did it. Guess they were crazy religious or something. He should have fit in better here.'

'You don't know crazy,' I said softly.

This startled him and his alarmed face pleased me. Luis would pause in appointments when I asked him about self-harm, but he was often reticent, so I hadn't questioned this normal response. Perhaps he had wanted to mimic his lost family. Perhaps it'd been only self-harm. Maybe both; I'd never know.

'Part of the reason I never liked him. I mean, who hurts themself?' he asked.

I pinned Owen with a glare. 'Speaking of the investigation, what were you two doing outside Hatchery the night Luis was murdered?'

'Is this an interrogation or a counseling session?'

'Did you go to your little room in the brothel above the saloon?'

He grinned. 'You found that. We liked to have our own space to fuck in.'

'You also took pictures of students when they were sleeping.'

Owen shrugged. 'We also like to put weird stuff we find outside in the food when we're on meal prep and kitchen duty.'

'Classy. Did you also wrap her in barbed wire?'

'The fuck I did. She accused me when she should have been pointing to Doc Douche. He was using her for something—'

I raised my eyebrows.

'Yeah, but she knew I was using her. It's different. He deceived her,' Owen said.

'How upset were you when you found out about Kristin's feelings for Dr Edwards?'

He leaned forward, one knee bouncing hard and fast, energy radiating from him like an electrocuted fence post. 'I wanted to kill her.'

I pressed my lips together. Since Owen found her body and

was her boyfriend, he'd be a prime suspect for her murder. So many pieces fit, but not the part of him dropping Ezra off in the prairie. He didn't seem aware Ezra existed. And while he'd targeted Luis, always bullying him, there still wasn't a strong motive for murder that I could see. Not unless he simply snapped at someone vulnerable.

I studied his face, knowing it was futile. Even if he were guilty, he wouldn't necessarily feel that way and show it. The least guilty could feel the guiltiest, accepting blame as a way to cope with loss. Accepting an illusion, a chimera, a mirage. Imagination versus reality.

Outside, grass waved furiously in the wind, which howled as the skies darkened. The pressure of a gathering storm spread through my office like an invisible gas.

'But you killed the rat instead,' I pressed on.

'I didn't like Luis much either; that where you're going with this?'

'Do you want to talk about Luis?'

'Fucking moron, that's what he was. Always mooning about.'

'Is that part of your plan? Be arrested for murder? Make sure you can never be free in society? Go from here straight to prison? Owen,' I said softly, leaning forward. 'Are you afraid to be out in the world?'

Owen's knee stopped jiggling. I couldn't read his face; it had turned to stone, his eyes glassy, mouth fixed in a straight line. There was a twitch in my chest, a roil in my belly. Outside, something creaked, straining against the wind, then crashed to the ground.

'Scared of what I'd do out there,' he said, barely audible,

fronting any other teenage boy, scared shitless, scared even of admitting it. He cracked his knuckles, those knuckles that had split so many faces.

He stood up and I jerked back against my chair, ready to spring up and toward the door if he lunged at me. Instead, he knelt, picked up the tissue box, set it on the table, and sat back down.

Tears shone in his eyes and he scrubbed them away roughly with a fist. 'She was supposed to go home soon. Was getting pretty excited about her shitty job. Wanted me to come visit her when I'm done here.' He shook his head, disdain darkening his face as tears glazed his eyes again.

Normally, I'd dismiss this show of emotion as manipulation, but something rang true about it.

'What a waste,' he went on. 'That night Luis died, we snuck out to steal gardening tools from Albert's shed. She thought it was romantic we were planting a garden together. She thought I was going to take care of her.' Owen rolled his eyes and laced his fingers together, squeezing tight until he made a single large fist. 'Stupid.'

'Pretty stupid,' I said quietly, wondering for how long he could bury the part of himself that cared for her. He may not care as much as she deserved, but there was something there.

Owen tried to nod, but his face slipped downwards like it was melting; his body folded forward. He sobbed raggedly, spine convulsing, shoulders shaking.

I let him cry it out. Out the window, tumbleweed rolled toward the fire pits under an electric blue sky, the shade a child uses to paint a sky on paper. The not-quite-real color of optimism.

I imagined the cathedral holding other kinds of assemblies

a hundred years ago, voices clamoring, bodies jostling, longing and heat rising like incense up, up, up, swirling between the beams, eddying into shadows. All they wanted was eternity. And then those people were expelled into the too-bright light before their graves and this building stood as an empty gut, waiting to be filled again, waiting for us.

Once Owen left, I pulled Ezra out of the closet and apologized, reminding him he had to stay with me at all times. He picked his teeth with a toothpick and his dark eyes betrayed nothing, no agreement or rebellion, just a steady scrutiny.

I needed to comb through my notes on Kristin's appointment to see if I'd overlooked anything. After taking Ezra with me to get coffee from the lounge, I poured over her file back in my office.

Letters began to swim before me, my mind flailing, vision watery around the edges. Fatigue. I downed more coffee and it tasted like ashes, dry and thick. I fumbled with the pages; fingers too loose in my joints. What was I doing, again?

The box of patient dictation tapes. I needed to review hers. Reaching down for the box, my hand touched nothing; waved at the floor.

It was gone. After calling Mrs Iden, I was in such a rush, I'd forgotten to lock my office door.

I stood up quickly and the room slipped sideways from me. Woozy, I swayed on my feet. The room swarmed around me and in a blur, Ezra rushed toward me, his expression more nervous than I'd ever seen it.

'I'm fine,' I tried to say, but my tongue gummed in my mouth and a strange sound escaped my lips.

I expected to find black dregs in my mug. Instead, white powder clumped the bottom and I dropped it. Shards of ceramic scattered across the floor. My head was rolling to the side as if I were falling asleep in a car. Ezra cried out, his voice disembodied and robust, a sound rich and high-pitched as a bird's cry.

I lost my sight before I hit the floor.

CHAPTER 35

My head felt full of cotton. The wool rug had carved its pattern on my arms, and my feet tingled with pinpricks. Awareness returned in gradual waves, tides coming in and retreating.

A throw pillow had been placed under my head, and my shawl, used during chilly mornings, had been draped over my body. I stared down at them in bewilderment.

Ezra.

'Ezra!' I called out, struggling to my feet. I swirled in a circle. My office was empty.

My muscles quivering under me, I sank back down to my hands and knees. I gripped my desk and pulled myself back up, calling his name again and again.

I searched the dining hall, lounge, and his bedroom. Panic was a spike in my chest; heat ripped up my spine. Lurching into my apartment, I yanked at the landline receiver, shakily dialing Cedar's number. The smooth surfaces of the laminate countertops, the ratty blue sofa, the piles of old mail and clutter on the table all looked foreign, the opposite of déjà vu, as if I'd never been here before.

The phone wouldn't stop ringing; I slammed it down.

Think, think.

I turned on the sink and began gulping water, pushing the medication out of my system. The door opened behind me and I jerked up so fast, I knocked my head on the faucet, reeling backwards, kneading my head.

'Lore?'

Cedar and Ezra stood in the doorway. I blinked, slack-jawed, taking in Cedar with his luminous eyes and broad shoulders, Ezra with his fine features and abundant dark hair.

I had to stop myself from hugging them, had to fight back sudden tears.

'He came and found me,' Cedar said, coming toward me. 'What happened?'

I took it as proof of Ezra's observational skills that he knew to find Cedar in Ennenock. Ezra napped on the sofa. Before he fell asleep, I sat next to him, his warm scent of prairie sage drifting over me. His palms were imprinted with crescent moons from his fingernails and I wanted to rub them away.

At the kitchen table, Cedar and I talked. 'Midazolam,' I guessed. 'Fastest acting benzodiazepine with a short duration.' It was also part of the cocktail used for executions by lethal injection.

'Who could have gotten their hands on it? Anyone prescribed it right now?'

'No. And when I do prescribe it, students have to take the pill in front of me, so I can monitor it. Unless someone broke into Dillon's medical cabinet, only Beverly, Dillon, and I have access. I already checked; my cabinet is up to date and hasn't been tampered with.'

'It could be the same sedative used on the other victims. When Dillon let me check his medical cabinet, it looked in order, but he could be manipulating the records or filling medications that he doesn't put in the cabinet.'

I didn't argue with this. There was only fiery rancor, a fixation: someone put something in my body. The violation stole what little stability I'd had left; someone couldn't get away with this.

'Are you the only one who drinks coffee from the lounge?' Cedar asked.

'In the afternoon, yeah. But why today?' I asked. 'The tapes were already stolen.'

It could be Dillon scaring me, making sure I got his message. Or a patient turning the tables, giving me my own medicine. A few times I'd had to sedate a patient against their will and never liked it. I hadn't thought of it as power, hadn't even felt it that way, but now I saw that it was.

'Maybe the person had already drugged the coffee, but then when you were away, they slipped in. You think there's evidence on those tapes? They stole them to see if the victims mentioned them?'

'That, or they want to witness how these murders are affecting people. Relishing the chaos of their handiwork.'

Cedar ran a hand over his face and sighed. 'I need to finish up at the scene, but I'll be back tonight. I want you and Ezra staying in here. Door locked, open to no one but me. Okay?'

This made me feel cornered, not safe or protected, and I glared at him. 'Don't use that tone.'

'Lore. When Ezra came and got me and I could tell it was about you . . .' Cedar trailed off, looking at the floor. He put his fist in front of his mouth, partially hiding his face. The last time I'd seen this gesture, his mother had been talking about Warren, and it meant: I'm holding this emotion at arm's length right now.

He shook his head and tried to force a laugh. 'Didn't know what I'd find when I got back here.'

A flock of birds passed the windows, their wings a nervous flurry. Ezra stirred in his sleep. I kept my hand out of reach, so Cedar couldn't take it. His touch would weaken me now, my reserve melting like a glacier.

'You remember that time we were both in New Orleans for that conference?' he asked. 'And we skipped out on all the sessions and took the trolley down Jackson to get to this absurd little bistro I wanted to go to? And after we got off the trolley, it started pouring, just buckets and buckets of rain, and we went running down the avenue, past all these gorgeous Creole cottages and mansions with their wrought-iron balconies and pillared porches. I remember your hair was plastered on your forehead . . . so dark, it looked almost black. And your eyes got so bright. We were laughing our asses off, standing on the roots of a cypress tree getting drenched. We were so soaked, we just rode the trolley back to the hotel, some dude next to us strumming a guitar, and I turned to you about to say something, and you just said, *I know*.'

His hand had been on my thigh. The air had smelled of moss and gasoline fumes, the sweat of stranger and jasmine. The memory was a cold glass of water, tunneling through me, bringing relief and waking me up.

'I hope you still know,' he said. 'Because it hasn't changed.'

I wished he'd said all this over a year ago, when I'd needed to hear it. But I also thought of the monarchs, the way they seemed tethered in their migration, how they found their way back even when something broke them apart. If we made it out the other side of this, perhaps we could salvage something of what we'd had before.

CHAPTER 36

Dusk came quickly. Green tainted the sky before the sun sank, and the sweet, pungent scent of a coming storm mixed with insect-song. Ezra put together a puzzle of a butterfly poised above a flower before moving on to playing with Deborah's snow globe. Beverly asked where he was, and I informed her he wouldn't be joining the other students for the evening.

'All the students must stay together in their rooms,' she said. 'He'll be safe there. Sheriff Anders and Agent Knox are patrolling the facility.'

'I want to keep an eye on him,' I told her.

'Not overnight. That is a breach—'

I hung up on her. Dark overtook twilight in the blink of an eye and an eerie stillness descended, no sounds from animals, no movement in the grass, only a gathering presence just outside my vision, and I knew this was going to be bad.

Once, Beverly had told me that in Hatchery's early days, a terrible ice storm had coated electrical poles, splitting them, leaving the students without electricity for three weeks before it could be repaired. She'd worried the candles and oil lanterns they'd used would lead to a fire, and I'd thought of Hatchery devoured by flames, a great torch under a black sky.

Lightning flashed in the west as the atmosphere gathered an electrical charge, a faint buzz in the night air. The radio announced a tornado and hailstorm warning in our county. These stone walls had stood for over a century; they'd been built for eternity. We would be fine.

Wind started up again, sounding almost human, shrieking and wailing across the expanse, thrashing the grass. Down in the garden, a weeding stool rolled like tumbleweed and splintered to pieces. Rubbing a knot in my shoulder, I stepped back from the window. Ezra must have sensed my fear because I felt him stiffen. Clouds scuttled east and thunder rumbled closer, building and building, until it cracked and rattled the windows.

Pure black fell as though a veil had dropped between us and the world.

No, no, no.

I stumbled toward the light switch and flicked it. Nothing. Tried it again, knowing it was futile. Ezra flared before me in a flash of lightning, still sitting at the table, snow swirling beneath his palm. My knees went weak and I felt lightheaded.

I could see Carson even now, squeezing himself small against the cold, only the crown of his blond head visible above the blanket. My hair was also light as a child's and I'd always wondered: if he'd lived, would his hair have darkened too?

Such dreams, such dreams as these, I know they mean no good.

Anyone could stalk along the hallway, winding up the stairs to the bedrooms, unseen. Something blew against Hatchery, the collision clattering as though something hard splintered against the stone walls. Ezra and I both jumped, the vinegar odor of our sweat tainting the room.

My skin had gone raw with glinting nerves, and I told myself to keep calm. You don't want to hallucinate now.

'I'll find flashlights,' I said, knocking over a chair as I stumbled forward. I found two in the small storage cabinet under the stairs and gave one to Ezra. He held his flashlight upside down on to the puzzle, the shapes becoming cartoonish, the colors garish under the concentrated light.

A knock sounded and I flinched, deciding to ignore it. But it sounded again, more insistent this time, a fist pounding.

'You stay there,' I told Ezra, but he scowled at me, his expression saying, *don't tell me what to do.* I knew he felt cornered inside during a storm; out of control. Nowhere to run to, now that his farmhouse swayed on its foundation like a rootless tree.

When I opened the door, Dillon's face floated in the darkness before me, lit from below with a candle. I threw my weight against the door but he pushed forward and wedged half his body in the open space. Fear left a bitter taste in my mouth. Knives were in the top drawer, right side of the sink, I reminded myself.

'I have candles,' he said, holding out five pale tapers and a small box of matches. 'What the hell are you doing? I'm trying to help.'

'Leave,' I said, still pushing.

Straining muscles visible in his neck, Dillon glanced past me at Ezra, who was still at the table, illuminated by his flashlight. He shoved the candles and matches at me and I let them clatter on the floor.

'We don't have a generator here,' he said. 'You don't want to burn out the batteries before dawn. I know you're upset but I want to apologize.'

'For trying to blackmail me or for sprinkling sedatives in my coffee?'

A stunned expression froze Dillon's face. He relaxed his stance, but I still kept pressure on the door. 'I didn't do that.'

I would've sworn this was honest, but I didn't believe it. 'Obviously, I don't need to say this, but since we're clearly not on the same page, I just want to be clear: We are done. Over. Done.'

'Yeah, I figured that when you spied on me and then broke into my office we might be splitting up.'

I wanted to slap him. 'Sure, now leave.'

'Lore, wait. I can't stop thinking . . .' Despite the warm glow of the candle, his face was pale and drawn, his eyes hollow as he stared past me into the darkness. 'She . . . she wanted to be a flight attendant.'

'What?'

'You know, serving on planes. She wanted to see the world as she worked.'

I could see it: Kristin smiling at an elderly passenger, offering them ginger ale before landing in Frankfurt; tidying up the cabin before taking off to Quebec. Was the allure partly in getting back to that day husking corn with her mother, listening to her travels on a driveway in the blistering heat, corn silk stuck on palms and the rustle of husks about her feet?

There was a side of her I hadn't seen, a side that honestly appraised what life had given her and was intent on figuring out how to play her best hand. That was more than most adults I knew were capable of.

'Kristin didn't like Helen,' Dillon said. 'Always said she belittled the students in private. There were rumors that once she flipped over a desk, that she occasionally had these outbursts—'

'Mania can present as rage. And it's convenient of you to toss blame on her, distract me from whatever shit is up your sleeve now,' I said, pushing against the door again.

He leaned forward, and the door inched open. 'You should be careful; you're starting to sound crazy. The drug trial has nothing to do with these murders. Don't make me the enemy. You never stopped to consider the good a drug trial could do. When Howard dies, how long do you think we'll have funding? His sons aren't thrilled with this place; they aren't going to allocate their inheritance here. The money will need to come from somewhere. A case study could reignite support.'

'All your talk about your vision for this place; you were biding your time, using these students.'

Color had gathered on his cheeks, and his eyes, golden as a big cat's, narrowed as he nodded in Ezra's direction. I strained against the door, trying not to pant, my feet sliding a few inches on the smooth floor.

'You weren't here then, but they were friends before.'

'Who? Before what?'

'Luis and Ezra. I saw them around on the grounds some, huddled together, back before Ezra disappeared. After Luis's murder, I started to think about it more. Why isn't Ezra talking?'

I slammed my body so hard against the door, Dillon was knocked backwards, off his feet. Clicks of the lock, that comforting metal, and I closed my eyes in relief.

CHAPTER 37

After setting the candles on the kitchen counter, I hesitated with the matches, weighing them in my palm before stuffing them in my jacket pocket. For an emergency.

I didn't love Dillon, but I remembered the hope us being together had given me. Under everything that had happened, I was surprised to still feel this simple, lesser heartache. Shaking my head to clear it, I sat down next to Ezra, the table so small, our knees nearly touched. I didn't trust Dillon's insinuation, that Ezra had special knowledge about Luis, but there was doubt lurking beneath my disbelief, a misgiving about my own biases.

'We need to talk more about that night – the night with the horse on the bridge,' I told him.

Leaning away from me, he clicked off his flashlight. I flipped mine on, trying to hide my frustration, my bones heavy with fatigue.

'Stop it,' I snapped. 'I'm trying to help. Were you planning to run away because you saw something?'

He shook his head. Then he flipped off my door, the walls, the ceiling, the windows, all of Hatchery.

I rubbed my forehead, tired of this taciturn, childish bullshit.

'You know, I dreamed of growing up in a place like this when I was your age. Dreamed of it. Some of you students have no idea how much people work to help you.'

It felt good to say it, but that feeling evaporated and left me ashamed. I thought he would flip me off next, but instead, he pointed to the candles on the kitchen counter and made a gesture with his hand of a closed bud blooming into an open flower.

'We're not going to light them,' I said. Don't make me regret telling you, I thought.

He raised his eyebrows: *Why not?*

'You know why.'

Satisfaction sharpened his features and he crossed his arms. I was beginning to sense myself – her – over near the window, and I was scared to shine my flashlight in that direction. We were running out of time.

With two fingers, Ezra made a motion of someone walking on the table. Then he pointed to himself and shook his head.

'I have no idea what you're trying to say,' I said. 'Why don't you just talk?'

Fury flashed across his face and he stood. He placed both hands at the edge of the table and flipped it, sending the snow globe soaring. The crash was barely audible above the thunder, but the shards glittered in my flashlight's beam, the angel figurine poised and penitent in her ring of broken glass.

It was just a snow globe. It didn't matter. But the heat in my body had been turned up to full boil, anger vibrating in me.

'You think breaking my things will give you the space you want? Guess what – people are always busting their way in. You hide away by the river, outside under the stars, in a homestead;

255

I don't care, someone will find you. You'll never feel safe because you'll never be safe. Sooner you come to terms with that, the better.'

His mouth pursed as if to ask, *Have you come to terms with that?* Then he clicked on his flashlight, picked up a piece of paper and crayon from the floor, and set it against the wall, writing something. He shoved it in my face.

Luis.

His handwriting was barely legible, scrawled as though with a non-dominant hand. But there it was: the first word he'd written since I'd found him.

The windowpane shuddered against the storm's pressure. Something without wings whirled past, illuminated by a lightning flash, tossed sideways by the wind.

'Luis? Luis, what?' I asked.

He made the motion with his fingers again and I realized it meant running away. My mind went adrift; shock flung it sideways. And then I remembered what Oksana had said: Luis was the one who stole the horse, not the killer.

He'd been trying to run away, and someone had stopped him. Kristin was moving home this week. Ezra had also been planning to run away. It was the commonality I'd been looking for: each victim was leaving Hatchery before they were killed.

Ezra snatched the paper back, ripped it, again and again, until it was confetti, and he tossed it up in the air in mock celebration and I understood. They were stopped. None of us recognized this was a prison to them.

He held my eyes, his look penetrating as if to say: *You should have seen this.*

I could feel her coming now in full force, the smell of charred flesh and singed hair, the ringing in my ears and sway of the room around me. I couldn't lose control in front of him; I needed to recover quickly.

'Don't let anyone in,' I told him as I hurried to the bathroom, my boots grinding glass to splinters. 'I'll be right back.'

The stench of mold in the drain hit my face as I clutched the sides of the pedestal sink. I gripped it, tighter and tighter, willing her away, my knuckles whitening.

How could helping someone be so mixed up with hurting them? Deborah. My brother. Luis. Kristin. No shucking that truth like an outgrown shell. It was within me; if I cut myself open to pluck it out, I'd find it in the tiny vessels feeding my marrow.

A clattering on the rooftop, the deafening din of rocks falling from the sky. Hail.

The glass doorknob twisted back and forth. The gales raged so loud, I couldn't hear the metal creaking against wood, the scritch-scratch complaint.

Sticky as sap, I felt that lingering residue of someone's gaze on me. I looked up from the mirror and there she was, regarding me with steady hostility. She had a faint smile, no lips to cover the white, large teeth, a charcoal smell, her melted, blackened skin with patches licked away to reveal the flesh underneath, the purple veins twisting against red muscle.

Leave, I begged, my jaw sore from clenching, heartbeat thrumming too fast.

She leaned past me, toward the mirror, the heat of her steaming the glass, and wrote in the vapor with a bony finger: *Not yet.*

*

Within a minute, she evaporated with the hail, and I flung open the door to find wind in my apartment. A window yawned into the night, shards glinting, and below it, glass and melting hail splayed across the floor.

'Ezra?' I called out, sweeping my flashlight over the tossed table and tiny kitchenette.

The deadbolt was unlocked, and I dashed forward, tripping over the shattered snow globe and sending it flying against the wall.

I laid my hand on the cold, smooth door handle. Thunder rumbled distantly now, backing away over the hail like a man pulling a cart full of pans, the clattering growing softer and softer.

Perhaps in mutiny, he'd unlocked the door, and then, perhaps, had regretted it. He'd run to get me, twisting the locked bathroom knob, and I hadn't answered.

CHAPTER 38

There was a chair outside my apartment, facing my door. No one sat on it now, but the person who had could have watched Ezra and me through the keyhole.

I was going numb again, softening around the edges like the hailstones in the grass, easing into oblivion.

Quick, quick. With this weather, he'd still be inside Hatchery, or at least on the grounds.

The hall was silent; students, likely wide-eyed in their rooms, blankets in a straitjacket around their tense bodies. The wallpaper's briar roses unfurled down the hall and I padded down an Oriental runner. A footstep sounded behind me; I whirled around.

My flashlight beam caught the glint of a blade and a scream escaped me as I stumbled backwards, colliding with someone else. Albert. He reached for me, hands flailing in the dark, and almost tipped backwards down the stairs.

I caught the collar of his shift and yanked him, clotheslining him back to safety.

Beverly opened her door, pulling her robe's sash tightly around her waist, and demanded, 'What's going on?'

Rubbing his neck with one hand, Albert lifted his lantern and illuminated a figure running down the hall, toward the study room. Cedar dashed up the steps with Sheriff Anders behind him, asking, 'Who screamed?'

'Someone with a knife ran into the study room,' I said.

Beverly's face had blanched, and she clutched about her chest as if reaching for her rosary. Doors cracked around us as Dillon and Helen came out of their apartments. Cedar cocked his gun and sidestepped down the hall.

'We know you're in there. Come out now,' he shouted. 'Drop the knife.'

A tossed knife clanked on the floor.

'You better not shoot me, motherfucker.'

Owen stepped out of the study room, hands up. Soon as Cedar lowered his gun, Owen lunged for the knife; Cedar sprang forward and blocked him, snatching it up.

'I'm not going to be unarmed with a killer on the loose. I have a right to protect myself,' Owen said.

'Absolutely not,' came a cold, low voice behind me. Turning, I was surprised to see Beverly had spoken, with an iron sternness in her posture, a blaze in her eyes, her long grey hair in a braid over her shoulder. Here was the woman who had run this place for thirty years. I wondered if the shock of the last few days had worn away and left a new resolve, returning her to herself.

I seized my moment. 'Ezra is missing. We must look for him now.'

Every head turned to me and people spoke over one another.

'He can't be gone.'

'Maybe it's a prank.'

'When did you last see him?'

'We can't scare the other children.'

'NOW,' Beverly roared. 'We will all search for him now. Wake the other children.'

Stance wide, Albert held firm. 'Beverly, we'll take care of this; you need to get your sleep—'

Beverly turned from him, crossed the stairway landing and flung open doors, shouting commands. Students climbed groggily out of their beds, looking at each other in confusion, some sinking their heads between their shoulders and sobbing.

This will scar them, a part of me thought. The other part was thinking of Ezra, and glad to have their help.

Everyone collected in the dining hall, where Albert lit candles for the students. They flitted past, carrying a dim glow with them, only their faces and hands illuminated, floating along disembodied and faintly golden. They crossed in the dark, calling to each other as they checked rooms, whispered voices between passing flames like monks in a monastery, keeping vigils and holy hours. I gripped my flashlight tighter and tried not to think of all those small fires.

Twenty minutes evaporated and the atmosphere of unified purpose shifted into bleak resignation. A dismal weight settled among the sleepless students, who stood bewildered in their pajamas, skin not yet soft with sleep. I could see it in their eyes, the gathering awareness that another one of them was gone, but gone in a different way – a disappearance with no trace, no trail of breadcrumbs.

It felt like Ezra was still within these walls. As if he'd transformed into the grandfather clock in the dining hall or the potted plant in the lounge, and refused to come out of hiding. Or could not.

Becoming more desperate, I almost ran into Helen at the cellar entrance in the kitchen. Her nose was reddened, as if inflamed by crying, her smooth skin blotchy.

'You go ahead,' she said. 'That place always creeps me out. Oksana was down there earlier.'

I frowned. 'Oksana? When?'

Helen shrugged. 'An hour ago? I'm not sure. She was dropping by her homemade tea, but then she heard what'd happened and hurried home.'

She was on the grounds when Ezra disappeared. My mind jumbled like a puzzle flipped over. I couldn't remember any time Oksana had dropped by to deliver tea; it wasn't something she usually did. The only times she came were when she had appointments with Beverly, during which she'd stood in the office, growling and occasionally swearing, insulting Howard's attempts to buy her land.

'We really should search the grounds,' Helen said, biting her lip. 'But no one can go out in this storm.'

I agreed without realizing it. Down in the cellar, I swept my flashlight over glass jars of preserves, a corked bottle of fermenting eggs, and vegetable bins. The stench of something rotting came from a crate.

What was it that Oksana had said? *Kids there don't know how well they got it.*

It hadn't seemed odd at the time; everyone is always making judgements about other people's lives, what they do and don't deserve. But now, a darker undercurrent snagged me.

She had been pleased that the students had given her a witch's name. Her horse. The dolls with the bodies, and the fact that

Kristin had been held, a gesture almost maternal, with a hint of a ritual. Like tucking a child in at night.

And all this time, Cedar and I had labored over the security footage and keys, trying to figure out how the killer had left and returned, when maybe the killer hadn't needed to enter or exit Hatchery at all, because they didn't live there.

I didn't want to believe Oksana could be involved, but I couldn't risk ignoring the possibility, so I slipped out the front door when no one was looking. We'd already lost too much time.

Despite my jacket, wind cut to my bones. The hail was already beginning to melt in thick, slippery piles and I stumbled and tripped over them as I crossed the dunes. Sand whipped into my mouth, choking me, and I buried my face in my arm as I lurched forward.

A sulfurous smell wrapped around me and the wind stopped so quick that a branch dropped from the sky. Wreckage was already strewn across the hills: bits of lumber, ripped shingles, a tire, clothing torn from a clothesline. I clambered over Oksana's fence, her garden before me shredded under the blinking sky. Clouds flitted east like fish in a black pond.

I pounded on her door. There was a rumble, like a train approaching from far away, becoming a roar. As if sucked through a straw, the wind started again, blowing straight, forcing me to bend against it, so I wouldn't topple over.

I looked west toward Hatchery. Lightning flared, illuminating a tornado half a mile to the northwest and Oksana on the porch beside me, silhouetted against the funnel cloud. She grabbed my arm and yanked me down the steps. She was shouting something at me, but the gale flung her words away.

Something with fur and flailing limbs sailed past us. A tree branch ripped from a trunk and careened into the dark. Oksana tugged me toward her barn, wrenched open a hatch in the ground and shoved me inside.

CHAPTER 39

Flare of a match, sizzle on a wick. She lit two more candles after the first. Sitting on an overturned bucket, I huddled in the corner. The stone cellar was tomb-like, with an arched ceiling curling overhead and cold, abrasive rocks at my back.

Masons jars on shelves rattled; the ground around us shook. Dust clouded the air and a long, low rushing filled my ears, then clattering and smashing, earth vibrating as the tornado scoured its surface. It felt like we could be sucked straight up, tossed for miles.

Suddenly, the howl ceased. Silence settled around us.

Oksana took the quiet as an opportunity to tell me I was a fool. 'Why in damnation are you out in this storm?'

'Ezra is missing.'

Her disgust melted away, replaced with concern. 'Again?'

I tried to sound calm, matter-of-fact. 'Do you know where he is?'

'Yes, I've hidden him in my cupboard. No, I have no idea where he is. Have you told Beverly?' She was fidgeting, fretfully smoothing her flannel shirt. I saw myself in her, born of a different time and place.

'Everyone there is up searching. Thought you may have seen him . . . at some point. I'd heard you were at Hatchery earlier, around when he disappeared.'

Her eyes narrowed on me. 'Are you accusing me of something?'

'No,' I said quickly. I didn't want to break whatever frail connection we'd built and was reluctant to believe this was anything other than another dead end. Liking her had turned me squeamish.

This seemed to settle her, and she sank deeper against the stones, plucking a feather from her shirt. An empty liquor bottle, a paperback with yellowed, curled pages, and large wood bins surrounded us.

Oksana noticed me surveying the cellar. 'Grandfather built this almost two hundred years ago. The hills change; this stays the same. After harvest day, we'd all enjoy a vodka down here, nice and cool, those blistering hot days. In winter, I'd take the baby down here and let it nap in a basket, nice and warm. People knew what they were doin' when they lived in caves.'

The underground, musty aroma made me claustrophobic. A roar began again. 'Is that another one?' I asked Oksana.

She shrugged. 'Might be. Might not be above us though. This is like sitting in a seashell; makes things sound closer than they are.' Her face tightened. 'That boy – Ezra. Maybe he's hiding. My kids used to curl in these potato bins during storms. Wanted to tuck themselves away. Maybe that's all.'

'I don't think so,' I said softly. Wait, I told myself. Patients revealed the most after long silences.

She shook her head aggressively, skin swaying beneath her chin. 'Place is haunted if you ask me.'

'Hatchery? Has something terrible happened there before?'

She squinted into some invisible place for so long, I thought she was ignoring me. Finally, she said, 'Thirty years ago, must have been, around when Hatchery opened. My kids and their friends were wearing those bell bottoms and peasant dresses and awful fringe vests. There was this attack. I didn't witness any of it myself. It was back when I was having another of my bouts. So many of those years when the kids were young blend together. But I saw a picture of the twins in the paper and read about it.'

She went on to tell me about Samhain, the All Hallows' Eve festival once celebrated at Hatchery, before the attack. She'd been to the one the year before, trying to make nice with the neighbors, but this one, her family had sat out. There had been jack-o-lanterns, divination games, the scents of apples and hazelnut. The students carved lanterns out of turnips and squash and set them in the windows for the souls of the dead as they revisited Hatchery. They lit bonfires and danced around them, playing games to determine who would live the following year. Pranks and disguises filled the night; students wore burlap sacks with holes and clustered on top of hills, pretending to be wandering spirits.

There were twins there at the time and one was on an experimental medication – that was the rumor anyway. Made him belligerent and hostile. Another student, an artistic boy who struggled with psychosis—

'What was his name?' I interrupted. 'The artistic boy?'

Oksana squinted again. 'John? Something common, old-fashioned. J something . . .'

I remembered the painting Beverly had been trying to clean

and repair the day after Luis's murder. She'd said he'd had bouts of psychosis. 'James?' I asked.

'Might be. Don't interrupt.'

She told me how the week before the festival, Twin One had attacked James, beat him black and blue. On All Hallows' Eve, when everyone else was busy merrymaking, James snuck up on one of the twins, and jimmied out his eye with a carving knife. Blood, screams, tumult, figures running in the dark, smoke dwindling to a wisp as wood turned to ash. Turned out he'd mistaken Twin Two for Twin One and gotten revenge on the wrong one. Maimed at, what, around ten years old? When it was all over, the twins had been expelled, and James had been taken to a children's prison.

'Shame,' she said. 'That boy was never right in the head. Didn't belong behind bars.'

'That's terrible,' I whispered. I was beginning to wish I'd never come here; what a mistake this all had been.

The pensive Oksana didn't last long; she smirked. 'After that, to keep my kids from sneaking out at night, I'd tell them the story of the one-eyed twin who prowled the prairie looking for his other eye, not able to rest. His eyeball rolls and rolls over the hills seeing everything, watching everyone.'

This nonchalance irritated me, spurred me beyond my peace-making. 'Agent Knox found dolls – the same doll you left with Luis – where Kristin's body was found.'

Oksana's head swiveled toward me, her face creased with irritation. 'I made dolls for the students years ago; most of them didn't have toys. Stopped when Beverly threw a hissy fit, claiming I was introducin' them to witchcraft or some other such nonsense. Maybe those're the same ones.'

'Doesn't explain why they were found with a dead body, in what had previously been a locked safe.' I knew I was giving her confidential information related to the crime but I couldn't stop myself.

'What *exactly* are you accusin' me of?'

'I'm just trying to understand.'

She scoffed. 'Bullshit. You don't accept that your way of seeing things isn't the only way. Kids these days, running around with their thoughts and feelings – someone needs to tell them: if you can think wrong, well, you can feel wrong too.'

I needed to approach this differently. 'Your photos – I know, you went through a time . . . with your daughter—'

She stiffened at the word. 'You think that because I was unwell at one point in my life, that I'd kill your students?'

I flinched. I was doing this all wrong. 'I just wanted to say that I understand how things can get out of control—'

Oksana leapt to her feet and flew toward me, grabbing both my arms above my elbows and lifting me up. Despite her strength, I felt her grip loosen, and tried to pull away from her, but her grip tightened again, then softened a final time before she let go. Pain glittered in her eyes. Her arthritis. She could grip things, but she couldn't apply steady, strong pressure for more than a few seconds. She dropped her hands from my arms and held them out between us, palms down. Her knuckles were swollen and lumpy beneath cracked skin, her fingers bent and twisted at odd angles away from their joints.

'You think I could strangle an eighteen-year-old girl? Beverly told me that's what happened. I couldn't kill her that way, even if I needed to save my own skin.'

Shame washed over me. 'Oksana, I'm sorry. I hadn't—'

She climbed up the ladder and threw open the hatch, cold air bursting inside. I pulled myself up after her, feeling as desolate as the wrecked landscape before me. In the starlight, I could see the hills, their forms faint and blue-hued. Some had bits of metal or wood strewn across them, others had been flattened like plateaus, and the smell of uprooted grass and flayed earth lingered in the storm's wake.

'You want to look through my house?' she asked, spreading her arms wide.

'No – I'm sorry – I—'

Oksana lumbered toward her house, slamming the door shut. I tried to remember the last few hours, trace the path that had led me here, but clarity was elusive. As I walked back, I followed a shallow, crooked trench, dug as if a claw had ripped along the belly of the earth.

CHAPTER 40

The electricity was still out when I made it back to the House. Beverly was up keeping watch, pacing the hallway of the main floor, and she informed me that Sheriff Anders, Cedar, and Albert had left to begin the search for Ezra. Dillon was talking a student through a panic attack and Helen was comforting the younger students, who had set up camp in the dining hall after becoming convinced their bedrooms were haunted. I wanted to join the search for Ezra, but Beverly insisted I stay in the building.

'This isn't over. I want the rest of the staff to stay in until the sun is up,' she said. 'The kids here still need you.'

I bit back an argument. She was right. The night wasn't over, and the students needed another familiar face keeping watch. I told Beverly I would change out of my wet clothes and keep an eye on things upstairs.

In my apartment, I pulled on fresh clothes so predictable, they were almost a uniform: navy trousers, wrinkled button-up, and combat boots. While I combed my unruly hair, I thought about Oksana's story. Subtracting the years, I realized Dillon had to be around the age of James and the twins. Or, the age James would be, if he were still alive. I hadn't met Dillon's family. Now that I thought of it, I hadn't even been shown photos, which wasn't initially odd to me, because I didn't go around showing photos of my family. But now I wondered if there was a reason he hadn't. People did invent fake histories sometimes.

Crying drifted down the hall, pressed up against my door. The cries softened and were replaced by a melodic sound, faint, but clear, someone singing the ballad: *but Lady Margaret lay in a cold, black coffin, with her face turned to the wall.*

I froze, head turned toward the door, glass tilted at my lips. It was the first time I'd heard it myself after months of dismissing the students' claims. It couldn't be. It sounded different than when Owen had sang it boisterously in the cafeteria. It might have been the echoing acoustics of the cathedral or my slipping sanity, but it reverberated and drifted past in an otherworldly, disembodied way.

The song dissipated and another voice replaced it.

He denies having suicidal thoughts. His affect is congruent with mood. He displays high levels of insight when discussing problems, though he has yet to identify . . .

My own voice. It was terribly calm, detached, almost robotic. The cadence was familiar, like a favored memory, often revisited.

I struggled against the break with reality, strained to maintain lucidity the way someone pieces together the image of an incomplete puzzle, slowly, with effort. Resting my head against the cabinet, I tried to breathe past the rising trepidation: after seeing things that weren't there for years, I couldn't handle hearing things too.

Considering this trauma and the meaning ascribed to it, his chronic

pain may be psychosomatic. Cognitive behavioral therapy will be needed
for him to more fully integrate the experience . . .

Trauma. Chronic pain. Albert. My stolen patient tapes.

I cracked my door open, expecting the tape to be playing in the hall, set outside my door like a May Day basket, mocking, planted with intention. But the halls were empty, my voice wandering from the students' rooms.

I crept toward it. The exposed wood beams of the vaulted ceiling curved like a rib cage over me; a female saint watched me from a gilt-framed oil painting. I skirted around the baroque bannister, its carved wood cold beneath my palm. Eight doors surrounded me, labeled into male and female rooms for the ages of Young, Preteen, Teen, and Fledgling. Apprehension sat in a knot between my shoulders as I opened the door of the oldest boys' room, those about to take flight.

Four students sat on the floor, my recorder in the middle. The box was next to Owen's thigh, lid askew, tapes visible within. They all looked up at me with uneasiness except Owen, who shot me an amused expression with a shrug.

'Should Albert really be working here? When he admits to thinking about killing people?' Owen asked.

I snatched up the recorder and box of tapes. 'Where did you find these?'

Everyone was silent. Tucking the box and recording beneath my arm, I balled my free fist. 'Did you steal them from my office?'

They shook their heads; Owen leaned back on his hands. 'Found them in the dining hall when Albert was handing out candles and everyone was searching for Ezra.'

I was too rattled to decide if he was telling the truth. Owen's gloating face made me wonder if he himself had stolen it as some gumshoe rubbernecker, looking for evidence. Or maybe he was telling the truth and the killer had abandoned it after a listen. A worm, tunneling into other people's minds, hungry for their misery.

'I liked listening to you talk about how bad I was,' Owen said. 'You sounded *so* concerned. I also was surprised I'm one of the only ones without a diagnosed condition! Am I the only sane one here?'

'There are different kinds of sanity. Some can't be diagnosed,' I said.

Owen's stare pulled at me; I felt a sharper aggressiveness beneath the placid surface than had been there before. A whittled determination.

I fought for a semblance of authority and shook the recorder at them. 'Everything on these tapes is confidential. You are not to share it with anyone,' I said.

The other three students nodded.

'Sure,' Owen said. 'I'll try not to let anything slip. But you know how I can be.' He spread his hands in a helpless gesture and I shut the door.

Back in my room, a note was waiting for me. Or more precisely, a torn page from a book with two lines of a poem circled in red: 'Some are born to sweet delight/Some are born to endless night'. William Blake, from 'Auguries of Innocence'.

This was the shudder of the web; the spider was coming closer. Back against the wall, I slid to the floor and sank my face against my knees. A sour taste lined the back of my throat and I thought, this person knows me. Knows that I drink coffee in the afternoon from the lounge but knows also that I've felt – and worried these students might feel – ill-born, ill-bred, less than. Knows the one thing you don't change is where you started. Scornful of our Achilles' heel.

It was a threat, but it was also more than that. Instructional, reprimanding, a headmistress with a long ruler pointing at an equation on the chalkboard. Clearly, I had upset this person and they wanted to correct me, in the old-fashioned way, punish me into my place.

I was tempted to stay down but was pulled to my feet by the thought of Ezra. He wasn't doomed. He'd already proven that by surviving, making a home out of a dusty shell and finding water in an abandoned well. He seemed to instinctively understand that the start or finish isn't the measure of a life; the way you endure is.

Out the window, a few clouds lay thin, long wisps, their undersides painted pink by early light. Vapor from the melted hail hung along the horizon line, smudging the contours of the dark hills beyond.

Below my window, the garden was destroyed: sprouts ripped up from their roots, the finely shaped rows obliterated. She, my hallucination, was down there, smeared with dirt. Same as the time on the road, I hadn't felt her coming and reared back in shock.

Maybe she didn't announce her appearance because like last time, when she'd held a funeral pyre for the rat, she was on a mission. Now, she knelt in the garden, clawing dirt to the side, digging and digging as if searching for bones.

CHAPTER 41

May 5, 2007

The electricity blinked on right after dawn. Sunlight scorched the trampled grass, heavy in its heat, drying away the small bit of moisture the storm had brought. Cedar had left me a new voicemail, telling me to meet him in Ennenock ASAP. His tone was clipped, irritated, which was understandable – he'd been up all night. But something else in his voice unsettled me that I couldn't put a finger on.

I dialed Mrs Iden's number, shame already burning on my face.

'Mrs Iden, this is Dr Webber—'

'I know I'd told you I'd be there early but that won't happen. I'm just leaving now. That storm last night knocked a limb on to my driveway, and Rick, my neighbor, used his chainsaw to break it down and move it. All set now. Be there soon.'

When I told her Ezra was missing, she fell into stunned silence. Then she erupted into questions I couldn't answer: *What happened, where is he, how could you let this happen again?* I took it, jaw clenched, wanting to tell her she wasn't asking anything I hadn't played on repeat the whole night long. By the time she was finished, I felt clawed to shreds. She couldn't join in with the search, due to her leg, but I promised to update her on any developments.

After I hung up, I flipped on the radio, searching for other words to drown out the rest as I finished getting dressed. The weather report announced that last night had been a dry storm; there hadn't been enough rain to relieve the drought. Ezra's snapshot of the twins lay on the floor, slightly crumpled, from where it had flown from the table the night before. Pulling on my jacket, I grabbed the photo and stuffed it in my pocket for a talisman.

Townsfolk from Augustine volunteered to search the grounds for Ezra again – a mother and her teenage son walking around the picnic tables, an older couple passing the Indian tree. Sheriff Anders nodded at me as he rounded the bell tower. It all felt like déjà vu, a similar image to the one from two months ago when everyone had searched for him.

The police force from a town an hour away parked in the circular drive and a few officers exchanged notes, leaning against the hoods of their cars. Owen stood outside Albert's door, taunting him, hands at his hips, chin tilted up to the sky to project his voice.

'How does it feel to kill somebody? Did you miss it too much?' Owen crooned, twisting his voice into a slight lilt.

'Shut up, Owen,' I said as I passed him. 'Leave Albert alone.'

Owen just wanted someone to take his anger from him, it didn't matter whom or how. If Kristin's killer couldn't be held accountable today, then Albert could be held accountable for confessed thoughts.

'Who would really decide to be here of all places, if they didn't have to be?' Owen called to me, kicking matted clumps of grass. 'What have you done?'

There was a widening in my chest and I spun toward Owen. 'Get back inside!' I shouted, pointing toward Hatchery.

Owen held up his hands, palms facing me. 'Geez, calm down. You are cuckoo.' His index finger spun in a circle near his temple.

I hurried onward, his voice dimming behind me. *Ignore him, ignore him.*

Ennenock bustled with activity. The team must have begun working before dawn, yet they still combed the ghost town. A tech exited the bank with a camera in one hand and an evidence collection kit in the other. A few uniformed police officers canvased the buildings east of the bank, creeping across half-caved-in porches. Voices hummed along the thoroughfare, and the more people Ennenock held, the more ruined it appeared, its decaying false fronts in sharp relief against the flurry of bodies.

Inside the bank, religious graffiti sprawled across the walls. Several crosses had stick figures hanging from them and what looked like a baby was cut in two. Uneven crooked letters said: *Their littles will be dashed to the ground.*

Cedar leaned against the doorframe of the bank's safe, a narrow, low-ceilinged room filled with shelves, where several techs bagged evidence. Kristin's body had already been moved but horror still twitched in me at the memory of finding Luis's body out beneath the hanging tree. When Cedar saw me, he jerked his head toward the street as if to say, *Wait out there.*

This unsettled me, and a few minutes later when he crossed the dirt road toward me, his stare was so angry, a chill passed through me.

'What—' I began.

'Let's talk over here.' Cedar grabbed my arm and pulled me with him past the hotel, toward the stables. He stopped in what had been the gravel paddocks, the fence around it half collapsed, leaning at odd angles.

'Were you waiting to tell me or just not going to tell me at all?' he demanded, arms crossed over his chest, head thrust forward.

I stepped back. 'What the hell are you talking about?'

'I didn't expect this case to be easy, but hell, Lore, I'm looking like a fucking idiot. Mitchell may even take me off and bring someone else in. And to think, I *asked* him for this case, to come out to the middle of nowhere, knowing I could see you again, try and make things right, only to find out I can't even trust you—'

'What—'

'This morning, when I'm meeting with the techs, Owen stops me, tells me he's nervous about Albert working here. Since he already confessed to wanting to kill people and it's on tape. The techs give me this look . . . apparently, it's on your dictation tapes. Meaning, you knew—'

Gritting my teeth, I ran my hands over my face, rubbing my eyes with the heels of my palms. That little shit.

Cedar's nostrils flared and he raised his voice, pointing at the bank. 'You're not the only one who cares about this. I was caught with my pants down – Mitchell has already talked about pulling me from the field after the raid and my extended time off—'

So, it was the embarrassment more than my omission that rankled him. I could understand that, but I was growing weary of his bossiness and inability to listen, his dismissal of my intuition. Even when we were kids, his eyes had sometimes glazed over when I showed him something I cared about: my plant collection or sketches, the colored rock I kept in my pocket. I became picky about what to share, hoarding other, deeper, discoveries.

'I wanted to wait until I had something solid,' I said. 'You know how many false confessions, rumors, attention-grabbing antics float around here? Beverly was baiting me, and while I do think Albert's the one who's been stalking me, I didn't think—'

'Isn't part of your job assessing patients' proclivity toward violence?'

A hot flush of anger made me lift my chin. 'That's exactly what I did. Thanks for pretending you know how to do my job.'

'I'd like you to do it better.'

I was struck with a new kind of pain, a lighter, more gauzy sensation of hurt that lay under the heavy weight of Ezra's disappearance. Cedar and I had finally been getting close to how we'd been, and now we'd cast off into different water altogether. We'd squabbled before, minor quarrels, but rarely had we attacked each other. We'd been each other's defenders.

'Look,' I said quietly. 'You don't get to take your stress out on me. You don't get to sail in here like last year never happened, convince me to help you out – even though I warned you it's a compromising situation – and get upset about me not being your puppet. You think I need you? Think I can't just turn around and walk away for good?'

Inhaling, he lifted his chin, looking slightly above me. Before, his arms had looked like a barrier; now, they looked like he was trying to hold himself together. My nails bit into my palm.

'I'm sorry—' I started.

'No, I'm sorry,' he said. 'I shouldn't have asked you. I didn't expect things to get so out of control. I thought . . . it would be different . . .' His voice had a faraway, echoing quality, as if he were speaking to me from the opposite end of a cave.

'I'm going to help you finish this.'

Cedar seemed to take this and weigh it in his mind, then nodded. It was an uneasy truce. Not knowing how to look at each other, we both glanced at the bank, its long shape stretching away from the road into tumbleweed territory beyond.

'Tentative time of death is around 9:30 a.m. yesterday morning,' he said.

'No hoof prints?'

He shook his head.

'Could the safe be where it started with Luis too?'

'I'd hoped we find something to indicate that, but nothing yet. We did find some hoof prints around the hotel and trace evidence matching the sweater he was wearing, so we're reworking some of that.'

Money in a safe. A guest in a hotel.

Something moved in one of the stables, a ghostly flicker, a translucent figure shifting. I blinked; saw that it was from wind blowing dirt from the loft down into the stall, sunlight turning it opaque and swirling.

Sweat glistened on Cedar's forehead and he swatted a fly away. 'This afternoon we'll be expanding the search for Ezra to the farms and ranches in the surrounding area. His homestead – the one he was in before – has already been searched. I'm heading back to Hatchery now to search Kristin's room, talk to her friends.'

As we walked back, he told me he was consulting with the

Nebraska State Patrol and Mitchell would be sending a few agents to help tomorrow, after the raid was finished.

'How is this one going?' I asked, not certain I really wanted to hear about it.

'Better than last time,' he said. 'But it'll be a long night for them.'

The grass rustled from the movement of a snake or rodent.

'We got a response on the APB,' he went on. 'Someone sighted a kid that matches Ezra's description at a truck stop in Kansas. Sounded like suspicious circumstances. Sheriff Anders is headed there now to check it out.'

'Ezra's not out there; he's here. I can feel it.'

'We have to check out every possibility.'

I let it go and told him about Luis's plan to run away, how all three victims were planning to leave. Not wanting to make him question my judgement, I left out my scramble through the storm to confront Oksana.

Cedar began to respond, but the crack of a gunshot stopped us in our tracks.

CHAPTER 42

Cedar and I exchanged a wordless glance as the hills echoed the gunshot's ring. I'd heard gunshots frequently since moving here; the winter had been filled with hunters on these country roads, their camouflage coats visible against a backdrop of vinyl seats and plastic dashboards, carcasses bumping along in the truck bed.

Touching my arm, Cedar raised his eyebrows in question. My pulse had sped up because I was thinking of Ezra. I didn't want to overreact; I could feel myself on the verge of it, all keyed up, that energy rubbing just under my skin.

'Maybe a hunter?' I suggested.

'I thought that was mostly fall and winter.' One hand rested on his holster and his other reached for his radio.

'It's furbearer season – bobcats, opossum, fox.'

'Sheriff Anders,' Cedar spoke into his radio. 'Heard what sounded like a single gunshot. Might have come from north of Ennenock; hard to say exactly. Could be a hunter, so notify heads of search parties just in case.'

'Will do. And I'll send someone to look into it,' Anders said.

'Thanks.'

The search parties for Ezra had already moved beyond

Hatchery's grounds. Someone was heading toward the river, poking around in the grass with a tall stick. A few others made dark forms against the bleached landscape, indistinct as a single brushstroke in a painting.

Owen was still yelling obscenities and other insults at Albert's house. 'If you're going to kill everyone else, why not go ahead and kill yourself?'

Something shifted in me. It was as though a curtain had fallen, separating one side of my mind from the other. What was true on the other side had ceased to exist. What existed now was a young man abusing an elderly man for thoughts he'd admitted in a private therapy appointment.

Two window boxes held peonies, their fragrance thick and the colors bright. I tried to focus on their fragility, so I wouldn't boil over, the image like a bubble: get too close, and it'd pop.

'An eye for an eye. Don't you want to give the world justice?' Owen stood with his arms outstretched on each side, as if he were a preacher giving a sermon. The sun a blister in the sky, turning his hair the color of an aged lemon.

People always had to say something. My aunt, loudmouthing at the funeral, as though she, who'd never lifted a hand to help us, had a right to pass judgement. I could still feel the texture of the brocade curtain between my fingers, the ridiculous tassels that swept across the floor as I pulled it over me, as if it were a shield. Albert should be left alone.

Through the window, I could see Albert at his kitchen table, spine arched forward, head resting on the table in front of him. Surgical tape closed a laceration on his neck where Owen's whip had licked him.

In a crime scene photo of a murder-suicide years ago, I'd seen a man hunched and sprawled over a table like that. The single gunshot. I'd asked Albert about suicidal ideation and he'd always denied it. But the patient who didn't want to be stopped always lied.

Owen had done this. Had driven Albert to do this.

I was half aware that I was shaking. And then running. Owen didn't see me coming.

'If you were gone—' he bellowed.

The thud of my bones against his bones. My shoulder smashed into his ribs and the word *gone* hovered in the air around us, like he'd spit it out and it'd fallen to the grass near us.

We sprawled on the grass and I rolled over, pinning him beneath me, my knees on either side of his waist, puffs of dust around us. Owen lay stunned and docile, seemingly shocked into astonishment and something like respect.

'He's a murderer—' Owen started.

With an open palm, I smacked him hard across the face; his jaw sent pain ringing up my arm.

'You killed him,' I whispered.

Owen opened his mouth to speak but I smacked him again.

Cedar was calling my name, but it sounded impossibly far away, back along the twisting river and cottonwoods at its banks. Owen lifted his arms to shield himself when I raised my hand again.

Cedar wrenched me away. He shouted in my face, but it took several tries before I could hear him.

'What the hell are you doing?!'

I blinked at him, slightly impatient. 'He drove Albert to suicide. Go look—' I pointed at his house.

Albert stood in his open doorway, framed by the peonies in their window boxes.

My mouth dropped open; I stared, completely dumbfounded. He was dead. He had shot himself.

Albert stepped off his front porch, a faint red indentation on his forehead from where he'd rested his head on the table. My eyes couldn't leave that mark. He looked like a schoolboy who'd fallen asleep during class, and now woke up, bewildered and self-conscious.

He'd fallen asleep at the table. Of course. He'd been up all night patrolling Hatchery and searching for Ezra. The gunshot may have been from a hunter after all.

Cedar helped Owen to his feet and Albert turned to me, his voice choked with dismay as he asked, 'What have you done?'

I sat on the short church pew in Beverly's office while she talked to Cedar in the hallway. Half-burnt candles from the night before left wax pooled on her desk in a small red lake.

I knew I was going to lose my job, but I felt weightless. Mea culpa, I thought, without feeling. Wasn't that a phrase during mass? It'd been so long since I'd attended with Cedar's family. In psychiatry, excessive self-criticism was associated with depression; in some religions, it was associated with spiritual health. The crucified savior above me appeared haunted by his own holiness, not of this world.

Beverly opened the door and stepped inside. My thoughts scattered and blood rushed to my face as what I'd done became real.

'Agent Knox told me what happened,' she said, leaning forward, hands splayed on her desk. Gossip from beyond the door, invasive chattering voices, filled the brief pause. 'Do you have an explanation? Was it self-protection?'

I shook my head, cheeks burning.

'This is the last thing we need with everything going on. A staff member attacking a student. You'd do us a favor if this had been provoked.'

'I have no defense,' I said, clasped hands in my lap.

Beverly's mouth tightened into an even firmer line, her lips disappearing entirely. 'Well, I have no choice. Your employment is terminated immediately. You'll have twenty-four hours to move out and will not have any more contact with students. Is that understood? Normally I'd have you escorted off the grounds but, in these circumstances . . .'

'I understand,' I said, though I didn't. I didn't understand what had happened to me at all. I stood up to leave but Beverly kept talking.

'My mother sang in vaudeville shows before rodeos. She'd paint her face beforehand; she loved being someone else. She'd always say to me, "Everything holds its opposite, the wicked and the good." And I thought, that's blasphemy if I ever heard it. I'm going to do something pure and honest.' Beverly shook her head and gave a short, humorless laugh.

I shifted uncomfortably on my feet. This wasn't what I expected – I expected Beverly to rant and rave at me, shake her fists, covered in a sheen of righteous indignation. Oksana had said Beverly seemed lonely, like she was aching to be understood. Perhaps that's all this was, but it also felt like a defense, an apology before an offense.

Before she could say or do anything else, I repeated, 'I understand,' and made for the door.

'Well, that's it, then,' she said loudly. She made a gesture like dusting her hands off, even though they were clean.

Outside the door, I was left with the lingering sensation that something more was coming.

CHAPTER 43

Wherever Ezra was, what could he see? Faded wallpaper in a basement? The shadow-filled backseat of a car? The earthen walls of a cellar?

Brushing dead seedlings aside, I knelt in the garden and began digging. She had led me to Ezra, she could lead me back. Something had been buried that would offer me a sign of where to look. It was comforting, the rhythmic gesture of scooping dirt, everything reduced to the sun on my back and the earth beneath my nails. It startled me to realize that Cedar had been crouching next to me for some time.

'What are you doing?' he asked.

I ignored him and pressed on, the sandy soil much heavier with the peat moss and compost mixed in. A worm twisted away and tunneled deeper.

'I need to tell you something,' Cedar said. 'You need to stop.'

'There's something here. I know it.'

'Lore, stop.' Cedar leaned toward me and tried to grab my wrists.

'STOP!' I screeched in his face. 'Don't touch me.'

'Lore. You're done. You're done.'

I leaned back on my heels. 'I'll find it later,' I said, though the spell was broken; I knew nothing was there. It was meaningless, actions that left no mark, that eroded faster than a landscape of sand.

'No, Lore, I mean you're done, for a while.' Cedar ran his hand over his head. 'I can't believe Beverly didn't tell you, but she reported your attack on Owen to the medical licensing board.'

Tilting my head to the side, I grinned at him; my eyes felt like they were rolling in their sockets. 'That's almost funny.'

'Lore,' Cedar said again, repeating my name over and over, presumably to ground me, but I still felt like I was floating. He stared at me until I drifted down, settling back into my body and the familiar aches in my neck and shoulders, the tightness I'd never been able to loosen. Tumbleweed snagged in the legs of a nearby picnic table.

'What?' I asked, not believing him.

'They may just suspend it. Doesn't mean they'll revoke it. I tried to convince her not to—'

No wonder she'd been acting penitent. Beverly wasn't firing me; she was destroying my career. Cedar had told her what had happened out in the hall while I sat in her office like a disobedient pupil. While I'd fully expected Owen to report it, it stung more that it had been Cedar. Perhaps he'd still been angry from our argument in the paddocks but I'd risked a lot to help him, had even warned him it wasn't wise, and he hadn't listened. Soon as I cracked he was first in line to leave me on the ground and point to where I'd fallen.

If I'd never gotten involved, Ezra wouldn't be in the hands of a killer. He'd be at the homestead; I'd be comforting my patients, oblivious to the details of the case. On some level I knew I was being irrational, oversimplifying things, but Cedar was knocking me off course yet again, shattering my already tenuous existence.

Cedar was still talking, now making excuses for Beverly. 'She knows Howard will ask how she handled it. Owen is a kid—'

'Kid?' I said. 'He can buy a gun. He can go fight in a fucking war—'

This was the defensiveness Beverly had been looking for, but I hadn't been able to summon it then.

'I knew you were a rule follower, but I'd never have guessed you'd inform on your informant,' I said.

'I wanted to be the one to tell her so I could construct a defense for you – give the attack some context. You don't want her finding out from Albert or Owen.'

'Covering your ass. That's what this is. Retaliation because I've embarrassed you once, and come hell or high water, you won't let that happen twice.'

'Lore, you're sounding paranoid. I should have known this would be too much.'

'You arrogant asshole. Too much for me, acting like you don't have baggage, like you have a clear head—'

'That's not fair.'

'I think you're happy I won't be able to work, because that's what you originally wanted, isn't it? For me to take some time off? Not unless I'm working for you, right? This is just another way of you telling me what's best for me.'

'This is why I didn't know what to do after Deb died. You always go on the offensive.'

'Yeah, I'm just too difficult.'

'You *are* difficult! You're fucking difficult! Why can't you let things go? I did try to be there for you. Later, once I got my own shit together.'

Months later, once I'd accepted he'd never return my calls, he rang my bell as I stood on the other side of the door, waiting for him to leave. He left a biography of the Brontë sisters, my favorite authors, on the doorstep, a lukewarm apology, typical for him, the kind that skirted discussing any actual problem. An olive branch. I left it where it lay, pages curling in the humidity, cover dissolving over the coming weeks of rain and sun. It was pulp when I finally tossed it, the words bleeding into each other, mute, senseless.

'Always on your terms, on your time. Like I'm a toy on a shelf, to be enjoyed when it's convenient,' I said.

'That's not true. Your way of thinking – it . . . this isn't healthy—'

'Healthy isn't real. It's a place we talk about that has no map because it doesn't exist. We just like imagining that it does.'

'I'm trying to help you, dammit. And if you can't see that, you're more out of your mind than I thought.'

'Well, you won't have to worry about me because we're done. You're on your own now.'

I found myself up in the Indian tree, watching clouds shift and sunlight paint the grass amber, gripping the branch so tight, it left red scratches on my palms. Tears kept building and I kept blinking them back, chest aching.

Cedar had been trying to help; I knew that. Why can't I let things go? I now realized my hallucination wasn't looking for something in the garden, she was digging her own grave.

All this time, I'd viewed Deborah's snow globe as a relic of my guilt, her saying, *This will remind you of what you've done to me.* But what if she gave it to me because after all our hours together, she cared for me? And meant the gesture as a gift, not an indictment?

What Oksana said kept reverberating in my head: *You can feel wrong too.* How many times had I told a patient that just because they felt something didn't make it true? Feelings did not always point you true north. There was a different, deeper intuition, beneath passing feelings, a kind of wisdom that only developed the more you listened to it.

I hadn't meant what I'd said to Cedar about health. I'd seen patients get better, seen them battle unseen currents as they rowed toward a more abundant shore. There may not be one destination, but that didn't mean you couldn't get somewhere else, somewhere better. And what else could lead me across uncharted water but a compass I'd had all these years, untouched, in the pockets of my memories? The people who stayed with me, who left their mark.

Like Ezra, with the monarch on his cheek, the buffalo below his dangling feet. The steady rise and fall of his chest as he slept, after he led Cedar back to me when I'd needed help. All he wanted was to run away, to flee when he felt frightened, but he hadn't. He wasn't any longer the boy I'd found on the kitchen counter eating ants, diving through a window.

I thought of Carson, not on that night, but the day before, when we played together at the hearth. After we'd grown tired of my book, we found a jar of marbles in the china hutch.

We flicked the marbles across the hearth, and Carson would howl with laughter if he knocked one of mine off. When we grew cold and tired and retreated to the couch, Carson grasped my hand in his.

'You're my best friend,' he had said as I tucked a blanket around him.

All that love. Everyone carried the love they'd been given, the way a pregnant woman carries a child hidden under her skin, the baby ready not just for birth, but to outlive her. To go into the future and change it.

I didn't have much time left; I'd be kicked off the grounds in less than twenty-four hours and Ezra had already been missing for almost twelve. Taking his photo of the twins out of my jacket pocket, I studied it again. The girls were barefoot in calico dresses, with pinafores and sunbonnets; half of a wagon wheel was visible behind them.

It was too much of a leap to think the twins in this photo were ancestors of the twins in Oksana's story, yet this possibility kept lurking, telling me that what had begun during Samhain was now ending with Beltane, thirty years later. They were opposites: Samhain's harvest festival and Beltane's pagan fires for fertility. New life, and life being cut down.

Looking more closely at the photo, I saw something in the corner, half shrouded by grass. A modern child's tennis shoe. It was an image of time slipping sideways as the children pretended to be in the past. Guising, tricking souls who'd otherwise come to haunt them.

CHAPTER 44

The students had gone out across the prairie collecting wildflowers, returning to drop them in a mound near the fire pits. When they gathered round it, I was cast back to the night of Luis's death, to the merriment amid the fires and smoke, trampling asters and prairie rose underfoot, releasing their dying scent into the night air.

But now, the students were mournful, and I caught also a shared gratitude that they had not been chosen for the autopsy table; out of this dwindling makeshift family, they were still here. It made me recall a lecture during fellowship on dysfunctional family dynamics: *Every group must have its sacrificial lamb.* A kind of sin-eater to purify the tribe; like Abraham, hand raised, ready to kill his own son.

Only Helen was missing from the memorial, and myself, uninvited. I stubbornly stood at its edge, waiting for Beverly to notice me. When she did approach me, I expected a scolding, but I wasn't leaving until my questions got answered.

'Dr Webber.' Beverly pinched the skin at her throat and blinked her watering eyes. 'I was hoping I'd catch you before you left.'

Her remorseful tone made me pause. 'I know what you did,' I told her.

'I wanted to apologize for my part in your . . . your . . .'

'Mental breakdown? Egregious lapse in judgement?'

She winced at these phrases. 'The footage above the front door. I thought it was you who exited under the umbrella because you've done that before – I've seen you go out at night. So I asked Albert to keep an eye on you. He wasn't supposed to scare you, just follow you around a bit, see if you were up to anything suspect. I was paranoid; I shouldn't have asked him to spy on one of the staff. Albert saw you out gardening with Ezra the morning Kristin . . .'

'So I have an alibi?'

'I'm terribly sorry.'

This reluctant attempt at kindness didn't make me regret that things were ending this way. I was still furious about her call to the medical licensing board and still not assured that her apology didn't have some ulterior motive. Albert's stalking could have been to prevent me from finding out their hand in the murders; not because they suspected me.

'Years ago, were there ever, I don't know . . . dress-up days? For the students? Historical reenactments or something like that?'

Beverly seemed flummoxed by this abrupt shift in the conversation and my complete dismissal of her confession. 'I . . . yes.' She frowned thoughtfully. 'We used to do these reverse field trips because it was too much hassle to take the students somewhere. This traveling museum exhibition used to come through each spring, a covered wagon pulled by horses, full of frontier-life memorabilia. There was a trunk full of antique clothing the kids could put on and get their photo taken. We stopped years ago because one of the students had a fit and broke the exhibit's china dishes.'

I felt that I'd stepped into a labyrinth, following a dark, curling path, uncertain where it would lead me. I had a theory and no proof: the twins in the photo hadn't attended Hatchery back when it was a church; they'd been students here. At least one was still alive and had returned, hiding somewhere under our noses. The students hadn't been inventing ghost stories when they claimed someone roamed the halls at night, singing a ballad about death.

Dillon was watching me behind the pile of flowers, his body tense and his gaze warning, as if to say, *Think about what you're doing.* Seeing him at the distance, knowing what I knew now, I couldn't believe I'd ever been with him.

Beverly looked apprehensive. 'Why do you ask?'

'No reason. Have to pack.' I hurried toward Hatchery, with no intention to pack. Cedar and I had missed something; I had to find it.

It was an overcast day and the foyer felt artificially bright and cheerful when I entered it. Pausing by the coat rack, I touched soft wool, sleek nylon, fuzzy yarn, smooth cotton, jackets and scarves of all styles. I thought of Oksana telling me about the attack between the twins and James at Hatchery all those years ago. How she had tried to place the time of the attack by what her own children were wearing. *Bell bottoms, awful fringe vests.*

Frowning, I fingered the collar of someone's trench coat. Before the internet and fast fashion, clothing trends in the rural Plains had been about a decade behind the rest of the country. I'd noticed that back when I was a child, my secondhand clothing already several years old – but even if it were brand new, it didn't match anything in fashion magazines.

There was a dark undercurrent tugging at the edges of my thoughts. Oksana had mentioned those years blending together and her recurrent bouts as she called them; it would be understandable if she remembered the incident unclearly. It could have happened twenty years ago, instead of thirty, and that would widen the possible ages of the twins today.

I was about to go to my office to look up the attack's date and newspaper photos when I heard footsteps upstairs. Startled, I caught my reflection in the bell tower door's brass knob, warped and small.

A buzz of nerves and curiosity goaded me up the stairs. Midway, I heard a scrape and a clatter, a jangle of metal. I clasped the smooth railing and proceeded on.

The hall was dim; whoever had walked down it must have turned out the light. Weak sunlight poured through a small round window at the end of the hall, silhouetting a figure before they disappeared into the study room.

I followed, trying to swallow the knot in my throat. The walls seemed to be closing in around me. Long runners cushioned my footfall, and all was silent, except my breath, which seemed to ring out loudly in my ears.

Standing with my back to the wall, I peered around the edge of the doorframe. I could only make out the outlines of heavy antique furniture, a velvet chaise lounge, ornate drapes, a French armoire, a dresser with apothecary drawers, a desk with mahogany carved wood. No one was inside in the room, as far as I could see.

You can't leave now, I told myself. Not without Ezra.

I took a small step inside. Nothing was out of the ordinary, no one was hiding behind the door. Except one of the armoire's doors was open and a foot moved inside it.

I froze. It was massive and stretched across half the wall, large enough for a person to fit comfortably inside. Perhaps it'd been built inside this very room, someone carving a ram's head and vines at the top with a very small knife.

A few footsteps sounded, muffled, as though from behind a wall. Then the armoire filled with light, which spilled across the floor and touched my feet.

I tiptoed forward, crouched, and pushed the door open further. It creaked and my heart leapt to my throat. No one here, either. There was something at the back of the armoire that looked like a small trapdoor on hinges.

The light didn't shine from inside the armoire. It shone from the room beyond, which the armoire hid.

CHAPTER 45

When I had first met Helen, I'd paused outside her classroom as she told the students a ghost story. In a one-room schoolhouse not far from here, the teacher went insane and chopped off the students' heads and placed them on their desks. Then she cut out their hearts and dropped them over the bridge, where to this day, they beat in the water below, shuddering the planks and any traveler who dared walk across.

What's another word for insanity? Helen had asked the students.

Mad, someone had said.

Maybe she wasn't crazy at all, Helen had said. Maybe she was angry.

Helen was the type of woman you'd forget was in the room, so unassuming and polite. She laughed when people's jokes weren't funny, smiled so they felt accepted, moved aside in crowded rooms. She never seemed to expect anyone to return her excessive consideration. So, when she stepped out of the armoire, I didn't believe my eyes.

I was hidden in the opposite corner of the study room, tucked behind a leather armchair that smelled of old cheese and cigars. Even now, she seemed to fold in on herself, shoulders hunching forward, slightly stooping, as if she could make herself so small, she'd disappear. Her posture, an apology for taking up space.

She didn't look around as she left. Of course not; she hadn't felt eyes on her these last few days as I had; she wasn't as worried as she should be.

It wasn't actually her who killed Luis and Kristin; it couldn't be. She was hiding or helping someone else. There was no time to call Cedar, not if Ezra was in there needing help or if someone lurking wanted to escape. I couldn't miss this chance.

Pulling my flashlight from my pocket, I crept toward the armoire. My tongue had gone dry, my heart keeping its dashing rhythm. Smelling of cedar blocks and lavender satchels, the armoire yawned like a giant mouth and I climbed inside, slipping through the trapdoor into a black beyond.

The chamber was long and narrow, with thick stagnant air and a single lightbulb hanging from the ceiling. I didn't pull the cord; couldn't risk the light shining into the study room, revealing where I was. Sweeping my flashlight into each corner, along the floor and across the walls, I didn't see another person.

Most of the objects dated back to when Hatchery had been a church and convent: stacked hymnals in a corner, a pile of nuns' habits on a pew, candlesticks and collection plates and Bibles, a broken butter churner, an icebox with a smiley face drawn in dust. A bell's tongue lay on a tattered rug with a design of tangled, forked vines.

This room had the original stone walls and the armoire had been placed in front of the doorless door-frame, hiding it completely. I wondered if Beverly even knew about this room, if in the chaos of the renovation it'd been intended as a storage room but had been concealed and forgotten. The wood floor moaned from my footfall, and my breath hitched.

At the far end, a dresser emerged from the shadows, holding a framed photograph. Identical twins stared back at me. Their hair was in a short, boyish style, but the faces were unmistakably recognizable. Perhaps around the age of eight, here was Helen's soft jawline and deep-set green eyes, the wide cheekbones and pale, arched eyebrows.

The personal history in her medical file was a lie. Or at least some of it was; she'd never told me about a twin. This wasn't a hideaway for someone else; it was her personal refuge, a lair. The twins of Ezra's photos weren't the ancestors of Oksana's story. They were the same people, and Helen was one of them.

Helen had been a student at Hatchery. But I spoke to her mother and she hadn't mentioned . . .

I beat back a surge of nausea, swaying slightly. The phone call had been short and brisk, made between appointments. I'd introduced myself as Helen's psychiatrist at Hatchery, and Mrs Lewis had sounded a bit stunned, confused, but had seemingly recovered and answered a few questions. She appeared to want to get off the phone quickly and this was a relief, since I was behind on notes. She must have assumed I knew Helen's history, including her time as a student at Hatchery, since I worked with and treated her. So she hadn't mentioned it.

Opening one of the drawers, I rifled through mail and old newspaper clippings. Several empty envelopes were addressed to an Agatha Lewis in Augustine, from electric and internet companies.

Another was from a real estate agent. Perhaps she kept a home for an alternate identity, I thought. Or – I glanced at the photograph – it could be for this secret sister.

The other letters were from former students asking for money from the foundation, as if mistakenly thinking that Hatchery had a mainline to Howard's finances: *I lost my job at the plant and was wondering if I could get some help. Not sure where to turn.*

The newspaper clippings detailed crimes, trials, and sentences: *Randolf was convicted of burglary and sentenced to five years minimum in a state facility.* Among these, an article announced the passing of artist and former student James Sevelt: *Inmate committed suicide at Wardburn facility yesterday after a prolonged breakdown . . .*

My grip tightened on the edge of the drawer, heat building in my chest, sending a trickle of sweat down my back. This was a collection, memorabilia of other people's failures. Helen returned here again and again, softening paper with her repeated readings, the way you polished silver until your reflection shone clear and bright in its curved surfaces.

The night of Luis's death, I'd knelt before the chest in the lounge and sought comfort in the words of strangers, their blissful stories of jobs and marriages, graduations and births. I knew they were snapshots; I knew they didn't convey the hardship, but those moments were still small victories. I hadn't questioned why there weren't other kinds of letters; I figured Beverly had responded to them or students mostly wrote with good news. How naïve of me, caught up in what I wanted to be true. Helen must have removed it from the mail, hoarding it like stamps or coins. I wanted a reminder that these students could lead rich, full lives. Helen wanted assurance that not all of them would.

My mind spun, trying to knit this together with the Helen I knew. I'd caught glimpses of scorn or impatience or animosity, but had dismissed it as frustration or fatigue, a natural reaction to dealing with difficult students. I myself just this morning had smacked Owen across the face, something far worse than I'd ever witnessed Helen do.

Opening the second drawer, I pulled out a small box with a charcoal scrawl across the lid: *extra bell tower key*. It was empty.

I had a thought I should have had earlier: Beverly kept the students' time structured in the evenings with chores and appointments. To escort them up the bell tower for the drug trial, Dillon would have had to take them out of class. Perhaps he told Helen he wanted more research space and she thought giving him the key would please him. Perhaps she knew more about what he was doing; perhaps not. My jaw clenched; my teeth ached.

An old, leather-bound book sat in the bottom of the drawer. It contained rows of deposits and withdrawals, dates that went back to 1889. On a back page, various combinations to the bank safe in Ennenock were written in neat, cursive penmanship. The last one was the one Cedar had needed, back before Kristin had been led inside and killed between those metal, near-empty shelves.

My hands trembled as I replaced everything. Laughter from another room startled me. I took a step backwards and stumbled against the broken butter churner, which toppled, crashing against the floor.

Hand over my mouth, I froze, waiting, hoping against hope that no one had heard. At my feet, a plaid blanket and pillow lay in a dirty heap. A little nest for a sleeping child.

Last night, when we'd lost electricity and Ezra disappeared; she'd taken him here. That's why we couldn't find him.

A small black box was half burrowed in the bedding. Picking it up, I saw it was an empty case for a revolver.

CHAPTER 46

Helen was gone, the door to her apartment wide open. I'd exited the secret chamber with an envelope to Agatha Lewis stuffed in my jacket pocket. Back in my apartment, I used my landline to ring Cedar, but it went to voicemail; I left a long, rambling message about my discoveries, pausing before I was cut off, wanting to apologize, but decided to save it until I could see him. Instead, I left Agatha's address, telling him where to find me. I'd gotten the collateral wrong with Mrs Lewis. I needed to do better this time.

My car boiled with mid-afternoon heat as I pulled up in front of a quaint one-and-a-half story that glowered amid freshly cut grass. The house had a concrete porch, an old oak in the front yard and plastic shutters framing two front windows. The siding had been painted a bright yellow recently and I wondered if Helen had been the one to paint it. Helen's car was not in the driveway.

Perhaps there was a basement to this house; perhaps that's where Ezra was moved after being sedated in that dusty lair of a mausoleum. I surveyed the outside first, knowing Cedar wouldn't be happy about this. *You can't go on the field*, he'd say, kneading his eyes with his knuckles, as if trying to push irritation back inside his body.

A fence obscured a small backyard with lawn chairs, a garden, and a watering can tipped on its side in the grass. I peeked through a small window in the garage, where a brown sedan sat in the dark.

Sunlight painted the insides of my eyelids red when I squeezed them shut, trying to compose myself, rehearsing my story. I knocked on the front door.

A woman with an eye patch opened the door. She stood there, holding the handle, not saying anything, waiting and watching me.

'Hello. Are you Agatha Lewis?' I asked.

Unlike the old photograph, she no longer looked identical to Helen; life had treated them differently and their bodies bore that. Agatha carried more weight than Helen. She was paunchy around her face, as if she battled constant low-grade inflammation, and her gaze seemed distant. I'd seen this before with patients taking strong medications.

'I am,' she said.

'Is – is Helen here?' I asked.

She didn't look surprised that I'd asked. 'Not right now,' she said.

'Can I come in? I'm Helen's friend.'

'I didn't know Helen had friends,' she said with the placidity of a glacier.

'Well, I'm Dr Lorelei Webber, her physician. She's . . . she's been having these mood swings and I thought I'd talk to her family. See if we can get to the bottom of it.'

Agatha frowned at this. 'She's always had those. I haven't heard of you.'

I searched for something that would bolster my claims. 'Just – just today in our appointment, she was humming that song, you know . . .' I hummed a few beats of the ballad that haunted the students at night.

Recognition sparked in Agatha's face. 'She used to sing that all the time when we were kids. A doctor at Hatchery introduced her to it years ago.'

I gestured to go inside, and Agatha shuffled out of the way, not quite inviting me in, but not stopping me either. The odors of vinegar and stale air gave the house a cloistered atmosphere. The entire drive I feared a stone-faced woman who'd slam the door in my face, so I was relieved she was passive and docile. She wore a lemon-colored cardigan over an electric-blue T-shirt and body odor wafted around her. Her hair was dark with oil at the roots; I guessed she bathed only once a week.

The entryway led into a small living room with an adjacent kitchen, where windows overlooked the garden. Brightly painted birdhouses clustered on the kitchen table next to a vase of dead flowers. A note was attached to the bouquet: *My life wouldn't be the same without you.*

'Did Helen get these for you?'

'No, she always buys herself Mother's Day flowers. She doesn't like me to throw them out.' Agatha pointed to several vases of dead flowers that lined the fireplace mantel.

I sat in a hardbacked chair while Agatha ignored me and fussed with rearranging the couch cushions. Small porcelain figurines on the windowsill, gold-framed photographs and an antique television all gave the impression of someone who had retired from life.

'So, like I said, sometimes I talk to patients' family members to get a more complete picture,' I said.

The word *family* made Agatha stiffen, as if I'd brandished a weapon. She kept her face down as she fidgeted with a doily, running her finger over its scalloped edge. I didn't mention that when I collected collateral, it was typically only by phone, not drop-in visits, but Agatha did not seem perturbed by the odd protocol.

'Let's start with your parents—' I said.

'I'm chatty when I'm nervous. Helen always tells me to stop talking so much.'

I shook my head. 'I don't mind chattiness. You tell me what you're comfortable with.'

She repeatedly brushed the sides of her face as though to push back hair, even though it remained tucked behind her ears. Her high, yet controlled anxiety put me at ease; I leaned forward, coaxing her on as she told me about how their mother had worked as a cleaner at a local hotel in a small town several hours south of Hatchery. They'd never known their father but were close to each other, inventing games and stories.

'Helen liked to tell people we could talk to their dead relatives for a dime. We made three whole dollars off Mrs Ingraham down the street. I believed her for a time, thought she really could reach the afterlife. But later, after we grew older, it was only me who heard voices.'

'Why were you and Helen sent to Hatchery?' I asked.

She petted her hair the way one strokes a dog behind the ears and shook her head. Her blunt affect did not waver through all of this, no emotion crossing her face, her voice remaining flat.

'Helen always said I was trouble, and once my mama lost her job and got sick, I was too much. So I got sent away but didn't do well without Helen. I . . . I felt like I was dead without her.'

She said the word *trouble* as though it belonged in someone else's mouth, parroting a word she'd been called many times before. I suspected she had become comatose at Hatchery, nonresponsive in a new environment without her sibling. I kept silent, coaxing her to go on with an encouraging smile.

'So they sent Helen to live with me. I was so excited, but Helen . . . she was not. She didn't like the clothes they gave us, the food, the schedule. She was furious when they cut our hair short during the lice infestation. Said our hair had been the one thing that made us pretty. And I'm sure she's told you about the attack—' Agatha gestured to her eye patch. 'That's why she won't take anything now, not even vitamins.'

'Because someone gave her a medication that didn't help her?'

'Made her worse. Helen always said it was a trick. An experiment on her, like a lab rat.'

'Why did she return to Hatchery if she disliked it so much?'

She squinted into the past. 'Helen said: "They never saw me for who I am. They need to be taught a lesson."' Seeming eager to clarify this for me, Agatha added, 'She is a teacher.'

This memory seemed to make her agitated and she began twisting her fingers. Fearing losing her, I switched subjects.

'Are you still in touch with your mother?'

Agatha frowned. 'She's dead. Died back when we were teens in a car accident.'

This gave me a jolt. When I'd spoken to her, I'd assumed Mrs Lewis was Helen's biological mother, who'd raised her since birth, across the South Dakota border. But she must have been a foster parent.

'Do you have any other relatives? Anyone in your family who shares your last name?'

'Lewis isn't my last name. Well, not the one I was born with. Helen wanted us to take on our foster parents' names; she thought it'd make us more part of their family, but it didn't.'

'How long did you live with them?'

Agatha's responses were becoming disjointed and bewildering, skipping through timelines, people, and places without connections. I did gather that the Lewises had a wheat farm in South Dakota and had fostered other children over the years. They hadn't liked how Helen would wander the house at night, claiming she had insomnia, when actually she seemed to be spying on them while they were sleeping. The Lewises arranged for them to leave after an incident with a dairy cow.

'I don't know what happened. Mr Lewis shot it and didn't like Helen being around. Apparently, she touched the hole where the bullet went in, got blood on her, fingerpainted with it.' A preoccupied expression creased her brows. 'Helen liked the farm, liked animals. She'd always recited that poem about death riding the horse, stopping for someone.' Agatha snagged me with a sharp glare, as if just now noticing I was there. 'Helen doesn't like when people talk about her.'

I held up my hands in a gesture of acquiescence. 'We're all done; that was helpful, thank you. Can I use your restroom before I leave?'

*

Two prescription bottles sat in the medical cabinet, but only one had a pharmacy label.

Helen Lewis. Risperidone, 6mg. Prescribed by Dr Dillon Edwards.

Ever since Agatha had opened the door, I'd wagered she had schizoaffective disorder, the far more common diagnosis for someone prescribed Risperidone. Helen had been faking a bipolar disorder for the prescription.

The other orange bottle had been labeled in Helen's handwriting: *midazolam, 1mg*. The sedative I'd been drugged with, probably the same one used on Ezra, Luis, and Kristin. Perhaps she'd helped him more with the drug trial than I'd thought and had access to his medical cabinet, stealing these one by one, hoping he wouldn't notice. And even if he did suspect the theft, he might not want to report her and risk his research.

Leaning against the sink, I massaged my temples, trying to think straight. I'd hardly slept at all in the last few days, and my joints ached, my limbs leaden and heavy. At the edge of the white shower curtain, the tip of a brown crayon was visible, lying at the tub's corner. I swiped the curtain open.

The drawing of a bison stretched across the white tile.

I remembered the way his thin legs had dangled over the cliff's edge, the velvet thickness of their fur, the way we peered down at them like descendants before a chest of heirlooms, hoping to find ourselves.

It broke me a bit. Ezra was talking to me.

CHAPTER 47

Agatha stood at the window overlooking the garden, white-knuckling a coffee mug. 'My mama used to bury my baby teeth. Said they'd sprout flowers.'

The image of children in the ground, their bodies fertilizing the soil, darted past me. Adrenaline was overtaking my fatigue, sending a buzz to my fingertips.

'Agatha,' I said. 'I know Helen has brought a student from Hatchery here. I need to know where he is now.'

'No children here,' she announced and tilted her chin up, pretending to be strong. I knew that gesture because I'd lived by it.

An ache settled in my chest. 'Please tell me where he is.'

Coffee sloshed over her mug's rim and splashed on the kitchen tiles as Agatha took a step backwards, hair tossing around her blanched face. 'Helen told me I was just seeing and hearing things. Sometimes I don't know what's happening. I think I do but I don't.'

'I need to find him, Agatha,' I said gently.

'Helen said you are not her friend, not one bit her friend.' Agatha nodded vehemently, reminding me of how Helen always seemed to be agreeing with herself.

This stopped me in my tracks. 'She's here?'

'I called Helen to tell her her doctor was here and she wasn't very happy about it. But then she said it didn't matter. Everything was going to be over soon anyway. She said that in the *quiet voice*.'

This seemed to fill Agatha with despair, and she opened a kitchen cabinet, then slammed it shut. She did it with another and another, head rolling, face crumpled. 'Helen has always taken care of me. She has always helped me.'

I wanted to assure her that she wasn't betraying the sister who'd cared for her all these years, but I couldn't make myself lie to her. Agatha ripped her hand through her hair, clawing her scalp and moaning. She was gasping now, and I knew she'd hyperventilate or hurt herself if I didn't calm her down.

I couldn't stand tongue-tied any longer. Dashing into the bathroom, fumbling in the medical cabinet, I broke a midazolam in two. When I returned to the kitchen, her eye was too wide, her face red, as she kicked over each chair. A birdhouse, intricately painted with yellow flowers, tumbled to the floor, its roof splintering.

'Agatha,' I said gently. 'Agatha, I need you to take this.' My tone reminded me of how Cedar sometimes talked to me, repeating my name like it was a spell he could cast me back into.

She swiped at my outstretched hand and I recoiled before the pill went flying from my palm.

Tears were streaming down her face and her knees buckled as she collapsed to the floor. I dropped on the floor next to her and squeezed the joint of her jaw until her mouth popped open. She cried out as I pressed the pill against her tongue and clamped her jaw shut.

Twenty minutes passed with us on the kitchen floor, the clock's ticking loud and insistent against my racing mind. Body growing limp, she rested her chin on her knees, eyes closed, hair tucked behind her ears. I sat close to her, monitoring her breathing, making sure she wouldn't have an adverse reaction.

I guessed it wasn't only the drug that calmed her; this process seemed to be familiar to her. How many times had Helen done the same thing? Bearing down on her with force, making her feel better.

Small red pricks of blood flecked the inside of her ears and the eyelid her patch did not cover. Petechiae. Caused when blood vessels in the skin rupture from pressure, often seen in cases of strangulation. So this was why Helen faked a bipolar diagnosis to get Agatha's medication: she didn't want to risk a doctor seeing these signs of abuse.

I bit my lip until I tasted blood. This was what I hated about forensics. You thought you were going forward, when really you moved backwards in time, finding new victims at earlier dates. The case you worked on was just the crime that was discovered, not the first committed.

I tucked Agatha into her bed before I left the house. She was sluggish and polite, wanting the covers all the way up to her chin. I didn't deserve to be near her: she wasn't my sister; she wasn't my patient. Yet I still completed the ritual Helen had begun, cracking the door the way a near-sleeping child requests.

In my car, I tried to gather myself together, hands trembling on the steering wheel. A neighbor slammed her front door and I jumped. A child playing hopscotch was called in to supper, for

315

heads to be bowed over pork and potatoes before the bath-time march. Suburbia had become a radio turned down low, only a fuzz of noise between square lawns.

I still hadn't heard back from Cedar and swore at my phone. Helen had Ezra somewhere else.

Think, think.

I thought of how she must have baited Luis and Kristin away from Hatchery. When she lured them away, they must have believed she'd had their best intentions at heart. Perhaps a goodbye gift, a special surprise.

What was it she said about Ennenock? *A city of ghosts, holding so many souls.*

Fire and brimstone, cities of the plain, Sodom and Gomorrah, tale of divine retribution for an unholy place. She'd killed there before; she'd do it again. If she took Ezra anywhere, she took him there.

A knock sounded on my window; my phone flew into the passenger seat. Startled, I blinked at Cedar before opening my door.

'What the hell are you doing?' he asked.

I'd never been so relieved to see him. 'Did you—'

'I got your message as I was driving into town for a press conference. I came straight here instead. You can't be on the field—'

'We don't have time,' I said, walking toward his car. 'She kept Ezra here, at her sister's, during the search around Hatchery. I think she's taken him to Ennenock. Are the techs still there?'

'They've packed up for the evening. We can scout it out but we're not doing anything until backup arrives.'

I buckled myself in. Cedar called Sheriff Anders and swore when he heard he was still two hours south after investigating the dead-end APB. The neighboring police force promised to dispatch an officer our way soon.

I filled him in on everything I'd learned from Agatha as he drove. He was quiet, except for a few follow-up questions, and tension hung in the air between us until we turned off the highway on to the dirt road ending at Ennenock. Helen's car was still in Hatchery's parking lot.

'I'm sorry about earlier,' I said.

He tossed a dark look my way and I chewed on a thumbnail as I scanned the road. My nerves were splintering again.

'Why can't you accept my apology?' I demanded.

'I don't want to,' he said. 'I'm the one who asked you to get involved.'

'You don't get to determine the validity of my apology.'

We jolted and bumped along, deep fissures catching the tires, the car's underbelly thudding so hard against packed earth, I thought the axle would break. Grass grew in clumps along the middle of the road and dust billowed behind us.

'Where do you think she is?' Cedar asked.

'Not the hotel or bank. She'll choose somewhere else. Maybe one of the buildings burned and rotted by that fire? With all that charred wood and debris, it'd be easier to hide someone, and she might think people wouldn't search it as closely.'

The car's back wheels hit a soft patch of dirt as we hit a pothole; we fishtailed, lurched sideways, the car tipping toward the ditch. We skidded to a stop at a tilt. The hanging tree loomed before us, leaves still young and half curled at the tips of branches.

'Let's go the rest of the way on foot,' Cedar said. 'Will be quieter.'

Climbing out, we started jogging. When the town hall came into view, wedged between the graveyard and bank, I grabbed Cedar's arm and pointed. Tied up at the hitching post, Oksana's horse stood calmly, black tail whirling to ward off flies.

'Just keep behind me,' Cedar whispered, once we got closer.

'We should each take a side,' I said. It was how they did it on the field; canvas the exterior before moving inward. It was foolish to go in blind. The horse twisted its head, fixing us with an unblinking black eye.

I could see Cedar's desire to reach out in the stillness of his body; the only time his arms hung at his sides was when he was wanting to yank something closer. But he resisted, swallowed, and nodded.

'Check all exits and entrances,' he said. 'You stay behind the Osage orange, head for the back of the building. We'll stake the place out until backup arrives.'

We separated; him with his palm on his holster, and my hands empty. The thicket of twisted branches and thorns formed a hedge stretching alongside the town hall. I almost tripped over a headstone, catching myself against a rotted fence almost felled by twisting grapevines. A nearby metal windmill screeched from the patchy breeze. Blood pulsed in my ears; I wanted to be able to see Cedar even if we were separated, let him anchor me.

A dragonfly buzzed past my ear, its blue torso iridescent and bright, and I flinched. Shards of glass flashed in the windows, obscuring dusky rooms still as caves with sleeping bats. The wallpaper had been bleached by the sun, ladies in a lemon grove dulled to sepia tones, interrupted only by a grandfather clock with a broken face.

A curtain swayed and I halted, squinting hard, trying to sort the shadows from one another. There was a clatter, the sound of knocking on wood. Breath fixed in my throat. Was it from inside the town hall? Footfall on old floors?

Up ahead, a low red sun hung next to a one-room schoolhouse, sod houses and shacks scattered beyond. The back door to the town hall hung slightly ajar. I crept forward, following the Osage orange.

An outhouse came into view. There was a creak and a scrape. Helen had wrenched open the outhouse's door and now stared within, one hand paused on the handle, the other holding a gun.

CHAPTER 48

Sunlight burst through the door's crescent moon. Gone were Helen's translucent blouses and fitted slacks; she now wore lace-up hiking boots and a fleece pullover and jeans, dressed seemingly for a long trail ride.

I clutched fistfuls of grass to keep myself from lunging toward them. I couldn't make out what she was saying but her voice, brusque and impatient, was also coaxing. As though she pitied him, yet that wouldn't persuade her to relent. Her tolerance must have worn thin, because she reached forward and yanked him out. He stumbled, gagged with a dirty cloth, hands tied in front; I realized the sound I'd heard had been him pounding from inside the outhouse, the noise muffled by distance. If I'd arrived sooner, or hurried down the hedge, maybe I'd have heard him before Helen had tethered Oksana's horse at the post.

'Move along. Want to be at the homestead before nightfall,' she said. She swept a dead leaf from his hair in a maternal gesture. 'I had to check a few things before we left, but now we're ready. The investigators made a complete mess of the bank and hotel.' She seemed insulted by this, a frown creasing her young face.

Ezra glared at her defiantly as she tugged him toward the open back door. A river of half-dried urine snaked down his pant leg. When I'd found him at the homestead, he'd looked wild, but now he looked captive and filthy in a way that frightened me more.

I spotted Cedar watching them from behind the corner of the town hall; I guessed he couldn't see me, shrouded by knotted branches. Why wasn't he training his revolver on her, commanding her to stop? I hoped against hope we could convince her to let Ezra go, tell her to escape alone. I'd gone lightheaded, waiting for him to move. Helen and Ezra's feet swished the grass, shadows shuddering after them.

Fog was rolling in, clouding the dying light, and they were becoming fuzzy and smaller. We couldn't let them out of our sight. Time began to feel like an empty hallway, expanding on and on, lengthening and never ending.

I scrambled out from under the low branches and Helen whirled around, her gun trembling, pointed at me. I held my hands up and took another step toward them.

'Stop or I'll shoot,' Helen said.

'Just let Ezra go. You can escape; just leave Ezra here.'

When she didn't respond, frozen with either calculation or indecision, I dared another step forward. The gun shook harder as Helen cocked it, her thumb clumsy, knuckles spasming. Out of the corner of my eye, I saw Cedar inching around the corner, coming toward us silently, his own gun steady.

I knew several things at once. Cedar was probably inwardly cursing me for coming out of hiding. Ezra was good at playing brave, but his reserve wouldn't last much longer. He might not cower in fear, but he'd dash away as he had so many times before, giving Helen a chance to send a bullet into his back. Holding her gaze across the thistle-strewn grass, I knew I'd hoped in vain: she wasn't going to let him go willingly.

Helen must have sensed Cedar, because she whirled toward him, jerking Ezra with her. A pit opened in my stomach; panic echoed within. Everyone was slipping away from me.

Something changed in Cedar's face: it registered understanding, then alarm. His body tilted toward the town hall. Helen fired at him and he dove, bullet blasting into plank siding. He scrambled behind the corner as I stumbled backwards. I was ready to duck behind the outhouse when I realized Helen wasn't aiming at me. She'd run for the back door, dragging Ezra with her, and disappeared.

It didn't feel like a choice, though that was what it was. Stepping over the threshold, entering the near dark of an abandoned building. Some choices seem like things that have already happened; you discover them like misplaced objects, thinking, oh yes, of course it had been here all this time. It could never be any other way.

Cedar was worried about me.

'I don't want you going in alone if something happens,' I said.

'Just stay behind me,' he said.

So, in we went. Ezra's terror seared my mind, and under it, I felt astonishment that fear could run so deep that it became its own kind of pain.

A long hallway stretched the length of the building, ending in the front foyer. On the right was the courtroom, filled with benches, and on the left were offices, littered with debris. We paused next to a doorless room, where an old spinning wheel turned, spokes blurring. Ezra must have touched it as he passed, leaving us breadcrumbs. Cedar scanned the entryway, kept his back to the wall, and darted in.

No one was inside. The room held remnants of a tailor and carpenter's shop: carved spindles, sawhorses, wagon wheels, wood and bolts of fabric, bottles of varnish and needles in tiny pincushions. Dust covered everything, rendering it soft and ghostlike.

The wall separating this office and the next had a giant hole, almost four feet wide and five feet tall. I tilted my head toward it and Cedar nodded. We slipped along the adjacent wall, eyes on the hole and the slowly rotating view of the other room, from where, between pauses in birdsong, I could hear breathing. Plaster cracked away from the jagged edge, revealing wood lath splintered in tiny, uneven teeth, and our boots crushed broken glass. My pulse thrummed faster and faster.

'Tonight, tonight, my plans I make, tomorrow, tomorrow, the baby I take,' Helen sang out.

We needed to see what she was doing in there. Cedar's spine was rigid, gun held close to his chest, as he leaned toward the hole. He pulled back behind the safety of our wall, moving his hand over his chest, mouthing *Ezra* to indicate Helen held him as a shield in front of her.

'Let's put our guns down and talk,' Cedar called out.

Silence grew heavy on our shoulders. I knew her; I could negotiate better with her. *I'll go*, I mouthed to Cedar, trying to step past him toward the hole. He snatched my arm and pulled me back, shaking his head. Dust swirled about our feet like eddies of displaced water.

'I can tell you're upset but I think we can work this out,' Cedar called out.

When she still didn't respond, I worried she'd left the room noiselessly and taken Ezra with her. Exchanging a look with me, Cedar curled his upper body around the edge; a swallow flew into our room through a broken window.

Time stretched thin and taut. Dazed at its new surroundings, the bird thrashed and wobbled toward us, lurching through the hole as though it were a doorway back into the outside world.

Helen's startled shriek. A gunshot's piercing crack.

Cedar jolted and cried out, crumpling to the floor while bullets punctured the wall behind us. My teeth shook in their sockets; my ears rang. I found myself on my knees, scrambling toward him. Distantly, I heard the thud of the bird smashing into a wall and footsteps pounding down the hall.

Blood poured from his shoulder. I grabbed a bolt of cloth, the board thumping with each roll until the fabric released. Pressing it against the wound, I bore down on it with all my weight. He moaned and writhed under my hands.

I had to save him. Pictures of the shoulder, its two main arteries and a nerve bundle, from anatomy textbooks, flashed through my mind. If mangled by a bullet, the blasted nerve bundle would lead to numbness, then loss of mobility in the arm. If the arteries were severed, blood loss would lead to death. A widening between my ears made me lean to the side and place a palm on the ground, fighting back dizziness. Straightening and swallowing, I told myself that wasn't going to happen.

I fumbled with my phone. No reception. I had to get him to

Hatchery, use the landline to call a helicopter from Omaha, get him lifted to the closest trauma center.

The calico fabric soaked through, leaving a gamy, metallic odor, and my hands grew slicker by the second. There was a pebble in my brain, an insistent voice commanding me to think again.

At Hatchery, Dillon would stand over Cedar, flabbergasted, while Beverly buzzed around behind, a cluster of indecision and handwringing. Oksana had been a combat nurse in Vietnam. She'd tended to trauma wounds before, even if it were decades ago. I didn't know if anything could be done to stabilize Cedar before the helicopter arrived, but if there was, Oksana would know.

CHAPTER 49

A flush of violet lingering near the horizon was pulled under. Oksana flung her door open once we reached the porch steps.

'C'mon now,' she muttered, as though I were dawdling.

Her kitchen table wasn't large enough, so we hustled him to her bed, a rickety iron-framed twin with a sagging mattress. I was surprised Cedar hadn't lost consciousness on the drive and told Oksana what happened while she cut the fabric away.

As I turned to find the landline, she grasped my wrist. 'That teacher – the blond one – took Adrik, my horse. I called you but no one picked up.'

A sea-foam-green phone hung on the wall next to the kitchen.

'It'll be at least two hours,' the operator told me after I gave them our location and Cedar's stats.

Hurry, hurry, I thought, squeezing my eyes shut. Re-entering the bedroom, I told Oksana and Cedar the helicopter was on its way.

She had pulled back all the soaked fabric and was peering at the wound. 'Good you were with him. Blood loss normally the biggest problem, but you got pressure on him fast. He's fairly stable. Bullet maybe came out the back.' She pointed to a chest at the foot of her bed. 'Clean bed sheet. Scissors in kitchen drawer next to sink. Gauze rolls in bathroom cabinet. Bring them to me, then put water on to boil.'

I hurried to do her bidding and when I returned after lighting the stove, she had cut two long strips from the bed sheet.

She waved me to come closer. 'Help me lift him.'

We rolled him on to his side, so she could press gauze against the exit wound. When she knotted the dressings tightly, Cedar lifted his chin and gritted his teeth, eyes screwed shut against the pain. Once the bandages were secure, we pushed pillows against his back, so his wounded shoulder stayed higher than his heart.

'Lore,' he whispered.

I sat down, taking his hand in mine. 'It's going to be okay. It'll be a bit of a wait, but they'll get you lifted to the trauma center—'

'It doesn't hurt like it should. My whole arm feels numb.' His voice was knotted and hoarse, his pupils so dilated, I felt as though I could fall into them.

'You haven't been shot before,' I told him sternly. 'You don't know how it's supposed to hurt.'

He started to laugh and I broke into a smile, but then he winced in pain and my chest went hard again. Glaring at me, Oksana grabbed a quilt from the top of the chest and spread it over him.

Outside, a gust slammed the barn door shut. Silence hung so thick in the room, it felt suffocating. I was desperate to get him something, to help somehow.

'Think you can sip some liquid?' I asked him. 'Keep your blood pressure up?'

'No water,' Oksana snapped. 'Body's in shock; don't stress it more.'

She beckoned me to follow her into the kitchen. Hesitant to leave his side, I reluctantly obeyed.

'Don't fiddle; waiting is best. Nothing else to do.' Her eyes narrowed on me; brow knitted in frustration. 'You should go.'

This sent me into a panic. Of course, she wouldn't want me in her house after my insinuations in the cellar. 'Please. I'm sorry about before. I can't leave him alone. I was out of my mind, I wasn't thinking straight, I'm sorry—'

She waved her hands back and forth impatiently. 'That boy. Sveta already has her saddle and bit on. Before you came, I was going to ride out myself, hunt them down. Now you go.'

I felt halved, wanting to go and to stay. Through the open doorway, I could see only Cedar's feet and legs covered by the quilt, and a set of Russian nesting dolls staring back at me from atop a dresser. If Cedar died alone in a stranger's house . . . I didn't know if I'd survive that.

She seemed to read my thoughts. 'He's stable,' she repeated. 'May lose the arm, but I'd bet on him coming through.'

They could be anywhere. I didn't have a chance of finding them. But it came to me, swiping aside these excuses: the homestead. By the outhouse, that's where she said she was taking him – back to the place he'd escaped, the haven where he'd thwarted her, so she could finish things.

It'd been years, but I'd once been good with horses. It would be faster to ride across the prairie as a crow would fly instead of zigzagging along country roads.

Oksana had already lifted her rifle from above the fireplace mantel, the same gun she'd pointed at me when I'd knocked on her door that first time. It was heavier than it looked; I wasn't accustomed to so much metal.

'The chamber holds only one at a time,' she said, handing me a small box of cartridges. 'You know how to load a gun?'

I nodded. I'd shot revolvers in a shooting gallery with colleagues from the bureau and given them a good laugh, often missing the paper target completely. On a hunting trip with Cedar and his brothers years ago, I'd shot a rifle a few times. I was better with a scope.

Back in medical school, my cadaver in gross anatomy had been a gunshot victim. The bullet had torpedoed through his abdomen, spinning like a rototiller through his stomach and intestines, pulverizing the organs. A rib bone had shattered, shards shredding the liver and kidneys.

Like Humpty Dumpty, a classmate had said. No chance to put him back together.

Never thought I could hold a gun, intending to do that to another person. Turn their insides into a war zone.

Beating back a wave of nausea, I stuffed the box of cartridges in my jacket pocket. Oksana patted my shoulder, her gnarled hand unexpectedly soothing. Her expression was tender and sad, as though she didn't believe this night could end well.

I stepped into the bedroom to say goodbye to Cedar.

'Lore, don't you dare—' he started, trying to pull himself up to sitting, beads of sweat trailing down his face.

'Oksana will radio Sheriff Anders. He'll meet me at the homestead. We'll probably both arrive at the same time.'

'He's still too far out. Don't—'

I squeezed his hand one last time. The terror of possibly not seeing him again almost swallowed me whole.

I could think only of the summer we'd worked detasseling corn, the humidity drenching us in sweat, bugs caught in our hair. He snuck into my row, scared me shitless with a pinch, and I pretended to be annoyed. Husks rustled around our faces when he took my hips and pulled me closer, stalks not yet above our heads. He smelled like kernels and sun-warmed soil, gold only the earth could give.

Hatchery loomed to the north, blue in the dusk, stone walls forbidding and bleak while I rode westward, toward the rickety old bridge over the Niobrara. Fog was drifting across its brown water and the cottonwoods were still shaking off winter's chill, making me worried about finding the homestead. Stars began to glint above with the vibrance of gold dust flung into an oil spill.

The rifle bumped against my back, its strap cutting into the side of my neck as Sveta's hooves thudded in a steady rhythm. I smelled wood smoke before I saw the fire. We crested a hill, and then, like a beacon in the night, there they were, silhouettes before the river, tossed into shape by flames.

CHAPTER 50

When I dismounted, Helen held me at gunpoint until I obeyed her command to sit with them by the fire. Rough bark scratched my palms as I sat on a fallen log. No turning back now. *Set your face like flint.* It was a saying Cedar's mother had framed in her house and I felt that now, finally, I understood it, understood what she must have known for years.

Dead wood was ablaze on a small mound of sand, flickering precariously close to dry grass. Ezra sat cross-legged, his face glowing in shades of saffron and amber, hands in his lap, no longer bound. This concerned me more than if he'd still been shackled.

'Ezra? Are you okay?' I called out.

She stepped in front of him, blocking my view. 'You'll speak to me,' she said.

The desire to snatch him away crooned in me with a terrible hunger. The horses grazed nearby, languid and oblivious. I wasn't sure if I could mount one with Ezra quickly enough to flee. If the fog grew thicker, the moonlight would no longer be bright enough to aim by.

The river churned about twenty feet away, framed by steep

331

ridges with a smattering of cottonwoods and pines. It curved like a scythe and we were in its hollow middle. The old bridge was at the bottom, about fifty feet away. We could run for it, but the ravine was closer. We could leap from it into the dark water below, but I didn't know if Ezra could swim or if I were strong enough to keep us both afloat. Or if we'd survive the impact – the drop was around thirty feet. And if we did make it, Helen could aim at us from above, shooting us like fish in a barrel.

She must have noticed my calculations because she lifted her gun to the sky. Ezra and I flinched from the deafening crack as it ricocheted between the hills. The horses dashed off, their hooves rumbling, sending tremors to my bones.

'You run across that bridge, I will hunt you down.' She held up a police scanner. 'Reports that old sheriff is heading to the homestead, so we wanted to catch you first for a little farewell.'

A gust blasted over the dunes and scoured my skin with sand as I tried to gather myself together. Get her talking, talk your way out of this.

'If you leave now, you could disappear. No one will find you,' I said. 'Just let me take Ezra and go.'

'Why not execute the two of you and then disappear?'

I had hoped to find her scared, to see a desire for survival in her eyes. But she was cold and resolute; she'd evidently accepted this was where it would all end.

'Back in March, why did you drop him off in the prairie?' I asked, trying to redirect her.

'All I've ever wanted is to get out of this godforsaken place and have a real life. Instead I'm stuck here with crazy people. And him—' She gestured to Ezra, who glowered back at her. 'He doesn't respect me at all, never has. He stole my favorite photo of Agatha and I from my office desk, sneaking around where he shouldn't be. Thinks he can do whatever he wants and run off. Wouldn't even respond when I'd ask him a question.'

'He's mute.'

'He could talk if he wanted to. He doesn't make an effort.'

I wondered if he'd witnessed something he shouldn't have, overheard her talking to Agatha on the phone, or saw her taking students to the bell tower. Whatever it had been, he was someone who defied her control.

'Why did you even return?' I asked. 'If you hate it so much? No one forced you to come back.'

Helen sneered at this. 'When I interviewed with Beverly, I waited and waited for her to recognize me, to congratulate me on becoming a teacher, and she never did. I was just another face, passing through. Might as well have been a ghost.' Her lip curled in disgust. 'Should have been like you and offed my sibling, so I could have a carefree life, huh?'

This hit so hard, my eyes stung in disbelief. Swallowing, I gripped the tree trunk more tightly, then let it go, forcing myself to stay focused. The fire's crackling and the river's roar were the only sounds for miles.

'You were easy to play with, always so earnest and empathetic,' she said.

I didn't know what she meant by 'play' at first, and then I remembered her showing me the newspaper clipping and old photos from Hatchery's early days, the malice I caught glimpses of during her appointment, the sedative in my coffee.

'It was fun making you so scared and confused,' she went on.

'Especially after I took Ezra from your apartment; thank God the storm was so loud, but I still had to carry him with one hand clasped over his mouth while he kicked like a wild banshee.' She cocked her head. 'Why do you sleep outside? That night Luis died, I watched you from my window and was worried we'd run into one another out there.'

That night Luis died. As if she were an innocent bystander, curious and frank. Next to her, Ezra didn't even squirm; he stayed tight as a coiled snake. Flames blazed upwards, but smoke bent sideways, pushed northwest by a wind so steady and unyielding, I had to lean slightly against it.

Pull her close with honesty and compassion. 'Sometimes I feel trapped,' I said. 'It must have been so difficult to come back here, after all those years.'

There was a flicker in her expression – of yearning or vulnerability or hope – but it vanished. Heat hissed in her eyes; the air felt brittle. Ezra had tucked himself almost into a ball, only his head jutting forward, so he could keep his gaze on me.

'You remind me of a doctor who was here years ago,' she said. 'She talked about me the same way you do on your tapes, always focusing on the negative, what's wrong with me.'

'I'm sorry that made you feel bad. I was trying to help. I'd like to help now.'

'Well, joke's on you because I was pretending. There are problems out in the world—' She pointed toward Hatchery. 'They're not found in me. That doctor thought I was depressed – well, I was depressed because I was here. She was wrong about me; couldn't see I was different than the other kids. And you – you always act like you have it all together. When I was crying by the chalkboard, I just knew you'd come in, try to comfort me, completely unaware. You're so fucking blind. A sheep. A sheep that would wander into a ditch and cry about it. You have to slaughter them just so they'll stop whining. Half measures don't work; you've got to go all the way.'

Helen was almost crying now, her face pinched and reddened, the muscles in her neck visible. In the distance, there was a sound of a rumbling growl, vibrating in this open space, then growing louder and louder, building to a bellow. Ezra lifted his chin, a slight smile on his lips. Buffalo.

This seemed to unhinge Helen even more. Straightening, her eyes narrowed to slits.

'You knew about it and said nothing,' she said, with the petulant air of a child demanding an apology.

It? What . . .

'The drug trial,' I said. 'You found out about it before Dillon even asked for your help . . .'

'He thought I was some love-struck teenager, could get whatever he wanted from me—'

I realized she'd returned to Hatchery, on some level, for a do-over, a chance to fix whatever had gone awry before. But once she got here and found out Dillon was experimenting on students as she'd been, she'd decided to burn it down. She might have hoped the investigation into Ezra's disappearance would expose the drug trial and when it didn't, she'd chosen students who seemed close to escaping her fate. Not only would a string of murders shut Hatchery down, but she'd be able to trap students there as she had felt trapped. It must have felt terrible to see someone set off to live your life, the one you thought you deserved.

'This place shouldn't exist,' she said.

'And the people who need it?'

Reaching out, she possessively brushed Ezra's hair back from his forehead. He winced. 'Some people are anchors.'

My nerves sparked even brighter. I wasn't reaching her; I was indulging her. We were up against the limits of empathy, where talking sours and turns futile. In panic, my mind swung inanely, a tongueless bell, empty and irrelevant.

We needed to make a run for it. Ezra blinked, catching my attention. Leaning to the side, he shifted his leg to flatten the grass in front of his hand. He was clutching something hard and dark in a fist with bloodied knuckles.

Fitting, that he'd found a rock.

Helen stared into the fire in a trance, pensive, readying herself. The gun's metal glinted in her hand when she bent forward as though to stand up. Time rolled like a stone against a cave's entrance, cutting off oxygen. My chest squeezed tighter.

The currents near us thrashed against steep banks and fish battled it, scales glittering, fins thoughtless and efficient. Indifferent to a few bodies under moonlight, nothing else held its breath, but I did.

Ezra's hand came up. The world tilted sideways.

CHAPTER 51

They became a flurry of limbs. Helen blocked his blow with her forearm, slammed the butt of her gun against his temple. Ezra crumpled to the ground. Leaping to my feet, I tucked the rifle against my shoulder and aimed, while Helen scrambled to her feet, raising her gun.

When I took another step, pain ripped up my leg and I stumbled backwards. As I fell, my finger jerked against the trigger. The bullet hurtled into the sky; the rifle recoiled, smacking my eye.

Several other shots rang out. Clawing at whatever had my foot in its teeth, I smelled rust. One of Oksana's coyote traps.

Helen was upon me, shoving me down, her foot pressed into my chest. I reached for the rifle, palm fumbling, stretching into the dark – it had to be close – when her gun nosed against my cheek.

'Found that when I stole the horse. Thought it'd be useful.' Her eyes seared me.

A click.

A hollow sound.

I lurched forward, grappling with the trap. It shredded my fingers until I pried it open and yanked my foot out. Helen collided with me, the impact of her body radiating up my spine.

Her hands were around my throat, whittling my breath to a thin cry. Before my vision blurred, I smashed the trap against her head, sending her sprawling. Clambering to my feet, I reached Ezra, who was just beginning to pull himself up, blood dripping from his chin. Bewildered, he seemed to have forgotten where he was.

I wrenched him to his feet; we ran behind an outcropping of dead cottonwoods and bluestem. Ezra's teeth rattled. I wanted to be sure Helen didn't have extra ammunition for reloading before we dashed across the bridge.

A lone figure on a dark pasture, fog curling around her, she was faceless and still. Then she flung her revolver down and picked up my rifle.

It was a one-shot, empty too. I leaned my forehead against the jagged bark in relief. She bent down, picking something up, and I was seized with fresh alarm. Even though I could only see her silhouette, I knew the movement. Pull the bolt open, slide the cartridge into the breech.

No, no, no.

I rummaged in my jacket pockets. The extra cartridges must have fallen out while we struggled. Instead, I pulled out a tiny matchbox. Dillon had given them to me last night, when the electricity went out during the storm.

Need to do a controlled burn or there'll be wildfires come summer.

After my talk with Oksana I'd looked up prescribed burns, entranced and terrified, watching videos online of blowtorches and mowed firebreaks. Tonight's wind was steady, blowing northwest toward the river. The canyon was almost a half mile wide, more effective than most firebreaks.

It would push Helen away from us, to the north or east, giving us time to reach the homestead ahead of her. Maybe help would already be there. And the smoke would grant us cover, smudging us into near invisibility.

I rubbed the strike strip with my thumb and let myself think of Carson, not as trapped in that house, but outside it. Playing in the rain during an April shower, small shoes splashing in puddles. How his face had glistened with water, the light catching it and making his skin shimmer. How his limbs had moved in long arcs because he hadn't yet learned to contain his own joy.

Carson in a rainstorm. Cedar on that knoll where we'd listened to the sounds of our neighborhood. Deborah telling me about her mother, dreaming aloud about the future. I'd been haunted by my love for them as much as by my failures and they were with me even now, urging me forward.

Ezra looked up at me and I squeezed his hand, rough with calluses, the kind of skin that outgrew baby softness too early.

I struck a match and it flared before my face.

Ezra quickly collected tinder: dry bark from the tree, leaves with browned and brittle edges, dead grass. I lit the small piles, watching the wind coax them aflame, pushing it into the bowl of the bank's crescent moon.

It started slow, but then it began to spread, snapping as it moved. A bullet struck the tree; a limb crashed near Ezra. I tucked him under my body. Smoke was building, rippling in black waves. I waited for her to turn and flee, but she didn't; she stood with a wide stance, loading again and again, blowing bits of wood from the tree.

We huddled together, listening to the blasts, shaking, as the fire marched toward her. It was almost licking her feet when I noticed she was shooting in the wrong direction – out southeast toward Ennenock. She stumbled; the rifle's tip hit the ground and she tripped over it, sprawling.

I recognized this. Before unconsciousness and death, smoke inhalation leads to disorientation, obscuring your vision. Why hadn't she run when she could?

The air around us was thick with fog but otherwise clear, tasting only of dust and stubborn primrose. Ezra and I ran for the bridge, our footsteps swallowed by the clamor. We ducked behind yucca along the opposite bank. Moonlight turned vapor violet-hued as it tumbled upwards, blurring stars.

Ezra's fingernails dug into my flesh. Helen emerged from the black haze. Her hair had caught on one side, fire zipping up toward her scalp. Clumsily, she turned in a semi-circle, staggered backwards, and dropped off the cliff.

Dark water churned; she didn't surface. Howls of a coyote mixed with the rumblings of buffalo to the north, their prehistoric shapes cresting a faraway hill. Flames leapt at the chasm, hungry and reaching, and flickered down to embers.

We walked back to Oksana's hand in hand, shoe soles stained black with soot, ashes trembling in the air around us. By the time we got there, a helicopter had already arrived and whisked Cedar into the sky. The smoke and gunshots had alerted Sheriff Anders, who had been halfway to the homestead. With another officer, he found Helen's body caught in the reeds further down the river, close to where Ezra and I had first met.

CHAPTER 52

One Month Later

Cedar carried a tray of mugs and a creamer jar out to the back patio, the dishes clattering against one another, coffee sloshing over the rims.

He was living at his parents' house while he recuperated; this weekend, they were gone, taking Warren to see a specialist out of state. We had spent long summer hours on this patio, up past our bedtimes, spying on neighbors when sunlight dimmed. Sometimes, a fat raccoon had stalked past us, startling us into laughter.

The house still held a sweet, tangy aroma and well-worn, cracked surfaces – the faded sofa by the window, split tiles near the kitchen sink – that'd made me feel safe. Despite this, I couldn't stop fidgeting. My childhood home squatted across the street, waiting for the wrecking ball. It was foreclosed during my fourth year of residency, when my father finally keeled over one bright August day, cells swollen with alcohol.

Ferns grew around benches with chipping green paint, perennials sprouting between pavers, the air thick with humidity and the smell of hydrangeas and undergrowth. Our knees almost touched, his nearness bringing a current threatening to sweep me up or flow right past me. I'd visited him several times in the hospital, but now there was no hospital bed or nurses or monitors between us. I wanted to let go, to move on, but not without him. How to let go of the pain I associated with him, but not lose all the rest? I wasn't sure what could be salvaged.

'Sorry,' he said, setting the tray down on a wobbly side table. 'Physical therapist says it will get better.' He squeezed his hand into a fist. 'Some.'

In the early hours of the morning, while I had given my account to Sheriff Anders, Cedar had undergone an emergency nerve transplant. His surgery went almost as well as hoped, preserving his arm, though only time would tell how much mobility he'd get back in his hand.

'I'm sorry, C,' I said. It was my pet name for him, which I hadn't used since the raid.

Massaging the middle of his palm, he regarded me shyly. 'What are you doing now . . .'

'That my medical license is suspended?'

His mouth tightened. After a six-month suspension, the medical licensing board would assess my case to see if it could be reinstated.

I pretended to be a good sport about it. 'Got a new apartment,' I said. 'Little one bedroom. May work somewhere close by. Post office or library? There's a small flower shop down the block.'

His eyebrows furrowed. 'I can't see you in a flower shop. Or a library or post office, for that matter.'

'Thanks for the vote of confidence,' I muttered. Truth was, the next job didn't matter so much as me no longer trying to earn the right to exist anymore. No longer becoming grist for a mill that didn't feed anyone.

And I was lucky. A week after I left, Howard had called, telling me he wanted to pay off my medical school loans because of my work on the investigation. Hatchery is my most important life's work, and you saved it, he'd said.

I wasn't so sure I saved it, but I took the money all the same. When I visited Oksana last week, she'd told me she saw some fancy cars loitering around the gravel drive and strangers wandering the premises. As if it were for sale.

Oksana had recently been to Omaha, attending a grandson's Ph.D. graduation. I asked her how she liked the city. She must have heard worry in my tone, concern over her being all alone out here, because she scoffed.

'Fine. Not near as fancy as they seem to think.'

'I never imagined you'd be impressed,' I had assured her.

Now, I felt lighter without the loans, but also lighter without the medical license. Lighter, but not exactly better. More like a balloon with a cut string, disappearing into the sky, uncertain where it will land.

'Mitchell told me you stopped by the station,' Cedar said. 'Thought you said you weren't going to step foot in there again?'

'It was on my way home from the grocery store.'

'He said you were a bulldog but wouldn't say what it was about.'

I'd informed Mitchell that his obsession with the second raid had left Cedar in a lurch, without the help he'd needed. Perched on the edge of his desk, I glared down at him until he agreed Cedar deserved a promotion after being sent out to the hinterlands with only promises of backup, which came too late.

'We found some of Helen's prints in Albert's shed,' Cedar said. I frowned, confused.

'The barbed wire on Kristin,' Cedar said. 'Still don't know exactly why she did it, given that she killed her a day later.'

Closing my eyes, I exhaled. I'd heard Kristin bragging incessantly to other students about leaving and starting a new life, even though she admitted her ambivalence to me.

'Maybe to knock her down a notch, terrify her into silence, but it clearly didn't feel like enough. Helen did tell me she didn't believe in half measures. What did Helen's autopsy report say?' I asked Cedar.

'Smoke inhalation.'

She'd waited too long to run. By the time she did, death was caught in her lungs. She had mentioned suicide in our appointment; perhaps that was the only true line she fed me. Or maybe her rage blinded her to what was actually happening around her, as it had done for most of her life.

Cedar was gazing at me in such a steady way, with such brightness, I was becoming uncomfortable. It felt like a wave about to crash over me, enveloping me, flattening me. I'd been wrong to come; there was too much between us.

'Well,' I said, slapping my knees with false liveliness, 'good to catch up, probably should head out.'

'Please stay. I owe you another apology.'

I froze, having expected him to respond with a joke; I could always count on him for banter and evasive language. I didn't know what to do with this serious, affectionate version of him. 'I was crazy, attacking Owen, digging in the garden. I know—'

'No, I mean before all that. When I abandoned you.'

This hurt, to hear him admit it. I thought I wanted it, but now, I wanted to flee. I was shaking my head, trying hard to shrug it off.

'Remember when we were kids and I made you a crown of daisies? You refused to wear it. It shriveled up on top of your dresser. It upset me so much that you wouldn't let yourself just enjoy something. Always had to carry your dark cloud. I thought, I'm going to be with someone happy, cheerful . . . and then, after the raid, I got it. How you were scared of joy.'

Pulse quickening, I stood up, ready to leave. 'We don't need to talk about it—'

'The night Deborah died, I gave you a cup of tea. Do you remember?' He stood up, the small table between us.

I nodded, then shook my head. I remembered very little of that night.

'When you brought it to your lips, it spilled down your chin. You stared at the droplets on your pants. There was a clock in front of you and you asked over and over what time it was, like you needed to be somewhere else. You kept saying, *I'm fine*, while you picked at your cuticles until blood smeared across your nails. You couldn't get off the floor. I had to carry you out – but there was still blood on my uniform, and it smudged your cheek, and when we got to your house I didn't know if you needed a bath—' His voice rose and cracked. 'If you got in water alone, I was afraid—'

'I'd slip under.'

He ran a hand over his face, eyes wet. 'I didn't know what you needed, that's what I'm trying to say. I didn't know how to hold you up.'

Seeing me like that must have felt similar to when, as a child, he'd seen his mother wail for her broken son. Not knowing what to do.

I plummeted, fell through space, wordless and afraid. When my grandmother was dying of Alzheimer's, my father took me to visit her. She didn't recognize either of us, but she was polite as we made conversation and flipped through her old photo album. When we paused on my grandfather's picture, she grinned proudly and said, 'Now, that's my David.'

She had trouble reading, soiled her pants at night, and couldn't say which year it was. But her love for my grandfather was beyond cognition, lodging somewhere else, not sullied by time or decay. I was scared this was how I felt about Cedar.

He moved around the table. 'But I still shouldn't have disappeared. That's what I'm sorry for,' he said.

Cornflower blue against his dark skin, the sleeves of his chambray shirt were rolled up, exposing his forearms, the familiar topography of his veins and moles. I already knew every inch of him, and still he was a mystery to me.

I let him reach me. He gathered me in his arms, and with my head against his chest, I caught the sharp scent of antiseptic mixed with his tangy aftershave.

'That night you went after Ezra, I could hear each second ticking by. It took all I had to not go after you,' he said, voice hoarse.

'You'd never have caught up,' I said, grinning into his chest.

He pinched my side and I tried to squirm out of his grasp, but he gripped me tight. A hot coal had dropped in my stomach, burning and tender and live. Honeysuckle clung to a neighbor's fence, its nectar bright and audaciously sweet. 'I always knew I couldn't catch you,' he said. 'Just wanted to know you.'

He tilted my chin up, kissed me, and once I came up for air, I was dizzy. We'd been circling each other for so long, this felt like a harbor, a stillness needed before the world rushed back in. To say goodbye to the people we were before, in this maze of ramshackle houses and weeds and splintered sidewalks and falling trees. To try again.

When I leaned back, he was giving me his familiar smile. 'I thought you should know – after you left, Oksana graced me with a performance on her banjo.'

I threw back my head and laughed. 'No.'

'I think she was worried I'd die of boredom, rather than the bullet, and thought she could remedy that. Sang some weird Russian folk tune about a rabbit.'

'And here we thought I was her favorite,' I teased.

'Now that she sang to me, we *know* you're her favorite.'

CHAPTER 53

The next evening, I sat in Beverly's office, waiting to see Ezra, who'd asked permission to show me something after curfew. It was almost dusk and Hatchery was already quieting down, students burrowed in their rooms, chatting softly or doing homework.

'Is he having trouble sleeping?' I asked.

Beverly nodded. 'Your snow globe helps. He sleeps with it and shakes it when he wakes from nightmares. Good calming mechanism.'

This would have pleased Deborah. I'd sent the broken snow globe to a repair shop and when I got it back, I'd mailed it to Beverly, asking her to give it to Ezra. Now, I shifted on the church pew, running my palms over its smooth, worn wood. I could have stayed outside but I wanted to be within these walls one final time; to revisit it as Helen had, daring demons to resurface, testing my composure. Patients are often mirrors, but she went beyond that. She, of the eventide ballad and agony souvenirs. She, my twin on fire.

'How's Albert?' I asked.

Beverly pursed her lips thoughtfully. 'He's surprised me. Keeps to himself less, eats in the dining hall more often. Sometimes even jokes with the students. I've known him for decades and didn't even know he had a sense of humor.'

'And Dillon?' I asked.

Her expression tightened and she rapped her knuckles on her desk. 'We both knew he'd land on his feet.'

I nodded at this. Last night, Cedar and I had stayed up late talking about the case. The light had faded, turning leaves around us a deep, rich green, and the air had hummed with dragonflies. Apparently, Dillon finally admitted to his drug trial. He also confessed that someone had stolen midazolam from his medical cabinet and he suspected Helen, since she used his keys when helping him. Instead of reporting it, he'd changed his inventory chart, so nothing seemed amiss.

Beverly smoothed the collar of her starched white button-up in a brisk gesture and clasped her hands in front of her. 'I heard some family friend of his gave him a job back east in private practice. Kristin's father has teamed up with an investigative journalist; they're filing a civil case against him. Malpractice. I'm worried they won't get far.' She squinted into the distance. 'He'd talked so much about how special Hatchery was and I was just happy someone was taking an interest. I should have realized he was up to something else.' She shook her head, her voice strained. 'I thought this was a safe place. I believed in what we were doing.'

Recognizing the brittleness of self-blame, I leaned forward, softening my posture. It felt like I was always working. 'It was safe, a lot of the time. Students have gone through here and done well.'

She sunk her face in her hands and muttered into her palms, 'I knew. I knew something was off with her.' When she lifted her head, mascara smudged at one eye's edge and her nose was pink.

'Some students complained about her – claimed she'd threatened them, that something minor could send her screeching. A few said she'd forced them to write terrible things about themselves on the chalkboard, these old-fashioned punishments of humiliation. But there are always accusations, most of them unfounded. And other students – she was so attentive with them and they blossomed under her. She was our best teacher; we'd never had anyone like her. I wanted to believe only the good things could be true.' Beverly bit her lip, blinking back tears.

I saw in the lines on her face, the sunken skin beneath her eyes, all the nights she'd spent awake and alone, trying to build this place. The reasonable worries that someone would come along and stamp it out, the sandcastles of our hours. I'd judged her too harshly for clinging to her own sacrifice, hoping it'd keep her warm. Life could erode your sense of self slowly, over years of accumulated pressures, the same way the wind reshaped these hills, decade by decade.

'Does it surprise you, that she came back here after all these years?' I asked.

Beverly shook her head. 'Initially, yes. I couldn't believe I hadn't recognized her. But then I remembered her from when she was young . . . she'd been so protective of her sister. She was loyal to her, and yet so full of anger that you could feel it coming off her like heat waves.'

Tucking strands back into her bun, Beverly tried to pull herself together and switched the subject. 'I'm still sorry how things ended, though happy your loans got paid off. It was the least we could do.' Her desk was already clean, but she whisked her hands across it, as if brushing off invisible dirt.

The least we could do. That was the phrase Howard had used, which had sounded so unnatural with his commanding personality. He had seemed the kind of wealthy man accustomed to telling people how *they* should be, not how *he* should be.

'It was you,' I murmured. 'Thank you.'

She gave me a stern look, chin tilted down, eyebrows slightly raised. 'He owed me a favor, after all these years, and I finally made him pay it. I hope it gives you a clean slate. Can do something else if you like. Though that'd be a pity because you always were good with them.'

'Will Hatchery close?' I asked.

Biting her lip, Beverly stood and rang a bell that'd sat on the windowsill, its frail, tinny sound filling the room. 'Bells were once used to drive evil spirits away. As if you could scare something into submission. Hatchery . . . will transform.'

Before I could ask what she meant, I felt a presence behind me, near the door. Spine stiffening, fearing it was my hallucination, I looked over my shoulder.

It was Ezra.

He led me west, toward the sandstone cliff where we had watched the buffalo bully each other for a scrap of land. Oksana would call me two months later, telling me the pasture we'd burned was now a field of sunflowers. Thanks a lot, she'd muttered. Now my barn is full of bees. But I could tell she was pleased.

Ezra was trying to suppress a smile, but the corners of his mouth kept twitching. We sat near the edge, facing the opposite cliff, where deep fissures trailed down its face, ponderosa pines growing indistinct in the darkness. I asked him questions: how he was feeling about moving, if he'd met his new guardian yet. He gave me an impatient look, and then regarded the scene before us with a level stare, apparently waiting for something.

A sweet, charred residue draped the region. As the trees became silhouettes, the sky and river deepened into a brilliant blue. Reduced to cobalt and onyx, simplified to a single shape, the landscape's starkness lifted something in me; my chest expanded. A breeze gathered up and held our breath.

I wanted to leave him with something special, some bit of advice, but none felt worthy of him. I thought of those letters I'd wept over, the students who'd surpassed the odds and surprised us all.

Time passed; stars appeared. And after the stars, tiny pinpricks of light formed above the river, blinking on and off, a flurry of flashes in darkness. Fireflies.

For the first time since we'd sat down, Ezra turned to me.

'Fire,' he said.

My throat constricted and I reached for his hand, squeezed it. Who else could remind me that some fires wouldn't consume, some would simply burn out, and others, others would light the night?

I could not feel all the happiness in me at that moment. But maybe that's what memories are for – maybe we can't feel fully happy or sad in each moment, so we revisit it again and again, all these visits accumulating, pulling water from a well over and over until we've drunk our fill.

Years later, I remind him of this when he arrives on my doorstep one early morning, haggard and terrified, holding wild-flowers – alyssum, thistle, snake-cotton – as a gift. We kept in touch sporadically; he is a new father to a beautiful son who looks just like him. Now, Ezra sits at the kitchen table, says Hatchery still haunts him and he doesn't know what to tell his son once he's older. As he tells me about his family, I consider the fates of those who became linked over those brutal few days.

Owen left Hatchery for Wyoming, where he rode bulls in rodeos before venturing further west to Nevada and lost contact with the wider world. I imagined him in a trailer on a sand dune, unbothered by solitude, and if not happy, then at least less troubled. I had a feeling he never forgot Kristin, despite his insistence that she didn't matter to him.

After Helen's death, Agatha was moved into a care facility, where I hoped she thrived, or at least, was allowed to age in peace. I never visited or inquired after her, worrying my presence would disrupt any new equilibrium she found.

Carly's anxiety improved and she was sent to a foster family in a nearby town. She wrote me occasionally through the years, telling me how she married the son of the hardware store owner, settling in the town when her husband inherited the store. After having a few kids, she began blowing glass and I'd travel to local art festivals where she displayed her work. She made yellow glass flowers like the ones that had dotted the Sandhills around Hatchery and I bought them, keeping them in vases around my house. One sits behind Ezra right now, catching the light, almost glowing like the fireflies had all those years ago.

Ezra tells me that during the May Day festival, smoke reached the homestead; burning was visible on the horizon. It took hours, but he walked across the hills to watch us, spying from tall grass, holding himself back, not wanting to be found. And later, he witnessed the murder, but hadn't fully understood what he'd seen. Only knew he'd been right to stay hidden.

It had made him feel insubstantial, he said. Ghostlike.

I listen, make him a cup of tea. You'll be more present to your son than you can imagine, I tell him. I remind him of the times he came alive before my very eyes: standing amid the monarch migration, witnessing buffalo on a river's island, coloring at Oksana's table, watching the fireflies. Tell your son about how the light reflected in the water, becoming so bright, you'd think the river was glowing.

How even after we left that night, a part of us stayed; not even the wind can wipe us away.

ACKNOWLEDGMENTS

With Gratitude

To Benee Knauer for shepherding this book through its many stages and never losing the faith; to Victoria Sanders for being the most steadfast, fierce advocate; to Stefanie Bierwerth for your clarity of vision and helping make this book so much better; to everyone at VSA and Quercus; I'm so lucky to get to work with you all.

To my writing group: Theodore Wheeler, Felicity White, Ryan Borchers, Amy O'Reilly, Bob Churchill, Drew Justice, and Ryan Norris; to Kate Sims and Tessa Terry for being the best book critics; this road would be so much lonelier without your friendship.

To my family for always being so supportive of my work; especially to Mandie Montag and Carter Quinn for indulging my flights of fancy.

To my sons and to my husband, for everything.